Book 3 of the Seeds of Civilization series

I0680959

TRÍANGLE

R.J. Archer

NWIDI Press ~ Portland, OR

This book is a work of fiction.
All names, characters or incidents are either
the product of the author's imagination or are used fictitiously
and any resemblance to any persons, living or dead,
is entirely coincidental.

Library of Congress
Cataloging-in-Publication Data

"Triangle" by R.J. Archer

p. cm.
ISBN-10: 0-9779109-3-8 (softcover)
ISBN-13: 978-09779109-39
Science Fiction, general

823.0876   2008922203

Published 2008 by NWIDI Press,
P.O. Box 230154, Portland, OR 97281, USA
©2008 by R.J. Archer.

Cover design by Diseño International, Portland, Oregon.

Manufactured in the United States of America.

"From the thrill and danger of deep-water dives and cloak-and-dagger escapades of secret intelligence machinations to the potentially deadly consequences of interaction with alien artifacts and the mysteries of the Bermuda Triangle, *Triangle* packs quite a punch and never slows down until the final word on the last page."

Daniel Jolley, Amazon *Top 50 Reviewer*

"Take a little of Graham Hancock's theories on Earth's ancient civilizations, mix in some Clive Cussler-type adventure and action, put on your scuba gear and grab your archaeological text books. Let me see...that's one part action, one part speculative fiction, one part underwater adventure, one part... aw, heck, don't classify it. Just read *Triangle*, the third and concluding novel in R. J. Archer's *Seeds of Civilization* series."

Larry Ketchersid, author of *Dusk Before the Dawn*
www.duskbeforethedawn.net

About the Series

The *Seeds of Civilization* series is loosely based on the theories of Graham Hancock and others who believe that highly developed civilizations existed on Earth thousands of years before the time generally accepted by mainstream academia.

If Hancock's theory that an advanced civilization existed on Earth 9,000 years ago is correct, one has to wonder whether or not there were even earlier civilizations, each lost to some cataclysmic event. What if the Mesopotamians weren't really Earth's first civilization but merely the sprout from a recently planted seed?

Acknowledgements

Although this novel is purely a work of fiction, it is based on a great deal of factual information from a number of sources. I would like to thank the individuals and organizations listed below and I invite you to look them up on the Internet and learn more about their fascinating work.

Angie Micol at Satellite Discoveries for satellite imagery; Paulina Zelitsky and Paul Weinzweig of Advanced Digital Communications who discovered the real "lost city of Cuba" in 2000; Dr. Manuel Iturralde of Cuba's National Museum of Natural History for his materials supporting the aforementioned discovery; Deborah Bartlett of Global Marine Systems (UK) for arranging my tour of the cable maintenance ship *Wave Venture*; William (Bill) Donato of APEX Institute and Drs. Greg and Lora Little of A.R.E.'s *Search for Atlantis Project* for an incredible amount of information on the discoveries and ongoing research near Bimini and, last but not least, Thomas "Doc" Rowe of Noland Corporation for introducing me to the real *Bionic Dolphin*.

For more information about this series, please join us at
http://www.SeedsOfCivilization.com

Prologue

(July, 2000)

Ka'ax looked up from his work and listened as the noisy, crude device made another pass over his outpost, 2,100 feet below the surface. From somewhere above, a ship was towing the object back and forth in a grid-like pattern. In all the time he had been assigned to this location, nothing like this had ever occurred before and Ka'ax knew this activity would have to be reported immediately. If his position were in danger of being discovered, it would have to be abandoned, like so many others in the past.

***

(September, 2002)

Frank Morton closed the manila folder he'd been reading and leaned back in his plush leather desk chair. The rest of the NWIDI team had left for the day and the small hangar/office complex at the south end of Boeing Field was quiet again. The sun had just set on another unusually warm September day in Seattle and the metal roof of the building was popping as it cooled. Frank closed his eyes and smiled.

It was hard to believe it had only been fifteen months since he'd won the $86 million lottery jackpot that had changed his life. Shortly thereafter, he and three friends had informally joined forces to investigate a mysterious black sphere they'd acquired in a small town north of Las Vegas. That investigation, now referred to as the *Tractrix Project*, had taken them from Seattle to the secret military installations of Nevada and on to the Maya ruins in Mexico's Yucatan Peninsula. Along the way, they'd gotten themselves involved in a murder investigation and attracted the unwanted attention of government agents, Mexican *Federales* and an ancient Maya priest. In an unexpected turn of events, they'd stumbled across a three thousand year old secret that suggested an alien origin to the Maya's advanced knowledge of astronomy and mathematics. Before long, Frank had begun to formulate a theory about repeated alien interventions into the affairs of Earth and Earthlings.

Later, Frank had talked his three friends into formally creating the Northwest Institute of Discovery and Investigation (NWIDI). His goal had been to devote a portion of his lottery winnings to the exploration of several unsolved archaeological mysteries that interested him. Although he was a retired aerospace engineer, Frank had always been fascinated by the apparent contradiction between what traditional anthropology preached and what modern archaeology seemed to be discovering. As a trained SCUBA diver, he was especially interested in the numerous underwater sites, like the famous Yonaguni Monument that had been found in the mid-1980s. These newly discovered artifacts and submerged structures seemed to confirm the "new age" theories that one or more civilizations had flourished on Earth long before the rise of Mesopotamia around 4,000 B.C.

Frank smiled again. It was seven months to the day since the NWIDI team had left this very hangar to investigate a sunken pyramid off the coast of Yonaguni Island, in southern Japan. Within two weeks of their arrival, the four accidental adventurers found themselves involved in a case of murder and international kidnapping in what the team now called the *Tsubute Project*. While attempting to solve the murder and clear their own names, they had uncovered a dark secret that had been hidden on the tiny island for more than 10,000 years—one that confirmed Frank's developing theory about "alien interventions."

When Frank and his long-time friend, Tony Nicoletti, returned from Yonaguni on the NWIDI Learjet, team members Jim Barnes and Linda McBride had remained behind for several months to investigate the underground passageways they had discovered beneath the island. In just a few weeks Jim had deciphered enough of the passageway murals to change the entire history of ancient Japan. Based on star maps and other information that had been found, the writings appeared to be at least 14,000 years old and they described a rich cultural history that probably dated back another 2,000 years. Overnight, the theories of Graham Hancock and others had been substantiated and mainstream anthropology was being forced to rethink the entire timeline of human civilization.

With the team now reunited in Seattle, the mood at the NWIDI headquarters was relaxed and upbeat. Best of all, Jim was receiving full credit for his discoveries and he was a rising star in the scientific community. When the team had first discussed the trip to Japan, back in early February, Jim had been reluctant to go because of pressure to publish by the University of Washington, where he was a professor. Now the University was begging him not to accept any of the dozens of prestigious positions he was being offered by other institutions.

Linda, a former newspaper researcher and detective at heart, had also continued to investigate Yonaguni, but her interest focused on the *tsubutes*—the ancient Ninja throwing weapons the NWIDI team had found in a tomb deep under Yonaguni's Mt. Urabu. It had been decided that her work would not be made public until it was better understood, but Frank knew it was just a matter of time before the rest of the world learned what he and his team already knew— that the red stones in the center of each of the twelve ceremonial *tsubutes* were some sort of alien technology that had been fashioned into the objects by the same ancient race that had created the murals.

Because of Jim's work, NWIDI was receiving a lot of publicity and Frank was bombarded with proposals for research grants and scientific partnerships. The most intriguing request to date, however, was the one he'd just finished reading. The file had come to him through an acquaintance at the Department of Defense, but it had originated at the "highest levels" of the U.S. government and it detailed a remarkable discovery that had been made two years earlier by a Canadian underwater exploration company called Deep Oceanic Research.

While doing some salvage work for the Cuban government, the Canadians had accidentally discovered what appeared to be a large group of megalithic structures just off the western tip of Cuba, at a depth of more than 2,000 feet. Additional investigations, done a year later, confirmed that the complex covers nearly eight square miles and appears to contain many pyramids, roads and buildings. Tests completed only two months earlier had concluded that the megalithic structures are made of granite—granite that had to come from more than 1,000 miles away. The new age folks were already hinting that this could be the location of the mythical lost city of Atlantis described by Plato in 350 B.C. And to complicate matters, Castro was prohibiting exploration by all American companies in retaliation for the U.S. trade embargo. Even National Geographic's offer to fund a multi-national expedition to the site had been refused. Now NWIDI had received an "official" request to learn all it could about the site without creating an international incident and Frank knew he couldn't decline. Not because of the origin of the request, but because, well, what if it *were* the remains of Atlantis? That would be an incredible archaeological find! Or what if this new site were somehow related to the alien spheres his team had discovered in the hands of the Maya or to the alien rubies they had found on Yonaguni? What if this much older site had been an alien base? What if it still *is*?

Chapter 1

When the telephone on his desk rang, Frank awoke with a jolt and realized he'd slept through the night in his office again—something that was happening far too often these days! As he reached for the handset, he glanced at the clock on his office wall and wondered who would be calling him at 4:00 a.m.

"Hello?" he mumbled sleepily.

"Frank? Buzz Edwards here. Sorry to call so early, but we've had an incident down in the Gulf of Mexico that may be related to that file I sent you. Have you had a chance to look it over yet?"

Nodding to no one in particular, Frank opened the file. "Yes, I have it right here. It's very…did you say an incident?"

"We think so, Frank. Details are still pretty sketchy, but early this morning two fishing boats were reported missing from the remote village of Las Tumbas, on the northwest tip of Cuba. If you've studied that file much you'll recognize the significance of that location."

Sensing that Edwards was being purposely vague, Frank followed suit.

"Were the Canadians in the vicinity?" he asked, referring to the underwater exploration team that had originally reported the megalithic structures more than two years ago.

"No, we've confirmed that their ship is tied up in Progreso, Mexico, but some mysterious signals we've been monitoring in the area suddenly stopped and one of the missing boats contacted the Cuban Navy with a distress call at almost the same time that we lost the signals. That boat's last reported GPS coordinates are almost identical to those of the underwater site and we don't think this is just a coincidence. How soon can you have your team ready to move?"

Frank was now fully awake and already thumbing through his card file looking for the phone number of his flight crew.

"Assuming the Learjet isn't down for routine maintenance, I think we can be wheels-up by noon my time, but I've only just begun to study this file. I haven't put together an operational plan or a materials list. Hell, I don't even know what you want us to do!"

"Frank, the site's in more than 2,100 feet of water and I doubt if you have any gear that works at that depth! Bring a swimsuit, some sun block and we'll figure the rest out after you get here. By the way, the part about the signals is a classified component of this mission that I couldn't include in the file I sent you. I'll fill you in when I meet you and your team in Cancun. I've made arrangements with the Mexican government to use a facility at the airport and we'll set up our base camp there. Call me once you're in the air and we'll work out the clearances you'll need to get through Mexican airspace."

"OK, Buzz, I'll get going on the arrangements at this end right away and I'll talk to you in a few hours." Smiling to himself, Frank added, "But I have to warn you—we charge a premium for rush jobs!"

Seven hours later, at exactly 11:00 a.m. Seattle time, the NWIDI Learjet lifted off the runway at Boeing Field and banked right on a course that would take it first to Albuquerque and then on to Cancun. The total trip, including a scheduled stop in Albuquerque for fuel and food, would take slightly more than six hours and put them on the ground in Cancun at about 7:15 p.m. local time. It had taken a Herculean effort to get the people, supplies and aircraft ready on such short notice, but they had done it and Frank signaled a hearty thumbs-up as he felt the wheels leave the ground.

"Great job, guys! I don't know what we're getting ourselves into, but we're doing it in record time."

As soon as the aircraft reached cruising altitude, Frank used the air-phone to call Buzz Edwards and give him an update on their arrival time. With the speaker phone on, Buzz provided the team with an overview of the logistics of the mission and they kicked around several ambitious plans. After nearly thirty minutes, Frank ended the call and looked at Jim.

"I'm sorry to have to kick you out in Albuquerque, Jim, but as Buzz just said, you're the only member of our team who can get into Cuba without arousing suspicion. Your name's been in the press a lot lately so the Cubans shouldn't be surprised by your interest in their island and we really need somebody on the ground out near the site. Are you up for this?"

Jim smiled and nodded. A year ago he had been the typical shy, retiring university professor you'd see in the movies but the publicity and exposure he'd garnered as a result of his discoveries on Yonaguni had changed all that.

"I've always wanted to visit Cuba and compare it to the neighboring Yucatan Peninsula. I guess I'm going to get my chance, huh?" he laughed.

"It won't be all grins and chuckles, my friend," cautioned former Army Ranger Tony Nicoletti. He and Frank had served together in the jungles of Southeast Asia during the Vietnam Conflict and Tony imagined that guerrilla fighters were the same the world over—be it Cambodia or Cuba.

"He's right," added Frank. "You need to stick to the script and play the part of the professor you really are, as if your life depends on it. If the Cuban authorities figure out what you're up to, you might end up staying on that island for a very long time!"

"I understand, and don't think I'm not a little scared," replied Jim, his face returning to its normal scholarly calm. "You guys just be sure you meet me at the designated pick-up point and don't leave me stranded out there."

For the next two hours the four principle NWIDI team members discussed what few details of the mission they knew and speculated about those they didn't. Buzz Edwards had hinted at a classified component to the mission during his initial call to Frank, but he hadn't brought it up during the conference call, so neither had Frank. They would know soon enough and Frank decided that there was no need to mention it to the team until he had the facts. They had enough to worry about already.

Once the Learjet was on autopilot, the husband-and-wife flight crew of Fitz and Susan Fitzgerald took turns sitting in on the discussions in the cabin in case questions of air travel were to come up. It happened that Fitz, the husband part of the crew, was in the cabin when the conversation turned to emergency evacuation plans.

"Fitz, where, besides, Cancun, can you set this plane down if we need you to pull one or more of us out?"

Fitz pulled a sheet of paper out of his pocket and un-folded it.

"Well, there's Grand Cayman, but that's 300 miles southwest of the site. Or there's Key West, Florida, 250 miles to the northeast. That's about it, I'm afraid."

"What about on the island of Cuba itself?" asked Frank.

Fitz' eyebrows rose and his eyes widened for a second before he replied, "Well, there's an airstrip at the U.S. naval base in Guantanamo Bay that's big enough for us, but that's farther away than the Caymans, and the Cubans would know we were coming in for sure. They have spotters all around that place."

Understanding Frank's line of questioning, Tony said, "Yes, but it's a mighty long swim to Grand Cayman or Key West. At least the Navy's facility is accessible by land. Granted, it would mean hiking the entire length of Cuba through the jungle, but at least it's possible. I think we should put together a contingency plan that includes Guantanamo, and that means knowing how to get emergency landing authority, how to approach the runway, and anything else you might need to know. And we need to gather this information without hinting to *anyone* that we might actually be thinking about doing it."

Fitz rubbed his chin thoughtfully. "OK, I'll get on that right away. I have some friends—former military pilots—who should be able to tell me how to get in and out without getting shot down by either side."

"But this is just a contingency plan, right?" asked an increasingly nervous Jim. "You're not expecting me to hike 750 miles through the jungle are you?"

Frank smiled. "No, Jim, a water approach is obviously the best plan. As soon as we get your signal, we'll meet you on the beach just east of Las Tumbas."

Jim left the team in Albuquerque and caught a flight to Miami. There he was to meet a CIA agent and receive the necessary U.S. travel documents for Cuba. He would stay in a Miami hotel until he received the order from Edwards to continue on to Havana and begin his journey to Las Tumbas. Officially, he was traveling to Cuba to learn about the island's earliest inhabitants. Unofficially, his mission was to learn as much as he could about the fate of the lost fishing boats.

As the airport van pulled away from the Learjet, Jim looked out the side window and waved. He was on his own now and on his way to Miami. The next time he would see his teammates would be in Cuba.

"Frank, are you sure this is the right thing to do?" asked Linda, sadly. "Jim doesn't have any experience in this kind of thing and he's not made of the same stuff as you and Tony. If he gets stopped by the authorities, he'll... "

"He'll unravel like grandma's knitting," finished Tony. "But as long as he sticks to his cover story, which is mostly true, he'll be just fine. He has a good command of Spanish and he's genuinely interested in the people of Cuba, so everything should be fine."

Frank put his arm around Linda's shoulder and squeezed gently. "Besides, my dear, he actually volunteered for this job. Before I had a chance to suggest it, he took me aside and asked if there were any way we could get him onto the island for a few days."

Linda spun around and studied Frank's face. "I don't believe it!"

"It's true," smiled Frank. "Now let's get back aboard before the Fitzgeralds leave for Cancun without us."

The flight path for the second leg of the trip took the Learjet out over the Gulf of Mexico just north of Corpus Christi and the three remaining members of the team stared out the window, marveling at the bright blue water. It was hard to imagine that millions of years ago a meteorite might have splashed down in this area starting a chain of events that eventually resulted in the extinction of the dinosaurs. It was even harder to imagine what strange events might be taking place on the ocean floor a few hundred miles east of here.

As they approached the Yucatan Peninsula, the weather worsened and dark, ominous-looking clouds began to appear below them. Twice during their final approach turbulence buffeted the plane causing Linda to clutch the armrests of her seat when the wheels of the Learjet finally touched the runway at Cancun International Airport.

As it rolled to a stop in front of an old metal hangar, Frank spotted Buzz Edwards waving from the tarmac. Frank had first met Edwards in the Yucatan city of Merida while on the trail of a mysterious black sphere. Later, it had been Edwards who had helped Frank secure the Learjet the team now used for travel.

When Fitz opened the cabin door, Frank was hit with a blast of hot, humid air that caught him off guard. The interior of the Learjet had been maintained at a dry 72 degrees and the heat and humidity of the Yucatan, now near the end of its rainy season, was a real shock to the system. At the bottom of the stairs, Frank shook hands with Buzz, who smiled and nodded toward the cabin door.

"I'm glad to see that you brought along Beauty and the Beast," he quipped, indicating Linda and Tony coming down the stairs.

"Yeah, these two, along with Jim Barnes, are permanent fixtures now. We also have a full-time flight crew and several support folks back in Seattle. Things have changed a lot since you and I flew back to Las Vegas last year...including *this*."

Frank indicated the Learjet with a sweep of his arm. "I owe you big time for this!"

"Glad I was able to help, Frank, but you know what they say—pay-backs are a bitch! This mission isn't going to be a joy-ride in the jungle, like your last trip down here. Now introduce me to your team and let's get to work!"

Buzz had met Tony briefly at an air strip in Nevada, but he had never seen Linda McBride and he was obviously taken by her looks and poise. The Fitzgeralds soon joined the group at the bottom of the stairs and they were introduced to Edwards.

"It's a pleasure to meet you all," he smiled. "We're setting up in this hangar behind me and you'll probably want to get the aircraft inside as soon as possible. I hear there's another storm only a couple of hours away."

Noticing Fitz' grimace when he indicated the hangar, Edwards smiled. "Don't be deceived by the outward appearance, my friend. This facility is jointly owned by the U.S. and Mexican governments and it's normally reserved for high-ranking officials, including the presidents of both countries. The outside is left a little rough for the sake of the Mexican taxpayers but I think you'll find the inside much more to your liking. Follow me, and I'll show you around."

A "yip!" from the top of the stairs stopped Edwards in his tracks. Looking back over his shoulder, he spotted the small, long-haired dog and exclaimed, "You have a dog on board?"

Susan slapped her thigh and called, "Come, Sandstrom!"

The dog raced down the stairs and ran to Susan's side, tail wagging.

"This is Sandstrom," introduced Susan, "and he travels everywhere with us. Sandstrom, can you say 'Hello'?"

The dog yipped and the whole group laughed. Tony knelt down and patted Sandstrom on the head.

"He takes a little getting used to, but he's an okay mutt. He probably saved my life in Japan, so I owe him one."

Edwards was obviously not excited about the presence of a family pet. "It's an interesting breed. Some sort of terrier?"

Fitz smiled at Edwards' discomfort. "Actually, he's Havanese—a breed that originated on the island of Cuba as a lap dog of the aristocracy. So this trip is his homecoming, so to speak."

"Yeah, right. Maybe he should have gone on to Miami with Jim, then, because we have a lot to do and damn little time to do it in. Let's go inside and get started, shall we?"

"I'm going to stay out here with the aircraft. As soon as you're ready, open the big doors and I'll taxi her in out of the weather," said Susan.

Edwards raised his eye brows at Fitz, who just shrugged and said, "She's the boss, so I guess I'm with you guys."

Susan, with Sandstrom in tow, returned to the Learjet and secured the cabin as Edwards led the rest of the group through a side door and into the hangar.

"Holly crap!" shouted Tony as they entered the main part of the facility.

Inside, the sheet metal exterior was replaced with smooth concrete walls that appeared to be at least a foot thick and the building was absolutely empty. There wasn't a sign of a tool or a piece of furniture anywhere. Besides the door through which they had just entered and the large metal door for aircraft, the only other visible object was a rectangular concrete box about ten feet tall and six feet on a side that stood in the back corner of the huge cavern.

Edwards fished a walkie-talkie out of a pants pocket and said something into the device. Seconds later, the huge aircraft doors began sliding to each side with a groan. As Frank, Linda and Fitz watched, Tony moved into the hangar and examined a barely-noticeable seam in the floor.

Within minutes, Susan had the Learjet inside the hangar with its nose-wheel positioned directly over a faint yellow "X" painted on the floor. Edwards herded the group over to the concrete box and spoke another command into the walkie-talkie. As the big doors began to close, he signaled Susan to remain in the cock-pit and then opened a nearly invisible door in the side of the concrete box with a key.

"Inside, everybody. We'll meet her downstairs."

The door opened into an elevator that barely held Edwards and his four fascinated friends. He pressed a button marked "D" and the car moved smoothly down. Several seconds later, the car eased to a stop. Edwards opened the door.

"Welcome to MX-2, my friends. You are now part of a very select group of individuals who even know this place exists. Needless to say, everything you see, hear and do from this point on is classified—*very* classified."

As the NWIDI team members gazed around at the glass-walled offices and hallways that seemed to go off in every direction, Tony asked the obvious question.

"What the hell is this place?"

"MX-2 is one of three such complexes in Mexico and part of a global network of more than two dozen facilities around the world. Their primary purpose is to provide hardened shelters for the world's leaders in case of an attack, but they're also used for research and intelligence activities that must be conducted in absolute secrecy."

"So is this similar to the bunkers we hear about in the U.S.—the ones where they take the President and Vice President every time there's another terrorist threat?" asked Linda.

Edwards nodded. "Yes, but only a few of our facilities are part of this shared network. And the President would only be brought here if he were outside the country at the time of an attack and if the nature of the attack made it impossible for him to return to the U.S. We have a reciprocal agreement with the other countries involved so that no national leader is left unprotected, no matter where they are in the world. There's always a 'safe house' within reach by air."

"Well, it's impressive, I'll give you that," said Frank. "But why here in Cancun? Isn't this hurricane country?"

Edwards smiled. "I know it doesn't feel like it when you come down in the elevator, but we're now more than 100 feet below the runway you landed on. This facility was designed to withstand a direct hit from the largest nuclear device we know of, so a hurricane poses no danger at all."

Suddenly, a deep humming sound seemed to come from behind a nearby wall.

"That would be your wife," Edwards smiled to Fitz. "This way, please."

Edwards led them down a tunnel to a door where a red light was flashing. Soon after the humming stopped, the light went off and Edwards opened the door. Inside, a small electric tug was towing the Learjet off the huge section of floor that had lowered it down from above. The perimeter of the lower room was filled with gleaming aircraft maintenance equipment and small, isolated work bays.

"They can do everything from routine maintenance to complete engine overhauls down here," said Edwards proudly. "Please feel free to take advantage of this facility if you need anything."

Fifteen minutes later, they were all assembled around a large oval table in a conference room somewhere deep inside the underground complex. Edwards had been joined by a man dressed in a dark, well-tailored suit whom he introduced as Javier Reyes. The man had a contagious smile and spoke flawless English.

"Javier is a scientist on loan to us from Centro Ecológico Cancun, a local group based here in the Yucatan. Javier, why don't you start by telling them a little about CEC and what you folks do?"

The man smiled and stood to speak.

"CEC is a non-profit, non-governmental organization that conducts scientific investigations into the health of the regional environment and reports its findings to the state and federal governments, to local developers, and to the local population. I'm an oceanographer and for the past five years my focus has been the study of the effects of regional agriculture on the eastern Gulf of Mexico—the waters that are responsible for much of this area's tourist business.

"About three and a half years ago, my agency purchased some unique underwater listening equipment to help provide insights into what's going on in our coastal waters. Almost immediately, we detected an unusual signal coming from the east, near the western tip of Cuba. At first we thought we were picking up a very strong sonar signal, possibly from a ship or a submarine, but we ruled out that theory when we realized that the origin of the signal was absolutely fixed—and more than 2,100 feet below the surface."

Javier paused to let the significance of his comments sink in. Frank spoke the words everyone else was thinking.

"The 'lost city' discovered by the Canadians!" shouted Frank

"That's right," interjected Edwards, "and we've been monitoring the signals very closely ever since they first announced their discovery back in 2000. So you can imagine our surprise this morning when the signals suddenly stopped—at exactly the same time one of those fishing boats sent a distress call!"

Chapter 2

By the time Javier Reyes finished his briefing, it was nearly 11:00 p.m. local time and the NWIDI team was feeling the effects of the long day that had begun in Seattle. Tony leaned back in the high-back chair and yawned loudly, setting off a chain reaction of yawns around the table, which, in turn, set off a chain reaction of laughs.

"I guess I'd better get you old timers to a hotel before you conk out," joked Edwards. "I've made arrangements for you at the Sun Palace Resort. It's just south of the main hotel zone and fairly close to this facility. The rooms are in your name, Frank, and the folks down there are used to dealing with us Americans. In fact, the property manager receives a monthly 'bonus' from the DOD to provide us with some extra amenities. I'll have a van meet you upstairs where you came in and I'll see you all at the hotel in the morning—shall we say 8:00 a.m. in the Bugamvillias Restaurant?"

Thirty minutes later, Frank dropped his suitcase inside the door and gazed around the luxurious room. It was more like a suite, with a large sitting area, a wet bar, a separate bedroom and a master bath. Two couches were arranged in an "L" shape on two sides of a large marble coffee table and they faced the balcony, which looked out over the lighted beach of the Caribbean. Before Frank could get his shoes off, the phone on the bar rang.

"Now what?" he said out loud on his way to the bar. "Hello?"

"Frank, it's Linda. I'm afraid there's been a mistake with the rooms—they must have given me your suite. I'll be right over and we can switch keys."

"It's not a mistake, Linda," laughed Frank. "I have a suite, too, and I imagine Tony and the Fitzgeralds do, as well. This must be part of the 'extra amenities' Edwards mentioned. Enjoy your room and I'll see you in the morning."

Frank placed the phone back in the cradle and smiled. It would kill Linda to think that she was getting better treatment than other members of the team! He hadn't taken three steps away from the bar when the phone rang again.

"Again?" he mumbled, turning back to the phone. This had to be either Tony or Fitz wanting to change rooms, and he was betting it was Fitz because Tony wouldn't think twice about keeping the best room.

"Hello," he answered with a smile.

"Mr. Morton?" asked a deep voice with a heavy accent.

"Yes, this is Frank Morton. Who is this?"

"That's not important, Mr. Morton. What *is* important is that you and your friends get in that fancy airplane of yours and leave Cancun immediately. We're watching you and we will not tolerate any further interference with our operations. To do so would be a fatal mistake for you all."

The line went dead and Frank stood there with the phone to his ear for several seconds before springing into action. He dialed "0" and waited for an answer. Thankfully, the night operator spoke passable English.

"This is Frank Morton in room 2012. I just received a call. Can you tell me where it originated?"

"No sir, I can't. I haven't transferred any calls to your room so it must have been placed from within the hotel."

"Are you sure?" questioned Frank.

"Very sure, *Señor*! All outside calls come through this switchboard and I'm the only one on duty right now. It must have come from one of the other guest rooms—or perhaps from the lobby or one of the restaurants. Is there a problem, *Señor*?"

"No, no problem. Thank you very much, *Señorita*, and good night."

In rapid succession, Frank called the rooms of Linda, Tony and the Fitzgeralds with the same message for each: "My room, five minutes."

Tony was the last to arrive, and he was carrying his shoes.

"Geez, Frank, a guy can't even go to the bathroom around here!" he complained.

Frank motioned them onto the couches and described the mysterious phone call.

"What bothers me the most is that this person knows a lot about us," he concluded.

"And he's here in the hotel," added Tony. "Or at least he was. Too bad we're not in Vegas—we could have security pull the surveillance tapes and maybe we could spot the caller."

"That's a good thought! I'll check with the manager in the morning and see if they have any hidden stuff they don't tell the public about. What's the matter, Linda?"

Linda was shaking her head and grimacing.

"If they know that much about us, they probably know about Jim, too, and he's on his own in Miami. I knew we shouldn't let him make that trip alone!"

"You're probably right about that," nodded Frank. "I'll call Edwards right away and have him alert the CIA agent meeting Jim. I'm not inclined to call this whole mission off just because of one phone call, but I want everybody on their toes from now on. Since the caller warned us to leave tomorrow, we should be relatively safe tonight. Tomorrow we'll figure out how to deal with this situation."

It was after 1:00 a.m. when Frank finally flopped onto his bed, exhausted. He had contacted Edwards, who had promised to pass the alert on to Jim's handler immediately. Frank had also spoken directly to Jim by calling the professor's personal cell phone but he had intentionally left out the part about the 'fatal mistake.' It didn't seem necessary to frighten the soft-spoken anthropologist until more was known about the nature of the threat.

The next morning, at breakfast, the mood was somber. When the last of the group returned from the buffet line and sat down, it was Buzz Edwards who spoke first.

"Well, the good news is that the hotel does have a few hidden security cameras positioned around the property and we'll have the tapes before we head back to the airport this morning. The bad news is that the hotel is pretty full and there was a big banquet last night, so there were a lot of non-guests on the property. It would have been easy for someone to slip in, make the call on one of the house phones, and leave without looking out of place. We'll check the tapes, anyway, but I don't expect much in the way of results."

"Great!" exclaimed Linda. "What about Jim? Has he been brought up to speed?"

Frank and Edwards both said "Yes" at the same time.

"I talked to his contact in Miami right after Frank called me last night," continued Edwards.

"And I talked with Jim directly," nodded Frank. Seeing Linda's surprise, he added, "Well, he does have a cell phone, you know. He promised to stay put until his contact shows up. After that he should be in good hands."

"So what's our next move?" asked Tony. "Obviously, our cover is blown here in Cancun and we don't even know who's mad at us."

"I have a plan," replied Frank, "but it still needs some fine tuning. I don't want to go into it here, but when we finish breakfast I want everybody to go back to their rooms and pack. We'll be checking out this morning with no explanation other than to say that our trip has been cut short. I'll fill you in on the rest of the details when we get to MX-2."

"Just what I need is more spy vs. spy intrigue!" said Linda. Looking squarely at Frank and Tony, she added, "I know you guys eat this stuff up, but I don't like it one damn bit."

Edwards and the five members of the NWIDI team re-entered the MX-2 hangar facility through the same side door they had used the day before. Assuming that they were being watched, they made a production of unloading their baggage and carrying it into the hangar with them. When they were securely inside and the metal door was shut behind them, Edwards signaled for them to drop their gear and follow him.

"I'll have someone come and collect your stuff right away. Let's get down stairs and find out what Frank's big plan is."

Frank stood at the white board at one end of the conference room. His team, Buzz Edwards and Javier Reyes sat at the large table waiting to hear what he had in mind.

"Here's what I have so far," began Frank. "As soon as possible, Fitz and Susan are going to file a flight plan for Seattle and take the Learjet as far back as Albuquerque with three volunteers from this facility—volunteers who look as much like Linda, Tony and me as possible. From Albuquerque, the Fitzgeralds can take the plane back to Seattle and wait for our call. Meanwhile, the three volunteers can return on commercial flights, one at a time. Hopefully, that will convince our mysterious friends that we've heeded their warning and gone home to Seattle."

When Frank paused, Tony asked, "And then what?"

"Well, that's all I have figured out, so far, but somehow we need to get away from here without being recognized. If our caller thinks we've gone home, maybe we can continue our investigation as we originally intended."

"I may be able to help there," said Edwards. "We've enlisted the services of a state-of-the-art British underwater cable repair vessel named the Atlantic Protector. It's based in the Bahamas and it's already headed this way. However, it's still about

500 miles out and too far to reach by helicopter. If we could get Javier and his folks to ferry you out to meet it, you'd be out of sight and headed in the right direction. I had hoped we would be able to spend the next couple of days planning and then I was going to chopper you out to the Protector once it was on station over the site, but this may work just as well. What do you think, Javier?"

Javier nodded. "We only have one boat large enough to make a trip like that, but I believe it's available and we'd be happy to take Frank and his team. In fact, we could plot an intercept course with the ship that also takes us above the site of the Canadians' underwater ruins, just to see if there's anything visible on the surface."

Linda wrinkled her nose. "I'm not sure I like the idea of spending an extended period of time on a ship, but at least we'd be out of here. What about poor Jim?"

Frank thought for a minute and then replied. "Okay, how about this? The Fitzgeralds lay over one night in Albuquerque to convince anyone who's monitoring us that the return trip was legitimate. The next morning they amend their flight plan and change the final destination from Seattle to Florida. Anyone watching will see the plane depart and assume it's headed home and no one in Florida will be looking for them. Fitz, find a place to hide the plane near Miami and contact us. If it looks like we need to abort Jim's mission to Cuba, he'll come to you and you can get him out of there in a hurry. Otherwise, you'll be relatively close by if we need you and away from the prying eyes here in Cancun."

Linda smiled and Tony slapped his hand on the table.

"I knew we kept you around for a reason, Frank. That sounds like the plan we should have had from the beginning. Now what about these boats—Javier's and the other one? What will we need logistically?"

Edwards pointed to Javier, indicating that he should go first.

"Our vessel is only a 90-foot research ship and space will be limited, but there's one triple-bunk stateroom the three of you can share if we leave some of the regular crew behind." Javier pulled down a roll-up map of the Caribbean from above the white board. "Based on our last location of the Protector, we should intercept her about here, 92 nautical miles northeast of the site." He pointed to a spot on the map and stepped out of the way so the rest could see.

"It will take about 21 hours to get there, so we'll have some time to strategize during the trip. As for equipment, I'd suggest you travel as light as possible. Two or three changes of clothes and your personal items are about all you'll have room for on our ship."

"And that brings us to the Protector," said Edwards, taking over from Javier. "She's a little more luxurious than Javier's boat—she's about 400 feet long and has 86 private cabins! They always have space available for visiting dignitaries and the skipper has assured me that there's plenty of room for the four of you. I think you'll be impressed with the ship. It's so automated that the builders claim it can leave port, travel to the site of a broken trans-oceanic cable, make the necessary repairs and return to port without a single crew member on board!"

"What about the depth of this site?" asked Frank. "How deep can the Protector work?"

"No problems there, my friend. She carries an ROV—an unmanned mini-sub—that's good down to 6,000 feet. And this ROV is a rolling, swimming underwater laboratory. It's as good as being there! It's better, actually, because there aren't any humans in harm's way with the ROV doing the work."

"Cool!" beamed Tony. "So what are we looking for with all these high-tech toys, and what do we do if we find something?"

Edwards frowned. "I'm afraid you're going to have to make that up as you go, Tony. The officers of the Protector are Brits and most of the crew is from the Philippines. We've cleared the officers for low level classified work, but a lot of these guys—and gals—are engineers. If you find something, they'll probably figure out what it is before you do, and we can't help that. Even the Navy doesn't have a ship with the capabilities of the Protector, so we're stuck with the situation. If the site turns out to have military significance, damage control will be up to the four of you."

"This gets to be more fun every minute," laughed Tony. "How soon can we get going?"

A short two hours later, Frank, Tony, Linda and Javier stepped off Cozumel's Municipal Pier and onto the research vessel *El Caribe* dressed as members of the Mexican Coast Guard. In their ball caps, sunglasses and bright orange life vests, no one could have recognized them as the same four who had carried their luggage into the MX-2 facility earlier that morning. Now they were each carrying military-issue blue duffle bags that held everything they were being allowed to take with them. As soon as the four newcomers were onboard and below decks, the ship slid away from its berth and out into the wide channel that separates the island of Cozumel from the mainland of Mexico.

Once they reached open water, the first mate knocked on their stateroom doors and gave them the "all clear." Frank, Tony and Linda had been assigned the triple-bunk room and Javier was sharing a double-bunk room with one of the crew members. One at a time, they used the ship's only bathroom to shed their uniforms in favor of shorts, t-shirts and sun screen. Soon they were all seated on the aft deck of the *El Caribe* watching the Yucatan Peninsula shrink into the distance.

"Well, that was interesting," commented Linda. How did I look in a uniform?"

"Not as good as you look out of it," grinned Tony. "I hope you remembered to pack that yellow bikini you had in Japan."

Linda blushed and Frank wagged his finger at Tony.

"Down, boy! There will be plenty of time to tease later. Right now, we need to put our heads together and come up with some sort of plan so we don't look like complete dunces when we board the Protector. Anybody have any ideas?"

"I heard Edwards suggest that our target might be a submarine," said Tony suddenly getting serious. "Is that even a possibility, at 2,200 feet?"

"Oh, sure!" replied Frank. "The Navy's USS Dolphin is rated to 3,000 feet and carries a crew of more than 50. And there are submersibles that have been down to 35,000 feet."

"Yes, but not for extended periods of time," replied Javier. "We've been monitoring these signals for more than three years and they've been non-stop until yesterday."

"Well, that's true. Nothing in anybody's fleet can stay submerged for that long," acknowledged Frank. "Maybe what you've been listening to is just an underwater beacon designed to provide a directional indicator to submarines in the area. If it's not ours, then maybe the Russians dropped it during the Cuban missile crisis to keep their subs from running aground as they rounded the tip of the island."

Tony laughed. "Are you suggesting the Russians built something that could actually last forty years? Come on, Frank, you saw the crap they sold the Viet Cong. Most of it didn't last four years, much less forty."

"Okay, then I'm out of ideas. Anybody else?"

"Javier, you say you've been receiving signals for more than three years," said Tony. "Can you describe them to us? Are they random, repetitive, or what?"

"Well, they're actually a mixture of everything. Over the time we've been listening, we've learned to recognize a number of repetitive patterns, but we also receive a lot of seemingly random stuff. Every minute of every transmission has been digitally captured and we continually analyze it by computer, but all we've learned is what I just told you."

"Wait a minute, did you say 'transmissions' just now?" asked Linda. "I guess I assumed that this signal was more or less constant, 24-7."

"Oh no, sorry if I gave you that impression," apologized Javier. "We receive regular bursts, or transmissions, at twelve hour intervals and they're so regular you could set your watch by them— 7:00 a.m. and 7:00 p.m."

"Interesting," mused Frank. "What are the shortest and longest ones you've ever received?"

"I don't have the exact numbers in my head, but they normally last about a minute and a half and the longest was just under eight minutes. Each transmission consists of a sequence of signals that is repeated twice in a row."

"And when was the long one?" asked Frank.

"Well, again, I don't remember the exact date, but it was about two years ago, in July, I think. As soon as we reach the Protector and have access to a computer, I'll get the exact answers for you."

"Yes, I'd appreciate that," nodded Frank, who seemed to be pondering some private mystery. "A one-of-a-kind transmission like that might be a real clue to what's going on down there."

"I agree," nodded Javier, "and we searched for a correlation at the time of the event but nothing turned up. We checked astronomical data, geological data—we even tried world news—but nothing seemed to check out."

"If you don't mind, I'd like to have Linda run that analysis again when we get aboard the Protector. Can we get her access to a computer?" asked Frank.

"Absolutely! Edwards didn't really make this clear in our briefing, but that $20 million ship is loaded with computer and communications gear and she was ordered this way solely to support your investigation."

"*Our* investigation, my friend," smiled Frank. "You're part of the team now, at least for a while. You and your organization have a three and a half year head start on us and we're going to need your help if we're to learn anything out there."

Javier smiled and glanced around the group, from Frank to Tony to Linda. "I appreciate that—and I look forward to working with each of you."

Javier's eye contact with Linda caused a slight blush and she looked away quickly.

After a light lunch, prepared by the ship's Second Mate, Frank suggested that they take turns getting some rest. The *El Caribe* would be passing almost directly over the site of the Canadians' "lost city"—the source of the mysterious transmissions—at 11:00 p.m. and he wanted everyone well rested when they got there. In an effort to provide Linda with some privacy in the cramped quarters, Frank suggested that she take the first shift in their shared room. He and Tony would nap later.

Along with the Coast Guard uniforms and duffle bags, Edwards had provided each member of the NWIDI team with a letter-sized, waterproof pouch to hold passports and any other documents they wanted to protect from the elements. Frank retrieved his from the stateroom and retired to the ship's galley to do some serious thinking. Meanwhile, Tony had struck up a conversation with one of the few English-speaking deck hands and Javier had gone to the bridge to review their course with the captain.

Frank pulled out the envelope he had originally received back in Seattle and studied it carefully. Periodically, he jotted notes on the back of the envelope and mumbled to himself. The pouch also contained several articles he had found on the Internet about the Canadian team's exploration activities and Frank made notes from those as well. Eventually, he stuffed everything back into the pouch and sealed it shut. Leaning back in his chair, he clasped his hands behind his head, closed his eyes and pondered what he had just read. He must have dozed off, because when he opened his eyes again, Linda had her hand on his shoulder and she was saying, "...to the room and stretch out."

"Huh? Oh, hi, Linda. Yes, I think I'll do that but can you round up Tony and Javier first? I have something I want to show you."

Five minutes later they were all seated at the small table in the ship's galley and Frank had the document pouch in front of him.

"I've been going over some stuff I brought with me and comparing it to the information Javier provided earlier today. I can't be positive until we know the exact date of that eight-minute transmission, but I believe it will coincide—to the hour—with the

Canadian team's first pass over the site with their side-scan sonar, which they did two years ago, on July 17th."

"So maybe the transmissions are automated warnings, designed to scare away large fish or something," guessed Tony. "Like whales or sharks."

Javier shook his head. "No, we've compared the sounds to every known marine voice and it's not even close."

"I think," said Frank, leaning back in his chair again, "that the transmissions are just that—transmissions from the site discovered by the Canadians to another site elsewhere. The repetitive portions of each message could be the equivalent of a call sign or a station ID and the rest could be a routine status report providing water temperature or other variable data. When there's unusual underwater activity in the area, the message is naturally longer, and when the activity is something like sonar signals the message becomes an alert."

"Wow, Frank, that must have been some fantasy I woke you from," laughed Linda. "I'm glad I didn't let you sleep any longer!"

"Laugh if you want, but I think you should take a look at this." Frank pulled a colored picture out of his pouch and turned it so the others could see. "It's a relief map of the ocean floor here in the Caribbean made with some brand new satellite technology. Can you see this incredibly straight groove right here? Well, the western end of it just happens to match the GPS coordinates of the place where we'll be at 11:00 p.m. tonight!"

"And what's at the other end?" asked Javier as the group hunched over the table and stared intently at the picture.

"An island in the Bahamas called South Bimini," scowled Frank. "You might know it as the home of Bimini Road, which isn't really a road at all but is something much more mysterious."

Chapter 3

At 10:30 p.m. the augmented NWIDI team met on the aft deck of the *El Caribe*. There was a nervous energy in the air as they anticipated their arrival over the site of the alleged underwater ruins—and source of the mysterious signals. The air was warm and humid, and a slight breeze was blowing from the south. Clear skies provided an incredible view of the stars and a full moon provided a ghostly illumination.

"Are we there yet?" asked Tony as he rubbed sleep out of his eyes and sipped from a cup of steaming coffee.

"Almost," replied Javier. "We've made better time than expected and the Captain said he'll shut down the engines when we're directly over the site. He's keeping a close eye on the GPS right now, but he'd like to join us once we're over the spot."

"The more eyes the better," nodded Frank as he slid a pair of oversized binoculars out of a worn leather case. "Since we have no idea what we're looking for, be alert for anything out of the ordinary. I don't really expect that we'll see anything on the surface, but our chances are much better now than when we return in the big ship."

Soon, the engines throttled down and stopped. Without the constant forward thrust, the *El Caribe* bobbed like a cork in the surf and the observers were forced to grab the ship's rail for balance.

In passable English, the Captain stated the obvious. "We have arrived at the coordinates I was given, but the ship's instruments don't indicate anything unusual. The radar shows no other vessels in the area and the water and air temperatures seem quite normal."

Even though the outside temperature was a balmy 78 degrees, Linda shivered as she stared out into the dark Gulf of Mexico and realized how insignificant the little ship was in the vast body of water that surrounded them.

Frank had been scanning the horizon with the binoculars when he suddenly froze.

"Captain, please turn off all the running lights and make the ship as dark as possible!"

Frank snapped the binoculars back up to his eyes as the Captain issued an order in Spanish into a small walkie-talkie he carried.

"What is it, Frank?" asked Tony. He cupped his eyes with his hands to shield out the surrounding light. "I don't see a thing."

As the ship gradually went dark, everyone stared intently in the direction Frank was looking. After a long silence, Frank lowered his binoculars and frowned.

"I don't see it anymore, either. Maybe it was just my imagination."

Aware of Frank's training as a forward air controller in Viet Nam, Tony knew that if Frank thought he saw something, it was probably out there.

"Yeah, right! What was it?"

"I thought I saw something moving out there at the very edge of my vision, but I guess I just imagined it," replied Frank.

After several more minutes of scanning the horizon, Frank lowered his binoculars again and said, "Captain, you can turn the lights back on. I don't think we're going to learn much tonight, so let's get underway and rendezvous with the Protector. Thanks for stopping, though."

As the engines came to life, Linda returned to the shared cabin and Javier went below to scrounge for a snack. Frank had slumped into a deck chair and Tony dragged another over to join him.

"Okay, old man, spill it. What did you see out there?"

Frank shook his head. "It was probably just my eyes playing tricks on me, Tony. I was trying very hard to find something and so I did."

"I don't believe you! Back in 'Nam, you could spot a bug on the back side of a tree from a mile away. What do you *think* you saw?" pressed Tony.

"Well, just for a second I thought I saw something sticking out of the water, but when I blinked it was gone."

"A periscope!" shouted Tony.

"That's impossible—you heard the Captain say there wasn't anything on the radar. Besides, it looked more like part of a sphere. It might have been something from one of the missing boats, but it was probably just my imagination. We'll check it out again when we get back here with the big ship. In the mean time, what do you make of the radio transmissions they've been monitoring? Pretty weird, huh?"

"Yeah, and obviously not a natural phenomenon, either. Irregular intervals, irregular signals—that's got to be the work of humans. In light of your recent sighting—sorry, *possible* sighting—I'm leaning towards the submarine base theory. Wouldn't it be something if those damn Russians have been lurking in the waters just off our coast ever since the Cuban Missile Crisis? They could be eavesdropping on our communications, monitoring our space shots from Florida or doing any number of other nasty things!"

Frank leaned back in his chair and ran his fingers through his hair, staring at the night sky.

"Tony, any functioning vessel would have to surface now and then, if only for routine maintenance and fresh air, and our Navy would certainly have detected a boat traveling to or from this site. But what if, as you suggest, the Russians brought a sub over here in the 1960s and lost it. For whatever reason, it sank and all hands were lost. Rather than expose their deed, the Russians decided to just leave it down there in 2,000 feet of water, assuming that it would never be discovered. Years later, the sea water finally corrodes some electrical wiring to the point where it causes a short and fires up a long-dormant distress beacon. Javier and his buddies come along three years ago and as soon as they drop their gear into the water, they hear the signals. Then these Canadians show up with their ROV and the beacon system reacts by sending out a more robust distress call. Maybe this sub has been lying there decaying for 40 years and now it's finally starting to break up. That would even explain what I thought I saw tonight. Maybe it was just a piece of the sub that finally corroded off and floated to the surface."

"Well, I like my version better," smiled Tony, "but yours probably makes more sense. I guess we'll find out for sure when we get our own ROV down there. But how does your theory explain the other reason we're out here—the missing fishing boats?"

Frank yawned in the dark. "I haven't worked that part out yet. At this point, there's no evidence the disappearance of the boats has anything to do with the underwater site or the signals."

Tony settled back and locked his fingers behind his head, lost in thought. After mentally reviewing the possibilities, he pressed the friendly debate. "And the sudden halt to the radio signals? How do you explain that?"

When Frank didn't answer, Tony realized that his friend had dozed off and he decided that sleep wasn't such a bad idea. Tomorrow they would be aboard the larger ship and there would be plenty to do.

Sunlight glinting off the ship's railing woke Frank at sunrise. Tony was snoring fitfully in another deck chair nearby so Frank quietly eased himself up and made his way to the hatch leading below deck. When he reached the small galley, he was surprised to see Linda, Javier and the boat's captain sitting at the table sipping coffee and chatting.

"Morning," he mumbled, heading straight for the coffee urn in the corner of the room.

"Good morning, Frank," replied an almost-too-chipper Linda. "Did you sleep well?"

Frank grunted a non-committal reply and when he turned back to the group they were engrossed in conversation again. He leaned back against the galley wall and asked no one in particular, "So, what's up?"

"The Captain and Javier were just explaining to me what their organization does and it's fascinating. Did you know that they're the only group currently monitoring the environmental health of the eastern Gulf of Mexico?"

"Uh, no, I didn't know that," yawned Frank. "What time do we rendezvous, Captain?"

"Pretty damn soon, I'd say," called Tony from the top of the stairs, "unless that big blue and white ship on the horizon is the Cuban Navy coming to blow us out of the water."

The Captain looked at his watch and stood up. "Your friend is right, Mr. Morton. We should be along side the Atlantic Protector in about thirty minutes. Please excuse me!"

The Captain bolted up the stairs and disappeared behind Tony, bringing the first smile of the morning to Frank's face. He patted Linda on the head as he returned to the coffee urn.

"I'd say he finds you charming, my dear. He seems to have lost track of time!"

"Well I haven't," grumbled Tony. "I sure hope we have something better than deck chairs to sleep on tonight—my back is killing me!"

Linda blushed and smiled sheepishly.

"I'm really sorry, guys, but you should have knocked on the door. There are three bunks in our room, you know. I would have come and reminded you, but once my head hit the pillow last night, I was out cold until about an hour ago."

"It's probably better that we slept out on the deck," laughed Frank. "Tony was snoring so loud this morning that I thought the Captain was sounding the fog horn!"

"Well, tonight we should all sleep good because I understand the Protector has arranged private officer's quarters for each of us," interjected Javier. "And speaking of that, we'd better go get our gear together so we'll be ready when it's time to make the transfer. I'll meet you all up on the deck in fifteen minutes."

At just past 7:00 a.m., Frank, Tony, Linda and Javier thanked the captain of the *El Caribe* for his hospitality and climbed into the large cage-like box the crew of the Atlantic Protector had lowered to the deck of the smaller boat. When the make-shift elevator was closed and secure, the captain gave the thumbs-up signal and the NWIDI team was hoisted up. Once aboard the Protector, they were greeted and shown to their quarters by Andrew Booth, the ship's First Officer.

"Master Roberts sends his regrets that he could not welcome you aboard personally, but he felt his presence was needed on the bridge while the two vessels are so close together," explained the 30-something merchant marine officer. "He would like you all to join him in the officers' mess in about an hour, if you're   up to it."

"Of, course, Mr. Booth," replied Frank, accepting for the group. "And we appreciate your hospitality."

"The Protector is, quite literally, at your disposal, Mr. Morton, and please, just call me Andy—everyone else does."

Stopping part way down a long hallway one flight above the ship's main deck, he indicated four doors and said, "Here we are— Staterooms 18 through 21. They're all identical, so I'll leave it to you to decide who sleeps where, but please let me know later so I can update the ship's intercom directory. To get to the Mess, continue down this hall to the end and then turn left. It's the second door on the right—you can't miss it. Shall we say about 8:30 a.m.?"

The staterooms were small but adequate. The furnishings consisted of a single bed, a clothes locker, a straight-back chair, a wash basin and a unit with a cupboard above, a fold-down writing desk in the middle, and three drawers in the bottom. All were made of metal and all were permanently attached to the metal walls of the room. A small bathroom in the far corner contained a toilet and a shower stall, also made of metal.

The team assigned themselves rooms in the order they were standing in the corridor: Javier in number 18, Linda in 19, Tony in 20 and Frank in 21.

"Why don't you all come down to my room after you're settled?" asked Frank. "We should probably have some kind of plan in mind before we meet with the captain, so bring ideas with you but give me time to shower and shave—say 15 minutes, or so."

A few minutes later the four had crowded into Frank's room and Linda had even thought to bring a notepad and pencil.

"Okay, let's get started," announced Frank. "We're obviously going to ask the captain to send the submersible—I believe they call it an ROV—down to see if it can locate anything visually. Does anybody have any specific requests or shall we just let these guys do their thing and see what happens?"

"How much do they know about the ruins?" asked Tony.

"Only what they might have read on the Internet, and that's probably nothing," replied Frank. "Given the potential archaeological significance of this find, it's been very poorly covered in the media, and that works in our favor. But the officers, at least, know we've chartered the ship and the senior officers probably know that the U.S. government is footing the bill. I think we need a good cover story before we meet the captain."

After a moment of thought, Tony chuckled and said, "Hey, how about if we tell them that we're UFO investigators looking for a flying saucer which we think crashed here a few days ago?"

"Tony, that's…" began Linda.

"That's just crazy enough to keep them from taking us seriously and off-the-wall enough to justify our presence," laughed Frank. "Tony, sometimes you amaze me! Okay, guys, here's the plan."

Over the course of the next hour, the crew pieced together a cover story about a non-existent UFO group from Seattle that had convinced the government to fund a trip to the next credible UFO sighting in order to defuse complaints about government cover-ups. They even decided to call the group NWIDI in case anybody got nosey. Casual research would, in fact, turn up a Seattle-based group called NWIDI!

"And if we do find something tangible, be it megalithic ruins or the rusted hulk of a Soviet sub, we'll act just as surprised as everyone else and explain that our agreement with the government requires us to report any findings to them," concluded Frank. "At that point, Buzz and his crew can come out here and take control of the situation and we'll head home."

As they filed out of the stateroom, Linda said, "I have just one question—what if we *do* find a UFO down there?"

The others were silent for a second and then burst out laughing all together.

"Good, one, Linda," roared Tony.

The captain of the Atlantic Protector could have been a character out of any recent Hollywood movie about the sea. A large, stocky man in his mid-60s, he had wavy gray hair and a full salt-and-pepper beard. His appearance, along with his deep voice and serious nature, suited his position of authority perfectly. He stood and smiled as the NWIDI team entered the officers' mess and remained standing until the guests were seated across from him at the large, rectangular table.

"Welcome aboard, folks! I'm Nigel Roberts, the captain of the Protector, although, technically, my title is Master rather than Captain. I've asked my senior staff to join us so we can better understand how we can be of service to you. To my left is my First Officer, Andy Booth, and to my right is the Atlantic Protector's Chief Engineer, Alistair Hopkins."

Frank introduced himself and the other members of the team. After briefly relating the cover story they had made up just minutes ago in his room, he nodded to the Captain, indicating that he was through.

"Ah, UFOs! Well that explains all the mystery regarding our orders and the urgency to get us out here. About all we knew when we left port was that the British government had asked our company to dispatch a ship at full speed to this location, where we were to pick up a group of Americans and provide whatever marine services were requested. Most unusual, indeed, Mr. Morton!"

"Well, I'm sorry for the secrecy, Captain, but we didn't actually make the request —that would have come from our government—and the whole sense of urgency probably got inflated as the request traveled through the various agencies involved. However, we very much appreciate your hospitality and we look forward to working with you. To be honest, we left Seattle on pretty short notice, too, so please excuse us if we seem a little disorganized. Most of our UFO investigations involve sightings in the sky, so we're really out of our element out here and we welcome any suggestions you or your staff have. And, please, I'm Frank and this is Tony, Linda and Javier. There's no need for formalities with us."

The Captain relaxed a little and smiled at the NWIDI team members. "Well, let's get to it, shall we? I assume the reason your government requested the services of a ship such as the Atlantic Protector is because your search will require the use of a submersible like our Poseidon 3, correct?"

"That's correct, Captain. There isn't much information available about this part of the Caribbean, but a survey done in this vicinity about two years ago indicates we may be looking at depths of 2,000 feet or more."

"The Poseidon is good for about three times that, so depth shouldn't be a problem. Do you know what kind of bottom conditions we'll be dealing with," asked Chief Engineer Hopkins.

"Not for sure, but that same survey reported a vast plain of fine white sand in this area, and I think that's where we should begin our search. We're not too far from a feature called the Cuban Shelf, a series of terraces that ultimately drop off thousands of feet. If our mysterious object ended up out there, we'll never find it, so let's start easy—maybe we'll get lucky."

What Frank wasn't telling the officers of the Protector, of course, was that the Canadian research team that had discovered the megalithic ruins two years earlier had reported its location as being on this same sandy plain. Switching back to his UFO cover story, he added, "I have some GPS coordinates that are based on several visual sightings. I suggest we start there and work our way out in a standard spiral search pattern. If your side-scan sonar picks up anything interesting, we'll deploy the ROV and check it out."

The Captain raised his eyebrows and asked, "Do you folks really expect to find something down there?"

"We're always hopeful," smiled Frank as he handed the captain the GPS information. "That's what keeps us going. However, you should be aware that the U.S. Government has a political stake in this expedition because they're trying to convince the public that there's no cover-up regarding UFOs. They don't really want us to find anything—they just want us to appear to be free to look."

The captain glanced at the piece of paper and then passed it on to his First Officer.

"Set a course, Mr. Booth, and let us know when you have an ETA. Mr. Hopkins, please prepare to deploy the side-scan sonar as soon as we're on station. That's all, gentlemen."

"Aye, aye, Captain," both men replied in unison as they stood and left the room.

When they were out of sight, the captain fixed a stern gaze on Frank.

"Okay, now that the pleasantries are out of the way, let's get down to business, shall we? I've been at sea enough years to know that this ship's day rate isn't being paid for a silly 'witch hunt' and I think I have a right to know why my ship and my crew are here. What's going on, folks?"

Frank leaned back in his chair and crossed his arms.

"As we told you, Captain, we're here investigating a reported UFO sighting..."

Tony could see the blood rising in the captain's neck so he jumped in to interrupt.

"Frank, he's right! We might as well lay it all on the table. Captain, we have reason to believe that there's a scuttled Russian submarine in the area and we think it's starting to break up. If there *is* a boat down there, we need to determine if it was powered by conventional or nuclear technology so we can better understand what kind of environmental impact it may have on the area— particularly the southern coast of the U.S. But until we know what we're dealing with, this information must be kept strictly confidential."

"Oh, course, of course!" nodded the captain. "I knew it had to be something more serious than a UFO incident!"

While the captain's face returned to its normal color and he relaxed a bit, Frank, Linda and Javier tried to hide their surprise.

"That explains why your government is involved and I'm proud to say that this ship and her crew are uniquely equipped to assist you in your search," beamed the captain. "And I thank you for taking me into your confidence—I'm sure your orders instructed you otherwise."

Frank recovered and nodded to the captain. "You're quite correct, but you and your crew will be the first to see anything we find, anyway, so our cover story is only delaying the inevitable if there's really a sub down there. However, we wouldn't want your crew writing home to friends and family about this if it turns out to be a false alarm."

"Quite!" smiled the captain. "Shall we go up to the bridge and see if Mr. Booth has an arrival time available yet?"

As the four NWIDI team members filed out behind the captain, Linda yanked on Tony's shirt. When he glanced over his shoulder, Linda mouthed the words "WHAT WAS THAT?" but Tony just shrugged and continued on. At the end of the line, Frank smiled to himself. Tony had told him that he liked that submarine story better!

At 4:30 p.m. that afternoon, local time, the Atlantic Protector arrived at the designated GPS coordinates and deployed its side-scan sonar. Frank, Tony, Linda and Javier had spent the last eight hours getting a detailed tour of the ship, meeting and having lunch with most of the ship's fifteen officers and relaxing in their private quarters. During a rare minute alone, Linda confronted Tony about his submarine story.

"Hey, I could see that Frank's weak UFO line wasn't going to cut it, so I pulled something out of the air," Tony replied unapologetically. "If you had a better idea, you should have jumped in."

The NWIDI team was now assembled on the bridge, along with Captain Roberts and his senior officers as the ship began its methodical search of the area. Not ten minutes into the sonar run, an instrument on the left side of the bridge began to beep loudly and the captain excused himself to confer with the young crewman who was positioned near the instrument. After several exchanges with the crewman, the captain turned to the four team members, who were collectively holding their breath.

"I think we found it, folks—right where you said it would be!"

Quietly, so only the other team members could hear, Frank whispered, "So now the question is, what *did* we actually find—a submarine or a UFO?"

Chapter 4

The sun was finally peaking over the eastern horizon, but Frank had been awake for hours, pacing back and forth across the sixty-foot-wide rear deck of the Atlantic Protector. The sonar discovery of the previous afternoon confirmed that something was definitely below the surface, but only live video from the ROV would tell them what it was and the captain had elected to wait until morning to put the ROV in the water. Now that it was finally sunrise, Frank was anxious to get started.

As he reached the starboard-side rail and started his turn, Frank noticed something floating in the water very close to the ship. From his vantage point, two stories above the surface, the object below appeared to be a very large milky-white plastic container of some kind but it was difficult to tell. Frank heard a commotion to his left and turned to see two crew members running from an open door of the superstructure.

"What is it?" Frank asked the two men as they joined him along the rail.

"It bobbed to the surface, just now," answered the man closest to Frank. "It looks to me like the cargo hold liner from a fishing boat. Are we looking for a sunken trawler, sir?"

"Ah, not exactly," stammered Frank, "but that's an interesting observation. Is it going to be brought aboard?"

"The captain is being notified right now, but I doubt it. We see strange things afloat at sea all the time and we generally leave them in the water. Once we hoist something aboard we sort of become responsible for it and tossing it back is like littering, if you get my drift. My name's Willis, by the way. I'm the ROV pilot and this here's my assistant, Hadley. We were getting ready for this morning's dive when we noticed this thing with one of our ship-mounted cameras."

"Pleasure to meet you both," smiled Frank, as he shook hands with the two crewmen. "How much has the captain told you about today's objective?"

"Just that we'll be looking for anything out of place on the bottom and that we'll be working for a bunch of Yanks," replied Willis too quickly.

As he realized what he'd said, he blushed and added, "No offense, sir!"

"None taken," smiled Frank. "And please call me Frank. I hope to be there, looking with you, so I'm sure we'll talk again, later. Good luck with whatever that thing is!"

Frank started forward toward the only door that he knew lead to his cabin. As he pulled the heavy metal door open, Tony almost fell out onto him.

"Hey, Frank! Out for a morning stroll?"

"No, I've been up for a while," he said, jerking his thumb over his shoulder, "but it looks like some flotsam just surfaced from one of the fishing boats, which may be what we picked up on sonar last night. I can't wait to get a look at the bottom!"

"Well, you don't have long to wait. I saw the XO in the officers' mess and he said the ROV is scheduled to go over the side at 0700 hours. That's less than an hour from now. He also said he's been trying to reach you in your room, by the way."

"I'd better go check in. Do you know if Linda and Javier are up yet?"

"Javier was in the mess talking to one of the crew, but I haven't seen Linda. I'm just going to get some fresh air and then I'll meet you at the coffee pot," laughed Tony. "You look like you could use some!"

Frank carefully followed the memorized path that would take him back past the officers' mess and to his cabin. All the passageways looked the same to him, and knew that he would quickly get lost if he weren't careful. When he passed the mess the smell of fresh coffee almost lured him in, but he wanted a quick shower and shave before the day got started. As he turned the corner to the corridor where the NWIDI cabins were located, he ran—quite literally—into Linda who was headed in the opposite direction.

"Ouch! Excuse me...oh, morning, Frank! I was just on my way to breakfast. Have you been up all night?" asked Linda.

"Hey, between you and Tony I'm going to get a complex! I can't look that bad, but yes, I've been up for a while. I'm just going to clean up and I'll catch up with you in a few minutes. Tony is out on the deck getting some air and I think Javier's already in the mess. Will you keep everybody there until I get back?"

"Sure," smiled Linda, "especially Javier."

Frank was half way through his shower before he realized the significance of Linda's parting comment.

"That's going to be trouble!" he thought, smiling to himself.

Thirty minutes later, Frank arrived in the officers' mess just as the ship's loudspeaker announced, "ROV deployment in fifteen minutes. Stations, please."

Frank chose a Styrofoam cup instead of a mug and filled it with hot coffee. Walking along the table, he passed Tony, Linda and Javier to seek out the executive officer.

"Good morning, Andy! Where can we get the best view of what's going on down there today?"

"Good morning, Frank. There's room for one of you in the pilots' shack but I'm afraid the rest will have to join me on the bridge. We have a live video feed up there but it's not like being at the controls."

Without hesitation, Frank replied, "I'll take the shack! Can you point me in the right direction and then see that the others get to the bridge?"

"Of course." Turning to a junior officer across the table, Andy Booth said, "Jamison, please escort Mr. Morton to the ROV pilots' shack. And if the rest of you will follow me, I'll show you to the bridge."

Frank settled into a small office chair that had been squeezed between pilot Ken Willis and navigator George Hadley. The "shack" was actually an eight-by-ten room just inside the door that Frank had seen the men use earlier. The three men sat at a console that extended the length of the room and across one end. In front of them was a double-high row of computer monitors and video screens, along with a staggering array of dials, gauges and switches. Willis sat in front of a joy-stick device and Frank could just make out a set of pedals on the floor under the console. Hadley sat to Frank's left in front of a unit that reminded Frank of the mixing console in a recording studio.

One of the video screens showed the twelve-foot-square, nine-foot-tall ROV Poseidon 3 suspended from a ship-board crane. As the ROV was moved slowly toward the side of the Atlantic Protector, Willis pressed a button on the console and the caterpillar-like tracks on the bottom of the ROV began to move. Another button stopped them and Willis spoke into the microphone of his headset. "Mobility check complete. All systems go for dive."

Frank watched as the ROV was slowly lowered to the surface of the Caribbean. Just before the tracks touched the water, a dozen more monitors came alive as Hadley flicked switches on his control board to activate various cameras aboard the ROV.

Frank's jaw dropped and Hadley explained. "We have
color, black and white and infrared on five sides—front, back, left
right and top. In addition, there are a couple more specialty cameras
on the front. The apparatus that's attached to the front of the unit is
a very sensitive metal detector used for finding buried cables."

"But I thought the cables were all fiber optic these days,"
replied Frank. "Aren't they basically very fine glass tubes?"

"Yes," nodded Hadley, "but they're wrapped in a protective
metal sheath and that's what we look for. Fortunately there isn't
much else down there that's metal."

Frank watched the monitors as the ROV descended below
the surface and began its journey to the sea floor, some 2,000 feet
down. The pictures on the video screens got dimmer and dimmer
until, just before reaching the bottom, Hadley turned on the ROV's
external lights.

"Wow!" exclaimed Frank. "This is amazing! I had no idea
there was so much life down there."

Willis and Hadley were silent for several long seconds until
a red light on the console illuminated and Willis said, "Captain, this
is ROV command. We're on the bottom and awaiting transfer
of control."

Several more silent seconds passed before Willis said,
"Roger that, we have control."

Frank looked questioningly at Hadley, who twisted the
microphone on his headset up and whispered, "Ken is now in
control of both the ROV and the Atlantic Protector. Since the cables
that connect the ROV to the ship must remain attached at all times,
we need to have the ship follow the ROV as it moves along the
bottom. This is all done electronically, of course, but it's a tense
time for the captain because he's relinquished control of his vessel.
Ken is going to take the ROV to the exact GPS coordinates you
provided and then we'll take a look around, 360 degrees. After that,
it's your call."

Frank's palms were sweaty and he felt a chill run down his
spine, but the only thing he could say was, "Man, this is *so* cool!"

As the ROV crawled along the smooth, sandy bottom,
Frank's eyes darted from one monitor to another but there was
nothing but more sand in every direction. The visibility was pretty
good, considering the depth, but there wasn't anything to see.

Eventually Willis said, "All stop. All stop." He turned to
Frank and said, "The ROV will continue to move a little more as the
ship comes to a stop, but we're essentially at the spot where we had

the positive sonar readings last night. As we remain still the visibility will improve a little and then we'll have a good look around."

As the pictures cleared, all three men studied the monitors, trying to make out anything that might explain the reading taken the previous night.

Suddenly, Hadley spotted something on one of the black and white monitors.

"There! Off the port side, about 25 meters away! I can't tell what it is, but there's definitely something out there!"

Willis alerted the ship above. "We've got something, bearing 268. We're moving to it."

As the ROV moved, the object grew from a vague dot to the obviously badly damaged remains of a commercial fishing boat. And it hadn't been on the bottom long, either!

Willis brought the ROV to a halt a few meters from the wreck and Hadley adjusted the external lights to provide the best possible illumination. Using a small control stick, the navigator slowly panned the site with a video camera.

The boat was more or less in-tact and at first it was hard to understand why it had sunk, but as the camera reached the back of the vessel, a hole the size of a baseball came into view.

"It looks like it was hit with a small rocket," commented Frank as he studied the monitor. "Probably a shoulder-launched weapon similar to those used in the mid-east against trucks and personnel carriers."

"How can a hole that small sink a boat that big?" asked Hadley.

"Ah, well if you could see the other side—the one that's buried in the sand—you'd understand," replied Frank. "These things are loaded with a tremendous amount of high explosive that's rigged to detonate a split second after the nose hits something hard. That way the explosion occurs inside the target vehicle, rather than outside. My guess is that the hole on the other side is the size of a small bus."

"That sounds like the work of terrorists or some paramilitary group," suggested Willis. "It was certainly no accident, though."

Frank nodded. "This is probably a case of bad guy versus bad guy, but we probably should report it anyway."

"We're recording all this," he told Frank. "Maybe the maritime authorities can figure out what happened, but I guess we've found the source of last night's sonar hit, huh?"

"It sure looks like it," agreed Frank.

And while the navigator's statement was probably true, Frank knew that the recent shipwreck wasn't really what he was looking for. It couldn't possibly be the source of the mysterious signals that Javier's group had discovered because those signals had stopped before this boat had sunk.

Disappointed, Frank leaned back in his chair and as he did so felt his head bump against something. Suddenly, a buzzer went off and an amber light on the console started blinking wildly.

"Oh, crap! What did I do?" asked Frank, as he shot back to an upright position and looked over his shoulder to see a panel of switches directly behind him.

Laughing, Hadley reached behind Frank and pressed a button to silence the buzzer. The light on the console continued to blink rapidly.

"Sorry, I should have mentioned that panel when you sat down," apologized Hadley, still laughing at Frank's look of terror. "You accidentally turned on the cable locator out in front of the ROV and it appears that it's sitting right over something metallic. Good work, Frank!"

"It's probably just something from the wreck, but let's check it out as long as we're here," said Willis. "Besides, it's good practice for me."

Using compressed air jets located around the outer edge of the rectangular metal detection grid, Willis carefully puffed away small amounts of sand while Hadley monitored a computer display.

"Whatever it is, it isn't moving," offered Hadley. "It's either pretty big or it's a ways down in the sand."

Willis continued to alternately work the bottom with the air jets and wait for the visibility to clear. After several minutes, he moved the ROV forward and backward, a meter in either direction. With each move, the signal strength dropped off significantly, indicating that the object they had discovered was relatively small.

"Well, now I'm really curious!" exclaimed Willis. "Let's bring out the heavy equipment, George."

Frank watched the monitors as a robotic arm, apparently attached to the upper portion of the ROV, came into view. Using a wide shovel-like tool on the end of the arm, Willis skillfully simulated a miniature back hoe and quickly cleared away sand.

At a depth of about one foot, one of the cameras caught a glint of light reflecting off something shiny.

The robotic arm disappeared for several seconds and when it came back into view the shovel tool had been replaced with what looked like a nozzle. Willis used a focused stream of compressed air to clear off the top of what was now clearly a rectangular metallic plate measuring about six inches by eight inches. As the dredging continued, Willis soon exposed the sides of a small box. Once again the arm disappeared and this time it returned with a retractable pincer-like device which Willis used to lift the box out of the sand. When the arm moved out of site for the final time, the box went with it.

"It's safely aboard the ROV," nodded Hadley, before Frank could even ask the question. "What a stroke of luck to stop the ROV right over it! And if you hadn't bumped that switch, we still wouldn't have found it. I'm curious to see what's inside because it was too deep to have come from the wreck we found."

"Right," mumbled Frank. He was staring intently at one of the monitors and had barely heard Hadley's comment.

Standing, so he could touch one of the monitors, Frank said, "What's this right here? Is this a glitch in the video or is there a ridge out there?"

Willis and Hadley studied the area where Frank was pointing and then Hadley realigned a camera with a powerful telephoto lens to get a better look.

"Damn, Frank, I think you're right!" agreed Willis. Into his microphone he said, "We're underway again, bearing 035, distance about 40 meters."

As the ROV closed on the feature Frank had spotted, it became obvious that the line was actually the edge of a feature in the sand, almost like the ridge of a sand dune. As the ROV approached the feature, the instruments indicated a slight rise in the sea floor. Willis stopped the ROV just short of the crest and made some adjustments to his controls.

"I'm going to approach very, very carefully, now, because I don't want to drive off a cliff. What did you call it, Frank?"

"The Cuban Shelf," replied Frank. "And, from what I've read, you definitely don't want to drive off the edge of that! Would the ship's winch cable hold us if something like that happened?"

"Us?" asked Willis. "Frank, I know this seems like the real thing, but we're still aboard the ship, remember? We're not down there with the ROV! And no, the winch cable probably wouldn't hold if it was suddenly snapped tight by the ROV falling over a cliff. We have to keep quite a bit of slack in the cables to allow for the pitching and rolling of the ship, so the ROV would fall a ways before coming to the end of the cable. Anyway, here we go."

Frank was glad the lighting in the control room was dim so the other two men couldn't see him blushing! But they had been so focused on the monitors that they had become like windows in the side of the ROV and it was easy to imagine being inside the vehicle, more than 2,000 feet below the surface.

The ROV had only moved a few inches when something flashed across several of the monitors.

"What was that!" shouted Hadley, grabbing the rod that controlled the video camera. "There's something out there on the port side!"

Suddenly the flash appeared in another set of monitors.

"Now it's out front!" This time it was Willis that shouted. "And it's headed east in a big hurry."

Hadley spun the front-mounted video camera to the right and was able to catch the blurred image of a silver object moving at right angles away from the ROV at high speed. It was gone in an instant and the three men sat there in silence for a minute.

Willis' headset crackled and Willis replied, "Yes, captain, we saw it, too, but it was too quick for an ID. Yes sir, I agree. I'll return control to you as soon as the ROV is back on level terrain."

Turning to Frank and Hadley, Willis explained, "The captain wants to get the ROV out of there, at least until we figure out what that was."

Hadley had returned the video camera to a forward position again, and Frank was studying a monitor.

"Ken, whatever we scared up left in a hurry as we approached this crest. I think we need to see what's over the hill, don't you?" asked Frank without taking his eyes off the monitor.

"The captain has ordered the ROV topside, Frank. I can't disobey…"

"Just a few more feet and this forward camera will have a view over the ridge. We have to take a look, Ken. Just another couple of minutes and then we can turn back," pleaded Frank.

"Leave the ship in position and use up some of the cable slack," said Hadley. "By the time the captain figures out which way you've moved the ROV, you'll be rolling back. I agree with Frank—we need to see what's out there."

Willis nodded and moved the ROV forward toward the ridgeline. Suddenly, the camera cleared the top of the "hill" and the view changed.

"My God!" yelled Hadley. "That looks like a city!"

Chapter 5

Willis, Hadley and Frank stared at the monitor in disbelief. They all knew it couldn't be possible, but the image on the screen appeared to be the faint outline of several structures, some tall, some smaller and rectangular, and one shaped like the step-pyramids found throughout Central America.

"Well, well, well!" exclaimed Willis, leaning back in his chair and smiling to himself in the dim room. "I think we've figured out why Frank and his team commandeered the Atlantic Protector! Just what *is* that, my friend?"

Frank didn't respond immediately, partly because he was trying to make up a reasonable answer and partly because he could hear the captain chattering wildly in Willis' headphones.

When Willis finally broke the silence in the small control room, it was to speak into his microphone.

"Roger that—ship's control has been returned to the bridge. Initiate recovery of the ROV."

Willis swung the small boom mic attached to his headset away from his mouth, leaned forward to put his elbows on the console and rested his head in his hands.

"Man, is he pissed!" mumbled the submersible's pilot. "As soon as the ROV is back on deck, he wants all three of us to report to his stateroom immediately."

Hadley was still staring intently at the bank of monitors, even though the rising ROV's camera no longer had a view of the mysterious skyline.

"I'll take full responsibility," offered Frank. "I encouraged you to move the ROV forward and, technically, this is my mission—so you were just following orders, Ken."

Willis, who was now busy monitoring the recovery of the ROV, looked up and said, "Thanks, Frank, but it's you he's mad at, not me!"

It took more than thirty minutes to get the ROV back onboard and stowed and, while Wills coordinated the effort, Hadley and Frank reviewed the images from the ROV's cameras. Hadley had converted the video footage into digital files and they reviewed them each several times, finally stepping through the view of the departing silver object, one frame at a time.

"There! Stop right there!" shouted Frank.

Hadley hit a key on the keyboard and zoomed in on the blurry object on the screen.

"There's no evidence of any propulsion system," commented Frank. "Given the acceleration that this thing had, there should be signs of a disturbance in the water around it, but I don't see anything."

Hadley moved forward and back, one frame at a time and finally nodded.

"You're right, Frank! I don't see a prop, so that would mean thrusters of some kind—but I don't see any evidence of air or water jets either. It's as if it were being attracted by a giant magnet off in the distance."

"But that would have affected the ROV, too," said Frank.

"Maybe the object we saw isn't made of steel," said Willis, looking up from his controls for the first time in minutes. "And maybe Hadley's magic magnet only attracts whatever the object is made of."

Forty minutes later, when the three men reached the door of the captain's office, Willis knocked.

"Enter!" boomed the captain's voice from inside. Willis glanced at Frank, rolled his eyes, and opened the door.

The captain was sitting at a small desk in his stateroom, which was about twice the size of the other officers' quarters. He looked up with a scowl and motioned the three men to a brown leather couch with a flick of his head. He stared at them for several tense seconds before he began.

"Mr. Morton, I don't know why you insist on treating me like a fool, but I assure you I don't appreciate it. Now just..."

"I'm sorry, Captain, but I..." interrupted Frank.

"You *what*, Mr. Morton? You have another lie to tell me? First we were looking for a UFO and then it was a submarine! Instead, we discover a recently sunken fishing boat and a mysterious underwater craft capable of incredible speeds. And, oh, did I mention a *whole damn city*! Now, just what is going on out there?"

Frank leaned forward and plopped his head into his hands for a second before responding.

"Captain, please forgive me for being evasive, but our orders are to provide only as much information as is absolutely necessary. The truth is that that we *were* looking for a UFO and we *were* looking for a submarine, or something like one. We also suspected there might be an archaeological site down there, but I can assure you that the silver object we saw was not on our list at all—that was a complete surprise. Please let me explain."

Over the course of the next fifteen minutes, Frank told the captain and the two ROV engineers everything he knew about the mission, including the mysterious signals, the discovery of the underwater ruins by the team of Canadians and the distress calls from two fishing boats just days earlier.

"I'm sorry I couldn't tell you this earlier, Captain, but we had no idea what we might find—and in case there was nothing to be found, we didn't want to let the cat out of the bag, so to speak. As it turns out, everything—and more—was here, so there's no use pretending any longer."

The captain leaned back in his desk chair and crossed his arms over his chest. His anger had transformed into bewilderment.

"I wouldn't have believed that story anyway, if I hadn't seen it with my own eyes, Mr. Morton. I'm not used to being deceived but I guess I'd have done the same thing, in your position, so let's forget it and move on. What's the next step? I assume the fishing boat is of no consequence and that we can just report it to the authorities. But what about that speedy silver ball? And what about the ruins?"

Frank thought for a minute, looked at the two men next to him on the couch and then back to the captain.

"I'm guessing the mysterious ball is long gone, but we should contact the Navy anyway. As for the ruins, there isn't a ship better equipped than the Atlantic Protector and I have a very high regard for these two beside me, so I suggest we learn as much as we can in the next few days."

"Yes!" shouted Hadley, before clamping his hand over his mouth in embarrassment.

"Contain yourself, Mr. Hadley," smiled the captain. "And what about you, Mr. Willis? Are you in agreement?"

"Absolutely, Captain!" replied a more subdued Willis. "This is the chance of a lifetime. I'd like to reconfigure the ROV slightly, but we *must* do this. Like Frank said, our vessel is uniquely qualified for this kind of work."

"Alright then, see to it, gentlemen. We'll reposition the ship immediately and re-deploy the ROV as soon as you're ready."

Willis and Hadley nodded to the captain and fled the room like their feet were on fire. When the door closed, the captain looked at Frank sternly.

"Can I assume that you're going to be absolutely truthful with me from here on out, Mr. Morton?

"Absolutely," repeated Frank emphatically. "Like I said, Captain, all our secrets—and then some—are out, anyway. However, I need to ask you to caution your crew to not pass on any of what they have seen, at least for the moment. We obviously don't know what we're dealing with here, and it could have national security implications."

"I understand. The only off-ship communications available to the crew is a satellite-based email system that I control and I've already taken it offline. I'll simply say that the system is down due to a hardware issue and that there will be no more email until we return to port. As for the radio operators, I'll have a talk with them shortly but they aren't authorized to transmit any messages unless they come from a senior staff member. What about contacting your Navy?"

"I have a satellite phone, so I'll call my contact in Mexico and he can pass the word. I also want to shuttle one of my team members out here from Miami and maybe the Navy can help out with that, too. If it's okay with you, I'd like to continue to monitor the exploration from the ROV shack, but I'd also like Tony and Linda to have a chance to review all the video from the cameras they weren't able to see on the bridge."

"I'll see to it. I must confess, this is all pretty exciting— even for an old sea dog like me."

Ninety minutes later the ROV was lowered back over the side of the Atlantic Protector and every person aboard the mother ship became totally immersed in the exploration of the sunken ruins 2,100 feet below the surface. As much as everyone would have liked to zip through structures, their ears and eyes were mounted on the ROV that, quite literally, moved at a crawl. To maximize their efforts, the captain and Willis had decided to conduct their survey in a series of one- to two-hour dives separated by a repositioning of the ship based upon what they were seeing. The ship, with the ROV aboard, could cover more distance in a few minutes than the deployed ROV could cover in an hour.

During the first dive, Frank, Willis and Hadley explored the perimeter of what appeared to be an outer wall. Only about a meter of it was exposed, but it was too high to cross without lifting the

ROV and the only opening was through an arched gate. The cable connecting the ROV to the ship above made crawling through the gate impossible, so the decision was made to explore outside the wall during the first dive. The team examined the construction techniques and looked for tooling marks on the large blocks that made up the wall. After an hour there was no doubt in anyone's mind that the wall was artificial.

For the second dive, the Protector was repositioned to lower the ROV about 50 feet inside the wall on a broad "avenue" that ran from the gate to a cluster of large structures. One of these structures was similar in design to the pyramid Frank had seen at Uxmal in Mexico's Yucatan Peninsula and he was eager to get some close-up video for comparison.

During the twenty-minute crawl from the touch-down point to the pyramid-like structure, Hadley used the ROV's onboard cameras to constantly scan the landscape but there was no sign of the silver object they had seen earlier. An odd assortment of sea life lived 2,100 feet below the surface, but none of it looked round and shiny.

As the ROV approached its target, it was apparent that a lot of sand had drifted into the areas between the structures and now hid the lower levels. To the left of the pyramid, a rectangular structure had what appeared to be a row of window openings below the roof line, but no doors were visible and Frank speculated that at least the entire first story must be buried in the sand. Nearby, a pointed, square shaft of stone poked through the sand like a boney finger. As the ROV crawled past the shaft, Hadley used one of the cameras to capture images of the glyph-like inscriptions etched into the near side.

"Any idea what they say?" asked Hadley.

"Not a clue!" admitted Frank. "I studied Maya writing a few years ago and these look similar, but I don't recognize a single character. Maybe when Jim gets here he can give us an idea what culture they're from."

"Jim?" asked Willis. "Who's Jim?"

"Jim Barnes. He's the anthropologist in my group," replied Frank. "Unfortunately, he was in Miami when we made this discovery, but I'm having him rushed out here right now. He'll be in heaven when he sees this stuff!"

"Hey guys, take a look at this!" Hadley was on his feet, pointing to one of the monitors. "It's a little tight, but that's the first sand-level entry point I've seen that we could squeeze the ROV through. Who's up for a peek inside the pyramid?"

When the ROV neared the opening, Willis rolled the unit back and forth a full length of the tracks several times to make sure the sand was stable.

"I know this is a huge discovery," he commented, "but I don't think the folks back in the U.K. would appreciate losing the Poseidon, either. If this sand is as deep as Frank thinks, there will probably be a very steep drop-off, almost like a sand waterfall, just inside the opening, so I need to stop this side of the threshold. That should give you a pretty good view with the forward cameras and lights, though."

The control room was ghostly silent as Willis rolled the ROV up to the opening. Since Willis was using a small camera mounted on the front of the ROV to maneuver the craft, the powerful flood lights had to be left off. Finally, he released his tense grip on the joystick and leaned back.

"It's all yours, boys. Let's see what's in there!"

Hadley flicked on a bank of powerful lights mounted across the front of the ROV and then turned on the forward camera that was equipped with the telephoto lens. A monitor directly in front of Frank flashed pure white and then blinked off.

"Hey!" shouted Hadley. "What was that?"

"I think you just fried a camera," replied Willis. "Kill the lights and give the camera a minute to reset. If you didn't melt the CCD, try turning the camera back on and then add lights very slowly."

Frank was on his feet with Hadley and all three men were wondering what could have caused the intense light to feed back into the camera lens.

Hadley flicked a switch.

"The camera's back on and it appears to be working. At least I don't have any error lights on my panel," he said.

"Well, maybe you got lucky," replied Willis. "Now slowly bring up one of the small variable-brightness spots on the cable guide. That's right—slower—stop, right there! Do you see that?"

"It looks like there's a light shining back at us!" exclaimed Frank.

Using a joystick, Hadley moved his small spotlight back and forth a few degrees and the image on the monitor followed.

"Well, I'll be damned!" laughed Frank. "That's our light, and it's being reflected off something!"

"But what?" asked Hadley.

"Leave the camera and lights just as they are," said Willis. "I want to try something."

Slowly, over the next few minutes, Willis maneuvered the ROV in and out of the opening, gradually changing the angle of the craft with respect to the threshold. As their view panned through nearly 100 degrees, the reflection of their own spotlight always remained visible.

When Willis brought the ROV to a stop in the threshold for the last time, he shook his head.

"I don't get it! It's as if the inside of this entire structure is covered with mirrors!"

"Not exactly," muttered Hadley, intently studying his instruments. "I've been doing some quick distance measurements and the reflections appear to be coming from a cylindrical surface just twenty-five feet away. I'm pretty sure that the structure at this level is more than twenty-five feet across, so I think we're looking into a room that may have served as a navigational beacon or a signaling room."

"That makes sense," nodded Frank. "A light placed near the opening would have been intensified just like our spotlights were. As we develop a map of this site, it will be interesting to see what would have been directly behind us—to see who or what was being signaled."

As a result of the discovery of the beacon room, Frank encouraged the team to move the next ROV mission to the opposite side of the pyramid. For one thing, it would establish the approximate size of the structure but Frank was also curious to learn if the original inhabitants of this now-sunken city had any special interest in whatever faced the beacon room. If similar rooms were found on other sides of the structure, that might indicate that it served, at least in part, as a lighthouse or a navigational aid. Frank had already formed his own opinion, but he decided to keep it to himself for the time being.

By the end of the first day of exploration, the Atlantic Protector was buzzing with excitement. Every person onboard, right down to the lowliest deck hand, was caught up in the historic significance of the images being sent back from the ship's ROV, Poseidon 3. More than once Frank had overhead conversations speculating on who built the city and why it was now more than 2,100 feet below the surface. For now, all communications with the outside world were being very strictly controlled, but he knew that once the Protector docked, the news would spread fast and he wanted his team member and friend, Jim Barnes, to arrive ahead of the rumors that would certainly develop. Frank paced back and forth under the huge octagonal helipad that stood on supports above the Protector's forward deck. As he checked his watch for the tenth time, his trained ear detected the faint sound of a military helicopter in the distance.

Frank greeted Jim as he climbed out of the UH-3H Sea King helicopter, ducked low and ran to the side of the helipad. By the time the two friends were down the metal stairs, the Navy helicopter was already disappearing into the distance.

"Sorry for the sudden change in plans, Jim. How was your flight over from Miami?"

"Wild!" smiled Jim broadly. "You must have built a real fire under the military, because they busted their butts getting me out here. The CIA agent that was babysitting me raced me to a Coast Guard station in Miami, where I was flown by plane down to the Key West Naval Air Station. From there I literally hopped out here by helicopter—I think we made three or four fuel stops along the way and the ride was really rough! So, now that I'm here, what's the big panic?"

Frank laughed, both at Jim's first experience in military aircraft and at his gross understatement of the discovery they had made.

"Well, we've just spent the day exploring what appears to be an ancient city that's about 2,100 feet below your feet. I just thought you might want to get in on what will likely be the archaeological discovery of all time, that's all!"

Jim's jaw dropped as he exclaimed, "No kidding! Is this the place you mentioned on our way down from Seattle?"

Since Jim had left the team in Albuquerque, he hadn't been in the briefings at Cancun's MX-2 base so he had only heard idle chatter on the Learjet.

"That's the place!" smiled Frank. "And we already have a mountain of work for you, so let's get you some chow and get you to work. The next ROV mission is about twelve hours away and we need your advice on where to dive."

"The next what? Who's diving?" sputtered a confused Jim as Frank led him by the arm down into the bowels of the big ship.

Tony, Linda, and Javier joined Frank and Jim in the officers' mess and got caught up on recent events while Jim ate. When Captain Roberts stopped by for coffee, Frank took the opportunity to introduce him to Jim and later, when Andy Booth, the ship's First Officer, dropped in, Frank made sure Jim got a room near the other team members.

"I'm afraid the rooms on either side of your block are both occupied, but there's a room available a few doors down the hall. I trust that will be acceptable?" asked the always polite Andy.

"I'm sure it will be fine," smiled Jim. "I doubt if they'll let me sleep anyway."

"Speaking of that," interrupted Frank, "We need to get you busy on some photos so we can plan tomorrow's dive schedule. Andy, is there a conference room onboard that we could use for a couple of hours?"

"This is it," said Andy, indicating the officers' mess with the sweep of his arm. "But we can pull this folding panel closed and give you some privacy. I'd offer you the entire room, but the tea and coffee pots are…"

"No, we wouldn't consider coming between a crew and its caffeine," laughed Frank. "This end will do just fine and we'll try to be brief."

"The next meal isn't until morning, so take your time. Until then, there will just be the occasional sleepy officer stopping in for a spot of tea. Nice to meet you Jim, and I expect I'll see you all bright and early tomorrow. The first ROV deployment is at 7:00 a.m., I believe."

Andy pulled the room divider partially closed and disappeared into the hallway.

"Nice guy," commented Linda. "He can't seem to do enough for us."

"Actually, I've found the whole crew to be extremely accommodating," nodded Frank. "They're treating us like royalty. There's something to be said for the British sense of courtesy and respect. Now let's get down to business here. You three give Jim as many details as you can remember from today's work while I run down to my room and get some notes. I'll be right back."

Minutes later, Frank returned and closed the partition as tight as it would go. He had a manila folder, several note pads and a hand full of BIC pens.

"Sorry, but that was all I could scrounge up on short notice," he said as he handed out the pads and pens. "Jim, are you up to speed?"

"Probably not," he said honestly. "It sounds like you guys had a busy day and my head is spinning with questions, but I'll sort it all out. I need some time to study these photos and compare them with my reference materials. Do we have access to the Internet?"

"I'm working on that, but for the moment, no. The captain had to shut down the link to help contain the news of our discoveries. Shortly before you arrived, I talked with him about getting service restored to just our quarters and he's asked the Chief Engineer to look into it. But for tonight, I'm afraid you're stuck with whatever you have in that tattered leather bag of yours."

"Well, I didn't really pack for a glyph decoding assignment," frowned Jim, "but I'll see what I can do. And there's certainly plenty here for me to digest tonight. These pictures of the silver ball thing are fascinating. And what's going on tomorrow that you wanted my input on?"

Frank snapped his fingers and opened the folder he had retrieved from his room. "Ah, yes, tomorrow. Here's a rough map of the portion of the site we've explored so far. The Xs indicate the positions where we've lowered the ROV into the water and these dotted lines are roughly the paths traveled by the ROV once it was on the bottom. After you've had a chance to look over all this stuff, I'd like your recommendations on where we should take up the search tomorrow."

"Oh, no pressure there!" exclaimed Jim. "Just how am I supposed to do that?"

"I'm hoping a pattern will emerge that will remind you of some other site you've studied, or that something will look very out of place—anything that will point us in a specific direction. Otherwise we'll have to continue making more or less random drops with the ROV and hope for the best. I don't know how long we're going to be able to keep our work out here a secret, and I'd like to make the best possible use of our time."

"Well, I'll see what I can come up with, but you'd better let me get started if you want any intelligent answers by morning. There's a lot to go through here," replied Jim.

"There's one more thing I'd like you to consider," added Frank as he pulled another sheet of paper out of his folder. "I showed this to the others on the way out here, but it took on new significance today. This is a relief map of the ocean floor in this general area. Do you see this odd looking characteristic right here? It's a perfectly straight feature on the seafloor running from South Bimini Island, in the Bahamas, directly to the site below us. I'd like your opinion on what it might be."

Jim studied the satellite image in disbelief.

"You said it had new significance, Frank. What happened today?" asked Tony.

"Two things. On the third ROV dive, we discovered what turned out to be a signal or beacon room of some sort on one side—and *only* one side—of the pyramid structure. It turns out that it faces straight down this feature, toward Bimini!"

Jim looked up, now more intrigued by Frank's story than he was by the image. "And the second thing?" he asked.

"That silver object we saw on today's first dive disappeared in exactly the same direction—toward Bimini!"

Chapter 6

After their brief meeting in the officers' mess, Jim headed to his room to get settled in and begin his analysis work. The rest of the NWIDI team went up on deck to enjoy the warm tropical evening and chat about the events of the day.

"Wow!" exclaimed Linda, as she leaned over the rail and stared into the calm waters of the Gulf of Mexico. "It's hard to believe that there's a whole city right down there. It really makes you wonder how much more is hidden under the oceans of this planet, doesn't it?"

"*Sí*," nodded Javier, "especially in this region, with its rich history of early civilizations. If the city below us turns out to be Maya or Olmec, it would change the history of the New World."

"Indeed it would, my friend," added Frank. "This is all new to you, but the rest of us have seen things in the last year that will change the history of all mankind, not just the New World. The ruins below may be ancient, but I'm here to tell you that the silver ball we spotted this morning is no ancient artifact. I think it's related to things we learned on Yonaguni Island and in the Loltun Caverns of the Yucatan—that we're not alone on this planet and that we haven't been for thousands and thousands of years."

Javier stared at Frank. "What?" he exclaimed.

For the next hour, Frank, Tony and Linda took turns bringing Javier up to speed on the discoveries the NWIDI team had made on it two previous "expeditions." The first, in the summer of 2001, had taken them to Las Vegas and on to the Yucatan, where they had learned about twenty mysterious metallic spheres and their link to the ancient Olmec and Maya. On their second outing, in early 2002, the team had traveled to the southern Japanese island of Yonaguni to locate the origin of an ancient Ninja tsubute. In the process, they discovered secrets about the island that still hadn't been made public. And now, barely eight months later, they had just witnessed images of a previously unknown underwater megalithic site that was somehow connected to a shiny silver craft with an unknown propulsion system.

During the long narrative, the group had migrated to a cluster of deck chairs that had been pushed up against the high wall created amidships by the superstructure that housed most of the living and working quarters on the ship. Javier was sinking into a state of near disbelief as Linda described what she, Tony and Jim had seen inside Yonaguni's Mt. Urabu and just as he opened his mouth to ask a question a speaker mounted on the bulkhead high overhead boomed, "Attention on deck! Mr. Morton, please report to the officers' mess immediately. That is all."

Frank raised his eyebrows and looked at his watch. It was 9:30 p.m. local time.

"Could Jim have found something already?" he pondered. Indicating that the others were welcome to tag along, he added, "Let's go see what's up."

When the four reached the officers' mess, there was no sign of Jim. Instead, a small group of men that included the captain, Willis and Hadley were huddled around the end of the long table intently studying something on its surface. As the NWIDI crew entered, Ken Willis looked up and greeted Frank with a broad smile.

"Frank! We thought you'd want to be here when we opened this up for the first time. In all the excitement today, Hadley and I completely forgot about it and we found it in the ROV's hold while we were preparing for tomorrow's dives."

The group parted to make way for Frank and he spotted the metallic box they had recovered on the first mission of the day.

"Well, I'll be damned!" he shouted. "I'd forgotten all about it, too! You mean you haven't opened it yet?"

"No," replied Willis. "It was your discovery—you should be the one to pop the lid, don't you think?"

"Well, I certainly appreciate that, but I only made the discovery because I banged my fat head into your instrument panel! Let's crack it open, shall we?"

Willis nodded to another crew member, who flicked on a digital video camera he was holding and when he nodded back, Frank picked up the box and examined it for a latch or other fastener. The box appeared to be made out of silver or pewter and it had ornate engravings on the lid and three of the four sides. What appeared to be the back and bottom of the box were more or less smooth, although they showed signs of age. The box was about eight inches long by six inches wide and appeared to be about four inches deep. Frank turned the object over several times looking for an easy way in and as he did so, he could feel a weight inside shifting and a faint clanking could be heard. He looked up questioningly at Willis.

"Yeah, we heard that to. There certainly seems to be something inside, doesn't there?"

Tony slipped his Leatherman multi-purpose tool out of its belt holster and opened the heavy-duty screw-driver blade.

"I think you're going to need this," he said as he handed it to Frank.

Gently at first, and then with increasing pressure, Frank tried to force the blade of the tool into a barely visible groove under the narrow overhang of the lid. Tony joined the effort by holding the box while Frank pried. Just as they were about to give up, the lid flew off and since Tony was holding the box upside down the lid and several metallic objects from inside clattered to the table. The room was immediately filled with an unbearable stench and cries went up from everyone present. Both Linda and Javier jumped back out into the hallway and the others held there noses and backed as far away from the table as possible.

"My God, what is that?" mumbled Willis through the hand he had used to cover his mouth and nose.

The captain, who had retreated to the corner nearest the tea and coffee, flicked on the room's exhaust fan and replied, "It smells like death—very old death."

"Death?" inquired Frank as the odor began to dissipate and find its way out through the fan's ceiling vent.

"When I was a youngster," explained the captain, "my uncle was the undertaker in Ely, a town out near the Fens in eastern England. One summer I went to stay with him and this smell is very similar to that of the old family burial vaults used out on the wetlands. Only this is much stronger!"

Tony was already recovering from the shock of the smell and reached around Frank to pick up one of the objects that had fallen out of the box.

"It looks like some kind of coin," he said as he flipped the triangular silver-gray object over and over in his hand.

"I'm not sure I'd be handling those things just yet, based on the smell that came out of the box," commented Frank. "Let's get some photos of them as they are and then I think we should clean everything—including the table—with a good strong disinfectant before we go much further."

Tony put the object down approximately where it had originally fallen and stepped back from the table. He sniffed his hands, wrinkled his nose, and said, "I think I'll go wash my hands! I'll be back in a few minutes."

"Hey, knock on Jim's door and ask him to join us, will you? He's in Number 15," Frank called to Tony.

A couple of minutes later Jim raced into the room.

"Tony said you found some...oh, wow!" he said as he caught his first whiff of the still foul air. "What *is* that?"

Slowly approaching the table, he spotted the objects on the table and promptly forgot all about the odor.

"Those look like coins," he said, repeating Tony's observation. "Where did you find them?"

"They were buried in the sand near the site of a sunken fishing boat we found this morning," replied Hadley.

"Only we don't think they have anything to do with the wreck," added Frank, "because they were buried at least eighteen inches into the sand. Hadley and Willis, here, had to dig them out with the robotic arm of the ROV."

"So how did you know they were there?" asked Jim as he covered his mouth with his hand and stepped closer to the table for a better look.

Hadley started to describe the incident in the ROV control shack but Frank interrupted and said, "Let's just say I used my head. I'll tell you about it later. Do they look familiar?"

Jim studied them for a minute and then stepped back away from the table.

"Nope, I can't say that they do. I've seen three-sided coins before, but they all had very rounded points and I've never seen anything with a triangular hole in the center. If these really are old coins, they'd be pretty hard to manufacture without some modern tools. The edges are just too sharp and well defined."

"So what are you suggesting?" asked Frank. "Are these things old coins, new coins or not coins at all"

"I just don't know. I need time to study them more closely and compare them to other coins, but to do that I need access to the Internet, and I don't..."

"Actually," said the captain from the corner, "I think we have that issue resolved, but it's going to require that you work on the bridge, Mr. Barnes. My engineer tells me that we can't isolate the staterooms on this level from the crew quarters on the deck below. However, the bridge is on a separate feed and we've already restored service up there. We can set you up on one of our computers if you don't mind the normal comings and goings of an operating bridge."

"Actually, Captain, I have my own laptop. If you could just create a small workspace for me and connect me into your network that would be fantastic."

"Consider it done! It will be much quieter up there during the first watch, from 8:00 p.m. until midnight, or during the middle watch, which runs from midnight until 4:00 a.m. Perhaps you could schedule your work on the bridge during those periods and enjoy the solitude of your stateroom at other times."

Jim glanced at his watch. It was nearly 10:00 p.m.

"Could I go up there right now?" he asked. "I could probably have some answers about these mysterious triangles by midnight and that would still give me time to work up some answers for Frank before morning."

"Of course. Mr. Booth will show you the way and help you get set up. And if you will all excuse me, I think I'll get some sleep myself. Gentlemen—and Ms. McBride—I'll see you all in the morning."

Pleasantries were exchanged all around and the captain left the room, followed by First Officer Andy Booth and Jim.

"We'd better leave, too," said Willis. "Hadley and I still have some work to do before the ROV is ready to go. See you all in the morning."

"Good night, guys," replied Frank. "And, hey, thanks for a great job today!"

Tony reappeared in the doorway carrying a one-gallon plastic bucket and looked around questioningly.

"Where is everybody?"

Frank explained and then eyed the bucket.

"Good idea! Let's get this stuff cleaned up and take a closer look at it."

One of the remaining officers offered to take charge of the washing process, although Frank was pretty sure he was going to "supervise" while a crew member actually did the dirty work.

"I'm down the hall in number 21," Frank told the young officer. "Would you let me know when the objects are ready to examine? And please don't use anything too harsh until we know what the material is."

"Of course, sir!" replied the man. "I was thinking just warm water and dish soap to kill the odor and then a rinse in hot water to kill any bacteria that may be hanging about. We'll be careful, I promise."

Frank nodded with a smile and helped scoop the box and its original contents into the bucket. It seemed like everybody onboard was eager to get to the bottom of the mysteries that Frank and his team had brought their way.

As the young officer lifted the bucket off the table, Tony raised his eyebrows and whispered to Frank, "I think I'll help with the washing. See you in a few minutes."

"Good idea," nodded Frank. Turning to Linda, he said, "Let's clean up this table, too, before we forget. And then would you and Javier mind reviewing some of today's video footage with me? We need to put together a solid plan for tomorrow's ROV missions and I haven't even started yet."

Frank had commandeered a small television monitor from the ship's supply room and a video camera from one of the officers so he could review video in his room. For the next forty-five minutes he and his two assistants fast-forwarded through as much tape as they could, stopping only when the blurred images showed an anomaly. They were so focused on their task that Tony's knock on the door startled them all.

When Frank opened the door, the first thing he noticed was Tony's bandaged hand.

"What happened?" he asked as he stepped aside to let Tony pass.

"Oh, it's nothing—just a reaction to whatever was on that coin I picked up, I guess. The Doc says it looks like an allergic reaction, so he put some kind of salve on it and then wrapped it to keep the salve in place."

"The Doc—my God, Tony, are you sure it's nothing serious?" asked a concerned Linda.

Tony set the towel-wrapped silver box on Frank's desk and shook his head.

"The Doc said it didn't look serious, but I'd recommend some care with this," he replied, nodding at the box. "He gave me some medical exam gloves for us to wear until we know this stuff is really clean, but we rinsed everything in boiling water so I doubt if they're still contaminated."

"Well, let's have a look," said Frank as he slipped into a pair of the latex gloves. "Anything would be more interesting than scanning video of sand!"

Frank opened the towel and laid it out on his desk. Inside, the box, its lid and five triangular objects had been wrapped in heavy plastic to prevent any possible contamination. As he carefully opened the plastic, he instinctively held his breath, remembering the horrible stench when the box was first opened. When he did breathe, his nose took in the faint aroma of citrus.

"Well, they certainly smell lemony fresh and clean," he smiled, mocking a TV commercial for cleaning products.

Donning surgical gloves, Frank picked up one of the objects and examined it closely. It appeared to be a perfect equilateral triangle about two inches on a side. In the center was a small triangular hole and the area between the outer edge of the object and the hole was almost entirely covered with raised figures resembling hieroglyphs. The other side of the object looked very similar, but Frank noticed that the symbols were slightly different.

"Interesting," he muttered. Linda had already put on gloves, so Frank carefully handed her the first object and picked up a second.

"They're all different," commented Tony. "Five coins, tens sides and no two are the same. If they really are coins their shape and size must have determined their value because there's certainly nothing else in common between them."

"They're beautiful." commented Linda as she passed the first object on to Javier, who had also donned gloves. "The detail is amazing and the holes seem to be perfectly centered. They almost look machine-made."

One by one, Frank, Linda and Javier examined each of the five objects without knowing what they were looking at or looking for. As Javier set the final piece down on top of the others, Frank noticed that he'd been stacking them with their sides aligned.

He reached across in front of Linda and rubbed the sides of the stack with his thumbs and fingers.

"They're exactly the same size," he observed. "Or at least they're so close to it that I can't feel any difference. We should get these to Jim and see what he has to say."

"That's already been taken care of," said Tony. "The guy in charge of the clean-up crew was the one with the video camera when you first opened the box. We laid them all out, side-by-side, and filmed both sides before I came down here. That video has already been taken up to Jim, along with what little he got earlier."

"Well, then I guess we just have to wait for Jim to finish his analysis and see what he thinks about all of this. In light of Tony's reaction, I think we should keep the box and its contents secured until we know they're safe. Let's put the triangles back in the box, replace the lid and wrap it back up in the plastic. Maybe we can scrounge up some duct tape and seal the package shut for now."

Just as Frank was replacing the lid, Jim burst through the door and squeezed into the already crowded room.

"Frank where are...there they are! I need to see the triangular objects!" shouted Jim, reaching for the box.

Tony grabbed him in a bear hug, momentarily pinning his arms to his sides.

"Hold on there, Professor!"

"Jim, you need to put these on before you touch anything," said Frank. "Tony had a reaction to the one he picked up in the officers' mess so we're being careful until we know they're safe to handle."

Tony released his grip on Jim and Linda handed him a pair of gloves.

"Okay, but look at these!" he said excitedly. "These are frame grabs from the video that was taken of them earlier.

Jim slipped into the gloves and took over the position directly in front of the box. He slowly removed the lid and began examining the objects while the other four jockeyed for position to see the prints that Tony had taken from Jim.

Tony slowly flipped through the print-outs several times before Frank asked the obvious question.

"Jim, what are we looking for here?"

Jim was intently studying the triangular-shaped objects and barely mumbled a reply.

"Look at the first photo—the one taken in the lunch room."

Tony shuffled through the pages until he came to the correct one.

"Okay, so what?" he asked.

"Now try to find a match with any of the other pictures," mumbled Jim again.

After several seconds, Frank said, "There isn't a match! Jim, what's going on here? Did we lose one?"

Jim laid down the last triangle and slowly turned to face his colleagues. His look of concentration transformed into a broad smile.

"No, we didn't lose one, Frank—the inscriptions on these things are changing! In fact, not a single one matches those pictures that were taken just a few minutes ago! They've all changed once again!"

There was a long silence and everyone stared at the triangles, expecting to see them change before their very eyes. Finally, Javier made the sign of the cross and broke the silence.

"But that's impossible, right?" he asked timidly.

"Apparently not," Tony sighed. "Leave it Jim to find the weirdness out here."

"What about that city you guys found this morning?" Jim shot back in his own defense. "Wouldn't you call that a little weird? Or what about this mysterious silver ball I've heard so much about?"

"He's right," Frank said to no one in particular. "Our mysteries do seem to be multiplying but let's stay focused on this one, shall we? Any thoughts, Jim?"

"Are you kidding? This is right out of a science fiction novel! Given enough time I might come up with some answers for the city beneath us, but these," Jim exclaimed, "are out of my league."

"Well, I'm afraid you just graduated to the majors, my friend. Like Tony said, you're our resident expert on weirdness. However, if you don't have any ideas yet, let's set this aside and focus on tomorrow's ROV missions. We can always come back to the triangles later."

"Okay, well I do have some thoughts on that subject," brightened Jim. "Before they brought me these pictures I was looking over some of the footage taken on one of the ROV missions and I definitely think we should get a better look at that feature that seems to lead towards the Bahamas. I only caught glimpses of it, but it's hard to believe it's a natural formation. I suggest we locate the end beneath us and do a little digging. Didn't you say they dug up this box of triangles with the ROV?"

Frank nodded. "They have a number of tools that can be attached to a remote controlled arm. What are we looking for?"

"Well, what little I can see reminds me of a ditch that's been dug, had something buried in it and then been filled back in. This seems to be a disturbance on the ocean floor in an unnaturally straight line and it just seems like a good place to start."

"Wow," smiled Linda. "I would have bet money that you would have suggested exploring some of those structures that are just barely visible in the later images. What's happened to the archaeologist I worked with on Yonaguni?"

"Oh, I'd love to explore the ruins," said Jim, "but there's probably a perfectly natural explanation for them. This odd straight feature, on the other hand, has me stumped and I'd like to have a closer look at it. Then we can go back to the ruins and do some real archaeology."

Frank pulled a map down off a shelf over his desk, partially unrolled it and handed one side to Tony. Holding the other side himself, he pointed to a spot near the left side.

"This is about where we discovered the pyramid-like structure and the feature Jim's interested in seems to lead directly to it. We've already set the ROV down approximately here and we know the bottom is relatively smooth and safe. Since we have exact GPS coordinates, how about if we go right back there and travel away from the pyramid this time? Once we pick up the sea-floor feature, we can either follow it back towards the pyramid or take some samples right there. If we find anything interesting we'll continue to investigate. If not, we can drop here, here and here to explore some of the other structures we think we saw."

Before anybody could answer, there was a knock on the stateroom door. Rolling up the map and squeezing past the others, Frank pulled the door open a bit to see who was there.

"Captain!" Frank said in surprise. "I thought you were going to bed for the night!"

"I *was* asleep, Mr. Morton, but something has come up and I wanted to personally let you know that we'll be getting underway very soon. There's a Cuban gunboat alongside and they've threatened to fire on us if we don't move into international waters within the hour."

Chapter 7

Frank's jaw dropped in surprise as he opened the door and invited the captain into the already crowded room.

"What? I didn't know the Cubans even had a Navy! Is this for real, Captain?" stammered Frank.

"I'm afraid so," replied the captain. "It isn't much of a boat, mind you, but they are insisting we move the Atlantic Protector immediately and the home office, back in London, has ordered me to comply. Because my company works with so many different governments, we must be very careful to not to provoke any—even the Cubans. I'm sorry, but we'll be getting underway in just a few minutes. We've been ordered back to our base on Andros Island in the Bahamas."

"No apologies necessary, Captain," frowned Frank. "I understand your position—and that of your company. I'm disappointed, of course, because there's still a lot of work to do here, but that will have to wait for another time. How far away do we have to move to satisfy the Cubans?"

"Well, we're about two and a half miles from the nearest land right now and they're claiming a twelve-mile territorial boundary, so..."

"Too far to do any meaningful work," interrupted Frank as he reached for the map he and his team had been studying before the captain arrived. As he opened the map, he traced the imaginary line that was the mysterious underwater feature.

"This is what we were hoping to investigate tomorrow morning. This feature seems to extend all the way back to South Bimini Island at a more or less constant depth of six hundred meters. As you can see, it stays very close to the Cuban coastline for quite a ways but they begin to diverge where the coastline turns southeast. Do you think we could interrupt our return trip for one ROV dive about here? This point is closer to the Florida Keys than it is to Cuba, so there shouldn't be any political issues, and it's far enough away from both coastlines to have remained fairly undisturbed. Also, can my team and I impose on you for a lift back to Andros?"

The captain studied the map for a minute before nodding slowly.

"We'd be happy to provide you passage back to Andros, Mr. Morton, and I think we can arrange a stop along the way. I'll need to clear this with London, but I don't see any problems. I'm a little concerned about locating this feature again so far away, but we can certainly give it a try. I need to get back up on the bridge, but please join me later and we can plot a course to intercept this line of yours."

The captain turned to leave the stateroom but stopped midway through the threshold and turned to Frank.

"I almost forgot! I don't know what this means, but the message from the Cuban vessel ended with a rather strange statement. It said, 'Tell the Americans this is their second—and last—warning.' Apparently they know you're aboard the Atlantic Protector, Mr. Morton."

With that, the captain turned and headed down the passageway. Frank turned to face his team, equally shocked by the captain's remark.

"The call at the hotel in Cancun!" exclaimed Linda. "They've been tracking us ever since we arrived in Mexico, Frank."

Frank and Tony both had the same thought at the same time and turned to Javier. As soon as he saw the expression on their faces, he backed up and held out his hands, as if to protect himself.

"I didn't tell a soul, I swear!" he shouted.

"Well, somebody did, and you're the only one who knew where we were headed when we boarded the *El Caribe* back in Cancun," challenged Tony. "The warning was directed to 'the Americans' which certainly excludes you doesn't it?"

Linda stepped in front of Javier and glared at Tony.

"Hey, wait a minute! You're jumping to conclusions here! There were several others on the boat and dozens more at the military complex in Cancun. It could have been any one of them, Tony. Javier's our *friend!*"

Frank stepped between Tony and Linda and held an arm out in each direction.

"Okay, let's all relax. Linda's right, Tony, and we owe Javier the benefit of the doubt. What about it, Javier? Did you know everybody aboard the *El Caribe*?"

"Uh, no, there were a couple of deck hands I hadn't met before, but the crew is the responsibility of the captain. The researchers work for Centro Ecológico Cancun, of course, but the rest of the crew are sailors, not ecologists. I'll call the office and have them checked out, if you'd like, but I find it hard to believe that anybody in our organization would have any interest in your team or that they would know anything about the site below us."

"Thanks, but I'll have Buzz Edwards check out the crew. He has access to resources we don't and if the Cubans are behind the threats, he'll be especially interested."

Shifting gears, Frank went into command mode.

"Tony, grab my digital camera off the bed and go shoot as many pictures as you can of the ship that's hassling us. I'd like to trace it back to a port, if possible. Linda, you help Jim secure the box and its coins and then start packing up this video tape. I want to copy it all to disk before we reach Andros, but for now I want it stowed safely away. Javier, you come with me."

"Frank," protested Linda.

"Relax, Linda. I just need his opinion on something. We'll be right back."

Once they were outside on the main deck, Frank glanced around to make sure they couldn't be overheard before addressing Javier.

"Javier, does your organization normally operate in Cuban waters?"

"No, not, as far as I know," replied a noticeably shaken Javier. "Our work is concerned with the ecological state of the Yucatan Peninsula and we have no interest in Cuban affairs. Besides, we couldn't influence them one way or the other even if we did object to some of their practices."

"What practices?" pressed Frank. "What's going on over there?"

"Well, we know for a fact that they still use the waters surrounding their island as a garbage dump. Millions of tons of garbage a year get hauled out to sea and most of it ends up on our side of their island," fumed Javier.

"Why on the Mexican side? It seems like Havana would be the biggest source and it's on the north shore."

"Yes, but the water is relatively shallow on the north and east sides of Cuba. On the other hand, there's a deep trench that begins just south of here and extends across the Yucatan Channel and down the entire length of Mexico's east coast, eventually touching the mainland in central Belize. Sooner or later their pollution will make its way into our water systems."

Frank realized that he'd hit a nerve with Javier but this information had nothing to do with the problem at hand.

"Okay, let's get back to your organization for a minute. How well do you know the captain of the *El Caribe*? He had an unusual accent that I can't place."

"Captain Ochoa has been with us since we acquired the *El Caribe* about three years ago, Frank. Before that he was a merchant marine and hauled freight to ports all around the Gulf of Mexico and down the eastern coast of Mexico. Why?"

"For some reason, that name sounds familiar to me. Do you know anything about his background?" asked Frank.

"I know he's been living and working in the Yucatan for a very long time, but I think he's originally from South America— possibly Columbia or Venezuela."

"Of course!" exclaimed Frank, hitting his forehead with the palm of his hand. "Now things are starting to make sense. Three of the original founders of the Medellin Drug Cartel were the Ochoa brothers!"

"Oh, I'm quite sure our captain is no drug smuggler, Frank, but even if he were, why would the Cartel be threatened by your team's presence?"

"Well, it just so happens that our Learjet was originally seized from a Columbian drug dealer by the U.S. Government. I'll bet the Cartel has been tracking that plane ever since its former owner was arrested!"

"Do you think they know about the sunken city? They certainly seem to be trying to keep you and your team away."

"Maybe—or maybe it has to do with the sunken boat we found today. And it looks like they're going to get their way, because I think I just felt the ship start to move. Let's go up to the bridge and take a last look around—we may not see this place again soon."

When Frank and Javier reached the bridge, Tony was showing the photos he'd taken to the captain. He waved Frank over.

"What's up?" asked Frank, as he peered over Tony's shoulder.

"I'd be willing to bet that's no Cuban Navy ship, Frank! Look right here—they've painted over something on the hull. And this machine gun looks to me like an old Russian PKT that's been modified to mount on the ship."

"They identified themselves as a Cuban Navy vessel and they're flying the Cuban flag, so I have no choice but to comply," said the captain defensively.

"Oh, I agree completely, Captain. In fact, if they turn out to be who I think they are, the sooner we get out of here the better," agreed Frank.

The captain returned to the task of getting under way and Tony looked at Frank and shrugged.

"After talking with Javier, I think it's quite possible that this *Navy* ship and our Cancun caller may be Columbian traffickers who think we've come to disrupt their drug business. Given the history of our plane and our recent associations with Edwards, it would be a pretty good guess on their part, don't you think?"

"Right! What was his name? Rafael, or something like that, right? But why would they be tracking the plane now?"

"I was hoping you'd dig into that for us," smiled Frank. "If we're really being tailed by drug dealers, we may have to convince them to turn their attentions elsewhere."

Tony beamed. "I smell a fight brewing!" he said as he collected the camera and left the bridge whistling.

After several delays, the Atlantic Protector finally got underway just before 11:30 p.m. Its first heading took it perpendicular to and directly away from the nearest shoreline. Once it was beyond the twelve-mile limit, the ship executed a gradual turn to the northeast and assumed a course that would take it directly to the northern tip of Andros Island. With the limited GPS data the ROV had collected during the day, Frank helped the ship's navigation officer plot the point where the Atlantic Protector's course would cross over the path of the seafloor feature and then went to bed. It would take the ship nearly twenty hours to reach the intercept point and Frank had been up more than eighteen hours when his head finally touched the pillow at 1:15 a.m.

He awoke to the sound of loud and rapid knocking on his cabin door. Through the fog of sleep he could just make out Linda's voice calling his name.

"Frank! Are you alright? Frank, open the door!"

"Just a minute," barked Frank as he crawled out of bed and opened the door.

When he opened the door, Linda burst into his room looking almost hysterical.

"Frank, are you okay? You've been asleep all day and we're almost to the intercept point. The captain would like to see you on the bridge right away."

Frank looked at his watch. It was 10:00 and from Linda's comments he guessed it must be 10:00 p.m., not 10:00 a.m.

"Thanks, Linda. I need to grab a quick shower and then I'll be right up. Please let him know I'm on my way."

"Are you sure you're all right? We've been worried about you all day, but you looked so exhausted last night that none of us had the heart to wake you."

"I'm fine, just over-tired, I think. I haven't slept well since we left Seattle and I guess I finally just crashed. Run along and I'll be right behind you, I promise."

As Frank showered, he suddenly recalled snippets of a dream he'd had during the night. He couldn't pull up any details, but he remembered the triangular coins and something about a message he'd deciphered. The message was about a trip to a distant place. What stuck out in his memory most was that he—Frank—had decoded the message rather than Jim.

"Jim would just die," he said out loud as he smiled and reached for his towel.

Frank arrived at the bridge at 10:30 p.m. on the dot and apologized to the captain.

"I just got worn out," he explained.

"I fully understand," replied the captain. "In fact several of my crew have reported to the infirmary with severe exhaustion. I think the events of the past couple of days have put some imaginations into overdrive and interfered with the normal sleep cycle. You're welcome to have the ship's Doc check you out if you'd like."

"Thank you, but I'm fine now; I just needed to catch up on some sleep. I understand we're somewhere near the seafloor feature?"

"Well, we're near the point you selected," smiled the captain. "Whether or not there's actually anything down there depends on how well you projected its path—and whether it extends this far out from the sunken city. I'm sorry to have disturbed you, but Willis and Hadley want to go over some mission details with you before they turn in for the night. We'll put the ROV over the side at first light and see what we can find."

The two ROV specialists came through a door across the bridge as if on command and joined the captain and Frank. Willis had several pages of photos showing the various robotic arm tools available and he spread them out on a large map table.

"There isn't room aboard the ROV to take everything on a single mission, so we'd like your input on what you think we might run into, Frank."

Frank studied the pictures for a minute and then selected several from the group.

"I think we'll need to dig," he said pointing to the first tool he'd selected. "And depending on what the bottom is like, we may need something like this to chip at the surface." He pointed to another of his selections.

Willis smiled. "So it's going to be a normal cable retrieval job, huh? We don't need any special tools for that, Frank. That's what the ROV was designed to do!"

"Yes, but what we're looking for is probably buried. Someone described the feature as looking like a trench dug to hold something—then later refilled."

"Just like our cables," said Hadley. "We often have to dig up buried cable, and we almost always bury it after we finish a repair, even if it was exposed before we arrived. The cable lasts longer because the sharks leave it alone."

"That's right! The cable locator I activated by mistake yesterday—the one we found the metal box of coins with. Only we don't know if there's anything actually buried down there and, even if there is, we don't know if it's metallic."

"We'll find it, Frank, and we'll take along these tools, just in case. Since there's room for a few more, Willis and I will pick out some other stuff and call it good. See you in the morning, Frank. Good night, Captain."

With that, Willis and Hadley were gone.

"Great guys," commented Frank. "It was amazing to watch them operate the ROV yesterday. At one point I actually thought I was inside the ROV itself."

"They're the best in the business," agreed the captain. "The reason they're assigned to the Atlantic Protector is because we encounter some of the most challenging undersea terrain in the entire fleet. There are thousands of islands in the Caribbean and each one is the top of a mountain. That presents unique obstacles beneath the surface. Our region also has some of the oldest cable still in service and it was originally laid with little or no information about what the bottom looked like. It keeps life interesting, I can tell you that."

"Well, tomorrow should be interesting, too. Captain, I'm going to leave you for now and go see if any of my team members are still awake. I'm not the least bit sleepy and maybe I can find someone to review video tape with me. I guess I'll see you at daybreak."

"Good night, Mr. Morton. As soon as my relief gets here, I'll be retiring myself."

Frank made his way down to the officers' mess where he found Linda and Javier drinking coffee at the far end of the long table. Several officers were standing around the coffee and tea pots and Frank guessed they were about to go on watch.

"How are you feeling?" asked Linda as Frank sat down with a steaming cup of coffee.

"Oh, I'm fine, I think. I've managed to mess up my sleep cycle, but I can deal with that. A few hours of watching ROV video and I should be sleepy again! How about you two?"

"I'm fine," nodded Linda. "How about you, Javier?"

"Yes, me too," agreed Javier. Between the discoveries of yesterday and the stories you told me about your other two adventures, it's been like a trip to Disneyland for me"

"Any word from Tony or Jim?" asked Frank. "What did you guys do all day while I was catching up on my beauty sleep?"

"We all had lunch together, but I haven't seen either one of them since," shrugged Linda. "Jim was all excited about the triangular coins, but it didn't sound like he'd made much progress with them since he discovered the changing patterns last night. And Tony, well, he's just Tony. I think he wants to go back and beat up the entire Cuban Navy, or whoever they were."

"He could probably take them, too," laughed Frank. "How's his arm doing?"

"He said the doctor looked at it this morning and doesn't think it's anything serious. It was still bandaged, though. Do you think we should check on him?"

"I'll stop by his room on my way back," said Frank. "You two enjoy the evening—we have a big day ahead of us tomorrow!"

Frank passed his own stateroom and knocked on the next door down. When he didn't hear any movement inside, he knocked again and shouted Tony's name. Inside, he thought he heard a chair being slid on the floor and then there was a thud. Pressing his ear to the door, he was able to make out a definite groan.

Minutes later the Officer of the Watch had Tony's door open and Frank stepped through to find Tony lying on his face on the floor. His desk chair was tipped over and a water bottle had emptied most of its contents onto the floor.

Once Tony was safely in bed in the infirmary, Frank raced back to Jim's room to check on him. The door opened on the second knock and Jim looked alert and excited.

"Frank! I was just coming to find you. I think I know what makes the coins change their patterns. I still don't know why, but at least I think I know how."

"That's great, Jim, but are you feeling okay? We just found Tony collapsed in his room and the Doc's attending to him now."

"Yes, I'm fine. What happened to Tony?"

"Well, he has that rash on his arm that showed up after he handled the unwashed coins—maybe it's related to that. And I'm just coming off a twenty-hour sleeping binge, so there's something weird going on around here."

"Really! I'm having just the opposite problem—I can't seem to go to sleep. I assumed it was just the excitement of the recent discoveries, but now that you bring up these other things, maybe…"

"I think we'd better all go see the Doc. Let's round up Linda and Javier and go check on Tony."

Frank entered the officers' mess to see Javier on his back on the large table. One of the officers was administering CPR and Linda was holding Javier's left hand. When she saw Frank in the doorway, she looked up with tears in her eyes.

"Frank, I can't get a pulse!"

Chapter 8

Before Frank could respond to Linda, a crewman rushed into the room carrying a yellow box about the size of a briefcase. In a matter of seconds, he ripped open Javier's shirt, attached two pads to the man's chest and yelled "Clear!" After the body on the table convulsed, he nodded to the man administering CPR to continue and grabbed the wrist Linda had just released. After a few seconds, he shook his head, reset the defibrillator and yelled "Clear!" again. As the entire room held its collective breath, Javier's pulse was checked again and this time the crewman smiled.

"We have a pulse! Let's get this man to sick bay—STAT!"

Four crewmen, two on each side, lifted Javier off the table and the man who had operated the defibrillator held Javier's left wrist, monitoring his pulse. As the patient and crewmen flew out the door, Linda broke into sobbing tears and Frank put his arm around her shoulder to comfort her.

Helping her stand, he guided her towards the door.

"That was close, but it looks like they saved him, Linda. There's something really weird going on around here and I want us all to get checked out by the doctor, once he's seen to Javier and Tony. Let's get to sick bay."

"Tony?" sobbed Linda. "What happened to Tony?"

"Jim and I were just coming to tell you that he apparently collapsed in his room and had to be rushed to sick bay. But when we got here, well, Javier was..."

"Oh, God!" cried Linda. "One minute we were talking about Maya ruins in the Yucatan and the next minute he wasn't breathing!"

By the time Frank and Jim helped Linda to the ship's tiny medical facility, Tony was arguing with the doctor about his condition and Javier was propped up on a gurney with his eyes open. Linda ran to Javier's side and hugged him.

"I'm so glad you're okay!" she cried.

"Hey, what am I—chopped liver?" complained Tony, still trying to get off the examination table.

"Down, boy," said Frank as he approached Tony. "You need to stay put until the Doc gives you the all-clear. In fact, I think you and Javier should spend what's left of tonight here in sick bay until we get a handle on whatever's hitting us. As the most recent victims, you two will be the best source of information for the doctor and maybe he can figure out if our temporary afflictions are somehow related."

"I'm not going to be anybody's guinea pig," insisted Tony as he sat up and swung his legs off the side of the table. Fortunately, Frank caught him just before he fell forward onto his face.

"Oh, boy!" he moaned as Frank helped him back onto the examination table. "I guess I'm still a little dizzy. Maybe I'll just hang out here with the Doc for a while."

"Linda, how are you feeling?" asked Frank. "You and Jim haven't really showed any symptoms yet, although Jim seems to be experiencing extreme hyperactivity. That would make you the last hold-out."

Reluctantly tearing her eyes away from Javier, Linda looked up at Frank.

"What? Oh, I feel fine, I guess. These medical emergencies aren't doing my nerves any good, but I feel fine otherwise. What is going on, Frank? What's doing this to us?"

"I suspect it has something to do with those triangular artifacts we've been examining, but I'm not sure. And if they are the cause, I don't understand why some of us are more affected than others. Tony I understand, because he actually handled one fresh out of the box. And I was holding the box when it opened, so who knows what I got splattered with. But Javier wasn't anywhere near the box when we opened it and he's only touched the coins once, while wearing surgical gloves. Jim, on the other hand, has been locked up in his room with them for hours and he seems to be only slightly affected. In fact, his insomnia may actually be the result of all the excitement and not have anything to do with the coins. I don't get it!"

"Maybe we should pitch those damn things back into the ocean," called a slightly groggy Tony. "There's something spooky about them."

"No chance!" cried Jim. "They could be the archaeological find of the century. They're a little odd, I'll grant you, but they aren't any spookier than the spheres of Loltun or the tsubutes of Yonaguni."

That was a statement no one could argue with and the room fell oddly silent as the four NWIDI team members dredged up their own special memories of the team's past adventures.

Taking advantage of the momentary lull in the room, the doctor spoke.

"So tell me about these coins you keep mentioning. Where did you find them? Were they covered with anything that might explain our medical mystery here?"

Frank brought the doctor up to speed about how and where the triangular objects had been found, about the incredible stench that was released when the box was first opened, and he even related the captain's comments about them having the smell of death. The only fact he left out was that the inscriptions on them seemed to be changing. It didn't seem to have any medical bearing and he hoped the other members of his team would pick up on his omission and understand that it was intentional.

"I see," nodded the doctor. "I'm not sure I completely agree with the captain, but maybe the odor was associated with some very old bacteria. It's possible that something decayed in the box while it was sealed and, if that's the case, the effect on individuals might be related to physiology rather then proximity. Is there any chance I can get a sample of something that came in contact with these objects before they were cleaned?"

"Tony, you were involved in that process. What about it?" Frank asked.

Lifting his head only slightly, Tony mumbled, "No, we washed everything, even the plastic bucket. And when we were done, we cleaned the entire area as thoroughly as we had cleaned the coins and the box."

From the gurney, Javier said weakly, "Frank, I used some paper towels to wipe off the table in the officer's mess before we cleaned it with soap and water. I think I tossed them in that tall trash can just inside the door—maybe they're still there."

"Good job, my friend!" exclaimed Frank. "Doc, if you can lend me a pair of latex gloves and a plastic bag, I'll see what I can dig up for you."

Ten minutes later, Frank returned carrying the bag gingerly between the fingers of his outstretched arm. He waved everyone out of his way and headed directly for a small room at the back of the main infirmary where the doctor had a microscope and other lab equipment set up. He stepped on the lever of a small trash can to open the lid and dropped in the bag, followed by his latex gloves.

"I don't know what you'll find, Doc, but I definitely felt the effects coming back again as I browsed through that can looking for Javier's paper towels. I suspect it's an airborne contaminant, though, because as soon as I had everything sealed up the effects started to go away."

"What about the rest of the trash in that can?" asked an obviously concerned doctor.

"Double-bagged and on its way to be sealed in a drum in the hold," smiled Frank. "One of your men is seeing to that for me. At first he was amused when he saw me digging through the trash, but once I explained our problem here, he seemed to know just what to do."

The doctor nodded his approval. "I'm sure it will be taken care of properly. Now I'd like these two to get some rest and I think the rest of you should do the same. Unfortunately I don't have the facilities for you all to stay here, but I don't think you should be alone behind locked stateroom doors until we know the full extent of whatever it is we're dealing with."

"Well, I'm staying here, even if I have to stand," insisted Linda in a tone that left no room for negotiation.

Frank raised his eyebrows, but the doctor nodded his approval, so Frank didn't challenge Linda.

"Okay, I guess I can hang out with Jim and we can sleep in shifts, if either of us gets sleepy. Otherwise, there's ROV footage to review and coins to examine. We're due to attempt our rendezvous with the sea-floor structure in a few hours, but I don't want anybody there who's not feeling one hundred percent, is that understood?"

Jim moved the mysterious box and its contents to Frank's room where the video equipment was already set up and the two went to work on their respective projects. After two hours of reviewing footage, Frank started to get sleepy again. Just as he was thinking about taking a short nap, he spotted something on the monitor that peaked his interest. He rewound and replayed the tape several times before disturbing Jim.

"Jim, can you take a look at this?"

Jim moved his chair over in front of the monitor and Frank pointed to a spot on the screen.

"Watch this area right here," he said as he moved his finger out of the way and started the tape.

"There!" Frank shouted as the object briefly appeared and disappeared from the screen. "Did you see it?"

"Yes!" replied Jim. "Play that again, will you?"

After a dozen replays, Jim leaned back in his chair and folded his arms across his chest in thought.

"So what do you think it is?" asked Frank, already knowing what he was sure he had seen.

"It sure looks like a submarine, doesn't it?" replied Jim. "It's faint and pretty far away, but that little 'hop' of the ROV brings it into view for just a second. It looks to be lying right on the bottom, so it's no doubt a wreck—maybe from the days of the Cuban Missal Crisis."

"But why didn't it show up on any of our sonar scans?" wondered Frank out loud. "Do you suppose the nearby megalithic structures could have confused the sonar and masked the sub's image?"

"I'm afraid I don't know anything about sonar, Frank," apologized Jim. "But wouldn't it be something if the Russians have known about this sunken city since the sixties and used it as a place to hide way back then? Maybe this sub was already in the area, ran into mechanical problems and ended up on the bottom where we see her now."

"Maybe," mumbled Frank, now lost in thought.

Jim slid back over to his coins and continued to examine the growing stack of digital photos he had taken of them. Periodically he would make some notes in a notebook, but mostly he just studied them and contemplated. Neither man realized how much time had passed until a knock on the door startled them both.

"Sorry to bother you, Frank, but it's almost time to put the ROV over the side." It was the familiar voice of Ken Willis, the lead ROV pilot.

Frank looked at his watch in amazement. It was 6:15 a.m.! He had watched almost six hours of video taken by two separate cameras aboard the ROV but the ghostly image of the submarine never appeared again.

Jim, who was closest to the door, opened for Willis and greeted him with a huge yawn.

"Sorry," he blushed. "I guess Frank and I worked all night. I'm going to run down to my room and catch a quick shower. I'll see you in the control room, okay?"

"Morning, Frank," said Willis as Jim slipped behind him and down the hall. "So what have you learned during this marathon all-nighter?"

"Ah, well, you'll have to see it to believe it," smiled Frank. "Can you take a minute while I queue up a tape?"

Willis nodded and took a sip from the Styrofoam cup he was holding. Frank loaded a tape, glanced at his notes and fast forwarded to the footage he had shared with Jim more than four hours earlier.

"Take a look at this and tell me what you see right here." Again, Frank indicated a spot on the monitor and then stepped back to allow Willis to get close.

"Stop!" said Willis a few seconds later. "Back up! Back up!"

Smiling, Frank rewound to the designated spot and pressed play again.

"I'll be damned!" shouted Willis. "That's a sub back there, isn't it? Frank, we have to…"

Willis was interrupted by a general announcement over the ship's loudspeaker system out in the hall.

"ROV deployment in fifteen minutes. All hands to your stations. Mr. Willis, please report to the control center immediately."

"We've gotta run, but I want to see that again when we get done, okay?" begged Willis. "That's just too cool!"

By the time Frank and Willis reached the ROV control center, Hadley was already there in Willis' seat with a pair of headphones on.

"Sorry, boss, but we had to start without you," apologized Hadley as he yielded the pilot's seat to Willis. "Where ya' been?"

"Frank was showing me some video we took yesterday. It seems we made quite a discovery and didn't even know it. Where are we here?" asked Willis, indicating the ROV's command console.

Hadley brought Willis up to speed and then took his own seat in front of the camera controls just as Jim arrived. Frank and Jim tried to stay out of the way by pressing their backs against the wall of the tiny room. In minutes the mission was under way and all attention was focused on the screens and monitors of the control room.

The Atlantic Protector was now holding a position over a point on an imaginary line than ran from the underwater ruins to South Bimini Island. They were exactly 24.76 nautical miles south of Key West, Florida, and 59.33 nautical miles north of the Cuban coastline—safely out of Cuban territorial waters and clearly closer to the U.S. than to Cuba. As the ROV descended on its cable, its onboard cameras showed nothing but water in every direction. There were no reefs, ridges or underwater cities here—just water!

When the instruments indicated that the ROV was nearing the target depth of 2,100 feet, Hadley pointed the forward camera straight down and turned on the lights.

"I don't see anything yet," he commented. "We should see the bottom come into view any time now, Frank. Our initial readings indicated that the depth here is just about what you predicted."

The control room was silent for a few seconds and then Hadley shouted, "There!"

Slowly, sea floor features began to appear on the otherwise gray monitor.

"All I see is a sandy bottom, so far," said Hadley as he adjusted the lights to provide some shadowing effect. "Nothing of any height at all—not even a good-sized rock."

Willis brought the ROV to a stop about six feet above the surface and turned to Frank.

"If I go any lower, we run the risk of kicking up huge amounts of silt and losing all visibility. What's your pleasure, Frank?"

Frank studied the monitor intently for a minute and then shrugged. "Well, there's certainly nothing of interest here. Can we move due north or south a bit and see if we spot anything?"

"Sure. Which way first?"

"Oh, how about north first," said Frank.

Willis spoke into the boom mic on his headset and the image of the sea floor began to move on the monitor.

"We're repositioning the ship rather than powering up the ROV. There's less chance of kicking up sand that way."

Frank couldn't feel the ship moving, but he could definitely see it on the monitor. After about five minutes, he lost patience.

"How far have we moved?"

Willis looked at a display and said, "About one hundred feet, more or less. Shall we head back the other direction?"

Frank nodded and Willis again spoke into the mic. After another five minutes he said, "We're just passing over the original dive site, Frank. Everything you see from here on is south of our target."

Once again, Frank glued his eyes to the monitor, but the scene remained the same.

"One hundred feet and counting," said Willis. "Shall we keep going?"

Frustrated, Frank said, "Give it one more minute and then I'll concede that this is a wild goose chase."

The words were no sooner out of his mouth when Hadley and Jim shouted, almost in unison, "There it is!"

Jerking his head back towards the monitor, Frank saw a definite change in the surface below. A strip of sand running diagonally across the monitor was noticeably raised and showed signs of having been disturbed.

Willis was immediately on the intercom to the bridge, but it took several minutes to stop the southward motion, reverse direction and carefully position the ship directly over the feature.

"How do you do that?" asked an amazed Jim. "How do you move a four hundred foot ship so precisely?"

"The magic of computers," beamed Willis as he released the joystick controls and punched a red button in front of him. "Everything is done by computers and GPS these days. And this ship has some very special thrusters on all four corners that can tilt and rotate in almost any direction. This button I just pressed basically told the navigational system to 'park it right here.' In normal weather, this ship won't move more than six inches in any direction, relative to the bottom, until I rescind the 'parking' command."

"Amazing!" exclaimed Jim, shaking his head.

"We probably have all the video we need," offered Hadley. "How about if we set the ROV down and do some digging?"

"Sounds good to me," nodded Frank. "If we stir up silt and lose visibility, so be it. We've come too far to not play in the sand!"

When the ROV touched down, a small puff of silt drifted up past the camera, but it quickly drifted off the screen to the right.

"Looks like we have a slight north-to-south current—that will help the visibility a lot," pointed out Hadley.

He had rotated the forward camera up almost ninety degrees so it was viewing the end of the ROV boom some ten feet in front of the ROV. Using an attachment not unlike a very small back hoe bucket, Willis carefully removed several inches of sand from the center of the feature. With the next bucket-full, the level of the sand had been reduced to that of the normal sea floor.

"Careful," cautioned Frank. "From here on, you could hit whatever's buried out there."

"Roger that," acknowledged Willis.

As he maneuvered the bucket, slowly filling it with sand, something shiny was exposed and he instantly stopped the operation.

"There, see it?" he shouted. "I can't believe I'm saying this, but it looks like a pipe or tube of some kind. Frank, you were spot on!"

All four faces were glued to the monitor as Hadley adjusted the ROV lights to provide more illumination.

"Can you move a little sand on one side?" whispered Frank. "I'd like to get an idea of the diameter of this thing."

"I'll give it a go," offered Willis. "Try not to rock the boat while I do this, okay."

Within a few minutes, Willis had excavated sand to expose the side of the tube, which now appeared to be approximately two inches in diameter. Its surface was a pearly gray color, almost translucent in appearance.

"Well, one thing's for sure," commented Jim. "It's definitely not a naturally occurring marine feature. There's no question that this is man-made."

"I wouldn't bet on that," Frank said softly. "Can you fold down the cable locator and see if it has any metallic qualities?"

The device Frank had inadvertently used to find the box of coins detected absolutely no metallic objects in the area.

"Okay, let's cover this thing back up and get out of here before the owners sue us for trespassing!" decided Frank.

As soon as the ship's winches began to hoist the ROV back to the surface, Frank left the small control cabin and Jim followed right behind.

"It's really cramped in there!" said Frank once they were outside in the sunlight. "So what do you make of it, Jim? It's not natural, as you said, and it would be one heck of an engineering feat, even if it were man-made. It's almost two hundred miles from here to the sunken city and the fact that we found it almost exactly where I predicted means that it's incredibly straight."

Jim shook his head. "Yeah, I don't get it, Frank. It's not part of the original city, because the tube is buried all the way to the site, which is now more then two thousand feet below its original position. That means that the tube was both installed and used after the city sank."

"Yes, but the ruins showed no signs of being disturbed in recent history," added Frank. "Except for the submarine, that is."

"Well that has to be it, then!" said Jim. "The Russians discovered the ruins and used the site to conceal their presence. When they lost a sub in a place where they weren't even supposed to be, they had to let the crew parish rather than give up their secret. Maybe the rumors we heard are *all* correct—to a certain degree. Maybe the site was both an ancient city and a secret sub base and maybe the Russians somehow laid in the tube—or whatever it is— to support the base. Maybe it's a giant fiber optic cable or something."

"Maybe. I just find it hard to believe that all that cable laying work could have taken place right under the nose of the U.S. Navy."

"So what's next, Frank?"

"Well the Cubans have run us out of the sunken city, so I'm going to do the next best thing—I'm going to find out where the other end of this tube goes. And I can't wait to see who's there waiting for us!"

Chapter 9

With the ROV safely back on board, the Atlantic Protector lifted anchor shortly after 8:00 a.m. and began the eighteen hour trip back to its home base on the north end of Andros Island. After stopping by sick bay to check on Tony and Javier, Frank and Jim retired to their respective staterooms to get some badly needed sleep. They had worked through the night—Frank on reviewing ROV video tape and Jim on the mysterious triangular coins—and they were both exhausted. Fourteen hours later, Frank was jostled awake by rough seas and when he made his way to the officers' mess for some coffee he was surprised—and pleased—to find Tony, Linda and Javier at the far end of the table eating a hearty breakfast. Frank sat down across from Linda, who was about as close to Javier as she could get without sharing his clothing.

"Apparently the doc has discharged you from sick bay," he smiled. "I take it he thinks you're all fit for duty?"

"We both had a good night's sleep, thanks to a shot from the ship's doctor, and woke up good as new," replied Tony. "I'm afraid Linda may need a chiropractor after spending the night in an office chair, but whatever tackled Javier seems to have been temporary."

"Well, I'm really glad to hear that, but both of you need to take it easy until you're sure this thing is out of your systems. Especially you, Javier! We almost lost you last night, you know."

"So I've heard!" Javier glanced at Linda and smiled. "The funny thing is, I never felt it coming on. One second we were drinking coffee right here at this table and the next second I was on a stretcher in sick bay feeling as bad as I've ever felt in my life. There was no warning at all."

"Has the doc come up with any ideas yet?" asked Frank.

"He hadn't when we left," answered Linda, "but that was hours ago. There seems to be a lot of activity on board, so I assume we're getting close to port. Maybe we should check in with him before he gets too busy."

Frank finished the last of his coffee and nodded.

"That's a good idea. On the way, we can look in on Jim. The poor guy worked all night on those coins and we didn't hit the sack until after 8:00 am this morning."

"He's been up for hours," laughed Linda. "I think he's up on the bridge using the ship's Internet access right now, but we had a late lunch with him about 2:00 p.m. He seemed pretty excited about something, but he wouldn't say what."

"Okay, let's go see the doc and then we'll track him down. We need to get our gear packed up and then I'd like to have a short team meeting before we dock."

The ship's doctor didn't have much to report on the strange illness that had affected all of them, to varying degrees, and that had almost killed Javier.

"I'm sorry, but I just don't have enough data to connect the dots," the doctor frowned. "Each of you was affected in a different way, and each to a different degree. I examined the residue I extracted from the paper towel Javier used to clean the table but I haven't been able to identify it with my limited ship-board equipment. Tomorrow morning I'm going to send a sample over to a lab in Miami, but it will take at least a week to get any results back. In the mean time, I suggest that you all—and especially you, Javier—pay attention to any unusual symptoms and see a doctor immediately if you sense anything out of the ordinary."

The doctor picked up a pad from his desk, scribbled a note and handed it to Frank.

"This is the name and phone number of a doctor on Andros Island that I highly recommend. I'll give him a heads up and you call him if necessary. That's an order!"

After leaving sick bay, the four NWIDI team members headed up to the bridge to find Jim. Just as Linda had said, he was hunched over his laptop at the far end of the bridge. He was so lost in his work that he didn't see the four approaching until Frank put his hand on Jim's shoulder and said, "How's it going?"

Startled, Jim let out a shout and snapped his head around to see his friends standing behind him. Suddenly embarrassed, he smiled sheepishly.

"Frank, you scared the crap out of me! How'd you sleep? Is everybody still feeling okay?"

"I slept fine," replied Frank, "and everybody seems to be fine for now, but the doc still hasn't come up with a cause. How are you doing?"

"Well, actually, I was just finishing up. I've been doing some research on the Internet about our triangular objects and I think I've found some interesting correlations."

Frank was surprised.

"You mean there's information about other coins like ours out there on the net?" he asked in disbelief.

"No, not on the objects themselves, but on the behavior they exhibit." Jim scanned the bridge and then added, "This probably isn't the place to go into detail, though. Let me pack up and we can go elsewhere."

Even though it was almost 11:00 p.m., the sea air was warm and the lights of Florida could be seen off the port side of the ship, so Frank decided to convene the team meeting on the deck where a group of chairs were clustered near the ship's massive superstructure.

"Let's start by going over what we know," suggested Frank. "We know that the ruins of an apparently ancient city lie on the ocean floor just off the western tip of Cuba. We know that some sort of tube, possibly a cable, extends from that site to a predictable point south of Key West and probably on to at least South Bimini Island. We know this object contains no metallic material—sorry, I probably forgot to tell anybody that, but we checked it with the ROV's cable locator on this morning's dive. We also know that the object was installed after the city sank because it remains buried right up to the point where it enters the pyramid, which implies that the pyramid—and therefore the rest of the ruins—was already on the bottom before the object was put in place. Jim, why don't you bring us up to date on the coins and coin box?"

"Well, we don't know much," Jim began. "We know they were found buried in the sand in the general vicinity of the ruins, but not within what appeared to be the city's outer wall. We know they are very regular in shape—in fact suspiciously regular if they are of any age. We know that contact with them made most of us sick and almost killed Javier. And, of course, we know that the symbols on them change whenever they are placed back inside the box and the lid is closed. What we don't know…"

Tony cut Jim off in mid-sentence.

"We know what?" he shouted. "When did we find *that* out?"

"Well, I've known about the symbols changing almost since my first contact with them, but it took me a while to realize that I could make them change at will by simply returning them to the box and closing the lid. The first few times it happened by accident while we were moving them from place to place and I didn't immediately make the connection. I now know that the symbols change whenever they're placed in the box and the lid is closed. I've tested multiple scenarios and I'm positive of this.

"As I was saying, what we don't know is what they're made of, what the symbols mean, where they came from or who buried them in the sand near Cuba. I also don't think we know that they're coins. In fact, I'm becoming more and more convinced that they're far more important than simple currency."

"Jim, up on the bridge you mentioned something about behavior of the objects. What did you mean by that?" asked Linda.

"Ah, yes! Just in the last hour I located an interesting reference to an ancient legend about objects that 'change their face when entombed.' Our triangles certainly fit that description, in a loose sort of way."

"What's the source of the legend?" asked Frank.

"Well, that's the interesting part—the legend is from some of the earliest Olmec writings ever found!"

"Are you talking about the same Olmec who hid the spheres in the cave at Loltun?" asked Tony.

"Exactly," nodded Jim. "It seems that our adventures have come full circle and brought us right back to the Olmec."

"Or whoever interfered with them," mumbled Frank. "What else do we know?"

"What about the submarine you found in the ROV video last night?" Jim asked.

"*The what?*" Tony shouted again. "Man, I take a little nap and all the rules change! What submarine?"

Frank explained to Tony, and the others who had spent the night in sick bay, about the image of a submarine he had discovered in the video taken on the last ROV dive at the ruins.

"The image is faint, but there's no doubt that it's a submarine lying on the bottom. It's listing slightly to starboard but I couldn't make out any other details in the video."

"I knew it!" Tony jumped to his feet and pounded his right fist into his left palm. "That ship that ran us off the site wasn't part of any Cuban Navy—they're hiding something down there, Frank, and we have to go back and dig into this. I know you're really into these triangle things, but this could be a matter of national security. What if there's an active sub base down there?"

"Calm down, big guy," replied Frank. "We'll turn all our info over to the feds when we get to Andros and they can go check it out. Besides, if there was a sub base down there, we'd have spotted it with the side-scan sonar."

"Did your fancy sonar see the sub you found in the video?" barked Tony. "Frank, we need to check this out now!"

"Tony, I agree that something isn't right in western Cuba, but you'd be so obvious out there on the peninsula that you'd be picked up in minutes. If we're going to get in there, we need to be a little less conspicuous. Maybe we could..."

"I'll go!" interrupted Javier.

"What?" Frank asked.

"I'll go," repeated Javier. "I speak the language, I could blend in with the locals, and I feel a little responsible, since it may have been my organization's boat captain that got us run off the site."

"No!" exclaimed Linda. "Javier, you're not a soldier! Frank and Tony love this G.I. Joe stuff, but you're not like them. You can't go..."

"...as a soldier..." This time it was Frank who interrupted. "...but you might get by posing as a photographer..."

"No!" interjected Linda again.

"...a photographer accompanying a beautiful American journalist on her quest to share the stories of remote Cuba with her readers back in the States."

"What?" Linda's eyes widened. "Oh, I like the sound of that much better. When do we leave?"

This time it was Tony objecting.

"Frank, that's crazy! These two couldn't fight their way out of a wet paper bag. They'll be snatched up in no time and then we'll have to go in and rescue them."

"But that's just the point," argued Frank. "Nobody would suspect that they're on an intelligence mission and all we really want, at this point, is intelligence. If they find evidence of any bad guys, we'll let Buzz Edwards and his boys take over. On the other hand, maybe the locals closest to the site of the ruins can shed some light on the place—who built it and when. Besides, you and I have some serious diving to do and neither one of them can take your place underwater."

"Well I still don't like it, but I guess they can't get into too much trouble just asking questions. How do you plan to get them into the country?"

Frank thought for a minute and then said, "I think I'll call the Learjet over from Miami and fly them back to Cancun. Edwards can use his resources at the MX-2 base to get them new identities and cover stories. From there they can take a commercial flight to Havana and make their way north and west to Las Tumbas, where Jim was originally headed."

"And what about us?" asked Jim. "You mentioned diving, but I won't be much help in that department."

"No, but you're the resident scientist and we're definitely on the trail of some out-of-this-world science," smiled Frank. "I have a feeling we're going to need your trained eyes to decipher whatever we find at the end of this ocean-floor cable. And maybe we'll capture a shiny silver ball for you to study!"

"OK, I get it," smiled Jim. "You two need a go-fer and I'm it!"

Everybody had a good laugh and then Frank glanced at his watch and got back to business.

"We're due to dock in about three hours, at 3:00 a.m. local time. We'll stay aboard tonight and get an early start in the morning. I'll rent a van to haul us down island to Andros Town and we'll have Fitz and Susan pick up Linda and Javier at the local airport around noon. The rest of us can check into a hotel and arrange transportation to South Bimini to begin the search for the other end of the mysterious cable. We'll keep our base of operations on Andros, though, because there's a pretty serious Navy facility there and if we need help, Buzz can probably arrange it for us."

"That's AUTEC, right?" asked Tony. "I've hauled a lot of classified freight to their mainland terminal in West Palm Beach. What do they do on Andros?"

"From what little I know, it's an undersea warfare testing facility. They provide a proving ground for defense contractors to test torpedoes, communications gear, submarine detection and cloaking systems—stuff like that. I once heard AUTEC referred to as the Navy's version of Area 51. It's conveniently located close to a feature called the Tongue of the Ocean—TOTO for short. It's a hole in the ocean floor that drops straight down 6,000 feet and it's a perfect place to test really secret stuff."

Linda covered her mouth and yawned.

"Wow, I guess I'm getting sleepy again. You're sure it's okay for us to stay aboard tonight, right?"

"Yes, I confirmed that with the captain before we got underway this morning. Actually, everybody's staying aboard tonight because the ship can't clear customs until tomorrow morning. And that reminds me—be sure to have your passports handy when you go ashore. Since we're not on the ship's manifest, we'll probably have some explaining to do and we'll have to clear customs separate from the crew. Does anybody have anything else to toss out before we call it quits?"

"Well, there is one more thing," said Jim. "When you went over the list of things we know about the ruins you didn't mention the silver ball you saw during the first ROV dive."

"You're absolutely right!" exclaimed Frank. "With everything else that's gone on the past couple of days, I'd almost forgotten about that. So, what do we know about it?"

After an awkward silence, Frank smiled and said, "Okay, so we know that it's round, shiny and capable of incredible speed underwater. Oh, and we're pretty sure it isn't metallic, either. Anything else?"

When nobody spoke up, Frank continued.

"If that's everything, let's call it a night and continue this in the morning. Since I've only been up a few hours, I'll try to reach the Fitzgeralds and Edwards before I turn in. Early tomorrow morning I'll find a hotel for Tony, Jim and me and arrange for transportation. Be sure to get up early enough to pack and square away your rooms. We don't want to leave a big mess for our hosts. See you all at 7:00 am in the officer's mess."

Frank followed the rest of his team down to the staterooms, retrieved his satellite phone and then made his way back up on deck to make his calls. Fitz sounded like he'd been asleep when Frank called, even though he said he hadn't. Frank apologized anyway, and briefed Fitz on the plan to get Linda and Javier into Cuba for a look around. Fitz agreed to have the Learjet at Andros Town airport by noon and bid Frank a good night.

Frank's next call, to Buzz Edwards in Cancun, lasted nearly an hour. They had been out of touch since the NWIDI team had left MX-2 and he wanted to know every detail about the ruins, the run-in with the Cubans and especially about the sub Frank had spotted in the ROV video.

"I want a copy of that video just as soon as you can get it to me," demanded Buzz. "And I'll have the captain of the *El Caribe* picked up for questioning in the morning."

"That might not be a good idea, Buzz," cautioned Frank. "If we're going to insert Linda and Javier into Cuba, we probably shouldn't stir up too much trouble. Maybe you could just have him tailed for now so you can grab him quickly once we have our folks back."

"Okay, but when the time comes I want this guy because I'm going to interrogate him personally! I'd be willing to bet anything, that this alleged Cuban Navy vessel had something to do with the lost fishing boat you found on the bottom. Now tell me everything you can remember about this undersea feature of yours?"

Frank related everything he remembered and ended with a question.

"Are you sure this undersea cable isn't part of some AUTEC experiment?"

"I don't think so, Frank, but I'll check into it. Listen, you need to get some rest, and I need to get to work on the details at this end. Call me when you get settled into the hotel and I'll let you know what I've learned from AUTEC. And I'll be looking for your Learjet here at the MX-2 hangar in the early afternoon."

By the time Frank finished his call with Buzz it was 1:30 a.m. and the lights of western Andros Island were just barely visible on the horizon. As he returned to his stateroom for some rest, Frank pondered the mysterious triangle-shaped objects that seemed to change their inscriptions whenever they were returned to their storage box. Would these "coins"—or whatever they were—turn out to be as alien as the spheres they had discovered in the Yucatan or the eight-sided disks they found on Yonaguni Island? Would the triangles lead them any closer to the truth about who had apparently interfered with the earth's earliest cultures—and why? Was the shiny spherical craft spotted at the underwater ruins evidence that this interference might still be going on?

"Well, we'll know pretty soon!" Frank said to himself as he closed and locked his stateroom door.

Chapter 10

As planned, the NWIDI team met in the officers' mess at 7:00 am. Frank had only managed about four hours sleep, and it showed, but the rest of the team seemed to be refreshed and ready for what promised to be an exciting day. Linda was especially animated, and Frank suspected he knew why.

"Are you two up for this?" Frank asked, referring to his recently conceived plan to insert Linda and Javier into western Cuba under cover as an American journalist and her Mexican camera man.

"Absolutely!" replied Linda.

Next to her, Javier nodded in agreement, but it was clear that he didn't share all of Linda's excitement.

"Any reservations, Javier?" questioned Frank.

"Some," he replied honestly. "I'm anxious to find out what—if anything—is going on in that part of Cuba because it's so close to eastern Mexico. On the other hand, I'm not eager to tangle with the Cuban government. I've heard they can be pretty ruthless and we'll be invading their turf."

"Frank, I really think you should let me go instead," objected Tony. "Like Linda often says, you and I like playing G.I. Joe, but these two don't have any training in this stuff."

"And that's exactly why they're the best candidates," replied Frank. "They couldn't act like spies if they wanted to and that will work in our favor. However, if either of you are uncomfortable with the mission just say the word and we'll come up with another plan."

Linda looked at Javier and waited for his response. After a second, he smiled and put his arm around Linda's shoulder in a quick—but conspicuous—hug.

"Perhaps my pessimism will balance Linda's optimism and we'll fool them after all," he laughed. "Besides, I've always wanted to see Cuba in the fall!"

During breakfast, the ship's captain came in and when he saw the NWIDI team at the far end of the table, he joined them.

"Captain, I don't know how we can ever thank you and your crew for all the support you've provided," offered Frank. "It's certainly been an amazing three and a half days!"

"That it has, my friend. I hope you and your team were able to meet your objectives. As for the crew of the Atlantic Protector, well, I can tell you it will be mighty hard to go back to routine cable maintenance after the adventure we've shared with the five of you! It's all my crew talks about and I'm afraid the entire island of Andros will know as soon as they step ashore."

"Well, that can't be helped, I'm afraid," frowned Frank. "I just hope it doesn't impact the rest of our work. Anyway, please convey our sincere thanks to your officers and crew. They were all great. And a special thanks to you, Captain."

A single blast from the ship's horn brought the captain back to business.

"I'm afraid I must excuse myself. That single means that the Bahamian customs agent is headed this way and I need to meet her to sign our entry papers. Since your names weren't on our outbound manifest, I'm afraid you will have to take your belongings and documents to the customs office down on the pier. I'm not sure how they will deal with your pick-up at sea or with the artifacts you're bringing into their country, but I wish you the best of luck!"

With Frank in the lead, the team solemnly marched into the small customs office at the end of the pier. A very tall, very black Bahaman man dressed in a white naval uniform looked up and raised one eyebrow.

"You must be Frank Morton," he said in a deep voice. "We've been expecting you. Please hand me you passports and then proceed directly to your van through that door. Mr. Morton, if you'll remain here, please."

Frank and Tony exchanged glances, and then shrugged. One by one, each member of the team laid their passport on the counter in front of the customs agent and went out through a door at the opposite end of the office where they had entered. Frank remained behind, as requested.

The agent opened each passport, checked the name against a list on the counter and then stamped each document. When he finished, he pushed the stack of passports across the counter to Frank and said simply, "Welcome to the Bahamas. Enjoy your stay."

Puzzled, Frank made eye contact with the man and asked, "That's it? Is everything okay?"

Without saying a word, the man turned the list he had been using around so Frank could see the signature at the bottom. Although he couldn't read the handwriting, the line immediately above answered his question. It read, simply, "From the Office of the President of the United States."

As Frank climbed into the front passenger's seat of the van, four sets of eyes stared at him questioningly.

Frank simply shrugged and said, "Apparently the President vouched for us."

Turning to the driver, he asked, "I assume you know where we're going, right?"

"Yes, sir. Arrangements had been made for you at the Bay Club."

And with that, the van pulled away from the Bahamian customs office less than five minutes after the team had entered it.

During the ninety-minute trip from the pier at Morgan's Bluff to Andros Town, Frank made idle chat with the driver and noticed that he didn't have the typical Bahamian accent that he had expected. The four in the back remained mostly quiet. They all correctly assumed that the driver shouldn't know about their plans and there wasn't much else to talk about.

Eventually the driver turned off the main road through Andros Town and onto a gravel driveway marked with a sign that read "Bay Club Resort and Marina."

"Well, this will be home for a while, so I hope it's everything Buzz said it is," said Frank. "Apparently upscale lodging is pretty rare around here."

The driver looked at Frank and frowned. "I'm sure you'll enjoy your stay with us, Mr. Morton."

"Ah, sorry. That didn't come out quite the way I meant it. So you work here at the hotel, then?"

The quiet black man smiled, exposing his bright white teeth. "No, sir, I own it."

The driver retrieved a letter-sized manila envelope from beneath his seat and handed it to Frank.

"Mr. Buzz Edwards asked me to give this to you. My name is Miles Adderly, by the way, and I'll do my best to make your stay a pleasant one."

The van rolled to a stop and Adderly turned to face an embarrassed Frank.

"Please come inside to register and then I'll show you to your rooms. Mr. Edwards only requested three rooms, so are..."

Before he could finish, Linda spoke up from the back seat.

"Two of us are leaving the island this afternoon, so we'll just hang out in Frank's room until it's time to leave for the airport."

"In that case, we'd better upgrade Mr. Morton's room to a suite. This way please."

The hotel was small and it certainly wasn't new but it was more than adequate. Frank apologized to its owner several times before he reached his room. As promised, Adderly upgraded Frank to a suite—a stand-alone building with two bedrooms, a full kitchen, a large living/dining area and a beautiful front porch view of the marina and the Atlantic Ocean. The rooms provided for Tony and Jim looked more like traditional hotel rooms, except that they each had a small refrigerator and a microwave and they had views of the hotel's swimming pool instead of the ocean.

After giving Tony and Jim time to settle in, the team reconvened on the large porch at Frank's unit for a strategy meeting.

"I've arranged for a charter flight to Bimini early tomorrow morning," began Frank. "I also hooked up with a dive operator on Bimini that's willing to take us to the area we're interested in. They'll provide all the gear we need but I sure wish I had my own stuff. We may be doing some pretty hairy diving, especially if we get into some of the blue holes up there."

"Blue holes?" inquired Jim.

"Blue holes are entrances to intricate water-filled cave systems which run underneath the islands and the sea floor around here," explained Frank. "They're a special treat for advanced divers and there are literally hundreds of them—many still unexplored."

"I knew I packed our dive gear for a reason!" beamed Tony. "It will be here at noon, or whenever the Learjet touches down."

"What?" asked Frank. "Based on what Buzz originally told us about the depth of the ruins, I thought we had agreed to leave the gear behind."

"We did, but there was extra room in the aft cargo area, so I threw it in anyway. I even tossed in Linda's stuff, but she probably won't need it in Cuba. I have another little dive surprise for you, too, Frank."

"What's that?"

"I called Jill a few minutes ago and she's flying in this evening. She's become an excellent diver since she moved to…well, since she moved. We haven't seen each other in a couple of months and she needed a change of scenery so she's coming up to help us."

"Ah, now that *is* a surprise, all right!" stammered Frank. "It will be good to see her again, though. It's been, what, more than a year, I guess."

"Is this the Jill from Las Vegas?" asked Linda.

"Sure, you remember Jill...no, I guess she had already left Vegas by the time you arrived to join us, huh?" replied Frank.

"Well, I've heard a lot about her," smiled Linda as she jabbed Tony with an elbow, "but we've never met. And I guess it will stay that way, because Javier and I will be back in Mexico by the time she gets here."

"True! Well, you can meet her when you come back from Cuba," replied Frank.

"If they come back," said Tony as he jabbed Linda back. "So, Frank, how'd you manage to make all those flight and dive arrangements so fast?"

Frank held up the manila envelope that Adderly had given him.

"Edwards anticipated almost everything. All I had to do was make the calls and provide the times. He seems to be pretty well connected over here."

"Interesting," mumbled Tony. "Now, why would an agent of the U.S. Department of Defense be so well connected in the Bahamian out-islands?"

"And why would he have access to a facility like MX-2?" added Linda. "I guess we'll have to ask him when we see him this afternoon."

That comment turned the conversation to a discussion of what the team hoped to gain from Linda and Javier's trip to Cuba. Once Frank felt that everybody was on the same page, he suggested that they all relax until the Learjet arrived. Tony decided to check out the pool, Jim wanted to test the Internet connection in his hotel room and Linda talked Javier into walking the boardwalk along the marina to check out some of the luxury yachts tied up there.

Three hours later, Frank was startled awake by the ring of his satellite phone. His neck was stiff from sleeping in the rocking chair and he rubbed it with one hand as he reached for the phone with the other.

The call was from Don Fitzgerald, the male half of the husband-and-wife crew that flew the NWIDI team's Learjet 60. Fitz, his wife Susan and their dog Sandstrom had just touched down at the Andros Town airport and would be clearing customs soon.

Frank asked Fitz if he would unload the dive gear Tony had secreted aboard and then suggested that he and Susan grab some lunch before their flight to Cancun.

Linda and Javier were nowhere to be found, so Frank walked up to the hotel office to make arrangements for transportation and to look for them. He was relieved to find them sitting beside the pool sipping a fruity drink and talking to Tony.

"The plane's here," he called as he approached. "Are you two still up for this?"

"As ready as we'll ever be," smiled Javier. "I assume Buzz has all the information we'll need?"

"Yes, he's handling all the cover details, so please give me a call before you leave Cancun and bring me up to speed. At this point, I don't even know what names you'll be traveling under or your itinerary."

"Yes, mom, we'll be sure to call," laughed Linda.

"Hey, I'm serious about this," admonished Frank. "I don't expect any problems, but if we do have to extract you we'll need all the details we can get. Make sure Buzz provides you with a satellite phone like mine and be sure you get me that number before you leave Mexico."

"Will do, boss," replied Linda in a more serious tone.

Frank suspected that she wasn't taking the trip seriously. Maybe she just saw it as an opportunity to spend some time alone with Javier, but he hoped he was wrong. He accompanied Linda and Javier to the airport in the van that was, once again, driven by Miles Adderly.

"Was the information provided by Mr. Edwards helpful?" Adderly asked as he left the hotel property and turned onto the main road.

"It was!" replied Frank. "How is it that you know Buzz, anyway?"

Adderly was silent for a moment and then replied, "My hotel often provides accommodations for visitors to the Navy's facility here on Andros and Mr. Edwards often makes 'special arrangements' for them."

"What sort of special arrangements?" inquired Frank.

Again there was a moment of silence.

"I've probably said too much already, sir. I'm afraid you'll have to direct your questions to Mr. Edwards. Are we going to the main terminal or are we meeting a private aircraft?"

Frank was puzzled over Adderly's comment and missed the question, so Linda jumped in.

"We're meeting a private Learjet with the letters NWIDI on the tail."

"NWIDI?" questioned Adderly. "I've never heard that acronym. Is that a new government agency?"

By this time Frank was back into the conversation. He responded to the driver's question.

"No, it's a small private corporation and we typically investigate ancient archaeological mysteries."

"And which of Andros' many archaeological mysteries are you investigating?" asked Adderly.

"Well, now *I've* probably said too much," smiled Frank. "But just how many mysteries are there out here?"

This time it was Adderly's turn to smile.

"More than most folks know about, I assure you," he replied. "Some evening we'll get together and discuss the topic in more detail, Mr. Morton. I have some artifacts in my study that you might find very interesting. But for now, let's look for that plane of yours. The airport service entrance is just ahead."

After bidding farewell to Linda and Javier, Frank helped Adderly load the dive gear and several other bags he had found into the van for the trip back to the hotel.

"It appears that you'll be doing some diving," commented Adderly as the van came up to speed on the highway.

"That's correct. The remainder of my team and I are heading off to Bimini tomorrow morning."

"To explore the infamous Bimini Road, no doubt," replied Adderly. "It's a very interesting place that's attracted a lot of American interest lately. It's not really a road, you know."

"Well, actually, that's not where we're headed, although I'd certainly like to dive the site if we can find the time. I understand there's a theory that it's actually the top of an ancient breakwater that once protected a harbor. Is that true?"

"It's quite possible. There are a number of megalithic features here in the out-islands that point to the existence of an ancient maritime culture. How much do you know about Andros, Mr. Morton?"

"Not much, I'm afraid, and I'd love to hear any details you'd be willing to share. Our original mission didn't include a trip to the Bahamas, so I didn't come very well prepared. And please, call me Frank."

During the rest of the trip back to the hotel and for an hour after they arrived, Adderly—who insisted that Frank call him Miles—provided a non-stop briefing on the history and background of Andros Island.

Andros, as it turns out, is the largest island in the Bahamas and it's actually composed of three major islands separated by meandering, salt water creeks known as bights. Its vast, mostly-unexplored interior is covered with dense forests of pine and mahogany. Thousands of kilometers of fresh water rivers are fed by rain water collected in the many caves. And, just a mile off the eastern coast of Andros is the third largest barrier reef in the world. Between the island and the reef the water averages six to twelve feet deep but east of the reef is the six-thousand foot deep Tongue of the Ocean that Frank had described to his team the night before.

Although Frank found the island's geography interesting, his interest really peaked when Miles mentioned several little-known underwater stone formations located off the northern end of Andros.

"The one called Andros Platform is most certainly another breakwater, similar to Bimini Road," explained Miles. "But the others appear to be walls or foundations, suggesting that large buildings once stood there."

"Very interesting," nodded Frank. "When we get back from Bimini, could you arrange for us to see these sites?"

"Of course! It's quite a long boat trip from here to the North End, but I have a friend who operates a dive boat out of Nicols Town and I'd be happy to make the arrangements. I might even come along, if you don't mind."

"Oh, so you're a diver, too?"

"I was a Navy SEAL for seven years before a back injury washed me out of the program," replied Miles proudly. "A long series of surgeries repaired most of the damage to my back, but by then I had a family and I was too old for the rigors of SEAL training."

"That's too bad, but it probably all worked out for the best. I think we're going to get along great, my friend, because Tony is an ex-Army Ranger and I was an Air Force Commando. We met during the closing months of the Viet Nam conflict and we've been friends ever since. I'd trust Tony with my life—in fact, I *have*, several times."

"Really?" exclaimed Miles. "Are you members of the TLC Brotherhood?"

He was referring to a name used by soldiers who had served—usually covertly—in Thailand, Laos or Cambodia. Since the U.S. military was never officially "invited" to operate in these countries, missions there were usually classified.

"You bet we are," smiled Frank. "How about you?"

"No, that was a little before my time, but some of the guys in my unit used to talk about the rescues behind enemy lines. That was gutsy stuff."

"It was all in a day's work back then," replied Frank. "But I like my work these days a whole lot better! I can't wait to check out these sites you've mentioned. Oh, and that reminds me! We're expecting another person to join our group here on Andros, so we may need another room, starting tonight. Do you have anything available?"

"I do, but if you're referring to Ms. Harris, Tony has already mentioned her arrival and he indicated that another room wouldn't be necessary. Has there been a change?"

"Oh!" said Frank. "I didn't realize they were...ah, no, no change. On another subject, we have a charter flight to Bimini scheduled for 8:00 a.m. tomorrow morning. Can I trouble you for another lift to the airport? Maybe I should rent a rig and stop pestering you."

"Nonsense! Besides, you don't know the island and there are a lot of places to get lost, especially in the interior. No, I insist that you allow me to provide your transportation. I can't promise I'll always be the driver, but the Bay Club van is at your disposal. Just give me as much notice as you can so I can accommodate other guests, too."

As Frank nodded agreement, he spotted Tony and Jim walking across the grassy area between the beach and Frank's front porch.

"Howdy, guys," greeted Frank. "What's up?"

"Nothing much," replied Tony. "We were just out looking around. But you'll never guess what we found tied up in the marina. Somebody has a sleek, one- or two-man water craft that looks like a big fish!"

"That would be my *Bionic Dolphin*," said Miles Adderly softly. "Once a SEAL, always a SEAL, I guess."

Chapter 11

After learning that Miles Adderly was a former Navy SEAL, both Frank and Tony saw him in a whole new light. Almost instantly he was a "brother"—a fellow Special Forces veteran— rather than a van driver or hotel owner and the three spent the rest of the afternoon sitting on Frank's porch swapping war stories. Jim, who had never served in the military, soon wandered off to his room to catch up on some research.

At 4:00 p.m. the alarm on Tony's watch interrupted the reminiscing.

"Jill's flight from Ft. Lauderdale is due in at 4:40 and I want to shower before we head to the airport," said Tony as he stood to leave. "I'll meet you guys back here in twenty minutes."

As Tony hurried off to his room, Miles raised an eyebrow and smiled.

"I take it those two are an item, huh?"

"It would seem so," nodded Frank. "But Tony has kept it pretty quiet. I knew he'd been down to see her a number of times, but I had no idea their relationship had moved beyond the 'friend-for-a-night' stage. I'm glad, though, because Tony has been on his own for a long time. They met in Vegas about a year ago and less than a week later it became necessary for Jill to disappear. Tony has traveled back and forth between Seattle and the Caribbean almost every month since."

"Disappear?" asked Miles.

"Yeah, it's a long story, but Tony and I—and later Jim and Linda—were in Vegas investigating an archaeological artifact that had been given to Tony by a man who turned out to be Jill's step-father. When he was murdered, Jill was spirited out of town for her own safety. The old man had accumulated a pile of money and the feds gave it to her and told her to get lost. She did—and, as far as I know, her stops in Miami and Ft. Lauderdale today will be the first time she's set foot back inside the continental U.S. since the day she left Vegas on a government aircraft."

"Artifact? Murder? Feds? It sounds like you guys had quite an adventure!" exclaimed Miles.

"I guess we did, at that," smiled Frank. "And not long after that Tony, Linda, Jim and I headed off to southern Japan for even more fun. I'll tell you all about it someday. Earlier today you mentioned some artifacts you would be willing to show me and I have something I'd like your opinion on. Maybe after we get back from the airport…"

"Absolutely!" beamed Miles. "But only if you let me buy dinner. We can have it served in my study where we can talk privately, if you wish."

"That would probably be best and thank you for the invitation. If you don't mind, I'd like to ask Jim to join us because he's our team science expert."

"I look forward to it! And now I suppose we should head up to the airport to pick up your friend. I have two other guests coming in on that same flight, so we'll have a full van coming back."

When Jill exited the Customs area and spotted Frank, Tony and Jim waiting for her, she let out a scream, dropped her bags and ran the twenty yards across the airport to where they were standing.

After a hug and kiss for Tony, she wrapped one arm around Frank and the other around Jim and hugged them as hard as she could.

Choking back tears, she whispered, "God, it's good to see you guys again!"

Tony collected Jill's bags from across the room and herded the noisy group out through the sliding glass doors and toward the waiting hotel van. When they arrived, Miles Adderly and two other passengers were already inside, so Frank pulled Jill aside and cautioned her not to say anything about NWIDI activities in front of the strangers.

As Jill stepped into the van, one of the other passengers turned and smiled at her.

"Hello again, Jill!"

When the man turned his head back towards the front of the van, Tony made a sign of breaking the man's neck and Jill chuckled.

Back at the Bay Club, the NWIDI gang dropped Jill's gear in Tony's room and went directly to the bar next to the pool.

"I'm so glad to be somewhere new!" Jill exclaimed as they settled into their chairs. "The Virgin Islands are beautiful, don't get me wrong, but I think I've visited every square inch of both St. John and St. Thomas and I was really getting bored with it all."

"Well, island life certainly seems to agree with you," laughed Jim. "You sure look tan, fit and happy. And Tony says you've been doing a lot of diving, too."

"I have! In fact, I just passed my Advanced Open Water test last Wednesday. I understand you plan to visit some awesome dive sites here—what's that all about?"

"We've made a number of pretty interesting discoveries in the eight days since we left Seattle," offered Frank, "but this probably isn't the place to discuss them. I assume Tony has told you about our trip to Japan last January."

"Yes, but the way he tells it, you three would all be Sushi right now if he hadn't been there to save you. I assume there's another version of that story?"

"Hey!" objected Tony with a laugh. "I had my moments over there!"

"Well, that part is certainly true," agreed Frank. "I fell off a cliff and got pretty banged up so Tony had to do the heavy lifting for a while but fortunately my brain was still working because…"

"Hey, again!" shouted Tony.

"So, what brings you guys to the Bahamas?" asked Jill. "Tony called me when you left for Cancun, but he didn't say anything about coming here."

"Again, this probably isn't the right place but we'll get you up to speed soon. In fact, Jim and I have been invited to dinner tonight with Miles Adderly. He's our van driver, hotel operator and a former Navy SEAL. Would you and Tony like to join us?"

Tony and Jill looked at each other and then back to Frank and said, in unison, "Na!"

Frank laughed and let them off the hook.

"Okay, but you two need to be ready to travel at 7:00 a.m. tomorrow morning. I've arranged a charter flight to South Bimini and I hope to be in the water up there by 10:00 a.m. Depending on what we find, we'll either make a second dive at our primary site or buzz up to Bimini Road and do a 'just-for-fun' dive. Bring a change of clothes, because we can't fly for twenty-four hours after our last dive. I thought we'd spend Thursday morning on the ground near our primary dive site. We can also make a stop at the alleged site of Ponce de Leon's Fountain of Youth, since it's only about a mile from the airport. Thursday afternoon we'll fly back down here and decide what to do next."

"What about Linda and Javier?" asked Jim. "When are they leaving Cancun for Cuba?"

"That depends on how fast Buzz Edwards can get their cover story put together, but certainly not before Thursday morning. Buzz is going to call me on my satellite phone once he has a firm itinerary. Fitz and Susan are on standby with the Learjet in case we need to go in after them, but I don't really expect any problems."

"How would you get in there?" asked Jill. "It's not like you can just fly that new airplane of yours into a Cuban airfield unannounced and pick them up."

Tony laughed and squeezed her hand.

"That's what Frank did for two years in 'Nam," he said. "He parachuted in, usually from low altitudes and often in scuba gear, and then swam ashore to rescue downed pilots."

"And frequently under the cover of night," added Frank. "If it comes to that, Tony and I would go in together, hook up with our two wayward travelers and make our way south to Guantanamo where we could get a lift off the island from the U. S. military. But, like I said, I don't expect it to come to that."

"Good," declared Jill, "because I don't want Tony pulling any of those crazy stunts! I had no idea you guys did that kind of stuff in Viet Nam."

"Well, actually, I didn't," smiled Tony sheepishly. "This would be my first low-level night jump into water. But, hey, what could go wrong?"

"Alright, you!" exclaimed Jill. "I haven't eaten since noon and I'm starved. Take me to dinner and then I have a surprise for you."

Jill gave Tony an exaggerated wink that everyone else could see and he actually blushed. As he got up from the table, he smiled at Frank and Jim.

"You two have fun talking about artifacts tonight. See you in the morning!"

As they walked away, Jim turned back to Frank, suddenly very serious.

"It sounds like you've put some thought into this rescue mission, Frank. Did you guys work this out back when you thought I was going to be the one going to Cuba?"

"More or less," replied Frank. "We've refined the plan a little since then, but yes, we would have come in for you if you had needed help. You didn't really think we expected you to make your way the entire length of the island on your own, did you?"

"Well, yes, actually I did, and the prospect terrified me. But this rescue mission sounds really dangerous, too. Why would you and Tony risk something like that?"

"Because 'leave no one behind' is a code Tony and I lived with every day overseas, Jim. That's just the way it is. Let's stop by your room and pick up the triangles and their magic box and then go see what Miles has to show us."

As promised, Miles had the restaurant's staff serve dinner in his private study in the back of the Bay Club's main building, the Great House.

As he finished off the last of his Filet Mignon, Frank leaned back in his chair and took in the warm, library-like atmosphere. One whole wall was lined with books and some of them looked very old.

"This is quite a place you have here, Miles," he said, complimenting his host.

"Well, I'm afraid I can't take much credit for it," Miles replied. "Most of this was already here when I bought the property and there are some first editions on those shelves that are probably worth a fortune. The old guy who built the original Bay Club was an academic—a history professor, I think—and when he died suddenly, his wife just wanted to liquidate everything and return to the mainland. Apparently she never liked it here and she was very anxious to get off the island. I've added a few volumes over the years, but most of this was his. In fact, that's what I want to show you—a couple of those books."

Miles indicated that Frank and Jim should move to a sitting area on the far side of the room while he retrieved a thick, leather-bound volume from the shelves.

"I found this one day, quite by accident," he said, laying the book on a small coffee table in front of Frank and Jim. "Open it and tell me what you think."

Carefully, Jim laid back the cover and gazed at the first page.

"It looks like Greek to me," smiled Frank as he peered over Jim's shoulder. "No pun intended."

"No, it's not Greek," mumbled Jim, "but it's very similar. Could it be early Phoenician?"

"Very good, Professor," nodded Miles. "According to several experts that I've sent copies of selected pages, this entire book appears to be written using a Phoenician alphabet that dates back to about 900 B.C."

"But why would anyone write a book in a language that died nearly 3,000 years ago?" questioned Jim. He examined several pages and then closed the book to study the cover. "This book certainly isn't that old."

"I agree," nodded Miles. "And yet, here it is. Let me show you something else I found on these shelves. Something that's even more puzzling."

He fetched another book and laid it on top of the first. He indicated that Jim should open it. Inside the cover, the book had a large rectangular cavity cut out of the pages and it contained what looked like a rolled up piece of parchment.

Jim removed the roll and looked up to Miles for approval before unrolling it.

"It's a map," Jim said almost immediately. "And the legend appears to be written using the same alphabet as the other book."

Frank reached around Jim and pointed to an arrow near the top of the five-by-eight inch document.

"If this elongated 'S' squiggle represents a Phoenician 'N' then this arrow probably points north. Any idea what this map represents?"

"I know exactly what it represents," smiled Miles. "That's why I have my little Bionic Dolphin tied up out in the marina. This map depicts a cave system that's just off-shore in front of the hotel. It's one of the many blue holes we're so famous for here in the Bahamas. After I discovered this map, I was making a couple of trips a day out there so I picked up the Dolphin to shuttle back and forth."

Frank and Jim both stared at the document wide-eyed. It clearly showed a system of three chambers connected together by tubes of varying lengths. Jim was the first to speak.

"There's no scale on the map. How long is this system, anyway?"

"I don't know," replied Miles. He pointed to a place on the connecting tube that joined the first and second chambers and added, "This is as far as I've been able to go because the passageway narrows here and I can't get into the second chamber with dive gear on. I've been out there dozens of times in the Dolphin looking for another entrance, but so far I haven't found one."

"So how far is it to your turn-around point?" asked Frank.

"About a hundred yards, Frank, but this map is very rough and not to scale, so you can't use that to extrapolate the distance to the last chamber."

"What's in that first chamber? Anything interesting?" pressed Frank.

"It's actually quite beautiful. I've seen other underwater caverns around the island that have stalactites and stalagmites in them, but the ones in this first chamber are really beautiful. In the morning there's quite a bit of light from the surface and it gives you the feeling that you're traveling into the jaws of a giant fish!"

"But, stalactites and stalagmites would mean..." blurted Jim.

"That this cave system was once dry. Yes, I know, but there are a lot of sites like this around here and they prove that the oceans were once much lower than they are today. For example, the bottom of this first chamber is about 90 feet deep. Using generally accepted data about the rise in the sea level, this cave system would have sunk below the surface about nine thousand years ago."

The three stared at the map for what seemed like minutes before Frank finally spoke.

"I'd love to see this place, Miles. A blue hole, in and of itself, is no big deal. But that fact that this one is depicted on a map that's hidden in this particular book makes it very interesting. Will you take me out there when we get back from Bimini?"

"Sure, I guess so, but I'd like to get credit for the discovery, if you don't mind. Discovering new geologic features is sort of a status symbol here on Andros and..."

"Not a problem, my friend, the credit will be all yours. Maybe they'll even name it Adderly Hole or some such thing. And now, we have something we'd like to show you. Jim, do you have the box?"

Jim retrieved his worn leather briefcase and carefully slid out the silver box Frank had accidentally discovered at the ruins near Cuba.

Miles' eyes widened in surprise as Jim set the box on the table next to the books.

"It's beautiful!" he exclaimed. "Where and when did you find it?"

"We found this box a few days ago," replied Frank. "It was buried a few inches under the sand at a site we were exploring off the western tip of Cuba."

"Cuba, huh? I wasn't aware of any sites in that area, but it's certainly a beautiful piece."

"Oh, you haven't seen anything, yet," Frank grinned. "Jim, show him what's inside."

Jim removed the tight-fitting lid and placed it to one side. One at a time, he removed the five triangular 'coins' and laid them out beside the box. When the last one clanked onto the table, Frank leaned forward.

"Ever see anything like that?" he grinned.

Miles' mouth was hanging open and his eyes had widened even more. Slowly, he nodded his head several times.

"Yes, as a matter of fact, I think I have," he finally managed.

Still in shock, Miles reached for the book that had contained the map. Turning the book over, he opened the back cover to expose the back side of the last page. There, all alone in the center of the sheet, was a triangular figure with a smaller triangle in its center. The space between the two triangles was filled with strange symbols similar, but not identical, to those on the five objects from Jim's box.

On a hunch, Frank picked up one of the 'coins' and placed it on the figure in the book. The size and shape was an exact match and the triangular center of the real object coincided perfectly with the inner triangle in the book.

"Wow!" remarked Frank. "I certainly wasn't expecting that!"

Chapter 12

Frank, Jim and Miles speculated about the origin of the triangular objects and the leather-bound book late into the evening. Frank's sleep schedule had been messed up since before they left the Atlantic Protector and when he yawned for the third time, he suggested that it might be time to retire for the night.

"We have an early morning flight to South Bimini and I'm beat," he told Miles. "Since we're going to be gone the better part of two days, maybe it would be a good idea if we left these triangle things with you. I notice you have a security system in this room, so I assume they'll be safe here."

"That they will," beamed Miles. "And it would be my pleasure."

Taking the box from Jim, Miles moved to the book case and slid some books apart to expose a small metal door with a combination lock in the center. He dialed in the numbers, placed the box inside, re-secured the door and replaced the books.

"There!" he announced. "Your artifacts, if that's what they are, will be safe until you return."

Frank raised an eyebrow and asked, "Did that come with the library, too?"

"No, that's an addition I made," smiled Miles. "On occasion I'm asked to hold large sums of money for some of my AUTEC guests and this does the job nicely."

Miles agreed to meet the NWIDI team in the lobby at 6:30 a.m. the next morning for the van ride to the airport and then showed Frank and Jim out through a back entrance of the main building.

The flight to South Bimini the next morning provided the NWIDI team with their first real view of the islands and the water surrounding them. All four were amazed at how much of the ocean floor was visible from the air and how shallow the waters appeared to be.

Talking loud, so as to be heard above the noise of the engines, Jim pointed down and asked, "How deep do you think it is?"

"It's deeper than it looks," boomed Tony in reply. "It's deceiving because the water here is so clear compared to what you're used to in the Northwest. I'd say it's probably thirty to fifty feet."

Jim looked surprised, but nodded. For much of the trip they each peered out their respective windows and marveled at the beauty below. They passed over numerous small islands that appeared to be uninhabited and around each the sand faded into turquoise-green water and, eventually, into progressively darker shades of blue. As they began their descent to Bimini, they could clearly see boats anchored in harbors and others speeding between the islands.

Frank had been very quiet—almost brooding—during the flight and Tony called him on it as they loaded their dive gear and overnight bags onto a cart beside the plane.

"Something eating you?" asked Tony.

Frank frowned and replied, "No, why?"

"You haven't said a word since we left Andros, Frank. What's up?"

Frank shook his head. "Nothing, I've just been trying to figure out the significance of the triangles we found off Cuba and how they relate to the drawing in Miles' book on Andros."

Frank had briefed Tony and Jill about the discovery during the van ride from the hotel to the airport but they hadn't seemed very interested.

Tony slapped Frank on the back and said, "Well, don't worry about that now, pal, we've got some diving to do! The mysteries can wait until tomorrow."

The van from Bimini Underwater Tours met the NWIDI team outside the small terminal and soon had them within a dozen yards of the coordinates Frank had emailed to them the day before. Their dive master's name was Ian Kingston, a tall, lean 20-something from London.

"Well, this is the spot, mates, but I still don't see why you want to dive here. The diving is much better over on the western side of the island."

"I know, Ian, but we're looking for something in particular and this is the spot where we were told to dive, so in we go," replied Frank.

The shoreline along the south coast of the island was rocky and difficult to navigate, but they finally made their way to the water's edge. As they prepared to start their dive, Frank turned and gave the "thumbs up" sign to Jim, who was standing on the bluff where they had left the van.

"So what's the terrain like down there, Ian?" asked Tony.

"I honestly have no idea," replied the young dive master. "When we received Mr. Morton's email yesterday I tried to find a chart of this area but we didn't have anything in the shop. I didn't even know the gravel road that brought us down here existed until yesterday."

"So why do you suppose that road was built?" asked Tony, adjusting the strap on his dive mask.

"Good question!" replied Ian. "For fishermen, maybe?"

"This gets more interesting by the minute," laughed Tony. "Let's go diving before I roast in this wet suit!"

With Jill at his side, Tony slowly walked out into the water until he was about waist deep. With the next step, he was suddenly bobbing like a cork and only his inflated BC kept him from sinking below the surface.

"There's quite a drop-off right here," he shouted.

As they moved out towards Tony and Jill, Ian asked, "So what are we looking for, Mr. Morton?"

"A friend of mine told me that an undersea communications cable used to come ashore right here," lied Frank. "When they put in a new cable, they just cut the old one off and tossed the end back in the water. My friends and I thought it would be fun to see what one looks like, so here we are."

Ian snapped his fingers. "That's what the road was probably for! I'll bet they had to come down here to inspect it periodically."

"You're probably right," agreed Frank. "Shall we go diving?"

When all four divers were bobbing near the drop-off, Ian gave the thumbs down sign that meant submerge. Slowly the four divers drifted down, staying as close together as possible. Tony's call about a drop-off had been right—they were descending a vertical wall completely devoid of vegetation. As dive master, Ian took a slight lead and controlled the descent. When they reached sixty feet, he signaled a stop and waited for the others to adjust their buoyancy so they were neither rising nor sinking. He pointed to each diver in turn and waited for the "OK" sign and then he gestured with his arms and shoulders to signal, "Now what?"

Frank signaled 1-0-0 and pointed down, indicating that he wanted to continue down to one hundred feet before making a decision.

Ian returned an "OK" and turned on his dive light before signaling the others to resume their descent.

By the time they reached seventy-five feet, the water had turned noticeably colder and Frank began looking for a reason. He moved the beam of his powerful dive light back and forth along the wall. Suddenly, his light caught the edge of something and he waved the light wildly to attract the attention of the others, who had already dropped several feet below him.

When the other three were back near him, Frank held his beam on the spot so they could see what had caught his eye. Moving horizontally along the wall, Ian led the group slowly toward the spot Frank had pointed out. The water around the divers continued to cool, and by the time they reached their objective, it was downright uncomfortable. There was also a strong current flowing away from the wall that made swimming very difficult.

The feature Frank had discovered was the edge of what appeared to be the entrance to (or exit from) a rectangular tunnel in the wall about the size of a garage door. Each of the divers took their turn at shinning their light into the opening, but the beams all disappeared into the darkness without revealing a back wall.

The four divers turned to face each other and Frank signaled a thumbs-up to return to the surface. Again, Ian took the lead and stopped the group at fifteen feet for their decompression safety stop. They were all cold, exhausted and anxious to discuss what they had just seen and the three-minute stop seemed like an eternity. Finally, their heads broke the surface and they all started talking at once.

"What the hell was that!" shouted Tony, shaking the water out of his hair.

"I don't know," replied Ian, "but I assure you it's not a documented feature that I've ever heard of."

"It was freezing down there," shuddered Jill. "Was there cold water coming out of that opening?"

"It was not only cold water, but I'll bet it was fresh water!" replied Frank. "Let's get ashore and get warmed up."

Once ashore, the warm rays of the sun soon made the four divers more comfortable. Jim joined them at the water's edge and Frank told him about their discovery.

"But this part of the island is less than a half-mile wide," protested Jim. "A fresh water source that large would have been discovered long ago. From what I remember in my reading, there are only a few sources of fresh water on the whole of Bimini."

"That's correct," nodded Ian. "And none of them could deliver the amount of water that seemed to be coming out of that opening."

"Ian, what's directly across the island from here?" asked Frank.

"Not much!" he replied. "Well, actually, I guess we'd be almost straight across from the small pool that some folks think is Ponce de Leon's legendary Fountain of Youth, but that's all it is—a small pool."

"Is it fresh?" pressed Frank.

"It's pretty murky, from what I hear, but it's not salt water, if that's what you mean."

"And the other fresh water sources—where are they?"

"Over on East Bimini there's a place they call the Healing Hole and further north there's the East Well. As far as I know, that's it."

"I'd like to look at those places on a map," said Frank. "Can we stop at your dive shop when we leave here?"

"Of course, Mr. Morton, but what about the communications cable you hoped to find? Have you given up on that?"

Tony looked shocked when Ian mentioned the mysterious cable they had traced more than two hundred miles from the ruins near Cuba to a spot just south of Key West. Frank had speculated that it continued on its absolutely straight course to the site they had just explored on the southern coast of South Bimini and he couldn't believe Frank had shared that secret with someone he hardly knew.

"Oh, I think my friend will forgive us if we don't find the cable he helped lay thirty years ago," replied Frank. "Besides, we might come back out here this afternoon, if you don't mind."

"Not at all," smiled Ian. "I was told you wanted to dive Bimini Road, but this is a lot more interesting than a site I've already seen a hundred times. I might suggest we return by boat, though. Maybe we can use the onboard depth-finder to find out how far down that wall goes."

"Excellent idea!" exclaimed Frank. "Let's do it!"

While Frank, Tony and Jill were getting out of their wet suits and stowing their gear, Ian grabbed something out of the van and scrambled back down to the shore. When he returned, he showed the others a spray can of florescent orange paint.

"I marked one of those big rocks so we can find the spot easier this afternoon," he announced proudly.

"I'm beginning to like this kid more every minute," laughed Frank.

At the dive shop in Port Royal, Ian produced a crude, hand-drawn map of the Biminis. Often described as two islands, Bimini is actually three separate land masses. The "V" shaped North Bimini is separated from East Bimini by a narrow salt-water creek, much like the two that divide Andros into three distinct pieces. It was East Bimini that Frank immediately focused on.

After a minute, he looked up at Ian and said, "Have you ever noticed this?"

Using the edge of a log book, Frank drew a light pencil line from East Well through the Healing Hole and on to the Fountain of Youth site.

"They're all in line with each other!" shouted Jim. "That's quite a coincidence!"

Frank continued the line across South Bimini and out into Nicholas Harbor, south of the island.

Tapping the map at the point where the line touched the southern shoreline, he asked, "Anybody want to guess where this is?"

"Get out!" cried Ian. "Is that the spot we just dove?"

"Well, this map is pretty crude, but I'm betting it is," replied Frank. "Before we return to Andros tomorrow I want to get the exact GPS coordinates for the other three sites, but I'd be willing to bet they're all on a perfectly straight line."

"And your friend's cable is there, too," added Ian. "That's just weird!"

"Yes, it is," smiled Frank. "It's very weird indeed."

The NWIDI team walked a couple of blocks to a local restaurant for lunch and to rest from the morning's cold dive. They tried to get Ian to join them, but he insisted on staying at the shop to prepare for the afternoon dive.

After they had ordered, Tony brought up the issue of the cable and the story Frank had told Ian.

"Before the dive he asked me what we were looking for, and I had to think fast," explained Frank. "On the outside chance that we might actually find it, I decided not to stray too far from the truth and once I started talking, that story about a friend being on the ship that installed the cable just seemed to flow out."

"It was a good cover-up, alright," smiled Tony, "but when he mentioned it I thought you'd spilled the beans. So what about the real cable—or whatever it is? Do you still think it's down there somewhere?"

"I do," nodded Frank, "although I'm not sure we'll ever find it. Remember, it was 2,100 feet deep at the Cuban site and just about the same depth at the Key West site. If that wall goes down that far, I'm sure that's where the cable will be—far too deep to dive. Until we discovered the wall, I had pictured the cable gradually rising as it approached the south island and either going underground at that point or connecting to some unknown device just off shore. Now I'm not so sure."

"It sure seems like that wall would have made it onto a map or chart or dive site list at some point," challenged Tony. "I'll bet you a beer it's not 2,100 feet deep."

"You're on!" Frank accepted. "Did anyone notice anything odd about that wall?"

"I did," answered Jill. "I've done a lot of wall dives in the Caribbean and you usually find all kinds of plant and marine life on the face of a wall, especially near the top. This one was nearly bare, and it didn't look like it ever had any vegetation on it, either."

"Very good, Jill! What about you, Tony?"

Tony thought for a minute and then his eyes widened.

"It was nearly smooth! In fact, it almost looked…"

"…artificial," finished Frank. "When we go back out there this afternoon, I'd like you both to keep your eyes open and make mental notes of everything you see. Tonight at supper we'll compare notes again. There's something very strange about that place and I intend to get to the bottom of it—no pun intended."

"I hate to be the rational one here," objected Jim, "but don't you think that if an artificial structure existed this close to the shore someone would have discovered it before now? Given all the diving that goes on in these parts, it's hard to believe there's a square inch of shoreline that hasn't been explored."

"And yet our dive master had never been there before," countered Frank.

By the time they returned to the dive shop it was nearly 1:00 p.m. and Ian was obviously eager to get started. He had already loaded their gear aboard the dive boat and he was busy studying a nautical chart when the NWIDI team arrived.

"Ready?" he asked eagerly. "It will take us about 40 minutes to cruise around Rabbit Cay and get over to our dive site. We were there just after high tide this morning, so it will be just after low tide for our dive this afternoon."

"Have you eaten?" asked Frank. "We don't want you fainting on us, you know."

"Oh, yeah, I always bring my lunch and I ate while I was getting the gear ready. Don't worry about me."

Ian flipped the "Open" sign over so it read "Closed" and locked the front door. Indicating a side door, he said, "Shall we?"

The dive boat was a large, well-equipped commercial craft capable of handling a dozen divers in comfort. Once Ian navigated out of the small marina and had the boat in open water, he called for Frank to join him on the bridge. He handed him one of the charts he had brought along and motioned for Frank to unroll it.

"It's the newest data I could find," Ian yelled over the noise of the engine. "I had a friend of mine from another dive shop drop it by while you guys were at lunch. It was done by your Navy about five years ago. Take a look at the bathymetric readings near the site."

Frank studied the map for several minutes and then rolled the chart up.

"Where's the wall?" he yelled back to Ian.

"I guess your Navy missed it!" laughed the dive master. "Or maybe they didn't want anybody to know it was there."

Frank returned to the main deck of the boat and told the others what he had just learned.

"What's odd," he concluded, "is that the chart indicates that the bottom gradually slopes away to a depth of about seventy-five feet more than three hundred yards out. We were that deep in less than 10 yards. It's as if they fabricated the whole shore line."

"But why?" asked Jill. "And how long did they think they would get away with it?"

"Well, nobody's reported the wall so far," said Jim.

"At least not that we know of," cautioned Tony.

He reached into his dive bag and removed a small, snub-nosed revolver, which he handed to Jim.

"Since you're going to be aboard alone, I want you to keep this close by. If anything tries to get onto this boat that doesn't look like one of us, shoot it!"

Jim accepted the handgun gingerly and Tony realized that Jim probably wouldn't pull the trigger if his life depended on it.

"Maybe I should stay up here with Jim," offered Tony, shaking his head in disgust.

"No, you dive," insisted Jim. "I'll be fine up here."

Tony started to argue, but Frank intervened.

"He'll be okay, Tony, and I don't think he needs the gun. How'd you get that through customs, anyway?"

"The same way I got guns into Japan, remember? There's a hidden compartment in the back wall of the lavatory on the plane. Its previous owner probably used it to smuggle drugs, but I prefer to stash away a little fire power for situations just like this."

"Very risky business, my friend," admonished Frank. "But I wonder if that secret compartment has anything to do with our Columbian friends? Maybe we'd better give it a good look-see the next time we're on the same continent as the plane."

"Maybe we'd better go over the entire plane," suggested Tony. "I found the compartment I use completely by accident and there might be others. Who knows what we've been unwittingly hauling around for the past year?"

Suddenly concerned for his unsuspecting flight crew, Frank turned to address Jim.

"Have you had any new thoughts on the connection between our triangles and Miles' book?"

Jim shook his head and frowned. "No, and it's really bugging me. The picture in the book and the real thing are just too identical to be a coincidence. And the book is just as big a mystery as our triangular objects are. Why does a book written in an ancient language look so new?"

"Maybe it's a copy," suggested Jill, who was sitting next to Jim on the long bench seat that ran the length of the dive boat.

"How could it be a…" Frank stopped in mid-sentence and snapped his fingers. "Of course! Miles told us he inherited that book, along with many others in his library, from his predecessor. Maybe the old man who owned the hotel before Miles made a copy of an ancient text and had it rebound. Jill, you're a genius!"

"Oh, I know," she smiled.

"Or maybe that book's just what it appears to be," mumbled Tony from behind Frank. "Maybe it's a relatively new book written by someone who still speaks Portuguese."

"Phoenician," corrected Jim.

"Whatever! Why do you guys always try to make things so difficult when the answer might be so obvious?"

Frank turned to face Tony and joined Jim and Jill in staring at him.

"Hey, I'm just saying that maybe there's no mystery here at all," shrugged Tony.

"But Tony, your suggestion would be more of a puzzle than Jill's," replied Jim. "The language used in that book hasn't been used in almost 3,000 years."

"Not that you know of," said Tony, raising his eyebrows.

The discussion about Miles' book was interrupted by Ian's yells from the deck above. The NWIDI team members looked in the direction he was pointing and realized that they were nearing the morning's dive site. Frank scrambled up the chrome ladder to join Ian and remind him to turn on the boat's depth finder.

"Already done, mate!" shouted Ian as he pointed to a digital readout on the instrument panel to his left. "But it can't be right."

Frank looked at the display and then back at Ian.

"One hundred ten feet. That's about what we guessed it would be, right?"

"That's in meters, mate. The bottom is more than 350 feet down!"

Chapter 13

"Now what?" asked Frank, knowing that three hundred fifty feet is way too deep for scuba gear.

"I have a plan. Let's get the boat situated and then I'll tell you what I have in mind," replied Ian.

Frank watched the depth as Ian slowly moved the boat towards shore. When the display suddenly changed from 110 meters to 1 meter, Ian manipulated the boat's engine controls and gently moved it back and forth until it was almost stationary right over the top of the wall. He toggled a switch on the panel in front him and the anchor dropped into the shallow surf on the island side of the wall. When he was satisfied with the orientation of the boat, he shut the engines down and signaled for Frank to precede him down the ladder to the main deck. Ian briefly disappeared down another ladder below the main deck and when he returned he was carrying what looked like a large yellow plastic back-pack.

"Okay, so here's the situation," he began. "We're right over the top of the wall, and the back of the boat is in deep water—more than 350 feet deep. Obviously, we can't get to the bottom with regular dive gear, but I can do it with this. It's called a closed-circuit rebreather and it's capable of depths of up to five hundred feet. I loaded it aboard earlier because I was afraid we'd run into something like this."

"I saw somebody diving with one of those back on St. Thomas," exclaimed Jill. "Don't they give you unlimited bottom time, too?"

"Well, not exactly, but they last a lot longer than a tank of air," replied Ian. "I need a few minutes to work up a dive profile so why don't you three get suited up and ready to dive. I'm going to ask each of you to station yourselves at a different depth as a backup, just in case I get into trouble and have to abort my dive."

Fifteen minutes later, Frank, Tony and Jill were in the water just off the back of the boat holding on to a heavy line Ian had dropped with an air tank attached to its end. Tony had been assigned the ninety-foot station, Frank the sixty-foot station and Jill the twenty-foot station. These were marked on the line with colored tape and the extra air tank hung from the end of the line, one hundred twenty feet below the boat. In addition, Frank was carrying an extra tank over his shoulder on a special sling.

"Okay, divers, I'll give you a five-minute head start and then I'm going straight to the bottom. I'll stay no more than ten minutes and then I'll begin my ascent. I'll stop at each check-point for five minutes on the way back up to decompress. When I leave your position, ascend with me to the next stop. When we reach Jill, we'll stay there ten minutes and then come back to the surface. Everybody clear on that?"

After receiving three "OK" signs, Ian shouted, "Divers down!"

Using the marked line, the three NWIDI divers descended slowly, clearing the pressure in their ears frequently. At the twenty-foot mark, Jill waved to Frank and Tony and watched them disappear below her. Frank and Tony exchanged "OK" signals at sixty feet and Tony continued on down. At about seventy-five feet, he was startled by a movement and looked to his right to see Ian waving as he passed by. As he watched the other diver descend, Tony realized for the first time that rebreathers, at least the kind Ian was using, didn't emit any bubbles. He also noticed that Ian had a dive light in one hand and an underwater video camera in the other.

"Gutsy kid," admired Tony.

Frank had marked the time that he reached his sixty-foot mark. He estimated that it would take Ian about five minutes to reach the bottom and the young diver had said he wouldn't stay there any longer than ten minutes. Adding another five minutes to get back to the first check-point, five minutes for his safety stop and five more with Tony should have brought him within sight five minutes ago. As his concern mounted with every passing second, Frank considered descending to Tony's position in case something had gone wrong, but he resisted the urge and made himself repeat the cardinal rule of diving—*"plan your dive and dive your plan."* Changing his position now could jeopardize those below him.

Suddenly he felt a rush of bubbles from below and spotted Tony's head. A little further down he could just make out the bright yellow housing of Ian's rebreather unit and he breathed an underwater sigh of relief.

When Tony and Ian had a secure hand-hold on the line at the sixty-foot mark, Ian pointed to the camera and nodded vigorously. Soon they were hanging on the line with Jill, impatiently waiting for the ten-minute decompression interval to expire. Frank noticed that Ian was constantly adjusting something on his rebreather's control unit and he wondered if something had gone wrong with the equipment. Twice he tapped Ian's arm and signaled "Are you okay?" Both times, Ian responded "OK" and then returned his focus to the control unit.

Finally, it was time for the four divers to make their way up the line to the surface. Frank was the first one to shake the water out of his eyes and when he looked up at the back of the boat he found himself staring into the barrel of a gun.

"Thank God you guys are safe," yelled Jim. "I was really getting worried and nobody told me what to do if you didn't return. I don't even know how to drive this boat back to the dock!"

"Well please don't shoot us," cautioned Frank. "Could you put that thing down and help us aboard?"

Jim looked down at the revolver as if he'd forgotten he even had it.

"Oh, yes, of course! Sorry about that, but I was getting really concerned—and a little scared, too."

As soon as the four divers were on board, Tony quizzed Ian about the camera.

"I take it you got some good footage down there?" he asked.

"Man, you're not going to believe it! The wall stays just as we saw it this morning all the way to the bottom—which was actually three hundred sixty-five feet, by the way—and there's this odd-shaped foundation or low wall on the sea floor!"

"It wasn't by any chance triangular, was it?" asked Frank.

"Yes! How did you know that?" exclaimed Ian.

"Just a hunch," Frank replied. "Did you see anything else? Any sign of the communications cable my friend mentioned?"

"Not where I was, but I didn't travel horizontally very far in either direction because I wanted to stay close to the drop line. However," he added, "the top of that triangle thing has these strange symbols all over it and the whole thing appears to be metallic, like pewter or something. Weird, huh?"

***

"I haven't been able to raise Frank all day," complained Buzz Edwards, "but I'll keep trying because he wanted to know the plan as soon as we had one. You two should get going or you'll miss your flight."

Linda and Javier had been in non-stop briefings almost since their arrival in Cancun the day before and now the plans were being pushed forward again.

"Are you sure we shouldn't delay this until tomorrow? Frank and the others should be back soon. I think today was the day they were going to Bimini."

"No, if we're going to make your cover stick, you need to be in Havana today. The conference we've signed you up for kicks off with a reception this evening and lasts through tomorrow. If you delay a day you lose the whole reason for being on the island."

"He's right, Linda," agreed Javier. We don't want to draw any attention to ourselves if we can help it and this environmental conference is the perfect excuse to be in the country."

"Alright, but I wish Frank knew we were leaving. He's our only way out if we get in trouble over there."

"Hey, I'm not entirely without resources, you know," said an indignant Edwards as he waved his arm to indicate the multi-level paramilitary installation buried deep beneath the surface near the Cancun airport. "And I promise I'll talk to Frank before you leave Havana Friday morning. In fact, I'll call my contact there right now and make sure he has Frank call me as soon as he arrives back on Andros."

Linda had met Miles Adderly and she trusted him to deliver the message, so she reluctantly gave in.

"Okay, then let's get this show on the road," she announced. "I'm tired of being in this overgrown root cellar anyway."

Earlier in the day, Linda and Javier had been given new identities, complete with passports and the appropriate ID cards. Linda was an American freelance writer specializing in stories supporting environmental causes and Javier was a Mexican photographer she had hired through a talent agency in Cancun. After a quick stop in Havana to attend the conference, they were going to spend a few days visiting some of the more remote areas of Cuba to gather background information on how well Cuba was protecting its natural resources. The Cuban officials had agreed to the visit because they never passed up an opportunity for favorable press coverage, especially if it could be had at the expense of the U.S. government.

Edwards accompanied Linda and Javier to the main terminal and made sure there were no glitches getting them on the Cubana Airlines flight.

Once they were through security and in the boarding area, Linda relaxed a little.

"I don't mind telling you that I'm a little nervous about this whole operation," she whispered as they found seats at the rear of the waiting area.

"Really? You'd never know just by watching your hands shake," laughed Javier, as he reached for her left hand, which really was shaking.

"Well, I never did care much for this cloak-and-dagger stuff the way Frank and Tony do, and we're headed for Cuba, of all places!"

"You'll do fine, Linda, and the Cuban authorities won't be surprised if you act a little nervous. After all, most Americans who travel from Mexico to Havana do so illegally."

"You're not helping, you know," frowned Linda.

After getting a fifteen minute late start, the plane finally landed in Havana at 5:00 p.m., local time. Linda and Javier had reservations at the same hotel where the conference was being held, and they took a taxi directly there once they cleared customs. Although he seemed friendly, the taxi driver spoke only Spanish, so Linda rested her head against the back of the seat and tried to relax while Javier carried on a lively conversation with the driver.

As traveling business associates, they had separate room reservations but Javier talked the desk clerk into assigning them adjoining rooms.

"Clever boy," smiled Linda as she unbolted her side of the door that connected the rooms and knocked softly.

"Who is it?" replied Javier playfully.

"It's Fidel Castro, wise guy! Now open the door."

The door swung open and Linda was confronted by a frowning Javier.

"In Cuba, one doesn't make jokes like that, Linda! This place is very different from the United States, where your President is fair game for every comedian and talk show host in the country. If the wrong person overhears you being disrespectful to Castro, you could end up in jail."

Linda quickly realized that he was very serious.

"Sorry! It was just a joke, but I'll try to be more careful in the future. This is going to be even harder than I thought."

Javier held out his arms and smiled to let her know it was forgotten.

"You just need to assume that every person you talk to is a government agent and you'll get along fine."

"I'll try, I promise," whispered Linda.

Linda and Javier arrived at the reception at 7:45 p.m. on the dot. Not early enough to be the first ones there and not late enough to be the last. The large meeting room, which would be configured with rows of chairs by morning, currently contained portable bars in three corners and a stringed trio playing softly in the other corner. Along one wall, a row of draped tables displayed literature from a variety of Cuban government agencies and each of the country's provinces. Representatives stood behind each table eagerly offering the materials to anyone who looked even a little bit interested.

Javier had changed into a dark suit and Linda was wearing a print cocktail dress that was a far cry from the jeans and polo shirts she had worn for the last few days. Javier soon noticed that Linda was catching the eye of many of the males in the room.

"I told you upstairs that you'd wow them, and it appears I'm right," smiled Javier as several sets of eyes followed them along the tables.

"Oh stop it! It's just because I'm the only blonde in the room, and you know it," blushed Linda.

The pair stopped at several tables and collected a small handful of brochures to make it appear that they were actually interested in the topic at hand. One of the last tables represented Pinar del Rio, the western-most province in Cuba.

When Linda spotted the name on one of the hand-outs, she nudged Javier with an elbow and hissed, "Smile, but keep moving. Don't look too interested at first."

After they had visited all the tables, they casually made their way back to the only one that really interested them.

Linda browsed the various pieces on the table and picked up several. She smiled at the handsome young man behind the table each time she took something, distracting him from his conversation with Javier. Finally Javier motioned her closer and introduced her to the other man who was now smiling from ear to ear.

"Linda, this is Ernesto. He's from Pinar del Rio, on the far western end of the island and they're doing some very interesting beach erosion work in his area. He thinks it would be excellent material for your article."

Javier picked up a small map of the province and held it so only he and Linda could see it. He indicated where the provincial capitol was located and then slid his finger over to the extreme western tip of the island, where the recently discovered ruins were located.

"I think we should check it out," he said out loud for Ernesto's benefit.

"*Mucho gusto, Ernesto,*" smiled Linda. "*Habla Inglés?*"

"*No, Señorita, lo siento.*"

Remembering Javier's caution in the hotel room, Linda decided not to trust the young Cuban's answer, just in case he was playing dumb.

"The preservation of beaches is something I'm really interested in! Javier, would you tell Ernesto about our travel permit and ask him if it would be possible to visit his province after the conference?"

As Javier explained the arrangement, Ernesto's face visibly lit up and he began nodding with each new sentence. Linda had noticed that the literature tables were being largely ignored by many of the reception guests and she was sure no one else had actually asked to visit one of the advertised projects.

After a lengthy discussion and some quick note taking on both sides, the two men shook hands.

Javier turned to Linda and announced, "Okay, it's all arranged. Ernesto has to return home tomorrow, but he's told me how to get to his city and we've arranged to meet there at 2:00 p.m. on Friday. He's offered to escort us to a project at Playa Las Canas, just south of the city."

"Excellent! *Muchas gracias, Ernesto,*" smiled Linda, turning to the young man who was beside himself with joy. He had not only interested someone in the ecological work of his remote province, but they were actually coming to see it first hand—and one of them was an American!

As Linda and Javier returned their attention to the reception, they noticed that other guests had gathered together in small groups, chatting and drinking.

As they started for the area where the trio was playing, Linda commented, "I've never understood why they call these things mixers. People just latch onto a friend or acquaintance and go out of their way to avoid the uncomfortable experience of actually meeting someone new."

"Perhaps we can change that tradition," said a deep, slightly accented voice from behind them.

Linda and Javier turned to find a well dressed, middle-aged Latino man no more than two steps behind them.

"I'm sorry to interrupt, but I couldn't help overhearing your comment, *Señorita*, and I couldn't agree more, so please allow me to introduce myself."

The man extended his hand to Linda and when she reached out to shake, he gently raised her hand and kissed it.

After a much less sincere hand-shake with Javier, he said, "My name is Antonio Olvera-Campos and I'm the organizer of this event. Please allow me to welcome you to Cuba, to Havana, and to my humble reception, Ms. Hollister."

"It's my pleasure, *Señor Campos*, and thank you for the last-minute invitation. Allow me to introduce my associate, Javier Martinez, a well-known photographer from Mexico City who graciously agreed to accompany me on this trip."

"Ah, yes, I've seen some of your work, *Señor Martinez*. You have a unique style and your portrayal of nature's beauty is very impressive. It's an honor to have you both with us. May I introduce you to some of my other guests?"

Linda soon learned that their host was the Cuban Minister of Science, Technology and the Environment, that he should be addressed as *Señor Olvera*, not *Señor Campos*, and that he was very well respected, at least by others at the reception. As a result of his introductions, Linda and Javier soon found themselves at the center of their own small group consisting mainly of other foreign correspondents representing small publications from across Western Europe.

As the evening wore on, Linda began to appreciate the hours Buzz Edwards had made her spend reviewing the details of her cover identity. As working professionals, the others were interested in obscure details such as where she went to school, other publications she had worked for and what stories she was currently working on. Fortunately, Edwards' analysts had worked that all out and developed a completely believable back story for the woman now known as Linda Hollister of Topeka, Kansas.

Later, in the privacy of their now-joined rooms, Linda and Javier reminisced over the events of the evening.

"The hardest part was when people addressed me as *Señorita* Hollister," said Linda. "I really had to pay attention and make myself respond to that name."

"Yeah, I had the same problem," laughed Javier, "but I want to know what Olvera meant by my 'unique style' and my 'impressive portrayal of nature's beauty.' I've never seen any of the photographs I'm supposed to have taken, of course, but they must be really good."

"Well, I wouldn't worry too much about it, because I doubt if he's ever seen any of them, either. That smooth-talker always knows exactly what to say—like any good politician. Tomorrow's going to be another day of this, though, so we both need to be careful about our cover stories and not get tripped up. That woman from Romania was driving me crazy tonight with her constant questions!"

"Yes, I know, and I'd be careful about that one," cautioned Javier. "Remember what I said earlier—always assume everybody's working for the other side."

"I'll remember. But, hey, the big news has to be the invitation to Pinar del Rio on Friday. How lucky was that?"

"Extremely lucky," replied Javier. "It was almost too good to be true, if you know what I mean, but I quizzed Ernesto pretty thoroughly and I think he's the genuine article. When we agreed to visit his province he got so excited I thought he was going to wet his pants!"

Linda rummaged through her briefcase and produced a map of Cuba that Edwards had provided. Unfolding it on the coffee table, she studied it for several minutes.

"Look at this," she finally said. "The province of Pinar del Rio covers the whole western end of Cuba and the city of the same name is right here. It has to be at least another one hundred fifty miles out to the tip of the peninsula, and these roads don't look very inviting."

"We'll have to figure that out when we get to the city," replied Javier, "but in less than seven hours we've managed to secure a legitimate reason for being in the area and I'd say that's pretty good work. After we reach the *playa*—sorry, I mean the beach—maybe we can ditch Ernesto and do a little sight-seeing of our own. He gave me the name of a hotel and I'll call them first thing in the morning to see if we can rent a jeep or a small four-wheel drive pickup somewhere in town. But I've had enough Cuba for tonight. I'm ready to hit the hay."

"Yeah, me too," agreed Linda as she folded up the map and put it away. "I'll see you in the morning, *Señor* Martinez."

"Hey, where are you going?" protested Javier as she walked towards the door connecting their rooms.

"*No hablo Inglés, Señor*," she replied without looking back.

When she reached the door, she turned to face the pouting Javier.

"I wonder what the real Linda would do?" she smiled.

And with three giant, running leaps, she landed face down on his bed.

Chapter 14

The NWIDI team members took turns watching Ian's five minutes of underwater video in the small viewfinder of the camera. It clearly showed the large triangular feature protruding from the sandy bottom and covered with symbols that resembled those on the "coins" back in Miles Adderly's safe.

"That's pretty amazing, alright," admitted Frank as he handed the camera back to Ian. "I thought that wall looked suspicious the minute I saw it, and this certainly confirms it."

"The wall?" exclaimed Ian. "What about that triangular thing? When I first saw it I thought it was the foundation of a building, but the top is too regular and it has those symbols on it. What the heck do you think it is?"

"Maybe it's just an architectural structure that fell off a passing cargo ship," shrugged Frank.

"Yeah, right!" laughed Ian. "As soon as we get back to the shop I'm going to check this out on the Internet."

Once Ian had the dive boat headed back towards the marina at Port Royal, Tony motioned for Frank to join him at the back of the main deck.

"The minute this boat touches the dock news of that video is going to be all over Bimini, Frank."

I know, and I don't like it, either! I need a few minutes to think of something, but in the mean time go talk to Jim and Jill and make sure they don't mention anything about *our* triangles. In fact, ask Jim to come back here, would you? I need to ask him something."

A few seconds later Jim joined Frank and shared the same concern that Tony had.

"What are we going to do, Frank? Ian's video clearly shows a man-made structure of some kind. By this time tomorrow there will be a thousand archaeologists on this island!"

"I'm working on that," nodded Frank. "In the mean time, answer this question for me. He said the bottom was three-hundred sixty-five feet down. How long ago would that have been dry land?"

"I don't know for sure, but I'd have to guess about 15,000 years ago, give or take a couple of hundred years. I can give you a better number when we get back to Andros. You're thinking that wall is the side of a structure, aren't you?"

"You saw it in the video, what do you think?" asked Frank.

"Well, I have to agree that it looks too perfect to be a natural feature," nodded Jim. "And then there's the triangular feature with the symbols on it—that's clearly not the work of nature."

"If I remember my maps correctly, the water is shallow to the east of Bimini, but drops off pretty fast on the west. Given that our dive site is on the extreme southwest part of the island, couldn't it have been in a small harbor on the coast of the much larger island that once existed here?"

"It's possible," conceded Jim, "but that's just a guess. There's no hard evidence of any ancient cultures around here that I'm aware of."

"I think Ian's video is pretty good proof," argued Frank. "Somehow we're going to have to…"

"Oh, no!" yelled Tony from the other end of the main deck.

"What's the matter, mate?" asked Ian, leaning over the rail of the flying bridge to look down at Tony.

"Oh, man, I'm really sorry, Ian! I don't know what I did, but I think I just erased your video tape. I just wanted to look at it one more time and I must have hit the record button by mistake!"

Yanking back on the throttle controls, Ian brought the engines to idle and flew down the ladder to the main deck.

"You couldn't have!" he cried. "Here, let me see that."

Taking the camera from Tony, he manipulated the controls for several minutes before he plopped down on a nearby bench and hung his head.

"I'm really sorry, man," repeated Tony.

Slowly, Ian lifted his head and glared at Tony briefly and then attempted a weak smile. "Well, I guess I can always shoot more video."

A few minutes later they were underway again, and Frank climbed to the bridge to apologize for Tony's actions and to plant a seed in the young dive master's mind.

"You know, Ian, I wouldn't be too quick to tell anyone about your discovery. If word gets out, someone else might stake a claim to the site and you'd lose any salvage rights. Maybe you should register the site with the government over in Nassau before you talk to anybody about this afternoon's discovery."

Ian was silent for several seconds before replying.

"That's excellent advice, Frank, but what about you? I only made the find because we were diving at coordinates you provided. Technically, it's your site, not mine."

Frank shook his head.

"No, you made the dive and you discovered the triangle. I still think it might be cargo that fell overboard during a storm, but who knows? I'm just glad we were along on the day of your big discovery. My teammates and I are really interested in that opening in the wall, though. Are you still up for taking us to the three fresh-water sites that seem to line up with our mysterious dive site?"

"Of course! I'd forgotten all about that, but we can do it this afternoon, if you'd like. Instead of stopping at the dive shop, we'll take the boat on up to Alice Town and I'll borrow a jeep from a buddy of mine to get us to the sites on the eastern island. Tomorrow we'll leave for the airport early enough to hit the third site on the way. Do you have a GPS unit?"

"I do," nodded Frank. "And thanks for being such a great guide, Ian. I'm really sorry about Tony's blunder with the camera but, like you said, you can always shoot more video."

That night the four NWIDI team members had dinner at an ocean-front restaurant in Port Royal. A light breeze was blowing in off the ocean and the temperature was perfect.

"So how long do you think Ian will stay quiet about today's dive?" asked Tony after dessert.

"I think I have him pretty focused on protecting the secrecy of his triangle discovery for now, and he's agreed to leave the issue of the wall to us. 'Dusty old archaeology stuff,' I think he called it. I'd love to explore the bottom of that wall for myself because I still think we'd find the end of the cable we've followed all the way from Cuba down there somewhere. I sure wish I were trained on that rebreather equipment he used!"

"How hard can it be?" asked Tony. "You're an experienced diver and it shouldn't be any different than adjusting to a new mask or a different regulator, right?"

"Well, I don't know about that, but I'm going to look into it when we get back to Andros. There seemed to be a lot more settings to fiddle with than I'm used to, but Ian told me he could stay underwater for up to ten hours at normal dive depths. Can you imagine what that would do for a search-and-rescue operation?"

"Or an underwater archaeology operation," smiled Tony. "Most of the work here in the Bahamas is happening at sixty feet or less, and, if necessary, you could shorten your bottom-time and go really deep to recover artifacts or whatever."

"Exactly!" agreed Frank. "And I already have a site in mind that I want to explore."

Thursday morning Frank was awake early and eager to get back to Andros but he'd had to push their charter flight up to 3:00 p.m. to provide the full twenty-four hours of decompression time suggested by most dive organizations. For lack of anything better to do, he spent more than two hours at a table beside the pool organizing his notes on the current project. It was hard to believe he'd collected so much stuff in just eleven days! His hand-written notes covered everything from the mysterious sonar signals that seemed to have come from the sunken ruins to rough sketches of the symbols he'd seen in Ian's video the previous day. There were also notes on the shiny silver ball they'd spotted off the tip of Cuba, and nearly every word Jim had shared about the triangular objects in the metal box.

About 8:30 a.m. Jim arrived, carrying a large pot of coffee and four cups.

"Where are the others?" he asked as he poured coffee for himself and Frank.

"I haven't seen them this morning, but when I turned in last night they were still partying at the bar. They're probably sleeping off a hangover, or something."

"I'd bet on the 'or something,'" grinned Jim. "Hey, I did a preliminary plot of the two fresh water sites we visited yesterday and, so far, your theory is holding up. Those two sites and the dive sight are in perfect alignment."

"I thought so!" shouted Frank. That reminds me, I need to let the dive shop know about our delayed departure time."

Frank pulled the satellite phone out of his backpack, called the shop and asked for Ian.

"Sorry," said the voice that answered, "but Ian isn't here. He said to give you his apologies but that he had something very important to take care of and that you'd understand.

"Right," replied Frank. "He's probably off to Nassau to take care of some business we discussed yesterday."

"I hope not," laughed the voice on the other end of the line, "because he left about an hour ago in our small dive boat. We'll have another bloke collect you and your mates for the trip over to the airport whenever you're ready to go."

"Did he go alone?" pressed Frank.

"No, his bird—sorry, his girlfriend—was with him. Why?"

"Listen, I need to get back over to the site where he took us yesterday morning, and I need to get there quick. How soon can you have somebody here with three full air tanks?"

When Frank hung up the phone, he shoved his notes back into his backpack and turned to Jim.

"Go bang on Tony and Jill's door and tell Tony I need him in the lobby in five minutes with his dive bag. And don't take no for an answer!"

Tony, with Jill in tow, arrived just as the dive shop van was pulling up to the hotel's main entrance.

"What's up?" asked Tony, huffing and puffing from running with both his and Jill's dive gear.

"Ian's gone back to the dive site, probably to re-shoot the video you erased yesterday, and his girlfriend is the only support diver with him."

As the van slid to a stop on the bluff overlooking the dive site, Frank handed a pair of binoculars to the driver.

"Is that your boat?" he asked, pointing to the only boat in sight.

"That's it," acknowledged the driver, "and that's Sarah onboard. I don't see any sign of Ian, though."

Frank slid open the side door of the van and jumped out.

"Suit up and let's get out there," he barked to Tony and Jill. "The dumb kid's probably already on his way down!"

Frank, Tony and Jill swam on the surface the short distance from the shoreline to the dive boat. The girl on board had recognized the van and when the divers approached, she lowered the dive ladder to allow them aboard.

"How long's he been down?" asked Frank without even introducing himself.

"About thirty minutes, and I'm starting to get worried because he said he'd only be gone fifteen. Who are you, by the way?"

Frank apologized and introduced himself and the others. He explained that they had all visited this site with Ian the day before but he didn't go into details about what they had discovered.

"Did Ian tell you anything about the dives yesterday?" asked Frank.

"Only that I wouldn't believe it until I saw it with my own eyes. I tried to pry more information out of him, but he just kept telling me to wait for the video."

"Is there another rebreather onboard?" asked Frank

"No, Ian's is the only one on the island, as far as I know," replied Sarah. "They take a lot of special training to use and nobody on Bimini is certified to train new users. Ian learned back in…"

"Frank, out there!" interrupted Tony. "Something just came to the surface!"

Before Frank could turn and focus on the spot, Tony was over the side and swimming away from the boat. When he turned back towards the boat, Frank could see that he had something yellow in his hand.

As Tony reached the dive ladder, he handed Frank a bright yellow dive slate—a five inch by eight inch writing device that divers often use to communicate with each other while under water.

Shielding his eyes from the morning sun, Frank read the message scribbled on the tablet—*"Sarah: There's something I must do. I'll come back if I can. Love, Ian."*

***

The day-long environmental conference was just about the most boring thing Linda had ever sat through and, to make matters worse, most of the presentations were in Spanish. Javier seemed interested enough, probably because of his work with Centro Ecológico Cancun, but even he couldn't stifle a few yawns by late morning. Lunch was a typical conference event with the attendees seated at large round tables pretending to show an interest in the work of their colleagues. Linda looked for the young man they had met at the reception the night before, but he was nowhere to be found. When Señor Olvera noticed her scanning the dining room, he immediately rushed to her side.

"May I help you find something—or someone, *Señorita*?" he offered in his too-smooth style.

"Oh, no, I was just looking for that nice young man from Pinar del Rio," replied Linda. "We're going down there tomorrow to see the work they've done with their beaches and I was hoping to chat with him some more."

"I'm afraid his delegation left early this morning, *Señorita*. However, I heard about your travel plans and I'd be happy to arrange transportation for you and your companion."

Olvera leaned close to Linda and spoke softly near her ear. "Be very careful while you're in the countryside—especially in the western province. We're not entirely happy with the situation there."

Olvera reached into the pocket of his suit jacket and retrieved a business card. He scribbled something on the back and handed it to Linda.

"This is my private telephone number," he said, returning to a normal voice. "If you need anything while in Cuba, please don't hesitate to call on me any time, day or night."

With that, the politician excused himself and was off to dote on another guest.

Linda leaned over to hand the card to Javier and whispered softly, "You'd better hang onto this. And what do you think he meant by 'the situation?'"

Javier shook his head and put the card safely away in his wallet. He couldn't help noticing the envy in the eyes of the others around the table but he smiled and continued eating.

The afternoon sessions focused on projects from outside Cuba and were presented in various levels of broken English. While this made them a little easier for Linda to understand, it didn't make them any more interesting and by the time the conference finally concluded at 4:30 p.m., both Linda and Javier were exhausted.

"I need a nap," declared Linda as she marched for the exit. "I'm beginning to think that sending us to this conference was Edwards' idea of a cruel joke, rather than an elaborate cover."

When Javier didn't respond, Linda turned to find him off to one side talking to the Romanian woman who had given her the third degree the night before. He seemed far too interested in the conversation to suit Linda, but she stepped out of the flow of traffic and waited for him to catch up.

"What was that all about?"

"It seems that we've achieved celebrity status—or at least you have—and we've been invited to a party tonight. Some of the foreign attendees are going out for a night on the town before they head back tomorrow, and we've been invited to tag along. Sounds like fun, huh?"

"Fun?" glared Linda. "Fun for whom? And if I'm the celebrity, how come she invited you, and not me?"

"Calm down, Linda," laughed Javier. "The invitation is for both of us, not just me, and her husband will be joining us tonight. He's a Cuban national who now lives in Europe and I thought we might be able to pick up some information about Pinar del Rio before we head over there. But if you'd rather not go, then…"

"A Cuban, huh?" smiled Linda as her jealousy melted away. "Let's go get me a nap, you party animal."

Linda and Javier met the six others in the hotel lobby at 10:00 p.m., as agreed, and the bellman escorted them to the waiting 20-year-old Volkswagen Vanagon that served as the hotel shuttle bus. After the eight conference attendees squeezed into the back seats, a large, heavy-set man dressed in black climbed into the front passenger's seat and the van eased away from the curb to merge into the heavy downtown traffic.

"Who's the extra?" asked Linda to anyone who happened to be listening.

"Our body guard," replied a male voice from the seat behind her.

The group made stops at several discos and at each one they had at least one drink. Linda looked for an opportunity to question the Romanian woman's husband, but his wife kept him on a pretty short leash. Finally the van delivered them to an upscale restaurant where a large table had been prepared for them in a private room. Linda made sure to get the seat next to the Cuban expatriate. Javier sat to her right and the Romanian woman was to the Cuban's left. In a stroke of good fortune, there was an unused chair to the woman's left.

A couple of before dinner drinks and an elaborate five-course meal put the partiers in a very relaxed and cordial mood, giving Javier the opportunity he'd been waiting for. Excusing himself, he moved down to the Romanian's left and engaged her in conversation, leaving the Cuban to Linda.

Linda had switched to plain tonic water when they arrived at the restaurant, and she was sure she was the only sober person at the table.

"I understand you're originally from Cuba," said Linda when she saw the man's wife turn to face towards Javier and away from her husband.

"*Si!*" the man replied, smiling broadly. "And I understand that you're not!" He laughed a little too loudly at his own joke and his wife turned to shoot him a glare before returning her attention to Javier.

"It's a fascinating place," continued Linda. "Have you traveled much of the island?"

"*Si, Señorita*, I have been to every corner of Cuba. When I was a young man I was a road engineer. Is that how you say it?"

"We'd probably call it a highway engineer, but I get the idea. That must have been very interesting work. What's your favorite province?"

"That would be Villa Clara, where I was born," replied the Cuban. "I love the mountains, lakes and rivers there."

"Mountains?" asked a surprised Linda. "I didn't know there were any mountains on Cuba, *Señor*..."

"*González. Rubén González, Señorita*, and yes, there are mountains on Cuba. Many foreigners think of Cuba as just a tropical island, but she is an island of many terrains. The highest point on Cuba is 464 meters above sea level and it's not far from my birthplace of Santa Clara."

"Really? And what about the rest of the island, Rubén? Are there mountains elsewhere?"

"Oh, *si!* In western Cuba, the Cordilla de Guaniguanico Mountains divide the province nearly in half and provide the proper climate and elevation for most of Cuba's tobacco crop—the finest in the world, I might add."

Now we're getting somewhere, thought Linda.

"That would be Pinar del Rio province, correct? My photographer and I are headed there tomorrow to visit a beach restoration project on the coast. Is the entire area mountainous?"

"No, the mountains end about eighty kilometers west of the provincial capitol and the extreme western end of the island is mostly flat, sandy plains. It also has many archaeological sites left by the original inhabitants of Cuba who fled to the peninsula in a failed attempt to escape the Spanish *Conquistadores*. Except for some small fishing villages, there isn't much on the peninsula and these days you can't even get out there."

"Oh?" Linda's interest was suddenly peaked. "Why is that?"

"It's become a rather lawless region and it's not safe to travel there. The federal government has even set up a check point outside the small town of Manual Lazo and only locals are allowed onto the peninsula itself."

"That's terrible!" exclaimed Linda. "Why don't the locals demand better protection from this criminal element?"

"Because the locals *are* the criminal element, *Señorita*. They're mostly Russian construction workers who were sent to Cuba with the missiles in the early 60s. Many of them were criminals in there own country and they were sent here as punishment. When the missiles were removed, the Russian government refused to take the workers back."

"I had no idea! Now I'm not so sure we should make the trip tomorrow," Linda lied. "I'm very interested in the beach project, but I don't want to put myself or my photographer in danger, either."

"As long as you don't travel west of the provincial capitol you will be fine," smiled the Cuban. "The tobacco industry is very important to Cuba and there are powerful men there who keep the *bandidos* under control. Just don't stray outside the city."

"Oh, we won't!" she lied again.

Chapter 15

Frank had the charter pilot circle the area immediately south of Bimini twice before beginning the 45-minute flight back to Andros. Four sets of eyes scanned the water below for any sign of activity, but Nicolas Harbor was deserted.

"It seems odd that they aren't at least searching for his body," said Tony as the plane started its climb up to cruising altitude.

"Well, the dive shop owner has convinced the local police that Ian had some kind of gas mixture problem and succumbed to nitrogen narcosis," replied Frank. "He attributes Ian's note to Sarah—the one we found on the diver's slate—to the fact that Ian wasn't thinking straight. They still have no idea how deep the water is at the dive site, but it's not like they could actually go after him. Either his body will surface or it won't. All they can do is check each day."

"I suppose," conceded Tony. "The dive shop owner obviously isn't a fan of rebreather equipment. It sounded to me like he was a little jealous that Ian had a $5,000 set-up that the more senior divers couldn't afford."

"Yeah, I picked up on that, too," added Jill. "Won't they eventually figure out that the water is much deeper than the charts show?"

"Oh, it's just a matter of time before somebody thinks to turn on a depth finder and then the cat will be out of the bag, but it's hard to say whether they'll request the equipment necessary to explore the bottom," said Frank. "It won't bring Ian back and unless they suspect foul play there would be no reason to order an investigation—especially one that would have to involve outsiders."

"What about plain old curiosity?" Tony asked. "Once they know the bottom doesn't match Ian's chart, somebody's going to want to know why."

Frank reached down and retrieved his briefcase from under his seat. He opened it, took out a large, folded piece of paper and handed it to Tony.

"You mean this chart?"

"Frank!" exclaimed Jill. "Why did you take that?"

"Ian had a hard time finding any information about the dive area, remember? He told us that this was the newest data available and that it was done by the Navy just five years ago. Well I intend to find out why this obviously incorrect chart was created. I'm betting somebody at AUTEC is behind it and I'm also betting that Buzz can find out who that person is."

"Do you think AUTEC knows about the wall and the mysterious foundation or whatever it is?" Jim asked.

"I do!" replied Frank. "And I wouldn't be the least bit surprised if they also know about the silver ball, the buried cable we followed over from the ruins and our triangular coins."

"But Frank," objected Jim, "why would Buzz and whoever he works for hire us to come all the way down from Seattle to investigate this stuff if AUTEC already knows about it?"

"Well, I'm still working on that part, but let's remember that the DOE didn't—and probably still doesn't—know about the flying saucer that's in Ben Kingston's lab at Groom Lake."

"Flying saucer?" questioned Jill. "I suppose that's another thing that happened after I left town, huh?"

"As a matter of fact, it is," smiled Tony. "And it's highly classified, so we can't talk about it while you're around, dear."

"Jerks!" she replied pretending to be indignant. "But back to Jim's point—I only met Edwards once, but he seemed pretty well connected to me. It does seem odd that he wouldn't be in the loop on something as significant as a 300-foot high submerged wall."

"Maybe Miles Adderly will have some ideas," suggested Jim. "He seems to be in AUTEC's good graces."

"That's a thought," nodded Frank. "You know, he made an interesting comment the other night that's been bothering me ever since. Jim, do you remember what he said when I asked him if his wall safe came with the library?"

Jim thought for a moment and then said, "Yes! He said something about being asked to hold large sums of money for visitors to AUTEC, or something like that. I wondered about that, too."

"Well, we'll know soon enough, because he's picking us up at the airport as soon as we land," said Frank. "Tony, when we get back to the hotel will you look into rebreather training for me? If there's none available on Andros, find out where the closest facility is and see if you can book me in for some training. "

"What about me?" asked Tony.

"And me?" added Jill. "I'll pay for my own expenses, if you'd like, but I'd like to try it, too."

"Sure, I guess," conceded Frank. "Jim, are you sure you don't want to get into diving, too?"

"I've never been so sure of anything in my life!" replied Jim. "You three go have your fun—I'll stay on dry land and watch over the triangular artifacts."

"Artifacts? Is that the official name now?" Tony asked. "You're convinced they're not coins?"

"The second I realized that the symbols can change on their own, they stopped being coins in my mind. Just imagine if the engraving on our own coins could change. You'd never know if you were holding a dime or a dollar."

"Did you say the engraving changes on its own?" asked Jill. "Man, have I got some catching up to do! Can I see these things, or are they top secret, too?"

"No, right now these are the sole property of NWIDI, and I see no reason why you can't see them," replied Frank. "We'll retrieve them from Miles' safe as soon as we get back and Jim can bring you up to speed while Tony checks into rebreather training."

"And you?" asked Tony. "What kind of trouble are you going to be getting into?"

"I'm going to discuss a possible field trip with our host, Miles," smiled Frank.

The charter plane touched down on Andros at 4:45 p.m. and the NWIDI team was back at the Bay Club Resort and Marina before 5:00 p.m. Since there hadn't been any other passengers in the van, Frank had already arranged to spend a few minutes with Miles after turning the artifacts over to Jim. Over a cold beer, Frank told Miles about the disappearance of their dive master, Ian.

"That's too bad," commented Miles. "Rebreathers are complicated pieces of equipment. They rarely fail, but when they do, there's usually not much a diver can do to save himself because the environment is so unforgiving."

"You sound like you know this equipment," said a surprised Frank. "Have you used one yourself?"

"Oh, yes, in fact I was an instructor in the Navy. SEALs are trained on almost every conceivable type of diving gear, but these days fully-closed rebreathers are used even on routine missions."

"In case an unforeseen situation comes up?" asked Frank.

"Well, yes, that too, but mostly because there's no tell-tale bubbles to tip off the bad guys. Of course the units used by the Navy aren't generally available to the public, but I might know where a couple could be found if someone were really interested."

"Could you teach me?" pleaded Frank.

"Probably," smiled Miles. "I've heard you Air Force guys are pretty slow, but I'm a really good trainer and I think I'm up for the challenge! Unfortunately, my back problems keep me from doing much high-tech diving because I'd be a real liability in an emergency. Rebreather diving isn't something you want to do alone, so you'll have to find another dive buddy if you decide to do anything very adventurous."

"Not a problem!" exclaimed Frank. "In fact, I can guarantee you a class of three as soon as you're willing to start."

"This should be fun! I haven't had a class of rookies in years," laughed Miles. "I'll meet you all on the dock tomorrow morning at 8:00 a.m. sharp! Any stragglers get push-ups as punishment!"

After finding no one at home in Jim's room, he knocked on Tony and Linda's door. From inside he heard a voice call "It's open!" so he turned the knob and let himself in.

Tony was just hanging up the telephone and Jill was huddled over the small desk with Jim. They were obviously examining the triangular artifacts.

"Bad news, Frank. There's no rebreather training on the island and it looks like the closest places are either Freeport or Nassau. Both involve long boat trips or flights, so we'd have to move there for several days."

"I have it handled," replied Frank. "It turns out that our resident SEAL can not only teach us, but he can also supply the equipment! Our first lesson starts bright and early tomorrow morning."

Hearing Frank's voice, Jill turned and said, "These things are incredible, Frank! They're even more amazing than the black spheres we found in Las Vegas."

Jill was referring to baseball-sized metallic spheres that had been the focus of the team's first investigation that began in Las Vegas and took Frank and Jim into secret Maya caverns in Mexico's Yucatan.

"Yeah, I know," replied Frank as he joined Jim and Jill at the desk. "Have you seen these critters change their stripes yet?"

"Yes! Jim was just showing me that. These things are really cool!"

"They also made most of us really sick the first time we touched them, so I want you to let one of us know if you start feeling funny," cautioned Frank. "We think the illnesses might have been due to something in the box when we first opened it, but you should be alert, just in case."

"I will. What can these things possibly be?"

All three men started to speak at once, but Frank and Tony deferred to Jim, the team's resident expert in all things weird.

"At first, we all thought they were coins like we said on the plane earlier today. Then, for a while I thought they might be some form of bizarre 'sticky note' device with a repeating message. But I'm not sure about that theory, either, because I haven't been able to document a repetitive pattern on any of them."

"So what's your current theory, Professor?" asked Tony.

"Right now I'm stumped," Jim replied.

"What about that triangular wall or feature we saw in Ian's video?" asked Jill. "Do you think those symbols also change?"

"Wow, that's an interesting thought!" laughed Jim. "But I don't think so, because even these don't change unless they're placed back in their box and the lid is tightly closed. I've tried peaking through a small crack but then they don't change."

"So whatever their purpose is, that box must be a part of the answer," concluded Frank. "Returning to the box reloads or rewrites them, so to speak. It gets them ready for another trip out."

Jim's face looked puzzled while he considered Frank's comments.

"That's an excellent observation," he muttered. "I'll look into that tomorrow while you three are out playing fish. But right now, I'm starving. Is anybody up for dinner?"

Part way through their meal at the hotel's restaurant, their host Miles Adderly stopped by to confirm their plans for the following morning.

"It's all arranged," he smiled. "My buddy over at AUTEC just received some new units that are state-of-the-art technology. This should be fun!"

"We're looking forward to it, too," replied Frank. "Hey, speaking of AUTEC, I have something I'd like to ask you. Can we step outside for a minute?"

Once outside, Frank explained the discrepancy between the Navy's bathymetric chart of South Bimini and what the NWIDI team had actually experienced.

"Gee, Frank, I find it hard to believe that they would intentionally dummy up naval charts. I'm not familiar with that area, but the difference between seventy-five feet and three hundred feet is quite a discrepancy. Are you sure the boat's depth finder was working correctly?"

Although he had omitted the details of their first dive when he had told Miles about Ian, Frank decided to lay all his cards on the table and hope the former SEAL wasn't an AUTEC insider.

"Are you kidding me!" shouted Miles out loud after Frank described the wall and the triangular "foundation" with symbols around its perimeter. "No wonder you want to get checked out on rebreather equipment! This is huge, Frank!"

"I know, and I really want to see this place first-hand. Listen, I'm trusting you to keep this under your hat, okay? We don't need every diver on the planet over there disturbing the site until we have some more facts. Don't even hint at the site to anyone else because one word to the wrong person and our cover will be blown. Somebody—and I'm betting it's somebody at AUTEC—knows about that wall and the feature at its base. I need some time to pursue other sources, so we need to keep a tight lid on this."

"You have my word as a SEAL," promised Miles. "But I think you're wrong about AUTEC. I've never heard any of the folks over there mention anything like this."

When the two men returned to the table, Tony shot Frank a questioning look and Frank signaled, "No" with a slight head shake. After Miles was out of sight, Tony pressed for details.

"Well?"

"I don't think he knows anything," frowned Frank. "I decided to tell him about the wall and foundation to test his reaction, and I think it was a complete surprise to him. Either that or he's a great poker player."

"Did you mention the silver ball or the cable leading back to the Cuban ruins?" asked Tony.

"No, there was no need. I figure the Bimini site is going to get rediscovered sooner or later anyway, but the ruins need to stay our little secret for as long as possible."

"Silver ball?" demanded Jill. Is this another thing I missed out on?"

"Ah, yes, I guess it is," laughed Frank. "I have a digital clip of it on my laptop if you want to see it later. Didn't Tony tell you about any of this?"

"I told her about the ruins, but I guess I forgot about the ball thing. Any ideas on that, Professor?"

"No, not yet," replied Jim. "I'm pretty sure it's some form of USO, but that's about all I have so far. As usual, you guys are able to come up with new mysteries much faster than I can research them!"

"Did you say U-*S*-O?" asked Jill. "What the heck is a USO?"

"An unidentified submerged object," replied Jim. "It's similar to a UFO except that it also travels underwater."

"Well, of course! Silly Me! Come on, Jim, is that something you just made up?"

"Not at all, Jill. There have been many reported sightings and some may date back to ancient Egypt. In fact, the area around Laguna Cartegena, in Puerto Rico, has been a real hotbed of alleged USO activity. Another active spot is off the coast of southern California"

"Well, I'd definitely like to see that video, Frank. I can't believe I took a short vacation to the Virgin Islands and missed both a UFO *and* a USO! You guys have way too much fun!"

"I wouldn't get too excited about Jim's USO just yet. It was a real anomaly over in western Cuba but now that we've tracked it back to AUTEC's neighborhood, it might have a perfectly logical explanation. This is, after all, the center of underwater research for the U.S. Navy. Who knows what they have swimming around out there?"

"Good point," agreed Jim, "but, again, I have to ask why Buzz Edwards would hire us to investigate the ruins if AUTEC already has a submersible traveling back and forth between there and here. That doesn't make sense to me."

"Or to me," agreed Frank, "but a lot of things about this area don't make sense. I assume you all know that we're technically inside the boundaries of the infamous Bermuda Triangle. And we're on the very edge of the Tongue of the Ocean, an underwater anomaly in its own right. Given all the reported aircraft and vessel disappearances in this area, doesn't it seem like a strange place to build the Navy's most top secret testing facility? Unless..."

"Oh, come on, Frank!" interrupted Tony. "You're not suggesting that the Navy had anything to do with all those disappearances, are you?"

"I'm just saying that it seems like an odd place to build a facility, that's all. You'd either have to be pretty confident that the Triangle's reputation is false or know for certain why it's true."

"Arrrg! You've gone off the deep end for sure, this time," laughed Tony. "Maybe your air tank was filled with laughing gas yesterday!"

Everyone except Frank laughed out loud at Tony's comment and when they stopped they realized Jill was choking. Tony turned in his chair and slapped her on the back several times, but that didn't seem to help.

"Call an ambulance!" yelled Frank as he raced around the table to help. As Tony's look of concern turned to one of real fear, Frank added, "Ill bet it's those damn triangles, again!"

Chapter 16

Friday began early for Linda and Javier, even though they had been out late the night before with other conference goers. When they had returned to their room after partying, a message had been waiting on their telephone from *Señor Olvera* instructing them to be in the hotel's lobby at 8:00 a.m. to meet their car.

"Any idea who—or what—we're looking for?" asked Javier as they stepped off the elevator and into the lobby.

"Not a clue," shrugged Linda. "Let's hope whoever's picking us up knows what we look like."

As they maneuvered their rolling suitcases through the throng of people in the elegant, high-ceilinged room, Linda spotted Olvera in the distance.

"There's the big shot himself," she commented. "Maybe he can tell us where our ride is."

"He's waving at us," said Javier when he finally picked the politician out of the crowd. "I think he's sweet on you, Linda."

Linda slapped him on the arm. "Knock it off! That's the most disgusting thing I've ever heard. But you're right—he's certainly trying to get our attention."

As they got closer, Olvera motioned for them to hurry and Linda started to get suspicious.

"Oh, no," she said under her breath.

"Right this way, please," called Olvera when they were close enough to hear him. "My car is blocking traffic and even government vehicles are subject to tow-away zones in Havana!"

Olvera guided them out through a side door of the lobby to a waiting Mercedes limousine. As the driver took charge of the two suitcases, Linda's laptop and Javier's camera case, Olvera motioned them into the open door of the long car then climbed in behind them. The rear salon of the limo had opposing seats and Olvera sat opposite them, with his back to the driver. For the first time, Linda noticed that the windows of the salon compartment were so heavily tinted that you couldn't see in or out.

When the door slammed shut, blocking out the noise of the busy street, Linda asked the obvious.

"Is this the transportation you offered yesterday, *Señor Olvera?*"

"*Si, Señorita.* Is it not satisfactory?"

"Of course it is, *Señor*, but this is not necessary. I'm sure you're a busy man and Javier and I would be happy to travel by bus and see some of the countryside."

The last thing Linda wanted was to be accompanied by a federal official on this leg of the trip. The plan had been to slip in under the radar, find out what they could and scoot back to Cancun before anyone caught on to their presence. Traveling around in a government limo wasn't exactly helping them keep a low profile.

As the limo merged into traffic, the Cuban loosened his tie and unbuttoned his collar in an uncharacteristically casual manner. The doors locked automatically and Linda began to feel uneasy.

Smiling broadly, he said, "This limo isn't quite the noble gesture it might seem, my dear. I scheduled this trip to Pinar del Rio months ago, long before I knew you would be visiting, and I just couldn't resist the opportunity to appear chivalrous in front of my other guests. But now I think it's time we discussed why you're really in Cuba, don't you agree?"

"What's going on here?" demanded Javier as he started to come out of his seat.

"Just relax, my friend," warned the Cuban. "Please don't make me restrain you—it's a long, hot ride in the trunk."

"I'm a U.S. citizen," shouted Linda. "You have no right to do this! I demand to be taken to…" Linda's voice trailed off as she realized her situation.

"Were you going to say 'embassy' my dear? Perhaps you've forgotten that there is no American embassy here. You are, as they say, up a creek without a paddle."

"What do you want with us?" demanded Linda. "We were invited to attend a conference on environmental issues and we've done nothing wrong."

"And no one is suggesting that you have, so please relax and try to enjoy the trip to Pinar del Rio. In the mean time, let's all get to know each other a little better, shall we?"

Linda nodded slightly and eased back into the plush leather seat of the limo.

"Sorry," she tried to cover, "but I've been a little nervous ever since we landed in Cuba—I guess that's something that's drilled into us back in the States. The truth is, this has been a very enjoyable trip—at least so far."

"I'm very glad to hear that," smiled the politician. "I think you'll find Cuba to be a very friendly place. Most of Cuba, that is."

"Are you referring to our current destination?" smiled Linda thinly.

"I am," replied Olvera. "As I mentioned at lunch yesterday, the situation there is less than ideal. That's why we're curious about your interest in the area."

"We have no particular interest in the area," Linda lied. "The young man at the reception seemed desperate for someone to talk to, so we stopped to chat. As it turned out, I do have an interest in beach conservation, so we hit it off immediately. When he invited us to visit their project, I was delighted, but we could just as well have ended up at the opposite end of the island."

"Well, if that's true, then your last-minute decision to attend our conference is indeed a stroke of good fortune, because the Cuban government would like to ask a favor of you."

"A favor?" laughed Linda out loud. "I thought the Cuban government was about to kidnap us!"

"I reserve that right as well, *Señorita*, but for now I'd like to ask you and your companion to conduct a small fact-finding mission for us. The two of you have been invited to the province as guests. As foreigners, and especially as an American, you may have access to information that we don't."

Reaching into his inside jacket pocket, the Cuban produced a folded piece of paper.

"I've prepared a list of questions we'd like to know the answers to, and all we ask is that you keep your ears and eyes open and learn what you can without arousing any suspicion. When you return to Havana, we'll meet again and you can pass along what ever information you've been able to gather. It's a simple request, no?"

"It sounds like spying to me," said Javier. "And it sounds dangerous. What's in it for us? What do we get in return?"

The Cuban glared at Javier for a moment and then smiled.

"You know, I've never cared much for Mexicans, *Señor*, and you're not helping change my opinion one single bit. But to answer your question, what's in it for you is a pair of diplomatic press passes that will allow you to travel anywhere in Cuba without interference. We're anxious to get the story out about Cuba's environmental efforts and we invite you to visit other parts of our country, if you wish."

Linda thought for a minute and then turned to Javier, who shrugged.

"OK, we'll find out what we can, but if—and only if—opportunities present themselves. We're not going to go snooping around where we don't belong," Linda lied again.

"Agreed!" smiled Olvera as he handed Linda the folded paper and two official looking ID cards. "I wouldn't flash those around in Pinar del Rio, but they'll open many doors elsewhere in Cuba. Oh, and there's just one more thing."

"Naturally," muttered Javier.

"We want copies of every photograph your assistant takes. If his camera is digital, we can do that when we meet in Havana. If he still uses film…"

"It's digital!" interrupted Javier. "And I'm sitting right here, you know. You don't have to talk about me as if I were somewhere else!"

"Such as in the trunk?" smiled Olvera. "Alright, my friend, apparently you understand the situation. You may keep and publish any photos you take, but we get a copy for our own internal use. Understood?"

Javier started to argue, but Linda intervened.

"We understand, *Señor*, and we agree to your conditions. But I'm curious—what are you looking for? What can you hope to find in a bunch of outdoor shots of a restored beach?"

"We don't know," frowned Olvera. "We just don't know."

The rest of the trip to Pinar del Rio was slightly more relaxed and the conversation focused on Cuba's efforts to survive in the shadow of its massive neighbor to the north. By the time they approached the outskirts of the provincial capitol, Linda had a whole different perspective on U.S./Cuba relations.

Suddenly the car slowed and the passengers could hear the sound of gravel under the tires of the limo. Linda shot an alarmed glance at Javier.

"We're stopping at a tobacco plantation on the edge of town where I've arranged to have a taxi meet us," explained Olvera. "If you were seen arriving in this vehicle, your information gathering usefulness would be greatly reduced. The driver's name is Carlos and he works for us. He will give you his telephone number and I urge you to call him anytime you wish to leave your hotel. If you don't, I can not guarantee your safety."

The car door opened suddenly and the bright sunlight temporarily blinded the occupants of the limo. A man in his mid-thirties helped Linda out and into the waiting cab while Javier exited the opposite side of the limo and made his way around the back of the limo to make sure their bags were properly transferred. Olvera lowered the salon's side window and waited until Linda and Javier were settled into the cab.

"Good luck and I look forward to chatting with you when you return to Havana," he called over to the cab.

"Thanks for the lift," waved Linda.

"Be safe, Ms. McBride," returned Olvera as the cab pulled away from the Limo.

On the way into the city Javier engaged the taxi driver in idle conversation in Spanish while Linda sat quietly, lost in thought.

A few minutes later, the cab pulled up in front of the Hotel Islazul, in the heart of Pinar Del Rio City.

"Welcome to our city," said the driver in perfect English.

Inside, Javier took care of the check-in and a bell boy followed them to the third floor with a luggage cart. Javier tipped the bell boy and closed the door. When he turned, Linda was sitting on the bed with her head in her hands.

Concerned for her health, he rushed to her side and asked, "Linda, do you feel okay?"

Slowly, she lifted her head and stared into Javier's eyes.

"He knows my real name, Javier! Olvera called me *Ms. McBride!*"

***

Back on Andros, Friday had begun with Frank, Tony and Jim pacing the floor of the emergency room waiting area where Jill had been taken earlier in the evening.

The choking that had started at the restaurant turned to full-body convulsions in the ambulance and by the time they reached the hospital Jill was unconscious. Following the ambulance in the hotel van, Frank had called the doctor recommended by the Atlantic Protector's medical officer and he had been waiting for them when they arrived at the emergency room. Jill was wheeled into the intensive care unit just after 8:30 p.m. and Frank, Tony and Jim were forced to remain outside in the waiting room.

At 12:30 a.m. a nurse came out to tell them that Jill was breathing on her own and seemed to be out of danger. The three men stopped pacing and relaxed for the first time since leaving the restaurant.

At 5:30 a.m. the doctor exited the intensive care unit and smiled at the three sleeping men slumped in the waiting room chairs.

The doctor cleared his throat and asked, "Are you the young lady's family?"

Startled awake, the three rubbed their eyes and tried to reconnect with reality.

"We're as close as it gets," mumbled Tony, getting to his feet. "How is she, doc? Can we see her?"

"Well, I think she's going to be just fine. Doc Jensen told me about your misfortunes aboard his ship and I suspect this was another case of the same thing. Other than keeping her comfortable—and breathing—there really wasn't much we could do. About midnight she started to improve dramatically and now I'm afraid that if one of you doesn't go in there and speak with her soon she's going to start dismantling the recovery room. Which one of you is Tony?"

Tony was smiling from ear-to-ear as he followed the doctor back into the ICU. Frank and Jim headed off to find some coffee and when they returned Tony was waiting for them.

"How is she?" asked Frank as he handed him a Styrofoam cup of coffee.

"She's tired, but otherwise she seems to be doing fine. They want to keep her here until this afternoon for observation, but all her vital signs are back to normal."

"Thank God," sighed Jim. "This is my fault, you know. I shouldn't have let her handle the triangles, but since I work with them almost every day I thought their effect on people had disappeared back on the ship. I'm really sorry, guys!"

"It's not your fault, Jim," Frank replied. "If anything, it's mine because I suggested that you show them to her in the first place. This is a lesson learned, though—no more 'uninitiated' are allowed to touch the triangles. From now on, we have to keep them confined to our own inner circle."

"I'm for throwing the damn things back in the ocean," said Tony. "We haven't learned anything useful from them and they've caused us a lot of grief. Jill's reaction was almost as bad as Javier's and, sooner or later, they're going to kill somebody."

"Not if we don't let anybody else handle them," argued Frank. "I understand your concern, Tony, but I believe the effect they have is a one-time event and we need to understand why they affect some—like Jill and Javier—so seriously while having practically no effect on others, such as Jim and me."

"Why?" challenged Tony. "Why do we need to know how they work? Why not just dump them into that six-thousand-foot deep hole east of here and be done with them?"

"Because," explained Frank, "I think they're the key to everything we've encountered since we left Seattle. I think they're connected to the sunken ruins off Cuba; I think they're connected to the silver ball we saw speed away from the ROV; and they're almost certainly connected with the dive site where Ian vanished two days ago. I believe those triangles are at least as important as the spheres we found in the Nevada desert or the tsubutes we found on Yonaguni."

Frank's revelation caught Tony off guard.

"Really?" he asked quietly. "But you believe that the spheres and the tsubutes are alien artifacts—do you think the triangles are, too?"

"I do," replied Frank.

"And I agree," added Jim. "There's no other explanation for the changing characters around their perimeters."

"But that would mean the book Miles found in his library is…" stammered Tony.

"It's also connected to the triangles. And the most amazing part of *that* puzzle is that it's a relatively modern connection. Based on its condition, I doubt if that book is more than a hundred years old and it may be much newer. That implies someone—or something—connected with the triangles was around here fairly recently. Do you still want to throw them into the ocean?"

Overwhelmed, Tony slumped into a chair.

"Well, no, not if they're really alien artifacts, but I don't want Jill anywhere near them. I've just gone through the worst night of my life, Frank, and I won't take that chance again. You have no idea how much she means to me and I don't know what I'd do if I lost her."

"Actually, Tony, I think I know exactly how you feel. When Donna died two and a half years ago, I had absolutely no reason to go on. And then, six months later, you showed up with that first sphere. I dashed off to Nevada and suddenly my life had purpose again. Come on, big guy, let's go find some breakfast and plan our next move."

As the three men left the hospital in search of food, Frank's thoughts returned to what he had just told Tony and the memories of his wife's death momentarily flooded in. Frank prided himself in being strong and analytical but every now and then these emotions broke through his façade. But by the time they found a small local restaurant that served bacon and eggs at 6:00 a.m., Frank had pushed those memories back into the mental vault where he kept them hidden away.

After breakfast, Tony insisted on returning to the hospital, so Frank and Jim dropped him off and then returned to the hotel in case Miles needed the van for an airport run.

"I'm beat!" sighed Frank as they climbed out of the van. "I'll let the front desk know the van is back and then I'm going to hit the hay. Shall we meet for lunch about noon?"

"Sounds good," yawned Jim. "I think the triangles are still in my closet. What should I do with them?"

"Hang on to them for now, but this afternoon we should find a more secure place to store them. Tony is right—we can't risk exposing anyone else to what Jill went through last night. Maybe we can put them back in Miles' safe for now."

"Okay, see you for lunch," yawned Jim again.

When Frank entered the office, the young woman at the front desk held up her index finger signaling Frank to wait and disappeared through a door. Seconds later she returned followed by Miles Adderly.

"How is she?" he asked without even saying "Hello."

"The doc says she's going to be fine," smiled Frank. "They're keeping her for the day, but she'll probably be back here in time for dinner tonight. And hopefully it will be a less exciting one than we had last night."

"Amen, brother! Do they know what was wrong with her? Did she have an allergic reaction to something she ate? I've been worried sick about her all night, Frank."

"Well, Tony ordered exactly the same meal so it certainly wasn't the food itself. It could have been an allergic reaction, but the doctors haven't said anything official yet. When she's feeling better I'll ask her if anything she ate yesterday was new to her and maybe we can track down the source. But right now I'm going to go get some sleep. It's been a long night, if you know what I mean."

"As a matter of fact, I do! I slept back there on a couch," said Miles, jerking his thumb towards the door behind him. "Shall we reschedule your first rebreather lesson for tomorrow morning?"

"Oh, crap!" exclaimed Frank. "In all the excitement, I'd forgotten all about that! Yeah, tomorrow should be okay, but I doubt if Jill will be up for it. I'll let you know for sure this afternoon after we pick her up. I might also need to borrow your safe again, if it's available."

"Any time, my friend," smiled Miles. "And I'm glad to hear Jill is okay."

When Frank reached his room, he hung out the Do Not Disturb sign and took a long, hot shower. Every muscle in his body ached from dozing in the waiting room chairs and he was dead tired. When he finally slid into bed, he was asleep before his head hit the pillow.

Seconds later he was startled awake by loud pounding on his hotel room door.

"Frank! Wake up! I've got to talk to you! Wake up!"

Frank forced his body out of bed and across the room. When he opened the door, Jim burst in waving his arms and yelling.

"They're gone, Frank! The triangles are gone!"

Chapter 17

"Are you sure?" questioned Javier. "I didn't hear him say *Ms. McBride*, but I wasn't exactly paying attention to him, either."

"I'm positive!" replied Linda almost in tears. "They've probably known who we are since we landed in Havana, Javier. What are we going to do?"

"Well, for starters, we're not going to panic. If they intended to detain us, they would have already done so. Except for our new driver, I doubt if anyone in this part of Cuba knows who we really are or why we're here. As far as the locals are concerned, you're a visiting freelance writer interested in the environment and I'm a Mexican photographer-for-hire. I suggest we try to get the information Frank wants and get the hell out of here as fast as possible."

Linda was up and pacing back and forth in the hotel room.

"That won't be as easy as you make it sound, now that we've agreed to be spies for the Cuban government!" she exclaimed. "At the very least, we'll be 'debriefed' when we return to Havana and I'm betting that's as far as we get. They could hold us on any number of charges, including entering the country with false identification."

"Ah, well, there *is* that," nodded Javier. "But it's not going to help to over-think this. If we can collect some of the information Olvera wants, maybe we can use that as our ticket out of here."

"I doubt it!" replied Linda. Digging into her computer bag, she produced a satellite phone similar to the one Frank carried. "Before we left Cancun Edwards gave me this but he told me not to use it unless we had a real emergency. I think this qualifies, don't you?"

Holding his index finger to his lips, he leaned close to Linda and whispered, "Not here! Let's wait until we're in the open in case this room is bugged."

With her suspicions fully restored, Linda's eyes darted around the room before she nodded in agreement and returned the phone to its hiding place. She motioned for Javier to follow her into the small bathroom, where she turned on the shower and the sink's two faucets.

Smiling, she whispered, "I saw that in a movie. We have to meet our young host from the conference in about an hour—any ideas?"

"Let me stash the phone in my camera bag, which I'll take with me. If we find an opportunity, we'll call Edwards and maybe Frank, too. Other than that, I think we should proceed as if we hadn't heard Olvera's comment. We're here to visit a conservation project, so let's do that so we don't arouse any suspicion among the locals. I think we just play it cool and be ourselves for now until we see who's doing what to whom. Are you up for lunch?"

Slightly taken aback by Javier's casual attitude about their current situation, she nodded and turned off the running water.

"Let's eat!" she announced, marching out of the bathroom.

When they were seated in the small, outdoor restaurant off the hotel's main lobby, Linda scanned the courtyard and was not surprised to see their newly assigned driver sitting at a table near the door. She smiled broadly and waved at the man, who acknowledged her with a barely discernable nod of his head.

"Guess who's here," she said while holding her napkin over her lips.

Javier, who had his back to the driver's table, replied sarcastically, "What a shock! Does it look like he's been here for a while or did he arrive just before us?"

Linda stole another look out of the corner of her eye and said, "There's an empty dish on his table, so it might just be a coincidence. Do you suppose he's staying here, too?"

"I doubt it. This place is too ritzy for a cab driver and staying here would blow his cover. That probably means that Olvera has another agent posing as a hotel employee, so be careful what you say."

"Didn't you make our reservations here?" asked Linda. "How would they be able to set that all up in less than twenty-four hours?"

"I did make the reservations, but the hotel was recommended by our conference friend, Ernesto."

"But he's on the other side," argued Linda. "Why would he recommend a hotel that was infiltrated by the government?"

"Remember what I told you the first night we were here? Always assume everybody's working for the other side!"

Javier indicated the approaching waiter with a flick of his head and the conspiracy talk ended for the time being.

After lunch, Linda and Javier made their way back into the lobby to await the arrival of their host, Ernesto. Both Linda and Javier made a mental note that the driver was nowhere to be seen.

They had no sooner seated themselves on a large leather couch at one end of the lobby when a smiling Ernesto appeared before them.

"*Buenas tardes, Señores!*" greeted the young man warmly. "*Me da mucho gusto verlos de nuevo!*"

As they stood to shake hands with the man, Linda remembered that he didn't speak any English.

"Great!" she mumbled. "What did he say?"

"He said that he's glad to see us again," said Javier. "I'll try to remember to translate everything but if we get to yapping away in Spanish, just jab me with an elbow."

"It will be a pleasure!" smiled Linda.

After several exchanges between Javier and Ernesto, Javier translated again.

"He's going to drive us to Playa Las Canas, the beach where the project took place, and when we return to the city he'll take us to his office. Apparently we've become something of celebrities and his boss is having a little afternoon party for us."

"What about our own driver?" Linda asked. "What about raising suspicions?"

"Well, I guess this is going to have to be the first exception to that rule," smiled Javier. "It would be even more suspicious if we insisted on taking a taxi when free transportation is being offered. Our friends in Havana will just have to be patient."

"Cool," said Linda to Ernesto. "I mean, *gracias, Señor.*"

Once they were in the car and headed out of town, Linda unzipped her day planner and flipped to a section of blank note paper.

"I'd like to get some background information on Ernesto for my article," she said to Javier.

Javier translated the request and their host beamed with delight.

"*Si, Señorita!*" he replied.

Over the course of the next thirty minutes Linda learned that Ernesto Flores had been born and raised on a tobacco plantation in a small town outside Pinar del Rio city. His father had been the general manager until his retirement a few years ago and his position and income had allowed Ernesto to attend the university in Havana. His childhood on the plantation had taught him a respect for nature and at school he had majored in agriculture and conservation. After graduation, his father had managed to pull some strings and get him a job at the local Bureau of Agriculture and from there Ernesto's own efforts had secured his current position with the provincial Ministry of Conservation.

Linda took notes furiously as Javier translated and she was surprised when Ernesto slowed the car to turn off the two-lane highway they'd been on since leaving the city.

"We're almost there," translated Javier. "The main road ends in a small fishing village and local vacation spot, but we're going about a mile down the beach to a community called La Coloma where a river flows into the sea."

La Coloma was barely a village, and the road from the highway had been unpaved most of the way. As they walked the short distance from the car to the beach, Linda was very glad she had opted to bring along her tennis shoes.

Ernesto delivered a lengthy discourse on the area in Spanish, which Javier abbreviated and translated.

"He brought us here because this is where the project ends and it's easier to see the 'before and after' effects of the work," said Javier.

As Linda scanned the area in front of them, there was a definite, visible boundary between the beach to the right, towards Playa Las Canas, and the beach to the left.

"To your left," translated Javier, "is Punta La Figa. It shows what is happening to many of the beach areas on the southern side of the island. The hurricane track that runs between Mexico and Cuba causes serious erosion and this side of the island is slowly disappearing into the Caribbean.

"To your right is about two miles of beach that is being protected by a man-made reef installed several hundred yards offshore."

Javier took a break from his translation work and gazed at the area himself.

"It really is amazing, isn't it?" he asked. "Ernesto said that they eventually hope to restore the entire area from here west to Cabo Francés. That's almost 75 kilometers of shoreline!"

"How much is that in English?" frowned Linda.

"Oh, sorry. About 45 miles, I think. Anyway, it's a pretty grand ambition, don't you agree?"

"Yes, but why stop there?" Linda asked, scratching in her notebook.

Javier shrugged and asked Ernesto.

"He says that's as far as they can go without permission from *Los Guanahacabibes*, who would never allow government workers to travel any further west."

"Really?" smiled Linda for the first time since leaving the car. "What can he tell us about these Guana…"

"*Guanahacabibes*," repeated Javier. "I'll ask, but let's not push it too much."

A minute later, Javier translated and Linda took notes.

"Ernesto explained that the entire Peninsula of Guanahacabibes is controlled by a group of '*Europeos*'—I think that's slang for Europeans—and that no one is allowed beyond the town of Manuel Lazo without permission."

"Well, that agrees with what Olvera told us except that he implied his side was in control of the check point. Tell him that I'd really like to see the western end of the Peninsula and ask him if he thinks they'd make an exception for an American journalist."

Javier asked and the young Cuban laughed out loud.

"I'll take that as a no," frowned Linda. "I'm curious about this artificial reef that Ernesto mentioned. Would you ask him what material they used for its construction?"

Ernesto's response was very animated and Linda could see that this was a topic of great interest to the Cuban.

"He says it's made from large blocks of stone arranged like an underwater wall. His team is especially proud of this construction because it's an environmentally friendly material that doesn't introduce any contamination into the sea. Apparently these blocks are readily available and can be found scattered all along the southwestern coastline. To create the wall they simply lift the blocks out of the sand with the hoist on a salvage ship, haul them over to the construction site and lower them into position."

"Really!" replied Linda. "Please tell Ernesto that I'm very impressed with the project and the ingenuity of the construction. Why don't you shoot a series of photos and then we can head back to the city?"

During the trip back Javier sat in the passenger's seat of Ernesto's small car while Linda sprawled across the back seat and reviewed her notes from the trip. Javier and Ernesto chatted away in Spanish but every now and then Linda would interrupt to get clarification about something she had written down or to fill in a missing fact. When she was satisfied with her notes, she reviewed the digital images on Javier's camera and wrote a short paragraph explaining the significance of each. Javier had taken a panoramic series of photos of the entire beach using both wide-angle and telephoto lenses. For his last few shots, Javier had turned his back to the sea and quickly snapped the desolate countryside. Something in the very last picture caught her eye and as she studied it more closely she let out a small gasp.

Handing the camera forward to Javier, she asked, "What's that on the far right of this picture?"

"Hmm," replied Javier. "If I didn't know better, I'd say it's a taxi cab."

***

Frank closed his hotel room door behind Jim and locked it.

"What do you mean, the triangles are gone? Are you sure you didn't stash them in another place?"

"Positive! I hid them behind an extra pillow on the shelf in my closet. That's what tipped me off. I opened the closet to get out my laptop and found the pillow on the floor. And the box of triangles was nowhere in sight!"

"Okay, calm down, Jim. There has to be a reasonable explanation for this. Here, sit down and take a deep breath."

Frank called the front desk and asked to speak with Miles. When he came on the line, Frank said, "Could you please come to my room right away? We have a bit of an emergency and I need to talk to you in private."

Less than a minute later, there was a knock at the door, and Frank opened for Miles.

"It appears that the box of triangles has been stolen from Jim's room. Can you tell me who might have had access to his room last night or this morning?"

Shocked, Miles joined Jim on the couch. He rubbed his forehead for a minute before speaking.

"It could have been any number of people, Frank. The housekeeping staff, certain maintenance folks, even me, for that matter. Are you sure..."

"We're sure!" said Frank curtly. "And I'm assuming we can take your name off the list, but we need to round up everybody else and get to the bottom of this as quickly as possible."

"I appreciate your concern, Frank, but most of those people have gone home and since today is Friday, some of them won't be back again until Monday morning. We could call the local police, but..."

"No, I don't want to involve them, at least not at this point," agreed Frank. "But there's something about those objects we haven't told you. Some individuals have a very serious reaction to contact with them. We think that's what caused Jill's close call last night and Javier nearly died aboard the ship we arrived on. We have to find that box immediately!"

"But they didn't have any effect on me," said Miles.

"That's because you didn't handle them," offered Jim. "There seems to be something that's absorbed through the skin and it doesn't affect everybody the same. I, for example, have felt no ill effects at all, but since our experiences on the ship I'm careful to wear latex gloves whenever I examine them.

"And in addition to the health risk, they have a significant scientific value. We need to get them back, Miles."

"Of course, of course," said Miles. "Let me get back to my office and see what I can do. In the mean time, I suggest you turn Jim's room upside down. We keep a pretty close eye on the day staff and it's possible that whoever took them simply moved them to another location until an opportunity comes along to retrieve them. We don't have this kind of problem very often, but we once found a lady's diamond bracelet hooked over the workings inside a toilet tank."

"Okay, we'll check, but we need to find them fast. You should alert your staff to the health hazard, but please don't mention anything about them being artifacts. The last thing we want to do is give the thief the impression that he—or she—has something valuable. We'd never see them again if that happened."

"I'm on it, my friend, and I'm really sorry about this."

With that, Miles disappeared out the door and Frank and Jim were close behind.

"This is terrible," moaned Jim as they rushed across the grassy area near the pool. "Whoever has them has no idea what they have."

"And no idea the danger they could be in," added Frank.

For the next thirty minutes Frank and Jim literally dismantled Jim's room. They tore apart the bed, removed the drawers from the dresser and night stand and completely emptied the closet. When the room didn't produce the triangles, they widened their search to the area around Jim's room, looking in garbage cans, flower beds and nearby shrubs. Frank was about to give up the search when he saw Miles running across the lawn waving his arms.

Frank ran to meet him, and shouted "Did you find them?"

"No, but Tony has been trying to call you on your cell phone. Apparently they just brought a very sick man into the emergency room and he called to see if you'd exposed anyone to the triangles. As it turns out, the patient's wife is a relatively new member of my housekeeping staff and was probably assigned to Jim's room today."

"The hospital!" shouted Frank. "I should have called him as soon as we discovered the theft! Let's get over there."

When they reached the waiting room, a woman was seated near the door sobbing. When she saw Miles, she let out a wail and began crying loudly.

"Let me handle this," he said.

Frank and Jim retreated to the other end of the room to minimize the intimidation factor while Miles took a seat next to the nearly hysterical woman and tried to calm her. Gradually, she settled down and stopped crying altogether.

After about ten minutes, Miles left the woman and rejoined Frank and Jim.

"Well, she admits to taking the 'silver box' but she claims she doesn't know where it is. She told me she gave it to her husband when he picked her up from work a couple of hours ago and she hasn't seen it since. About thirty minutes ago she went out to their garage and found him in convulsions on the floor. She called an ambulance, and the rest of the story you know."

"It's obviously in their garage," said Frank. "Let's go get it!"

"Hold on, there, Frank," cautioned Miles. "We can't just go raid private property, you know."

"But it's okay for her to steal from our hotel room, huh? Give me a break! You tell her that if she gives us permission to search her garage for our property, we won't press charges for the theft. Otherwise, I'm going to ask the local constable to arrest her for theft. And since the box and its contents could be worth millions, it will be a felony charge—or whatever they call that here in the Bahamas."

Miles frowned, but crossed the room, spoke with the woman and returned.

"Okay, I have the address. It's a small place on the other side of Fresh Creek. She said the garage door should still be open."

Minutes later, Miles pulled the hotel van into the short driveway and turned the engine off.

"Are you sure this is the right place?" asked Frank. "The garage door looks closed to me."

"This is the address she gave me," replied Miles, "but I can call the office and have someone check her personnel file."

"That might be a good idea," said Frank as he climbed out of the van.

While Miles made the call, Frank went around to the side of the garage, where he found a window. Shielding his eyes with his hand, he peered in through the window but it was impossible to make out details because the sun was directly behind him and it was reflecting off the dirty glass. Suddenly, he heard a crash inside, as if something had been knocked over, and saw a rectangle of light appear in the back of the garage.

"Miles! Around back! Somebody's making a run for it!"

Frank raced to the back of the garage just in time to see the outline of a figure disappearing into the underbrush. Just before Miles rounded the other side of the garage, Frank thought he heard a loud splash.

"Did you see anyone?" asked Miles.

"Yeah, sort of. What's down through there?"

"Fresh Creek, the same body of water that runs along side the hotel, why?"

"Because I think our intruder just went for a swim," replied Frank. "Did you get through to the office?"

"Yes, and this is the same address she put on her application," nodded Miles. He turned the knob on the rear entrance to the garage and the door opened. "Let's check it out."

Inside, the garage was dark and cluttered. Frank made his way to the other end and opened the big door.

"I'm afraid our fleeing visitor may have beaten us to it, but let's have a look around anyway."

A crude workbench along one wall of the garage was littered with greasy car parts and assorted tools, but there was no sign of the box or its triangles. Cardboard boxes full of assorted junk covered a large portion of the floor and a rusty wheel barrow was parked near the large door.

In one front corner of the garage, Frank spotted an unfinished particle-board storage unit with double doors on the front. As he swung them open, he smiled broadly.

"Bingo!" he shouted. "Over here, Miles."

The metal box that had been dug out of the sand off the coast of Cuba sat on the middle shelf among various cans of paint and small boxes.

Miles started to reach in to grab the box but Frank pulled him back sharply.

"Hold it!" he shouted. "Do you want to end up in the hospital, too? Hand me that plastic bag on the bench."

Frank picked up a metal rod that was lying nearby and used it to slide the box into the bag. As it landed in the bottom, Frank heard the tell-tale clank of triangles rattling around inside.

"It sounds like we recovered the whole package but I want Jim to check the contents to be sure," he said as he tied the bag shut. "Let's lock this place up and get back to the hotel."

As Miles maneuvered the van around the potholes in the gravel road that led away from the house, Frank kept his eyes focused in the direction of the river Miles had called Fresh Creek.

"How far is it to where this empties into the Atlantic?" he asked as they finally reached pavement.

"It's about a mile from the house to the inlet by the hotel, why?"

"I was just thinking about that figure I saw run from the garage," replied Frank. "It would take a human about thirty minutes to make that distance, right?"

"Uh, longer than that, I think. When I was a SEAL I could do 1,500 meters in just over twenty-five minutes, but I was in pretty good shape back then and a mile is more like 1,600 meters."

Frank glanced at his watch and smiled.

"So if you put your foot in it, we could probably make it back to the hotel before any normal person could make the swim, right?"

"Are you suggesting I'm not normal?" laughed Miles as the van picked up speed.

When the van pulled up to the entrance of the Bay Club, Frank grabbed the plastic bag containing the silver box and ran for the hotel's marina on the southern shore of Fresh Creek, just west of where it flowed into the Atlantic. Miles went through the lobby to drop off the van keys and exited the back door to meet Frank on the main dock.

Frank had crouched down at the end of the dock with the plastic bag between his feet and he was staring at the center of the channel.

"What are we looking for?" asked Miles.

"I don't know," replied Frank. "Anything out of the ordinary, I guess. I don't actually expect to see somebody swimming by here, but I never heard the sound of a motor, so maybe a sea kayak or something like that."

The two men stared across the three-hundred-foot-wide channel for several minutes without speaking.

Suddenly Miles pointed and shouted, "There! Straight out from here, dead center in the channel—see that ripple?"

It took Frank a few seconds to locate the disturbance Miles was indicating, and no sooner had his eyes locked on to it than it abruptly changed direction and headed straight for them, picking up speed as it moved.

Frank grabbed the plastic bag with one hand and Miles' arm with the other. As he glanced back over his shoulder, he yelled, "Run!"

Chapter 18

Nothing more was said about the mysterious taxi in Javier's photo, but Linda couldn't help glancing out the back window every few minutes to see if they were being followed. As Ernesto approached the city, he asked Javier a question, Javier answered and then translated for Linda.

"He asked if we wanted to stop by the hotel to drop off my camera gear and I said yes—is that okay with you?"

"Absolutely!" replied Linda. "I was hoping I'd be able to freshen up before we meet his co-workers. I'll be quick, I promise."

When they reached the hotel, Linda and Javier went to their adjoining rooms and changed into clean clothes. The heat and dust of La Coloma had left them both feeling gritty but Ernesto was waiting in the hotel's loading zone, so there wasn't time for a shower—a quick wash-up had to suffice.

When Javier knocked on the connecting door, Linda called for him to come in.

"Wow!" he said, as he opened the door and entered her room. "When did you get that?"

Linda twirled in her cocktail dress and said, "You like? I bought this in Seattle before we left for Cancun. You don't think it's too much, do you?"

"Quite the contrary," laughed Javier. "It brings a whole new meaning to the phrase 'little black dress.' Are you ready?"

"I guess so. After what Olvera told us, I'm a little nervous about attending a social gathering with a bunch of locals, but maybe we can use the opportunity to work on that list of questions he gave us, huh?"

"Yes. In fact, this may be our only opportunity," replied Javier. "We saw the project earlier and we'll meet the folks responsible for it in a few minutes—after that there really isn't much else to use as an excuse for staying here. At this point, I don't see any way to get the information Frank wants, do you?"

"No, not yet, but I haven't given up yet. Let's go—we've kept poor Ernesto waiting long enough. We can talk about this later."

"But not here," reminded Javier.

When they arrived at Ernesto's office, Linda and Javier were surprised to see that someone had taken the time to put up party decorations and balloons around the office. A large table in the center of the room was covered with an assortment of home-made foods, and several bottles of wine were chilling on the end of someone's desk.

"Wow!" said Linda as they entered the office to a round of polite applause. "Javier, please tell them that we're overwhelmed!"

"I think they can tell by the looks on our faces," laughed Javier, "but I'll tell them anyway."

He addressed the dozen or so people in the room and expressed thanks for such a warm welcome. A man in his sixties, dressed in a suit, rushed forward and shook hands with both Linda and Javier.

"We are honored to welcome you to the Ministry of Conservation, *Señorita Hollister* and *Señor Martinez*. My name is *Eduardo Torres Garza*. Please allow me to introduce my staff."

The minister introduced each person and gave his or her title, but Linda couldn't begin to remember them all. She did, however, pick up on Ernesto's title of Project Manager.

After everyone had filled a small paper plate with items from the table, Torres poured wine and toasted the guests in Spanish. Most of the staffers spoke little or no English, but the few who did gravitated towards Linda and engaged in polite conversation. Mostly, the discussions focused on conservation or journalism, but a girl in her early twenties caught Linda off guard.

"So, why did you really come here?" she asked.

A familiar voice behind Linda shushed the girl and ordered her away.

"Please forgive my daughter," the man continued. "She's at that age, if you know what I mean."

Linda turned to find Torres standing behind her frowning in the direction his daughter had fled.

"That's okay," smiled Linda. "I was that age once, too. Besides, from her perspective, it's probably a logical question."

"Well, I can tell you that having a visiting American journalist in my office has significantly elevated my social standing in the community," he smiled. "But I can't help wondering what brought you here myself. Pinar Del Rio is very remote, even for Cuba. Our own government rarely visits us, much less foreign correspondents."

"We came to see your beach restoration work, of course, and it's really a fascinating project. The change you've made to the beach is very dramatic and your project should become a model for coastal communities around the world. But, as for remote, I hear the western end of the peninsula is much more remote than Pinar Del Rio."

"What have you heard about that place, *Señorita*?" asked her host with a frown.

"Only that the residents don't like strangers, *Señor Torres*, and I get the feeling they consider themselves to be outside the control of the local government. Is the peninsula similar to our Native Indian reservations—a small pocket of federal land that isn't responsible to state and local laws?"

"That's an interesting comparison," Torres replied. And then, in a quieter voice, he added, "Except they don't respect our federal authorities, either. I've been monitoring the situation, unofficially, for years and I believe they must be connected to some group outside Cuba."

Suddenly very interested, Linda asked, "Why do you say that?"

"Because, the goods that pass through the check-point in Manuel Lazo couldn't possibly support the population out there. Additional supplies must be coming in by boat."

Pretending to be uninterested, Linda replied, "Couldn't the government just send someone down to see?"

"I'm afraid not! The only way for an outsider to get down there is in a box. And by box, I mean a coffin."

"Well, it's a good thing I'm not headed that way" Linda lied. Changing the subject, she added, "I'd like to know more about those stone blocks you used to construct the breakwater. What can you tell me?"

Linda and Torres talked for quite a while, but they were eventually interrupted by an employee who whispered something in Torres' ear.

"Ah, please excuse me, *Señorita* Hollister, but it's nearly 5:00 p.m. and my staff normally leaves before now. However, no one wants to be rude and leave without saying good-bye."

"How nice!" Linda replied. "May I say something in English and ask you to translate for me?"

"Of course!"

Linda turned to face the main portion of the group and said, "Thank you very much for your hospitality and kindness. As I told

Señor Torres, I think your project should become a model for coastal communities around the world and I promise to do what I can to make sure people hear about your success here. *Señor Martinez* and I would also like to thank you all for being so kind and for this celebration in our honor."

Torres translated and the beaming staffers applauded, this time more vigorously. Torres said something more and apparently excused the staff, because the room was nearly empty a minute later.

"They're a loyal group," he smiled, "but it *is* Friday afternoon."

"And we should be leaving, too, *Señor*. Thank you very much for this opportunity and, as I said, I will try to spread the word. You may find yourself hosting foreign journalists on a regular basis!"

"That would be my great pleasure," smiled Torres. "May I offer you a ride back to your hotel?"

"Thank you, but I'm sure you have things to take care of here. We met a very nice cab driver this morning who offered to be our personal chauffeur but, so far, we haven't accepted his offer. If I can use a phone, I'm sure he'll be here shortly."

Linda joined Javier, who was talking with Ernesto and a woman about the same age.

"Are you ready?" he asked.

"I am. I just called our driver and he'll be here in a couple of minutes. Apparently he was in the neighborhood."

"How convenient," said Javier sarcastically.

On the way down to the street, Linda and Javier exchanged notes from the event.

"I was able to get some information that I think will be of interest to our friend in Havana," offered Javier. "How did you do?"

"I also collected a tid-bit or two, and I think I know how we're going to get ourselves to Las Tumbas," she replied.

"I can't wait to here *that* plan," frowned Javier as the taxi pulled up in front of the Ministry building.

Back in their hotel rooms they changed into casual clothes and Linda asked Javier to help her download the photos of their coastal trip to her laptop so she could study them. Sitting cross-legged on the bed, Linda browsed through the images.

"Javier, you missed one. You didn't give me that last photo—the one that shows that interesting car." Her vague reference to the taxi was intentional because they were still operating under the assumption that their room was bugged.

Javier cycled through the pictures on the small screen of the camera twice and then signaled for Linda to join him in the bathroom.

After turning on the water in the shower and the sink, Javier whispered, "It's gone! Somebody deleted it while we were out!"

"I knew it!" whispered Linda. "I'll bet this is Olvera's handy-work!"

"No doubt. He did tell us not to leave the hotel without his driver so I'm not surprised that we were followed to the coast and then to the party, but if the driver was with us, that means someone else was in our rooms. And now I think we have to assume we're being monitored all the time."

"And that's how they knew my real identity!" hissed Linda. "I'll bet they accessed my laptop back in Havana!"

"But you had it with you the whole time except..."

"Except the last night, when we were invited out by your lady friend from Europe!" exclaimed Linda. "That whole 'evening on the town' was probably a setup!"

"We really need to call Edwards and let him know what's going on over here. We could turn up missing and they wouldn't even know where to start looking—or who to suspect! We need to get away from the hotel to a location they wouldn't have expected and therefore wouldn't have already bugged."

Linda thought for a minute before replying.

"Well, like you said, we haven't exactly followed instructions regarding our driver, so how about if we dream up a day trip for tomorrow? Maybe something out into the countryside? Sooner or later he'll have to use a bathroom and one of us can make the call then."

"That might work," nodded Javier. "Let's go have some dinner and when we get back we need to thoroughly examine my camera case and your computer bag for bugs. We should also go over whatever clothes we're going to wear tomorrow, especially belts and shoes."

"Maybe we should just buy new stuff after we eat," smiled Linda. "I have an NWIDI expense account, you know."

Javier turned off the water and they opened the bathroom door. Neither one noticed the tiny red light above the screen that covered the exhaust fan.

***

Frank and Miles sprinted the short distance to the double doors leading into the lobby and, once inside, turned in unison to stare through the glass at the object approaching the place where they had just been standing. Just feet from the dock, the disturbance beneath the surface suddenly reversed direction and retreated as fast as it had approached. The instantaneous course change created a huge splash and Frank thought he saw the surface of something shiny through the spray.

"What the hell was that!" shouted Miles as he caught his breath.

"I think I have a pretty good idea," puffed Frank. "Did you see how fast it was going when it reversed direction?"

One of the hotel desk clerks came running over and asked, "Are you okay, Mr. Adderly? What's going on out there?"

"Yes, we're okay, Donald, thank you. We just had a bit of a scare from some of the local marine life. Everything's fine now."

As the young clerk headed back to the front desk, Miles signaled Frank to follow him into the library where he had first been introduced to the triangles.

After he closed the door, Miles pointed to the plastic bag Frank was still carrying.

"It was after those triangles, you know," he said.

"Yeah, I kind of figured that. That's why I had them on the dock between my feet—as bait. I guess it worked, huh? Can I use your phone?"

Frank dialed Tony's room, but there was no answer. When he tried Jim's room, Jim picked up.

"Jim! You got back from the hospital, obviously. Do you know where Tony is?"

"He and Jill are here in my room. Hold on."

"Frank, I have some bad news," said Tony when he came on the line. "The man they brought into the emergency room died about fifteen minutes ago. As soon as we heard, the three of us got out of there before the police started asking a lot of questions."

"Oh, no! I'm really sorry to hear that but it wouldn't have happened if his wife hadn't stolen the triangles from Jim's room. I think the three of you should come down to Miles' library—Jim knows where it is. And have him bring a pair of surgical gloves."

When Tony, Jim and Jill arrived, Frank handed Jim the plastic bag.

"Will you check this out and make sure we still have everything? We found them in the dead man's garage."

While Jim inventoried the box, Frank motioned for the others to be seated.

"And that's not all we found. When we got there someone—or something—fled out the back door and into the brush. A few seconds later, I heard a loud splash, as if the intruder had jumped into Fresh Creek. Miles and I raced back to the hotel and I used the bag as bait. Sure enough, a few minutes later a submerged object raced towards us and when we took off it reversed direction and headed back out into the channel and eventually out to sea."

"So you think that whatever you saw at the garage was looking for the triangles and then it came after them again down at the dock, huh?" asked Tony.

"I'm not sure. What I saw at the garage definitely walked upright and looked humanoid. What we saw charging the dock looked very much like something we saw at the Cuban ruins."

"The what?" asked Miles. "Did you say Cuban ruins? You mentioned Cuba the other night, but I had no idea you were talking about an archaeological site."

"Well, the other night we weren't being chased by something that walks upright and swims like a rocket," laughed Frank. "After today, I guess you're officially in the NWIDI club."

"And not a moment too soon," said Miles. "When the local police question my former employee and find out that her husband may have died as the result of contact with your triangles, they're most definitely going to want to impound them as evidence. I may be able to help you out there."

"I'm listening," replied Frank.

"As I may have mentioned, I have some contacts at AUTEC," continued Miles." If you want to keep your triangles out of the hands of the local police, the safest place for them is in the custody of the U.S. Navy. The locals will assume they're part of a classified project and when my former maid learns that she may have stolen U.S. Government property, she'll forget she ever saw them."

"Are you sure the police won't hassle us?" asked Frank.

"I'm quite sure, because I have some contacts there, too," smiled Miles. "It's what I do, Frank."

Frank turned to Jim, who was just finishing his inventory of the box. "What do you think, Jim? Are you willing to turn them over to the Navy?"

"Well, I suppose that's better than handing them over to the Bahamian police, but I hate to give them up at all. I don't understand how they work, but I think, in time, I could piece together enough character sequences to start making some sense out of them."

"You wouldn't have to give them up," said Miles, "as long as you're willing to do your research at AUTEC instead of here at the hotel. I'm sure the Navy would be willing to provide you a small workspace if you'd be willing to share whatever you learn from them."

Jim furrowed his brow and frowned. "Frank, they're technically your discovery. What do you think?"

"I'd much rather have them in your control, even if that means accepting Navy oversight, than lose them altogether, so I guess we should take Miles up on his offer. Everybody agree?"

Frank scanned the team for objections, but they were all nodding affirmative so he shrugged and turned to Miles.

"Make the call, my friend. I don't suppose you have a contact in the Navy's R&D group, do you?"

"As a matter of fact," smiled Miles as he dialed a number on the library phone.

Several minutes later, Miles replaced the handset and addressed Jim.

"A Navy Shore Patrol unit will be here in about ten minutes to escort you and your triangles over to AUTEC. An ensign named Mallory will meet you at the gate and help you secure the triangles for tonight. He didn't think they could get you a workspace this afternoon, but at least you'll have them locked up. He's also going to get you started on the paperwork necessary for access to the base and to your specific area. If everything goes according to plan, you should be back in business by tomorrow morning. Be sure you take your U.S. passport for identification—and make it very clear to Mallory how dangerous these things can be."

"Well, it's been nice knowing you, Jim," laughed Tony. "You're in the Navy, now!"

"Hey, wait a minute! I'll be able to leave the base, won't I?" asked Jim.

"Yes, of course," grinned Miles, "but once you see the facilities over there, you may not want to. AUTEC serves as a testing facility for a lot of government contractors, and they have a number of individual labs all set up for visiting scientists.

Apparently this is their slow season, because Mallory told me you could pretty much take your pick."

"Cool!" smiled Jim. "This could be fun after all."

The intercom line of the phone buzzed and a female voice announced, "Excuse me, but there's a car here for a Mr. Barnes. Is he there?"

"Yes, Shirley, he'll be right out," replied Miles.

As Jim slid the box back into the plastic bag, Frank said, "Give me a call when you get back this afternoon and we'll all get together for dinner, okay? I can't wait to hear about this fancy new lab you've managed to swindle out of the U.S. taxpayers!"

Later that evening, Miles invited the NWIDI team, including the recovering Jill, to dinner away from the hotel.

"Not that there's anything wrong with our food here," he had laughed, "but I thought a change of pace might do everybody some good."

The place Miles had selected was a very small local restaurant at the north end of Andros Town. When they arrived, several tables had been pushed together and the rest of the dining room was empty. Seeing the surprise on Jill's face, he explained.

"It's actually a very popular place, my dear, but I took the liberty of reserving the entire establishment for the evening. The staff is preparing a special menu of typical Bahamian foods so you can get a taste of the culture—no pun intended."

When they were all seated and had been served drinks of their choice, a large black man dressed in cook's whites approached the table and took up position behind Miles.

"Folks, I'd like you to meet my third cousin on my ex-wife's side. This is Calvin, and he'll be your chef for the evening. Calvin, what's cookin', man?"

There was obviously a close bond between the two and Calvin replied with a jolly belly laugh.

"Well, folks, we've prepared a sampler that we think you're really going to enjoy. We'll be starting off with appetizers consisting of conch fritters, peas and rice and a special sweet potato soufflé. For the main course we're preparing chicken souse, grilled local fish, lobster curry and a vegetarian guava duff. These will all be served with conch salad, steamed rice and local vegetables. For dessert, we've prepared banana pudding, carrot cake and some delicious coconut candies. All the dishes will be served 'family style' so you can sample as many of them as you like. I hope you enjoy a taste of the Bahamas—which, by the way, is the name of this joint!"

As soon as Calvin disappeared into the kitchen, two teenage girls began serving the appetizers and the dinner conversation turned to Jim's afternoon at AUTEC.

"So what did you think of the place?" asked Miles between fritters.

"It's an incredible place, I'll give you that!" replied Jim. "A little more regimented than I'm used to, but the facilities are awesome. There are labs outfitted for acoustical research, chemical analysis and the study of various physical properties. And, Frank, you should see the data center! Each individual work module is equipped with a PC of enormous capacity that's connected to this main computer room. I picked a fairly simple module to begin with, because I want to see if I can crack the code of these symbols with the computer. Mike—Ensign Mallory, that is—is a cryptographic specialist and he's going to work with me on this part of the analysis. After that, I'll probably move to a chemistry lab and try to determine what the triangles are made of."

"See, I told you he'd defect to the Navy," laughed Tony. "Just don't forget your friends when you're rich and famous!"

"Any chance we could get in for a tour?" asked Frank. "I'd like to see what you're up to."

"I don't know, Frank. I've only been there a few hours and I don't know what the rules are, but I'll check. Or maybe Miles can arrange it."

Miles nodded.

"I'll see what I can do. You both have security clearances, if I remember from your files, so I should be able to arrange something."

Frank's arm froze in mid-air reaching for another piece of grilled fish.

"From what files?" he demanded.

"Oh, did I forget to mention the Department of Defense files?" he replied sheepishly.

Chapter 19

Linda and Javier had dinner at a small seafood restaurant directly across the avenue from the hotel and planned their day trip with the help of a map printed on the placemats. There was a loop, of sorts, that ran south along the mountains from Pinar Del Rio, through San Juan y Martinez to Isabel Rubio. Here, the road turned north through Guane, crossed a low pass and ran back up the north side of the mountains where it eventually turned east and south back to Pinar Del Rio. The entire trip appeared to be about one hundred miles long.

"This should be a nice drive," smiled Linda. And then in case they were being overheard, she added, "We should be able to get some really great shots of the tobacco country that this province is famous for, don't you think?"

"I agree," replied Javier, playing along. "And they will provide a good contrast to the pictures I took on the coast earlier today."

After dinner, they browsed the shops on both sides of the street in the block where the hotel was located. Linda bought a pair of walking shorts that looked like safari gear and Javier bought a pair of typical white cotton pants and a matching shirt. In another shop, they both found leather sandals and hand-made belts and next door Javier bought a medium-sized back pack that would hold his camera and some basic accessories. At a souvenir shop next door to the hotel Linda picked up several bottles of water and a canvas beach bag that had Pinar Del Rio crudely painted on one side. Inside, a label sewn into the bottom seam said "Made in China."

Back in their hotel rooms, Javier used the note pad on the nightstand to caution Linda.

"Inspect everything you plan to take tomorrow very carefully," the note read.

After propping chairs under each room's door knob and checking the two windows, Javier wrapped his digital camera in an extra shirt and put it in the back pack along with a case containing several filters. Another small box held an extra battery and several memory cards. He put his passport and Olvera's diplomatic press pass into a small zippered pouch on the front of the back pack and then positioned it between the pillows on his bed.

When Linda finished packing her beach bag, she put it next to the back pack and joined Javier on the bed. They drifted off to sleep watching Cuba's version of late-night television.

The next morning they awoke early and dressed for their outing. Javier called the phone number Olvera's driver had given him and made arrangements to meet in the lobby after breakfast. Javier scanned the room and then used hand signals to ask Linda if she had the satellite phone and laptop. She nodded and pointed to the beach bag, which she had slung over one shoulder.

After a light breakfast in the hotel restaurant, Linda and Javier entered the lobby to look for their driver. They were not surprised to find him waiting for them.

"We'd like to take a trip into the country-side before we head back to Havana," said Linda as she pulled the placemat out of her bag. "What do you think about this?"

She showed the driver the route she and Javier had planned the night before and the driver nodded.

"Those are well traveled roads, *Señorita*, and the scenery is very beautiful. It's an excellent choice."

As the taxi made its way through the heavy morning traffic, Linda and Javier took in the sites and let the driver concentrate on his driving. There were pedestrians and bicycles everywhere and Linda was amazed that they made it out of the city center without hitting someone. Gradually, though, the volume of traffic decreased and the driver glanced in his mirror to make eye contact with Linda.

"Is this your first trip to Cuba?" he asked.

"Yes, can't you tell," replied Linda who was gripping the armrest on the door a little tighter than necessary. "But so far, I'm very impressed. It's like stepping back in time to a period when life was simpler and more relaxed."

"That's an interesting observation," smiled the driver. "Some would call Cuba 'backward' rather than relaxed."

"You speak very good English, Carlos. Did you study abroad?"

"No, *Señorita*, I've never been off the island of Cuba but I attended a private school in Havana where English was a required course. My teachers would be pleased to hear your compliments."

Once outside the city of Pinar Del Rio, the highway became a narrow, two-lane paved road comparable to a secondary highway in the United States and the traffic restricted the speed to about forty-five miles per hour. After nearly thirty minutes of driving, the congestion began to increase again.

"We're entering the town of San Juan y Martinez," announced the driver. "As we leave town, we'll be going up into the mountains and there will be some vistas on your left that you shouldn't miss. I'll try to drive slowly, but there are no turn-outs until we reach Boca de Galafaro, about twenty kilometers from here."

As the driver had promised, the views were incredible, but Linda had a hard time enjoying them because the road narrowed and became very crooked. At one hairpin turn she let out a scream and admonished the driver.

"Be careful, Carlos! We almost went over the cliff!"

The driver smiled in the mirror and replied, "I've never driven off a cliff yet, *Señorita*."

Mercifully, the road straightened out once they started downhill and the long descent was much more enjoyable for Linda. Javier and the driver resumed their conversation in Spanish and Linda enjoyed the landscape.

As they entered the outskirts of Isabel Rubio, the driver announced, in English, "There's a major intersection ahead where this road meets the one we'll take back and another one that goes southwest to Sandino. I need to stop for gasoline because once we start north there are no more stations until we get back to Pinar Del Rio. This would also be a good opportunity to stretch your legs and use the facilities."

Linda waited until the driver's eyes were focused back on the road and then nudged Javier, who responded with a very slight nod. This might be their only chance to use the satellite phone to call Edwards!

Carlos eased the taxi to a stop at one of a dozen or more fueling islands in the large facility and said something to the attendant who approached the car.

"Refreshments and restrooms are in the main building, over there," he pointed. "I'm going to the restroom myself and then I'll move the car out of the way and wait for you, but please take your time."

Linda and Javier grabbed their bags and walked slowly towards the building Carlos had indicated. When they were away from the taxi, Linda whispered, "I doubt if I can make the phone work in the restroom, but I'll try if I have the opportunity. Otherwise, I'll slip around back while you keep him busy."

Linda was in the restroom for several minutes while Javier pretended to shop for candy and kept an eye on the door. Shortly after Linda went into the women's room, Carlos, who had reached the facilities ahead of them, came out of the men's room and joined Javier. When Linda came out, she shook her head slightly and started for the door but before she could get outside Carlos spotted her.

"Are we ready to continue?" he asked, smiling.

Back in the car, Linda fumed at their bad luck. The whole trip had been planned for this one event and now they had missed their opportunity. Noticing her agitation, Javier reached over and took her hand to comfort her. Just as he did, something slammed into the front of the taxi and his head hit the back of the passenger's seat with a thud.

Javier was seriously shaken but as his head cleared, his first thoughts were for Linda. He looked over to see her wiping a trickle of blood from her nose, but otherwise she appeared to be unhurt. The driver hadn't been so lucky.

A crowd of passers-by had quickly gathered around the wreck and two men were trying to pry the driver's door open. Javier forced open his door and helped Linda out the right side of the car while the men reached in to check on the driver, who was bleeding from his forehead.

Without thinking, Javier reached into the back of the taxi and grabbed his back pack and Linda's beach bag before helping Linda away from the wreckage and onto the sidewalk. As they turned to view the damage, they could see that an ancient, rusty pickup truck had hit the taxi head on just as it was exiting the gas station. The old man driving the truck appeared to be shaken but it was Carlos who was receiving all the attention. The men had managed to get him out from behind the broken steering wheel and had him on his back on the sidewalk where they were attending to a gash on his forehead. Within seconds, the air was filled with the sound of sirens and an ambulance screeched to a stop next to the taxi. By this time, the crowd had grown quite large and Javier gently eased Linda back behind the on-lookers.

"Are you okay?" he whispered.

"I think so," Linda replied, "but poor Carlos didn't fare so well. What should we do?"

"It looks like he'll be okay," said Javier, pointing to the gurney being lowered out of the ambulance. "They'll take him to the local hospital and see to his injuries, but that leaves us with a bit of problem, doesn't it?"

Linda suddenly came to her senses and recognized the opportunity the accident had provided. She looked carefully up and down the street and then grabbed Javier by the arm.

"Come on!" she said. "Let's get out of here before the police show up and start asking questions.

Protesting, Javier followed. "What about the driver?"

"Like you said, he'll be okay. Now follow me and don't look suspicious."

The two made their way back down the street that Carlos had traveled to reach the gas station until a slight hill hid them from the crowd gathered around the accident. Linda looked around and spotted a small market down a side street.

"Down there!" she pointed. "When we get to the shop, ask someone how to get to the local bus station." She fished the placemat map out of her bag and studied it. "I'll just smile and keep quiet so they don't know I'm American."

Javier got the directions Linda requested, thanked the old woman in the shop and started back to the corner where they had just been.

"So what's the deal?" asked Linda as they reached the corner.

"We continue down the hill, away from the accident until we come to a stop sign. There, we turn right and the bus station is two blocks down the street. We must have driven right by it in the taxi!" exclaimed Javier.

As they made their way down the broken sidewalk that lined the cobblestone street, Linda rummaged in her bag until she found her wallet. Without lifting it out, she checked the bill compartment.

"I still have six thousand pesos left, how about you?" she asked.

"I have forty-five hundred," replied Javier. "I counted it back at the hotel and I haven't spent anything since we left. So we have just over four hundred dollars between us, which should be plenty to get us from here to Pinar Del Rio and from there back to Havana."

"Oh, no, my dear, we're not going in that direction! We're going west, to Las Tumbas, remember?"

"You can't be serious, Linda! We don't have anything but the clothes on our back and we'll never get through the check-point at Manuel Lazo on a bus!"

"We don't have to get *through* the check-point, silly, we just have to get *to* it. Like I told you yesterday, I have a plan."

***

Miles' revelation about the Department of Defense files the previous night had come as quite a surprise to Frank and that, along with the spicy food Tony had goaded him into trying, had kept Frank awake a good portion of the night. He was standing at his patio door squinting at the Saturday morning sunrise over the Atlantic when there was a knock at his door.

"Who is it?" he called.

"Time to go diving," replied Miles' voice. "You guys stood me up yesterday, but you're not getting out of it today."

Frank had completely forgotten about the rebreather lessons he'd talked Miles into and as he shuffled towards the door he tried to think of a plausible excuse.

Frank opened the door to a cheerful Miles who was carrying an armload of gear and a pot of coffee.

Handing the carafe to Frank, he smiled and said, "Here, I thought you might need this. Where are the other two?"

"Tony told me last night that Jill is still feeling pretty weak and he wants to stay nearby until he knows she's not going to relapse. Maybe we should forget about this rebreather stuff."

"Oh no you don't! I'm all pumped up about doing some training again and you're not going to bail on me, even if you're the only student. We have some technical things to go over before we get in the water, so pour us each a cup while I get set up."

Frank took a sip of the strong Bahamian coffee and then returned to watch Miles.

"I'd like to talk to you about those DOD files you mentioned last night," he said as Miles worked.

Miles pulled a manila folder out of his dive gear bag and handed it to Frank.

"I thought you might. Here's yours, but I have to have that back when you're done looking at it," said Miles, without taking his eyes of the task at hand.

Surprised, Frank accepted the folder and opened it. The first page, titled "Present," included a recent photo of Frank and a summary of his life since winning the $86 million lottery jackpot fifteen months earlier. Frank was amazed at some of the details in the narrative, including a note about his brief encounter with a woman named Alex in Merida, Mexico.

Frank skimmed the remaining pages and when he finished he noticed that Miles was staring at him.

"Is everything in order?" he asked with a smile.

"No, everything is *not* in order!" replied Frank angrily. "Why was this information collected and, more to the point, why do *you* have it?"

"Easy, Frank. I have it because your friend Buzz Edwards sent it to me. You'll have to ask him why it was collected, but I'm sure you realize that the U.S. Government doesn't engage the services of civilians without analyzing everything there is know about them. I don't have all the details, but I understand that most of the work you and your team did in Japan is now classified Top Secret. In just the past two weeks you've discovered a previously unknown ancient site and a box of triangular objects that defy physics. Of course they're watching you, Frank! What would you expect?"

Frank was silent for many seconds.

"I don't like being spied on by the very people I'm trying to help," Frank finally said quietly. "I would have gladly provided most of this information, but I don't like being spied on."

"And neither would I," replied Miles. "That's why I showed you that folder. During our little party last night it became obvious to me that you didn't know you were being monitored so closely. Little private jokes that you and Tony obviously thought were just between the two of you are covered in detail in that dossier. I just thought you should know."

Frank was quiet again.

"I appreciate that, I guess," Frank finally said. "So how do you fit into all this? You're obviously more than a retired SEAL who happens to own a hotel up the road from the Navy's secret test facility."

"I can't tell you that, Frank. I'm sorry, but I just can't. Are you ready to talk about diving."

Surprised by the sudden change of subject, Frank stuttered, "Yes, I guess I'm ready. The rest of this I'm going to have to think about."

Frank tossed the folder onto the couch next to Miles, who slid it back into the gear bag without another mention.

"Okay, then pull up a chair and let's talk about exotic, mixed-gas diving, shall we?"

After an hour of "classroom" instruction, Miles led Frank out to a large boat tied up along the pier beside the hotel. A crew of three locals was already aboard and as soon as Frank's feet were on the deck, the engines came to life and the boat slipped quietly out into the Fresh Creek channel and headed for the open ocean.

Frank remained quiet during the ten-minute trip to the dive site, and Miles didn't attempt to engage him in conversation. As the crew lowered the boat's forward anchor, Miles joined Frank on one of the long benches that ran down each side of the main deck.

"Time to gear up," he said.

Frank stood and gazed at his surroundings for the first time since they had left the dock. The Andros coastline was just barely visible off the port side and the water was a consistent blue-green typical of the region.

"We're in about sixty feet of water but the blue hole I showed you the map of is nearby in case you feel adventurous," explained Miles. "Let's get you hooked up and take this thing for a test spin, shall we?"

The two deck hands helped Frank into the rebreather and adjusted the initial gas levels while he monitored the hose-mounted control panel, trying to remember everything Miles had told him earlier. Miles handed him a full-face mask, something he'd never used before, and explained why.

"This mask has full two-way communications built in," said Miles. "You and I will be able to talk to each other and the crew up here will also be able to monitor our conversations. If we get into trouble, they'll know immediately. I'm going to hook your regular mask to your BC in case you need to switch to my emergency air supply."

Frank noticed that Miles was wearing conventional scuba gear and said, "Hey, what's up with that?"

"I'm carrying your compressed air supply in case something goes wrong with the rebreather," replied Miles.

Frowning, Frank asked, "Does that happen often?"

The crewman helping Frank laughed and said, "Only when the diver messes with it, my friend. The rebreather is very smart— divers not so much!"

Miles smiled and said, "Not very tactfully put, but true, just the same. As we descend, you'll be mixing your own gas. If I had to be watching my own equipment, I wouldn't be able to keep an eye on what you're doing. We'll do it this way the first couple of times until I know you've got the hang of it and then I'll use a rebreather, too."

Frank nodded and lowered the odd-feeling mask. "Testing, 1, 2, 3," he said.

"I read you loud and clear," replied a strange voice from somewhere.

Miles lowered his own mask and pointed up to the captain, who had donned a headset equipped with a microphone. "He's got our back," said Miles. "Let's get wet!"

Once in the water, both divers showed the captain the "OK" sign and Miles initiated the dive with the thumbs down sign.

As uncomfortable as the oversized mask had been on the boat, it was quite the opposite underwater and Frank quickly adjusted to breathing comfortably through his nose rather than gripping a regulator in his clenched teeth.

"This is pretty cool!" he said out loud.

"I thought you'd like it," came Miles' slightly distorted voice, "but don't forget to watch your console. What's your oxygen partial pressure?"

"Uh, 0.65—too low, isn't it?"

"A little. Inject a little oxygen and then watch it as you descend. We'd like to see it at about 1.2 when we reach bottom. I know it's a distraction, but it's a part of tech diving."

"Got it," replied Frank. "I'll stop gawking around and pay attention."

When the two divers touched bottom, Frank's depth gage read sixty-three feet and his partial pressure display showed 1.193.

"How are we doing?" asked Miles.

"Right on the mark," replied Frank. "Where's this blue hole you mentioned?"

Miles turned a full circle scanning for a sign of the feature and then said, "We must have drifted a bit on our way down, but it has to be nearby. Follow me as I swim a spiral pattern until we find it. And keep an eye on that console!"

After about five minutes of searching, Miles spotted what he was looking for.

"There it is!" he said. "It's just behind that rock outcropping up ahead."

As they drifted over the outcropping, Frank saw the opening in the ocean floor.

"It looks like it goes straight down!" observed Frank. "Somehow I expected something horizontal, not vertical."

"It's actually a hole in the ceiling of a fairly large cavern, Frank, so once we're inside we'll move horizontally. I've never seen another diver out here, so I might be the only person who knows about this place. As you can see, the surrounding area is pretty barren and there isn't really anything else to attract people to the area. I found this one day while I was cruising around in my Bionic Dolphin."

"Amazing," replied Frank. "How deep did you say it is?"

"The cavern below us is about thirty feet high, so that would put the bottom at about ninety feet or so. At the far end there's a tunnel that slopes down quickly but, as I said the other day, I've never explored it because I can't get my gear through. Go ahead and drop down through the entrance and I'll meet you just inside."

The two divers slowly drifted down to within a few feet of the bottom and adjusted their buoyancy to allow them to slowly swim around the chamber without getting their fins too close to the bottom. Stirring up the silt would change the cavern's crystal clear water into a murky mess and make it very difficult to find the opening in the ceiling.

Frank had gotten into the habit of checking his rebreather console every minute or so, and when the O_2 level dropped to 1.1, he tapped the button that allowed more oxygen to enter the system. Looking back over his shoulder, Miles noticed the activity.

"Everything okay back there?"

"Just making a minor adjustment," replied Frank. "How long is this thing good for?"

"At this depth you're probably good for six hours or so, depending on your breathing habits."

"Six hours! That's amazing! What about depth?"

"Well, with a little more practice you should be able to get down to at least four hundred feet, but of course you couldn't stay very long—no more than ten or fifteen minutes. Pretty cool, huh?"

"I'll say!" replied Frank. "Why doesn't everybody use this stuff?"

"Well, it's expensive and technically complicated but it's also dangerous because it allows you to go places where you absolutely wouldn't survive an equipment failure. And for the typical sport diver, it's also not necessary. How many folks do you know who want to stay underwater for six hours at a time?"

"Yeah, I see your point."

Frank had been so preoccupied with his console that he hadn't noticed the long, slender stalagmites and stalactites that filled the back two-thirds of the cavern.

"Wow! This place is amazing!"

Miles turned to face Frank and held up his arm so the two wouldn't collide.

"You seem to be doing okay, so let me show you the best part of rebreather diving. I'm going to go up and exit the cavern so you can't hear my bubbles. You hang out here for a couple of minutes and experience the absolute silence of the ocean at depth. When you've had enough, come on out and we'll head back to the boat."

Frank swam a lazy circle in the front portion of the cavern while Miles went up and out. With each passing second, the sound of Miles' bubbles diminished until the cavern was absolutely quiet. Frank stopped moving his fins and took in the silence, as Miles had instructed. In all his years of diving, he'd never realized how loud scuba gear was! The silence was suddenly broken by a shrill alarm and Frank grabbed at his console to see what was wrong.

In his ears, Miles was yelling, "Frank! Frank! Are you okay?"

Chapter 20

Linda and Javier made their way to the local bus station without incident. Before entering the old, run-down building, Linda retrieved the satellite phone from her bag and called the number Edwards had programmed into the unit. The phone rang several times before a stiff male voice on the other end answered.

"Command Center. Please state your business."

"Uh, hello, this is Linda McBride," stammered Linda. "I'm calling for Buzz Edwards."

"Stand by while I connect your call, ma'am," came the curt reply.

"Go for Edwards," said the familiar voice of the DOD agent.

"Buzz, this is Linda. Listen, I don't have much time but I wanted to let you know that Javier and I are in a place called Isabel Rubio and we're going to catch a bus down to Manuel Lazo, where there's apparently a check point that controls all access to the Peninsula. You should also know that our cover's been blown because yesterday the official in charge of the environmental conference called me by my real last name."

There was a pause before Edwards replied.

"Sorry," he finally said, "but I'm trying to write this all down. If the official you're talking about is a guy named Olvera, he's a friendly. But I need to find out how he got your name because we certainly didn't give it to him. He was supposed to assign a chaperone to keep an eye on you two—what's happened to him?"

"You mean you knew about all this?" shouted Linda. "Why didn't you tell us what was going on? We've been playing cloak-and-dagger ever since we landed!"

"I didn't have any of the details until after you had left Cancun and apparently you haven't had the phone on, because I tried calling several times and all I got was an out of service message."

"Oh, well, I've kept the phone off so it wouldn't give us away," softened Linda. "I think you need to check up on this Olvera, though, because he has us on a spy mission for the Cuban government and he's threatened to hold us in Cuba if we don't cooperate. Anyway, our car was in an accident a few minutes ago and the driver was hurt bad enough to need medical attention. We slipped away during the confusion and we're headed west on the next bus out of here. For now, at least, nobody knows where we are."

"That's too bad," replied Edwards, "because your driver would probably have taken you right to the check point if you'd asked him to. But if there's a check point, why are you continuing on? Catch a bus back to Havana and we'll make arrangements to get you out of there."

"The whole reason we're here is to find out what's going on out there on the peninsula," exclaimed Linda. "So far, all we've done is play hide and seek with your so-called *friendlies*! I have a plan to get the information we came here for. If it doesn't work, we'll get back to Havana and call you."

"That sounds like a really bad idea to me, but at least leave the phone on, will you?" laughed Edwards. "I'll let Frank know in case he wants to start planning a rescue mission."

"Whatever! But do *not* pass our plans on to this Olvera character. The Cuban government doesn't have control of the peninsula and he has his own agenda. I'd prefer not to be part of it."

"Roger, General McBride! Listen, you two be careful over there and call me at the first hint of trouble. Got that?"

"Got it!" returned Linda as her finger pounded the End button on the phone. "What a jerk!"

"Well, that sounded like it went well," smiled Javier. "I take it our friends in Havana are—or at least were—on our side?"

"Can you believe that?" said an irate Linda. "But I still think Olvera has his own plans for us and I don't trust him one bit." Jerking her thumb at the bus station, she said, "Let's do this!"

Inside, Javier purchased two tickets to Manuel Lazo while Linda waited discretely away from other passengers.

"Everything okay?" she asked when Javier joined her.

"I got one raised eye brow, but no comments," he replied. "The bus leaves in about twenty minutes. It stops at every wide spot in the road and we have a layover in Sandino so it's going to take almost two hours to travel twenty-three miles but that will give you plenty of time to explain this plan of yours to me."

The bus to Manuel Lazo was at least thirty years old and it was as rough as a buckboard, but at least Linda and Javier were able to find a row of seats near the back that gave them the privacy to talk.

"Okay, lady, let's hear this plan of yours," demanded Javier.

"Well, it's not really that big of a deal. Ernesto's boss gave me the idea when he said something about the amount of provisions that pass through the check point. I figure, all we have to do is hide along side the road, jump into the back of one of those trucks, and off we go!"

Javier stared at her wide-eyed and she finally asked, "What?"

"I'm waiting for the rest of your idea! Please don't tell me that's all there is—what's the trick?"

"There's no trick, Javier, and please don't mock me. What's wrong with my plan?"

"What's wrong is that there *is* no plan!" he said in disbelief. "We hide along side the road, jump in the back of a moving truck and enjoy the ride to Las Tumbas? That's not a plan, Linda, that's a recipe for disaster. Look around you—what if there's no cover beside the road and we're seen? And we stand out like sore thumbs, you know. Besides, what if the truck we pick isn't even going to Las Tumbas, but instead to one of the little villages along the way? I can't believe it!"

"Hey, lighten up, will you?" replied Linda. "We have way too much invested in this trip to quit without getting what we came for. There's something very strange going on just off the tip of the peninsula and I plan to find out what it is. Frank is depending on us, but if you want to head back to Havana, then you go right ahead! I'll catch up with you later."

Javier was silent for a minute.

"You know I can't do that, Linda, and I'm sorry I didn't realize how important this is to you. But if we're going to pull this off we're going to have to get very lucky for all the reasons I just mentioned. I certainly don't have a better plan, but I do have some information that might help your plan."

Linda smiled. "My plan can use all the help it can get, so let's hear it."

"Well, when I was talking to Ernesto and his girlfriend yesterday, I tried to work the peninsula into the conversation. The girl mentioned that she had family in Manuel Lazo, but that she hadn't seen them in years. The other thing I picked up is the fact that the check point is about two kilometers west of town, on the road to Las Tumbas."

Linda wrinkled her brow. "Interesting, but how does that help?"

"Well, we wouldn't want to stow away in a truck in town, only to find out that it was going to be searched later, right? If we can find a way around that check point, we might actually make your plan work."

"Good point. But our best chance to sneak around any guards would be at night, wouldn't it?"

"Yes," smiled Javier, "and if I can just remember that girl's last name, we might have a place to hold up until dark."

When the bus bumped to a stop at the Manuel Lazo station, Javier still hadn't been able to remember the last name of Ernesto's girlfriend and he was beginning to wonder if he'd even heard it.

"Maybe we should just find a hotel nearby," suggested Linda.

"In this town, strangers checking into a hotel without a reservation would be like sending up a signal flare," frowned Javier. "I was hoping we could pass as relatives here to visit our family. Besides, sneaking out of a hotel in the middle of the night could be tricky. Follow me—let's try something."

Javier led the way out into the afternoon sunlight and headed for the first taxi he saw. He said something to the driver, who thought for a second, snapped his fingers and said, "*Si, Señor!*"

Afraid the cab driver might understand some English, Linda just smiled and remained silent as she and Javier climbed into the back seat of the small Nissan sedan. Ten minutes later, the taxi came to a stop in front of a small bakery on the edge of town. Javier paid the driver and helped Linda out. After a friendly exchange with the driver, the taxi pulled away.

"So I take it you remembered her name," said Linda as she looked up and down the street.

"No, but I remembered the girl saying that her uncle owned the best bakery in town, so that's where I told the driver we wanted to go—to the best bakery in town!"

"So you have no idea whether this is the right place or not," laughed Linda. "Great move!"

"Well, if this is the right place, we'll have a place to stay. If not, we'll buy some bread and try again."

***

The sound of the alarm had scared the daylights out of Frank but before he could react the alarm stopped. His pulse was racing and he was breathing hard.

Outside the cavern, Miles yelled into the two-way diver communications system again. "Frank, answer me! Are you okay?"

"Yes, I'm okay, but I don't know what that noise was all about. I'm headed up so you can check out my gear."

When Frank stood on the sea floor bottom outside the cavern entrance, Miles physically examined the rebreather pack and then checked Frank's console.

"Ah, ha!" he exclaimed as he stepped one of the digital displays through a sequence of readings. "It looks like you stopped breathing for several seconds. Were you holding your breath, Frank?"

"Uh, yeah, I suppose so. I was concentrating on the remarkable silence down there and all I could hear was my own breathing. I stopped for just a minute to listen. Is that what set off the alarm?"

"Probably," replied Miles. "The computers in these rebreathers are pretty smart. The one I use has been modified and it has all the noise-making features disabled, but yours is right off the shelf. Let's get back to the boat."

Back at the hotel pier, Frank offered to help with the cleaning and stowing of the dive gear, but Miles' crew wouldn't hear of it so he wandered off to look for the other NWIDI team members. It was only 9:00 a.m. but, with all the excitement of the dive, it seemed like noon.

Frank spotted Tony and Jill having breakfast on the patio adjacent to the restaurant.

"Morning!" he called. "How are you two feeling after that exotic food last night?"

"We're doing great," laughed Tony, "but how about you? You tossed down a lot of spicy stuff—spicy for you, that is!"

"Hey, I've already been for a dive this morning, my friend, so don't start on me! What's on tap for today?"

"Jim left for AUTEC about an hour ago and he suggested that we come over to see his set-up," replied Tony. "Jill wants to do some shopping, so I thought we could drop her in town and then check out Jim's new digs. Later, when we pick up Jill, we can find some lunch before coming back to the hotel. What about you?"

"I have no real plans and a visit to AUTEC sounds like fun. Other than that, I'd like to do a little investigation into the strange object that Miles and I saw in the river. I think I'll spend the afternoon in town at the local library."

"Sounds too boring for me! Maybe Jill and I will try some easy diving this afternoon, if she feels up to it, but I think you can count us both out of that rebreather training. Shall we go check up on Jim?"

Thirty minutes later, Frank and Tony climbed out of a taxi near AUTEC's main gate. Jim's new research associate had supposedly made all the necessary arrangements, but as they approached the gate a tall, muscular Navy SP stepped out of the guard house with an M-16 rifle held diagonally across his chest.

"Please state your business," he said firmly.

"Frank Morton and Tony Nicoletti to see a civilian named Jim Barnes," answered Tony in his most menacing voice.

The Navy shore patrolman wasn't impressed. "Wait here, please."

A minute later the SP returned and seemed more relaxed. "This way, gentlemen. I have some paperwork for you to sign and I've notified Mr. Barnes that you're here. He will be here to escort you in shortly."

By the time Frank and Tony finished signing the typical "I will not tell" documents and received their visitor badges, Jim had arrived. He seemed happy and upbeat, even for Jim.

"Hey, guys, you're just in time! We're in the middle of a very interesting experiment. Follow me."

As they chatted, Jim led the others two blocks straight in from the main gate and then two blocks to the left, down a row of narrow, single story concrete buildings. Each structure had a painted steel door in the middle of the twelve-foot-wide front and each door had a sign head-high on it that read "Authorized Personnel Only" followed by a building number.

"Nice neighborhood," snickered Tony.

"These buildings are the individual labs I told you about. They're mostly for civilian defense contractors. The Navy helps conduct tests at sea and then the equipment is brought back here for analysis. Here we are, Building D-11."

Jim pressed his thumb into an indentation just above the door handle and there was an audible click. Holding his thumb in place, he rotated the handle down and the door swung open.

"Very high tech," commented Frank as they entered the twelve by twenty-four foot room.

"There are often competing contractors working here at the same time," explained Jim. "The security is mostly to prevent industrial espionage, although I must say I sleep better knowing the triangles are locked up in here at night. There are only two of us in the whole world that can get in here."

"Sure, if you don't count the guy who made the locks and the one who controls the access codes," smiled Tony. "But it sure beats your hotel room closet. What's the experiment you mentioned?"

"Ah, yes! It's over here," said Jim. "Please don't touch anything, guys."

Jim led the way to a metal workbench that ran across the entire back of the building. Various glass enclosures with exhaust hoods broke the smooth upper surface and a small sink was integrated into one end. The back wall was dotted with electrical and gas fittings, much like a high school chemistry lab.

Approaching one of the enclosures, Jim slid the glass front up to expose a triangle resting on a glass Petri dish.

"We've been immersing this one in various gaseous environments," explained Jim. "Initially, we were looking for chemical reactions to pure gasses such as helium, oxygen, nitrogen and things like that. We were looking so hard at the surface of the object that we almost didn't notice this."

Jim picked up a small digital camera and snapped a picture of the triangle. He then lowered the front of the enclosure and entered some codes using a keypad and digital display located beside the enclosure. A red light on the hood came on, blinked several times and then changed to green. Jim flipped a switch that illuminated the interior where the triangle was.

"Take a look," he said proudly,

Pressing their faces close to the glass front, Frank and Tony squinted at the triangle.

After a second, Tony rolled his head towards Frank and whispered, "I don't see anything different, do you?"

"No. Me neither," replied Frank

"Shall we stand up and tell him, or should we let him think we see whatever it is he's been imagining?" smiled Tony.

"Guys, I can hear you, you know. And we had the same problem until a few minutes ago. Here look at this."

Jim handed his two friends the digital camera and motioned for them to look into the enclosure again.

"The symbols have changed!" shouted Frank. "And without putting it back into the box!"

"That's right," beamed Jim. He keyed some more codes, the lights sequenced again and when the green light came on he opened the hood and removed the dish holding the triangle.

"Now what do you see?" he asked.

Comparing the triangle to the image on the small screen of the digital camera, Frank announced, "Wow, they're back the way they were!"

"Yeah, wow," added an unimpressed Tony. "That and a dollar will buy you a cup of coffee. What does this mean, Jim?"

"The procedure I just went through was to remove all the air from the enclosure and replace it with pure methane gas—CH_4. That's when you saw a different set of symbols. When I removed the methane and put air back in, the symbols returned to their previous state."

"Like I said, what does this mean?" repeated Tony. "When you put them in the box, the symbols change permanently, right?"

"That's correct," nodded Jim. "Our working theory is that the closed box, for whatever reason, emits a gas that is made up of methane and something else. When we find the something else and add it to our environment in the enclosure, we think the symbol change will be permanent, just like it is inside the box."

Before Tony could ask what it all means again, Frank slapped him on the back and shouted, "And that correct mixture, once you find it, will represent the triangles' native atmosphere! From their home planet!"

"That's what we're thinking," smiled Jim. "And that's not bad for less than a days' work, is it?"

"Not bad at all, my friend!" smiled Frank. "Does knowing that the atmosphere is methane-based tell you anything concrete?"

"Not really," replied Jim. "In our solar system, the Jovian planets—that's Jupiter, Saturn, Uranus and Neptune—all have methane-rich atmospheres, but nothing suggests that any of those planets support life and the triangles came from a pretty advanced society. More likely they're from a gaseous, Jovian-like planet far from here."

"Well, it looks like you made the right decision by joining forces with the Navy. You would never have figured this out in your hotel room!" laughed Frank.

"Yes, and please don't mention this to Miles because we're keeping a lid on the alien artifact theory so the Navy doesn't censor us. You know how the government feels about UFOs! Let me show you a couple other places I've been granted access to and then I need to get back to work."

"Actually, we were hoping you could join us for lunch in town," said Frank. "Jill is doing some shopping and then we're going to meet her and eat away from the hotel for a change."

"Oh, I don't think I should, guys," apologized Jim. "Stan— that's Ensign Mallory—is in a staff meeting right now but he'll be back in about fifteen minutes and then we have a lot of work scheduled for the rest of the day."

"You're really enjoying this, aren't you?" asked Tony.

"You know, I've spent most of my professional life in a classroom, and I always thought I enjoyed it. Then Frank talked me into going to Las Vegas, the Yucatan and Yonaguni. That field work was a real thrill for me, but this—the lab, the challenge of unraveling a secret unknown to science—this is as good as it gets! Right now, I don't care if I ever see another classroom."

"Well, finish showing us around so you can get back to it," laughed Frank. "We need to meet Jill in about an hour."

Even though he had only been on the base part of a day, Jim seemed to know his way around and he had access to more of the facility than Frank would have guessed. And the facilities were impressive, to say the least.

"That place sure makes our renovated hangar back in Seattle look like a dump," commented Frank as the taxi sped them away from the base to meet Jill for lunch.

When they caught up to her, Jill was loaded down with shopping bags so they chose the first restaurant they saw and piled into a booth near the door.

Before they had even ordered their food, their lunch was interrupted by a call on Frank's satellite phone. When the call ended, he looked concerned.

"What's wrong?" asked Jill.

"That was Edwards," replied Frank. "He just received a call from Linda and Javier and it seems that they're heading to Las Tumbas in the morning."

"But that's a good thing, right?" asked Tony. "Isn't that why they went to Cuba in the first place?"

"Yes, but Edwards sounded a little worried, so now I'm worried, too! He's still doing some checking, but apparently the peninsula we sent Linda to investigate is controlled by rebels or some paramilitary group that's not friendly to the Cuban regime.

And Edwards' contact in Havana has apparently made some vague threats towards Linda and Javier."

"But a group unfriendly to the regime would probably be pro-US, right? I'm sure they're okay."

"You're probably right, but I think we should be ready to extract them, in case that becomes necessary. While I'm at the library will you make sure that we're ready to move if we have to? I'm going to call the jet in from the mainland in case we need it and you can impress Jill with some of the resources we have at our disposal."

"Yeah, right!" laughed Jill. "But seriously, I want to help any way I can. And don't forget I am—or at least I was—a nurse. I should be a part of any 'away team' you put together."

"I appreciate that, Jill, and we'll certainly keep your medical training in mind. Hopefully it won't come to a rescue operation, but they may be walking into something much bigger than any of us expected."

Frank used the satellite phone to call Fitz and Susan, the group's husband-and-wife Learjet crew. After delivering Linda and Javier to Cancun, they had flown the plane to a small private airport outside Miami where they'd been able to arrange inside storage until they were needed again. Frank instructed them to return to Andros Island as soon as possible and join them at the hotel until they had more news about Linda and Javier.

"They'll be here tomorrow morning," said Frank. "Will you guys make arrangements for them at the hotel when you get back?"

After lunch, Frank walked the short distance to the library. He had his laptop and plenty of paper just in case he turned up any information about strange sightings around Andros. Meanwhile, Tony and Jill returned to the hotel to prepare for the arrival of the flight crew and the possible emergency departure of all or part of the NWIDI team. Jill called the front office to reserve a room for Fitz and Susan while Tony used Jim's laptop to start preparing a rescue plan. After about fifteen minutes, he leaned back in his chair and said, simply, "Crap!"

"What's the matter?" asked Jill, who had turned on the room's small television.

"Well, it looks like weather might be a factor. There's a tropical storm passing Jamaica and the weather service is predicting that it will grow to a hurricane during the next twenty-four hours— just before it passes over the western tip of Cuba!"

Chapter 21

The aromas inside of the bakery were delicious and Linda really hoped it was the right place because she already had her eye on a pastry that was making her mouth water. Javier had engaged the elderly man who had come from the back when they entered and the conversation seemed to be friendly, although Linda couldn't understand a word.

Finally Javier pulled her away from the showcase and said, "Linda, this is Humberto. He doesn't speak any English, so just say '*mucho gusto*' and smile. I told him you don't speak any Spanish."

Linda repeated the phrase and flashed her widest smile at the man, who said something in Spanish and waved his arm in a broad arc.

"He says that he's very happy that we stopped by and that you're welcome to anything in the store," laughed Javier.

"Oh, I couldn't," blushed Linda. "But there is this Danish over here that looks absolutely sinful and I wouldn't want to be rude by refusing his hospitality."

Javier laughed again and translated Linda's comment to the old man, who rushed to fetch the pastry Linda had indicated. As he was handing it to her, he was joined by a woman of approximately the same age, who had also appeared from the back. Humberto made the introductions and the woman said, "*Vengan, vengan!*" and motioned for Javier and Linda to follow her through the door behind the counter.

Immediately behind the customer area was a large room with several ovens at the far end and work counters running down both sides. This was obviously the bakery proper, but the woman kept going, through another door and into a modest living room area. A quick glance around told Linda that the couple's house was directly attached to their business.

The woman, whose name was Carina, tried to speak to Linda in Spanish and Javier had to remind her that Linda didn't understand. After a short conversation, the woman disappeared into the kitchen and Javier indicated that they should sit on the nearby couch.

"She asked you what you would like to drink," explained Javier, "and I suggested iced tea. I hope that's okay."

"Perfect! So I take it you got lucky and found the right bakery on the first attempt, huh?"

"Well, not exactly," smiled Javier. "Here she comes—I'll tell you later."

Linda, Javier and the woman passed the next thirty minutes chatting. That is, Javier and the woman chatted and Javier translated the conversation for Linda.

Promptly at 2:00 p.m. the man appeared and Javier told Linda that they had been invited to join the couple in their afternoon meal.

"Wow," said Linda. "That's really nice of them, especially since they don't even know us. Please ask Carina if I can help."

Javier did and wasn't surprised when Carina wouldn't hear of it. He and Linda were guests, after all!

The meal consisted of multiple courses and ended with a delicious fruit pie, no doubt from the bakery. Linda had tried to follow as much of the conversation as she could and she was pretty sure she had heard the name Las Tumbas mentioned several times. She couldn't wait to get the details from Javier, because he was so engaged with Humberto that he had stopped translating soon after they had moved to the dining table.

When Carina poured the second cup of strong, dark coffee, Humberto and Javier rose from the table. Linda raised her eyebrows, as if to ask, "What's up?"

Javier shrugged and replied simply, "Cigar."

In spite of Carina's protests, Linda helped carry dirty dishes into the small kitchen and then returned to the couch with her coffee while the older woman busied herself putting the food away. About fifteen minutes later, the two men returned to the room reeking of cigar smoke. Humberto joined his wife in the kitchen and Javier took a chair next to Linda.

"What a stroke of luck!" whispered Javier.

Linda wrinkled her nose and asked, "How is a smelly cigar lucky? I didn't even know you smoked."

"I don't, but this time it was worth it because he's going to help get us to Las Tumbas!"

"Get out!" shouted Linda. "How's he going to do that?"

"Shhh! Every afternoon he bakes fresh bread and other items that get delivered to Las Tumbas the same night and he knows how the supply system works. He's offered to help us get through the check point."

"But why?" whispered Linda. "What could you have possibly told him that would make him take a risk like that? "

"I told him that you're an American correspondent and I'm your photographer and we're here to do an expose on Cuba's untamed 'wild west'—the Peninsula de Guanahacabibes. Pretty good story, huh?"

"Yeah, good one!" replied Linda. "But that doesn't explain why he would offer to help us."

"Well, while we were eating, he complained that he had to bake all afternoon and I thought that was kind of odd, because bakeries usually prepare their goods early in the morning so they will be fresh. Later he said something about being up at 4:00 a.m. every morning to bake for the store, so I asked him about the afternoon shift and that's when he told me about his Las Tumbas connection. Apparently he's forced to supply bread for the peninsula or lose his business. They've even threatened his family if he doesn't cooperate."

"Who are '*they*'?" asked Linda, glancing into the kitchen to make sure she wasn't being overheard.

"He wouldn't say, but he's clearly afraid of them and I think he believes your story might change things here and out on the peninsula."

"No pressure there," frowned Linda, "especially since I'm not even a real reporter! So how are we going to do this?"

Javier explained the plan he and Humberto had worked out and Linda listened intently.

When Javier finished, Linda thought for a minute and then nodded.

"That might just work," she smiled. "And when this is all over, maybe I *will* document the situation out here. I'm not exactly a journalist, but I worked for a newspaper for years and I think I know a thing or two about a good story."

That night, under the cover of a new moon, the baker delivered his cargo to a run-down warehouse on the edge of town. It was a delivery he made routinely, five nights a week, but tonight his truck also contained Linda and Javier.

Carina had found them some dark clothes to wear and they were stretched out under a tarp in the very front of the truck's cargo area. Humberto had covered the tarp with bags of fresh bread and created a low 'wall' with boxes of pastries. From the back of the truck, the tarp was invisible.

The truck slowed to a bumpy stop and Humberto called back to Javier.

"This is as far as he goes," translated Javier. "We just have to wait here until the driver from Las Tumbas shows up and then we're on our way."

While Humberto's plan wasn't without risk, it did solve the problem of the check point because vehicles driven by "insiders" weren't searched—or at least that's what Humberto had been told.

They'd been waiting less than five minutes when Humberto pounded three times on the back of his cab—the signal that the other driver had arrived and that he would be leaving them. Linda and Javier overheard a muffled exchange between Humberto and the other man and then their truck started moving again. The sounds from the tires changed from dirt to gravel to pavement and soon the truck was up to highway speed. After about fifteen minutes, the driver started down-shifting as he brought the truck to a stop.

"The check point," whispered Javier as he squeezed Linda's hand.

The cargo portion of the truck was enclosed with canvas sides and top, and the back was open, except for the tailgate. As the sound of laughing and the smell of cigar smoke drifted in, Linda wondered how much longer they would have to remain motionless before the driver resumed his drive west. Her thoughts were interrupted by a loud sound from the back of the truck.

"One of them is headed this way," whispered Javier.

Motionless, they listened as the tailgate was lowered and one of the two men climbed up onto it. They could hear him working his way towards the back, rummaging through boxes, and it was clear he was looking for something.

Suddenly he shouted, *"Ya lo encontré!"* and retreated towards the back of the truck. The sound of boots hitting the pavement and the tailgate being latched back in place brought a small sigh of relief to Linda.

"He found whatever he was looking for," whispered Javier. "This must be his lunch break. After he picks up the truck full of fresh bread he comes out here and shares some of it with his buddy before continuing on. How are you doing?"

"I'm terrified, actually," replied Linda softly. "This sounded like a much better idea earlier today."

Ten minutes later they were rolling down the highway again and the driver had loud music playing in the cab. Javier slowly pushed the tarp back and stuck his head up to look around. When he was satisfied that they were still alone in the back of the truck, he carefully pushed back the tarp and motioned for Linda to join him at the tailgate, where they could see out and not be overheard by the driver.

"Another hour or so and we'll be home free," he said quietly. "We need to stay alert and try to figure out exactly where and when this guy makes his first stop. After we've had our look around Las Tumbas, we'll try to catch a ride back to Manuel Lazo with him and hook up with Humberto again. And, with any luck, our friend up front won't know we made the trip either way."

Linda was studying the landscape as Javier talked.

"It's sure desolate out here," she commented. "I don't see a light of any kind on either side of this road. The only sign of civilization is the faint glow of the city directly behind us."

"Maybe they don't have electricity out here," offered Javier.

The two fell silent for many minutes and then Javier suddenly hissed, "Get down!"

As Linda ducked down below the top of the tailgate, she saw a single, bright light rapidly approaching the back of the truck.

"A motorcycle," she said as the high-pitched whine of the engine passed. "And he's in a hurry, too."

The motorcyclist gave the truck driver a quick beep of his horn as he passed the cab and then the pitch of the engine increased and faded away as the motorcycle raced on ahead. Light rain had started to fall, the first they had seen since arriving in Cuba.

Eventually lights began to appear along the road and the stowaways tried to make out features. The truck down-shifted a couple of gears and Javier thought they were coming to a stop, but instead the driver made a gradual right turn and then brought the truck back up to speed.

"Uh, oh," whispered Javier. "We may not be going into town after all. We may be headed for another remote warehouse, just like at the other end."

"Well, at least we'll have a better chance to get away," replied Linda. "But if we have to wait until morning to find our way into town, I hope we can find some shelter. This rain looks like it could get pretty serious."

The truck passed several complexes that each had a single outdoor light on a pole. In the inky darkness, the structures appeared to be low, single-story buildings with no windows. On the far side they could just make out a low ridge.

"Missile silos!" exclaimed Javier in a whisper. "I'll bet these are some of the missile silos that initiated what you Americans call the Cuban Missile Crisis."

"But why out here?" asked Linda.

"What better place for them? There aren't many prying eyes out here and they have an unobstructed view of the southern U.S. I'll bet the Gulf of Mexico is just beyond that ridge, which hides the silos from passing ships and..."

Javier was cut off by the sudden downhill pitch of the truck and the appearance of walls and a roof that enclosed the road behind the truck.

"We're headed down into an underground structure!" cried Javier. "Be ready to jump!"

**

After searching the small local library for nearly an hour, Frank finally found what he was looking for—a three-year-old article on page five of the local weekly newspaper about a UFO sighting near Morgan's bluff, on the north end of the island. It took him a minute to make the connection, but he finally remembered that Morgan's Bluff was the name of the area where the Atlantic Protector had docked when they first reached Andros.

The library's newspaper archive was stored on microfilm so there wasn't any way to do a global search for "UFO." The only way to find anything was to read every article in every issue and he soon tired of the slow process. After printing out the one article he had found, Frank hailed a cab and returned to the hotel.

"So, tell me about this storm," frowned Frank as he sat down across from Tony in the hotel room.

Jill had fallen asleep on one of the two queen beds in the room but Tony had continued to search the Internet for information on Tropical Storm Dessie.

"Well, it just passed over Jamaica as a strong tropical storm and its projected path will take it directly over the peninsula," replied Tony. "If it's not already raining there, it will be soon and Tropical Storm Dessie is expected to increase to at least a Category 1 hurricane by the time it reaches Cuba."

"And when will that be?" asked Frank, scribbling on a note pad.

"In about 36 hours, Frank, but the weather in the area will be deteriorating from here on out. If we're going in after them, we need to leave now. And I mean within the hour! How soon can we get the Learjet here?"

"Not until tomorrow, I'm afraid, and I wouldn't risk the crew or the aircraft in those conditions, anyway. We'd have to make a very low-level approach directly into the path of the storm in order to have any chance of surviving the jump and that would put the plane in a very bad situation."

"What are you two talking about?" demanded Jill.

She had apparently awakened when Frank knocked on the door and she was now sitting cross-legged on the bed.

"You're not seriously considering jumping out of an airplane into a hurricane, are you?"

"No, not yet," replied Tony as he studied a map of Cuba on the laptop's screen.

Frank had picked up his satellite phone and dialed somebody while Jill was questioning Tony and he held up his index finger to signal them to be quiet while he completed the call.

He pressed the End button and said, "No answer, so wherever they are, there's no way to reach them."

"But I thought a satellite phone was good anywhere in the world," objected Jill. "Maybe she doesn't have it turned on."

"The satellite mode only works if the special antenna is pointed at the satellite," replied Frank, "and she'd have to be expecting a call to do that. As for having it on, Edwards said he specifically instructed her to leave it on at all times, but who knows. We'll just have to wait for them to call us because even if we had a way to attempt a rescue, we don't have any idea where they are. Let's hope they can find shelter and wait out this storm."

"There won't be another weather update for six hours, so how about if you show me how to use that full-face mask you were talking about. If we have to go in with dive gear, being able to communicate would be a real plus!"

"Good idea! Shall I see if Miles has time to give you a rebreather lesson, while we're at it?" asked Frank.

"No thanks," Tony returned. "If I'm in a difficult situation already, the last thing I need is to be worrying about my gear. At my age, I think I'll just stick with my trusty scuba gear, thank you!"

Frank laughed, but Tony had a point. On the other hand, the extended bottom time provided by the rebreather could be invaluable in a rescue mission.

"Okay, but I'm going to get in another dive or two with the rebreather before we go after Linda and Javier. Jill, are you interested in trying it out?"

"I'm afraid not, Frank. My close call last night gave me a whole new perspective on adventure."

"Okay, but you don't know what you're missing!" smiled Frank. "I'll go get my gear and meet you in the lobby. If Miles isn't available, maybe we can just dive from the pier."

"Don't forget the mask," called Tony.

Miles was tied up in meetings all afternoon, but his boat was available and he called the crew to make arrangements for the dive.

"You did pretty well this morning," he cautioned Frank, "but don't get too cocky out there. These things can kill you if you aren't careful. And remember—no holding your breath!"

"I promise," smiled Frank. "Any suggestions as to a dive site that would be good for mixed company? Tony and Jill are diving in conventional scuba gear."

"As a matter of fact, yes! There's a good spot in the bay just beyond the channel opening. You'll see lots of interesting creatures that hang out where the fresh water mixes with the sea and the smooth, sandy bottom makes spotting critters easy. I'll let the crew know where to take you. Enjoy!"

The boat ride to the dive site was a short ten minutes, but it took another fifteen minutes to connect Tony's regulator to the full face mask. While the two crew members worked on the mask, Frank went up on the flying bridge to talk with the boat's captain.

Like the other two crew members, Captain Jimmy was coal black and spoke with the distinctive Bahamian accent.

"Captain, I know Miles gave you a specific dive site for us, but I'd like to get a feel for how this rebreather handles at depth. Is there a wall or drop-off somewhere close by?"

"Yes, sir, there is," beamed Jimmy. "But I don't want no trouble whit da boss. Are you sure you know how to use dat ting?"

"I think so. Miles had me inside a blue hole on the first dive, but I'd like something with fewer challenges for my first solo," smiled Frank. "A nice, vertical wall would be perfect."

"Okay, den," nodded the captain. "We'll move da dive spot a little and when you reach da bottom, swim a little ways south and there be da wall."

After a check of the communications system, Frank, Tony and Jill slipped below the surface and regrouped on the bottom, about forty feet below the dive boat. Once everybody was settled, they instinctively gave the thumb-and-index-finger "OK" sign and then Frank remembered that he and Tony could talk.

"Tony, can you hear me?"

"Loud and clear, Frank. Hey, this thing is really cool!"

"I know, and the captain can monitor us from the boat. Captain Jimmy, are you there?"

"Roger dat, my friend! You all have yourselves a safe dive and yell if you need anything. Over."

"Thanks, we will," replied Frank. "See, isn't that cool?"

Frank noticed Jill waving her right arm like she wanted to be called on in a classroom.

Pointing, he said, "Oh yeah, I forgot that Jill can't hear us. She probably wonders what's going on."

Tony used a dive slate to write her a brief message and she nodded. Making a motion with her hand, she signaled, "Let's go diving!"

"I'm going to head south a bit where there's supposed to be a wall," said Frank. "Would you mind coming along and hanging out while I run this contraption down a bit deeper?"

"Hey, it's all underwater to me. Besides, the marine life is usually more interesting near a wall—lead the way."

They found the wall in just a couple of minutes and swam out past it to get a look back at the top. Where the bottom had been mostly white sand, the vertical portion of the wall was covered with coral and plants that had attached themselves to the dark rock face.

"How deep is it here?" asked Tony.

Turning on his powerful underwater light, Frank replied, "I forgot to ask but you two should stay above sixty feet so you don't have any decompression issues. I'm just going to drop straight down right here and get a feeling for how this thing responds as the pressure goes up. I won't be long and I'll be on the radio."

"Okay, be safe!" said Tony.

When Frank was out of site, Tony wrote Jill another message to explain what was going on. He suggested they explore the top portion of the wall and, side by side, they gradually glided down the face, leveled out at fifty-five feet, and cruised along the strange anomaly in the ocean floor. In no time, Tony spotted a small octopus hanging on the wall and pointed it out to Jill. She'd made dozens of dives during her year in the Virgin Islands, but the marine life here was much different.

Meanwhile, Frank was still descending slowly, stopping frequently to check his rebreather console and to take in the sights.

As he passed the one hundred fifty foot mark, he made a mental note that he was now deeper than he'd ever been. At two hundred feet, he stopped to examine some interesting markings on the surface of the wall that showed up when he shined his light on them. Other than the normal tightening of his wet suit due to the pressure, he felt like he was in a pool. The rebreather had adjusted to the depth and his breathing was very relaxed and easy. He knew that at this depth with regular scuba gear he'd be suffering from a serious case of nitrogen narcosis, if he were still breathing at all.

Glancing at his watch, Frank noted that he'd only been descending four minutes, so he decided to press on a little further.

At three hundred feet, he decided he'd pushed his luck far enough. The pressure here was more than ten times the pressure at sea level and he knew some equipment wasn't rated for use at such extreme depths. As he turned to face the wall for his ascent, he caught a glimpse of what looked like a reflection off to his extreme left. He twisted his head, but there wasn't anything there. Fearing that he might be having a reaction to the depth, the gas mixture or both, he started up immediately. Every few seconds his eyes would tell him there was something just out of his view on the left or right but he couldn't ever actually spot anything.

Frank slowed his ascent to a stop at two hundred feet and grabbed on to an outcropping on the wall. Using techniques he'd learned thirty years earlier in the military, he closed his eyes and concentrated on his breathing to control his growing feeling of anxiety. Very slowly, he turned his body until his back was against the wall and he was facing out towards the open water. Feeling very much in control again, he opened his eyes and focused. His pulse rate immediately shot up when he saw a dozen or more shiny spheres gathered around him in a wide arc about twenty feet away!

Spinning back to the wall, Frank released air into his BC and began an emergency ascent.

After several minutes of leisurely swimming, Tony signaled to Jill for a U-turn and they ascended to the top of the wall for their return. It was also time to check in with Frank.

"Frank, how are you doing?" he asked.

When there was no reply, Tony tried again. And again there was no reply.

"Captain, can you hear me?" Tony asked.

"Yes, sir, but nothing from your friend, I'm afraid."

Chapter 22

The truck careened down the ramp and into the lower floor of a huge structure with Linda and Javier clinging to the tailgate for dear life. When the vehicle leveled out, Javier guessed that they had gone down three or four floors below ground level into what appeared to be a large, empty warehouse. Several rows of parking spaces were painted on the smooth concrete floor but the driver was cutting diagonally across the shadowy area and there were no other vehicles anywhere to be seen.

Javier leaned close to Linda and said, "When we stop, we need to be ready for anything. We may have to hide in here or we may have to make a run for it."

Javier removed a small pocket knife from his back pack and carefully slit the side panels of the truck from top to bottom on both sides before returning to Linda's side.

The truck started to slow down and Javier whispered, "Ready?"

When the vehicle finally came to a halt, the music in the cab stopped and the driver opened his door. Linda and Javier held their breaths and listened as his footsteps moved off in the direction of the front of the truck.

"Quick, get over the tail gate but stay low until we get a fix on him. And keep your eyes open for anyone else," instructed Javier.

Once on the ground, each took a different side of the truck and peaked around the large dual tires on either side.

"He's over here," whispered Linda from the right side. "He's in an office a few yards away talking on a telephone."

"There's no cover this way," replied Javier. "What about over there?"

"I can't tell, but he's facing this direction and if we make a run for it he's sure to see us. Wait, it looks like he's hanging up. Here he comes!"

Linda ducked back behind the tires and waited for the inevitable, but when she didn't hear approaching footsteps, she risked another look. The driver was on the phone again, only this time he had his back to them.

"Okay, go now!" cried Linda as she ducked low and raced for the nearby wall to the truck's right. Several large steel drums provided cover and when they were safely out of sight, Linda let out a huge sigh.

The driver soon returned to the truck but instead of getting back behind the wheel, he walked around back, leaned casually against the tailgate and lit a cigarette. Less than a minute later, the sound of a motorcycle disturbed the silence as it raced down the ramp and across the huge, underground facility. It slid to a stop behind the truck and the cyclist removed her helmet to reveal a mane of long, blonde hair. She kissed the truck driver passionately and then replaced the helmet while the man climbed on behind her. As quick as it had appeared, the motorcycle was gone, leaving the warehouse empty except for the truck.

"I'm betting that someone will be along shortly to move the truck," said Javier, speaking in a normal voice for the first time since leaving Manuel Lazo. "Let's get out of here while we can!"

A quick scan of the immediate area didn't reveal any doors, so they were forced to make their way towards the brightly lit office where the driver had used the telephone. At the back of the office there were two doors. One opened into a well-lit stairwell that led up and the other opened into a dark hallway that continued towards the back of the structure, away from the ramp leading to the surface.

"Too many lights," warned Linda as she opened the stairway door and glanced up. "If somebody *is* on their way here, that's where they'll be coming from. I vote for the hallway."

Before Javier could express an opinion about moving deeper into an unknown building, the door at the top of the stairwell slammed and their decision was made for them. They dashed through the hallway door and listened until they heard the truck engine roar to life. Linda flipped on a light switch that lit the few working lights and they moved quickly—but quietly—away from the office. They passed several doors but when Javier tried the knobs, they were all locked.

"This could be a dead end," whispered Javier. "If they're all locked, we'll have to go back."

"It doesn't look like this place has been used in a long time," Linda observed. "There's a door down at the far end. Let's check that out before we give up."

When they finally reached the end of the hallway, the door turned out to be made of steel, rather than wood, unlike the ones they had passed.

"This looks more promising," Javier commented as he turned the knob.

He had expected it to be locked, like the others, and he nearly fell down when the door swung open effortlessly.

"Careful," cautioned Linda as she stepped through the opening into a dark room that smelled of machinery, grease and sea air. "Let me see if I can find a light switch."

The switch she finally located turned on a single bulb above the door and provided just enough light to show that they were at one end of a large, mostly empty room. Several rows of seats, like long park benches, were positioned in the middle of the room and the scene reminded Linda of an old train station back home.

Using a switch outside the door, Javier turned the hallway lights off and eased the metal door shut.

"There must be another switch somewhere in here," he said hopefully. "Let's see what we can find before we head back."

During their examination of the room, they discovered a closed tin garage door on the long wall to the left and a large set of steel doors on the opposite. These opened vertically and reminded Linda of an old freight elevator she had once seen in a department store. As they examined the steel doors more closely, Linda picked up a familiar smell.

"The ocean!" she said. "This is probably an elevator up to a dock where they receive supplies."

"And passengers?" questioned Javier, indicating the benches.

"Sure, why not?" replied Linda. "Ernesto's boss implied that the locals were trading with a group from off the island— maybe this is the transfer point. Goods—and maybe people—arrive by ship, unload on a dock somewhere above us and are brought down here to be shipped out."

"Well, it would be a good way to hide the supply operation from spy satellites," agreed Javier. "They could unload at night and bring the stuff immediately down here for storage and distribution. That garage door probably leads to a connecting warehouse and, eventually, back to where we arrived in the truck."

"So what do you think?" asked Linda. "Have you seen enough? Shall we go back to the stairway—or try the elevator?"

"Well, if our theory is correct, there's more likely to be activity up above *now*, during the night. Maybe we should hang out here until morning and then try the elevator. If it works, we'll take our chances on the dock. If it doesn't—and judging by the surroundings, I'm guessing it won't—then we'll have to try the stairway. However, we know that's used because we just heard someone come down into the office. My guess is that there's office space above the warehouse and we're more likely to run into people in that direction."

"Well, frankly, I'm beat and I could really use a nap so hanging out here for a while sounds like a really good idea, but we're pretty exposed if someone comes in. Let's see what's behind those doors down there," said Linda indicating two standard doors at the far end of the room.

One of the doors turned out to be an empty closet but the other door revealed a small office, complete with wooden office desk, chair and several metal filing cabinets.

"This is more like it," smiled Linda as she entered the room and turned on the single overhead light. "Maybe we can find another chair somewhere and nap until morning."

"I don't need a chair," replied Javier. "You go ahead. I'm going to look around a bit but first I'm going to turn off that light at the other end. Leave the door open so I can find my way back here, okay?"

When he returned, he retrieved a flashlight from his back pack and turned off the overhead light. Linda was already asleep in the old, dusty chair so he closed the office door and moved to the filing cabinets. All three were locked so he propped himself up in a corner and soon fell fast asleep.

Awakened by the beeping of his watch alarm, Javier glanced at the face to see that it was 6:30 a.m. Sunday morning. He had slept sitting up for more than six hours and his neck was killing him but he laughed out loud when he saw that Linda had moved from the chair to a fetal position on the desktop sometime during the night.

"There's nothing funny over here," mumbled Linda without moving. "I'm starving! Are you ready to see what's above us?"

"I guess so, especially if there's hot, black coffee up there," replied Javier.

They gathered their back pack and beach bag and slowly cracked open the office door. There were no signs of life in the big outer room, so they quietly made their way across to the elevator doors.

Javier carefully examined the seam where the doors came together and Linda watched him with interest.

"What are you doing?" she asked.

"A little trick I learned from watching James Bond movies," he smiled. "I stuck a hair across the opening last night and it doesn't look like it's been disturbed. I don't think this thing has been used in years."

"Well, I hope it's safe," frowned Linda. "At least we're already at the bottom, so it has nowhere to fall!"

Javier pushed the upper door upward, which automatically lowered the bottom portion. The walls of the elevator car took on a soft white glow that bathed the interior in indirect light.

"That's a pretty fancy elevator for a dump like this," pointed out Linda. "Are you still sure this is a good idea?"

Javier nodded reluctantly and signaled Linda to proceed ahead of him. Once inside, Linda sought out the control panel to the right while Javier manually closed the large steel doors. As the doors touched, there was a single chime sound followed by a hissing sound. Javier jumped back as two horizontal doors, apparently made of the same material as the sides and back or the car, slid shut, followed by more hissing.

"I think we're sealed in," he said with a slight touch of panic in his voice.

"That's nothing! Check out these buttons!"

Javier crouched to examine the symbols on the three buttons. After a minute, he stood back up with a puzzled look on his face.

"It looks like a little Greek. Maybe they bought this thing overseas or maybe it's a used one. Due to the U.S. embargo, Cuba does a lot of trading with Europe, you know."

"Well it sure doesn't look as old and dilapidated as the rest of this building, so I'm feeling a little safer than I was feeling a minute ago," smiled Linda. "Are you ready?"

She pushed the top button and squeezed Javier's hand as unseen motors came to life. As the elevator started to move, Javier and Linda looked at each other in disbelief.

"It's moving sideways!" shouted Linda.

***

As Frank passed through one hundred fifty feet on his way to the surface, alarms sounded on the rebreather console so he slowed to a stop and clung to an irregularity in the wall's surface.

"*Are you injured?*" asked a voice. "*Do you need help?*"

Inside the full-face mask, Frank smiled to himself. Apparently some defense mechanism had kicked in and was making him settle down and take stock of his situation. Holding on to the wall with his right hand, he held up the now silent console and studied the digital display. As far as he could tell, everything was back to normal except for one blinking red light that was labeled "Decompression." Frank assumed that his panicked ascent had exceeded the rebreather's ability to correct his gas mixture but as he pondered what to do about the problem, the light went off.

"I'm okay now," Frank said out loud, just to hear his own voice. "I just freaked out for a minute."

"Frank! Frank, is that you?" Tony's voice boomed in Frank's ear. "Are you all right?"

"I'm fine," replied Frank. "I'm about a hundred feet down the wall and on my way back up. I got a little carried away and confused the rebreather, but everything seems to be okay now. I need to come up slowly, though, so why don't you two head back to the boat and I'll take my time so I don't get the bends."

There was a pause on the other end and then Tony replied, "Roger to half that. Jill's on her way to the surface, but I'm staying right here until I see your ugly head above the wall."

"That's not necessary. I have plenty of breathable gas. I'm just taking it slow so the rebreather can adjust things as I change depth."

"Whatever. But I'm waiting right here until you show up," replied a defiant Tony. "And you check in every couple of minutes or I'm coming down after you."

Twenty minutes later, the crew helped Frank and Tony out of the water and out of their gear.

"Well, that was certainly fun," laughed Frank as he brushed his wet hair out of his eyes.

"You had us worried for a while, old man!" replied Tony. "What happened, anyway?"

"Nothing, really. I drifted down to three hundred feet—I never did find the bottom of the wall, by the way—and then I started right back up. I think the sudden change in direction must have messed with the rebreather because I started seeing these glimpses of light just out of my field of vision. I was afraid the equipment was failing, so I panicked and started up too fast. At two hundred feet I even imagined that a bunch of spheres like the one we saw in Cuba were following me, but I finally got my act together and calmed myself down after I heard you ask if I needed help. It's been a long time since I was that spooked underwater. I had forgotten what it feels like!"

Tony looked confused. "I didn't ask if you needed help, Frank. You must have been hearing things."

One of the crewmen handed Frank a towel and whispered "Best not tell da boss 'bout dem spheres. He thinks he's only one what knows 'bout 'em."

Before Frank could respond, the man had disappeared down a short ladder that led below the main deck.

"So, have you learned your lesson about diving alone?" asked Jill sternly as she sat down beside Tony. "You scared the hell out of us, Frank!"

"I'm sorry, but there really wasn't anything to be concerned about," he smiled. "I don't know what happened to the communications gear, but physically I was fine. I think I just spooked myself, that's all."

That evening, Frank, Tony and Jill decided to meet Jim in town for dinner. He had called to excuse himself again, but Frank wouldn't hear of it and told him that if he wouldn't come to dinner they'd bring dinner to him. They met at a small Thai restaurant within walking distance of AUTEC's main gate and had the place mostly to themselves.

While they were waiting for the food to arrive, Frank brought up the subject of the DOD file Miles had showed him early in the day.

"Do they have one on me, too?" questioned Jill. "I haven't really been involved in your spy games, you know."

"Well, I didn't specifically see a file on you," smiled Frank. "Miles implied that it might have something to do with the Top Secret blanket the government threw over our expedition to Japan and, if that's the case, you were probably off their radar until you showed up here. Now, however, you probably have a nice thick file like the rest of us."

"And mine is going to get even thicker," said Jim, "because today the Navy started processing me for a security clearance of my own. I guess they figure that if I'm going to spend time at AUTEC they should look into my background, huh?"

"Well I can understand that," frowned Frank, "but it really bugs me that they'd spy on me—on all of us—when we've cooperated with them every step of the way. Poor Jim has given up the best parts of two missions because they classified his discoveries and it's beginning to sound like this one is headed in the same direction."

"Oh, man!" exclaimed Jim. "Do you really think so? I assumed the security clearance was just a formality."

"If they even suspect the triangles are alien artifacts, they'll hide them where they'll never be found again," agreed Tony. "They will be at the bottom of that Hole in the Ocean thing in a heartbeat."

"Tongue of the Ocean," corrected Jim. "And they'd better not try to take my three triangles away from me!"

Frank and Tony looked at each other and then at Jim.

"Three?" asked Frank with raised eyebrows.

"Hey, do I look stupid enough to hand them all over to the Feds?" smiled Jim. "Give me a little credit, please."

"You sneaky devil!" shouted Tony. "Smart, but sneaky! Where are the other two?"

"I have them hidden in the lab on base," smiled Jim. "I wanted them to be safe and where they wouldn't hurt anybody else, but where they would be in my control only, so I put two in my pocket on the way out there the first time. When the box was opened in the lab, it contained three triangles and I hid the other two the first time I was left alone. Even Ensign Mallory doesn't know about them."

"Maybe not," warned Frank, "but Miles does and he seems to be pretty tight with the folks at AUTEC. It's a gutsy move, Jim, but be careful, okay?"

"I will, but from what I hear, you're the one that needs to be careful. I hear you had a little excitement diving this afternoon!"

"Actually, I think Tony and Jill had all the excitement," replied Frank. "I was fine, except for an anxiety attack and some brief hallucinations."

"Hallucinations?" asked Jill. "I didn't hear about that! Sounds like a touch of nitrogen narcosis to me."

"That's what I assumed, too," nodded Frank. "However, one of the crewmen said something strange to me once I was back on board that has me wondering. Right after I started back up, I started seeing flashes or bright objects just out of my field of view. I tried turning, but I couldn't ever see anything. When I stopped to let the rebreather equalize, I turned towards the open ocean and thought I saw a bunch of spheres shadowing me and that's when I panicked!"

"You hallucinated about spheres?" pressed Jill.

"Well, I thought so, but that brings me back to the crewman. He overheard me telling Tony and he warned me not to tell Miles about the spheres, because Miles thinks he's the only one who knows about them or something like that. I didn't get a chance to question him further, but now it strikes me as a really odd comment."

"You know, I've had an uneasy feeling about that guy since the day he picked us up at the ship," said Tony. "I always get the feeling he's telling us half-truths and holding back information. I don't trust him, but in a friend rather then foe kind of way. Do you know what I mean?"

"Well put!" replied Frank. "And I know exactly what you mean. He's provided everything we've asked for but I always have the feeling he knows more than he's saying. Like the DOD files—he did take upon himself to tell me about them this morning, but he's had them since we arrived on Andros—and maybe before that!"

"And he knows all our secrets," frowned Tony. "You guys showed him the triangles and now they're locked up at AUTEC."

"Yes," frowned Frank, "and I made the mistake of telling him about Ian's discovery at the bottom of the wall over on Bimini. He also has a general idea that we explored some ruins near Cuba. However, I don't think he knows about the silver sphere we chased out of the ruins."

"Well, it sounds like he does know about spheres—he just doesn't know that we know," replied Tony. "And I vote we keep it that way!"

"Agreed," replied Frank. "But I'd like to find out how much he really knows without tipping our hand. If I could just get him to dive with me, maybe…"

"Frank!" shouted Jill. "You're not seriously considering another dive with that contraption! Are you crazy?"

"Yes to both questions," smiled Frank. "The equipment is safe, Jill, it's the diver that was screwed up today. Do you remember your first open-water dive? Do you remember how incredible it felt to be totally immersed in a world you knew you didn't belong in? Well, that's how I felt today at three hundred feet. I've probably made a thousand dives in my life and today's dive felt just like that first one. It's the call of the unknown—of course I'm going back!"

Sunday morning Frank was up early and ready when Miles called his room. They had arranged to meet at 6:30 a.m. sharp for the sixty mile drive north to Morgan's Bluff for another rebreather lesson and to dive some underwater caves that Miles wanted to show Frank. During the trip, Frank tried to use his library discovery to pry information out of his driver and dive instructor.

"Say, Miles, I was in the town library yesterday and I ran across a story about a UFO sighting up here at the Bluff. Did you ever hear anything about that?"

"There are a lot of strange sightings up this way," laughed Miles. "Which one was this?"

"It was about three years ago, I think. The newspaper said a lot of people saw it, including a local police chief, if I remember correctly."

"Ah, yes, that would be the infamous Constable Harney! He's been crowing about that ever since it supposedly happened. What a clown that guy is!"

"So there wasn't really a sighting?"

"Oh, yes, there was a sighting, alright, but like I said, there are a lot of sightings up this way. Most folks think they have something to do with AUTEC tests but a few are pretty hard to explain, even for AUTEC. In fact, I found the cave system we're going to dive quite by accident one day when I was up here checking out a sighting report."

"Really?" asked Frank, trying not to sound too interested. "Were you on official business or was it just personal curiosity?"

"This was strictly personal. Somebody from Red Bay reported objects entering and leaving the water at a high rate of speed and the story caught my interest so I did some investigating and eventually I found the blue hole system we're going to dive today."

"*In and out of the water*, huh? Any idea what shape they were?"

"Sure, Frank, they were shiny spheres, just like the one you and your team saw."

Chapter 23

The compartment Linda and Javier found themselves in continued to accelerate smoothly sideways for several seconds and then it began to decelerate just as smoothly.

"What's happening?" screamed Linda. "Javier, what's going on?"

Javier put his arms around Linda and held her as close as he could. Against the force of the acceleration, he inched them into a corner of the rectangular room and pressed against the smooth walls.

"I don't know, but I'm beginning to think this wasn't such a good idea," he whispered. "We seem to be slowing down, though, so be ready."

The elevator car or room or whatever it was, hissed to a stop and the interior became absolutely quiet.

"Welcome to Disneyland," said Linda to relieve the tension. "Now what?"

As if on queue, the doors they had entered through slid silently open and a chime sounded.

"I'd say that's the end of the ride," added Javier as he indicated the open doorway. "After you, my dear."

"Oh no you don't!" she replied. "If there are any big burly Russians out there, I want you leading the way. I'll be right behind you."

Linda held back while Javier picked up his back pack and stepped through the large opening into total darkness.

As soon as his body broke the plane of the doors, the walls of a room took on a glow similar to the interior of the car and the car's walls dimmed to darkness.

"*Please exit the transporter*," a soft voice said.

Linda pressed against the back wall even harder.

"Who's there?" she whispered.

"*Please exit the transporter*," the voice said again.

"Linda, look at this!"

This time it was Javier's voice, and it was coming from somewhere outside the car. Linda rushed to the door, looked both ways and spotted Javier a short distance away to her right.

"*Thank you*," said the voice. And with that, the doors hissed shut and any hope of retreat was lost.

"Linda, look! We're underwater!"

Javier was pointing to a small, round opening in the wall just past the now closed doorway.

"Well, that can't be good," she replied. "Where do you think we are?"

"We weren't moving very long, but it was impossible to judge how fast we were traveling," replied Javier. "What do you make of this room?"

"It looks like it was built by the same folks who built the transporter," replied Linda as she scanned their new surroundings.

"The what?" asked Javier.

"The *transporter*. Didn't you hear the voice telling me to get off the transporter?"

"The only voice I've heard in hours has been yours, Linda. Maybe you imagined it. Anyway, let's check this place out."

The room was essentially a cube about twenty feet on a side except that all the corners were rounded. The walls, floor and ceiling were all covered in a beige material that had the texture of pool table felt. There were no chairs, tables or other furniture. The lighting was indirect and it seemed to be radiating equally from the walls and ceiling.

While Linda stood in the center of the room and took in the big picture, Javier examined the walls carefully.

"It doesn't look very functional," Linda finally said. "And the interior decorator didn't have much of an imagination. What are you looking for so intently?"

"A call button," replied Javier. "When we got in the—ah, transporter—at the other end, you pressed a button to send us here. Doesn't it make sense that there would be a call button to bring it back?"

"Yes, I suppose it does," agreed Linda. "Unless no one ever goes back."

"Now you're just being morbid!" laughed Javier. "This technology is way beyond anything we've seen in Cuba, and I'm curious who it belongs to, but I'd also like to get out of here someday. Right now, I don't see any way to do that. Even the doors we entered through seem to be gone."

"That's impossible! They're right over... hey! What's going on?"

Linda's question was answered immediately. *"Please board the arriving transporter."*

"There!" she called to Javier. "Did you hear that?"

"Hear what, dear?" he asked.

"Please board the arriving transporter," he heard.

"Oh yeah, I hear it. Something about an arriving transporter. I guess we're going back after all.

Seconds later, a small door opened in the wall opposite where they had entered the room and Linda gasped in surprise.

"Please board the waiting transporter," the voice repeated.

"Now what are we going to do?" asked Linda. "The recording just keeps repeating 'Please board the waiting transporter' over and over."

"I'm not sure we have a choice, dear, but I only heard it once and even then I'm not so sure I *heard* anything as…"

"As *thought* it!" cried Linda. "You're absolutely right!"

Pushing her fingers into her ears as tight as she could, she yelled, "Can you hear us, too?"

"Yes, and it's not necessary to shout. Please board the waiting transporter," said the soft-spoken voice.

"It's in my head," she told Javier. "That voice is in my head!"

"Mine too!" exclaimed Javier. "It just asked me why you're shouting!"

"Please calm down and board the waiting transporter. There are no other options."

"Javier! Quick! Through the door! I think it's serious about this!"

As Linda ducked through the low doorway, the interior of a spherical chamber came to life with the now familiar glow. It wasn't quite tall enough to stand up in and it contained two opposing, offset high-back seats. Linda stepped through to the seat facing right and Javier piled into the closer one that faced left.

Again, they heard the chime and hissing sound that preceded the closing of the door. Linda gripped the hand rest on the seat in anticipation of sudden acceleration, but this time there was no movement. Instead, she detected a faint sweet smell and looked to Javier for an answer.

"Gas!" was the last thing she heard before she passed out.

Aware of faint sounds around her, Linda slowly opened her eyes and let them focus. The blurry, blue and white blob resolved into sky with high, fluffy clouds. Her brain was receiving no sensations from the rest of her body but she assumed she was lying on her back looking up at the sky. Or maybe she was dead.

"Is this what death feels like?" she asked herself.

"*You are well,*" said the voice again. "*The sedative was necessary to protect you during transport. You are safe now.*"

"Where am I?" questioned Linda silently. "Why can't I feel my body?"

"*You are well,*" replied the voice. "*Please be patient.*"

"Where am I?" screamed Linda again.

"Linda, is that you?" asked Javier's voice from nearby.

"Javier! Can you hear me? Am I speaking out loud?"

"Yes, I can hear you. Have you been hearing that voice, too? I can't move my muscles. I can't even turn my head towards the sound of your voice, but I can definitely hear you."

"I was told to be patient. Maybe whatever they did to us will wear off soon," replied Linda optimistically. "Any idea where we are?"

"I hear waves lapping against a shoreline, so maybe we're on the beach near the warehouse. Hey, wait, I think I can smell the ocean! I couldn't smell anything a minute ago."

Over the course of the next ten minutes, Linda and Javier gradually regained their motor control to the point where they could turn their heads from side to side and they discovered that they were lying head to head on a grassy area a few dozen yards from the edge of a cliff that looked out over open water. Linda could see her beach bag to her left and she remembered the satellite phone that had been in it.

"If my phone is still around, I'll call Frank as soon as I can move and we'll get some help out here," she promised Javier. "I'm sorry we got you into all this."

"Linda, if we get out of this alive, will you marry me?"

***

Frank looked at Miles with a mixture of anger and surprise.

"How long have you known about our encounter with the sphere?" he asked the former Navy SEAL.

"Since the day it happened," replied Miles without taking his eyes off the road. "It's part of my job, Frank."

"It's beginning to seem like everything I do is part of your job, Miles, and I'm getting pretty sick of..."

The ring of Frank's satellite phone cut him off in mid-sentence.

"Hello, this is Frank Morton," he said without taking his stare off Miles.

"Linda! Where are you? What do you mean you don't know? Near the ocean? There's a hurricane headed your way, woman! You need to find shelter immediately. No, we can't get the plane into Cuba until after the storm. Are you on the sat phone Edwards gave you? Okay, then read me the coordinates and I'll get back to you in a few minutes. Okay, got it. I'll check this out right now and call you back in a few minutes. Be sure you leave the phone on and keep the antenna pointed towards the satellite if you can. Yeah, you, too. Bye."

"Change of plans," he told Miles. "As you probably just heard, that was Linda. I didn't understand what happened to them, but they were knocked out by some kind of gas and when they regained consciousness they found themselves out in the open near the ocean. I need to get a fix on these coordinates and get them some help if I can."

Miles glanced at the numbers Frank had written on a hotel notepad and immediately pulled off onto the shoulder of the road.

"That can't be right," said Miles as he studied the pad. "Are you sure these satellite phones of yours display the phone's location?"

"Positive, why?"

"Because this latitude is about even with Miami—and that's more than 150 miles north of Cuba. In fact, it's even north of here! And the longitude is wrong, too."

Reaching between the seats of the van, Frank retrieved his briefcase from the floor behind his seat and rummaged through it until he found the piece of paper he was looking for.

"That's impossible!" he shouted. "Absolutely impossible!"

Frank handed the paper to Miles, who compared it to the coordinates Frank had taken from Linda.

"It's the same spot, alright. Where is it?"

"South Bimini Island—the spot where we dove with Ian!"

"Frank, that's impossible! Either she gave you the wrong information or the phone's GPS unit is broken. How could they have gotten from Cuba to Bimini without knowing it?"

"I have no idea," replied Frank. "Is there an airport on this end of the island?"

"Yes, but it will be a tight fit for your jet, if that's what you're thinking."

"Is it doable?" demanded Frank.

"Yes," replied Miles as he pulled back out onto the road and continued north. "The airstrip is about five miles ahead at New Town. Tell your pilot the chart code is MYNT."

Frank called Fitz' cell phone, but he got voice mail. Next, he tried the hotel phone number Fitz and Susan had given him the night before but he was told they had already checked out.

"No luck?" asked Miles as Frank lowered the phone.

"No, they've already left the hotel. They may be at the airfield in Miami Lakes or they may already be in the air headed this way. I guess we'd better turn around and head back to your hotel until they show up."

"Let me see your phone," said Miles, holding out his hand.

Miles dialed a number and spoke with someone for several minutes. Frank heard him repeat the New Town airport code at least twice.

"Done!" announced Miles as he handed the phone back to Frank. "You were right—they were just entering Bahamian air space. The Air Traffic Controller at AUTEC was able to contact them and they've been diverted up here. They should be on the ground in about fifteen minutes."

"How do you do that?" asked Frank in disbelief. "Is there anybody you don't know or have contact with?"

"Not on Andros," smiled Miles, "and not on Bimini, or any of the other western out-islands. Like I said earlier, Frank, it's my job."

Frank called Linda back and confirmed the coordinates displayed on her phone. When he told her that she and Javier were not on Cuba but were actually on Bimini, she laughed out loud.

"Frank, have you been drinking?" she asked.

"Just stay put. I'm on my way," Frank assured her before hanging up.

Within minutes, Miles brought the hotel van to a stop in front of the small building that served as the airstrip's terminal and administration building. When they entered the front door, Miles turned left, away from the waiting room.

"Follow me," he called over his shoulder. "I know the airport manager."

"Of course you do!" mumbled Frank as he followed Miles down the narrow hallway and through a door.

"Frank, this is Peter. Peter, Frank owns the Learjet that's inbound. Have you made contact with them yet?"

"Yes," replied the large man. "They should be coming in from your left in just a few minutes. I've been speaking with a gentleman, but apparently the pilot is a lady."

"Fitz—you've been talking to Fitz, and his wife, Susan, is piloting," acknowledged Frank. "Actually, they're both licensed to fly the plane, but she seems to get the tougher assignments."

"And who is Sandy?" asked the man at the desk that served as a control tower and communications center. "The gentleman also mentioned a Sandy."

"That would be Sandstrom, their dog," replied Frank. "He goes everywhere with them, but they hardly ever let him fly."

"Say, what!" said the man as he snapped his head around.

"Just kidding!" laughed Frank. "Listen, as soon as they're down, I'm getting aboard and we're heading to South Bimini. Can you file a flight plan for them so we can keep our ground time to a minimum?"

"Certainly, my friend, but we hardly ever get a plane like yours in here. Are you sure you wouldn't like to stay for a while?"

"Another time, maybe, but right now I have to get to Bimini as soon as possible. Miles, I'm going to get my dive gear out of the van. How do I get out on the tarmac?"

"I'll help you," replied Miles, "but just what are you planning to do with dive gear on Bimini? Maybe I'd better come along, too."

"No, that won't be necessary. I just want to have it along in case I need it. Besides, you need to get the van back to the hotel. I'll meet up with you later today and let you know the details."

"Okay, but I'm holding you to that! If they're really there—and I seriously doubt that they are—I want to know how it happened."

Twenty minutes later, Frank was aboard the Learjet and they were at the west end of the runway waiting for clearance. Fitz had briefed him on the takeoff procedure and he had the upmost confidence in his flight crew, but he knew both Susan and Fitz were a little nervous about the short runway. To make matters worse, the wind was blowing from the east, which meant they would be taking off right over the small municipality of New Town. If they didn't make it, well, Frank tried not to think about that as the two powerful engines behind him came to life and the aircraft strained against the brakes.

With a sudden jolt, the Learjet lurched forward and raced down the runway at full throttle. After what seemed like an eternity,

Frank felt the wheels leave the ground and the nose of the plane pitched up at an unusually steep angle. Seconds later a cheer from the cockpit eased his fears and he relaxed a bit.

"We're over open water and we didn't hit anything on the way out," reported Fitz via the intercom. "How about a round of applause for our flight crew?"

Frank was the only person in the cabin and he knew Fitz and Susan couldn't hear him, but applause seemed in order so he smiled and clapped.

As soon as the plane rolled to a stop on Bimini, Frank threw open the cabin door and ran down the steps to a waiting driver that Miles had arranged to meet the plane. Frank gave the man instructions to the rocky beach where Ian had taken them a few days earlier. When the small car stopped at the end of the gravel road, Frank jumped out.

"Wait here!" he shouted as he headed for the water line.

Frank jogged along the shore line, scanning to his left for any signs of Linda or Javier. After about a quarter of a mile, he came to a place where a high cliff dropped straight into the water and effectively cut off the shore line. While he was surveying the area and trying to decide what to do next, he heard a vaguely familiar voice.

"Your friends are near. Go back the way you came and follow the path up the hill."

Frank spun in place and yelled, "Who's there? Who said that?"

There was no reply, so Frank retraced his steps, watching for anything that looked like a path. He finally located a worn area in the short grass that covered the hillside and he turned away from the water. The path wound its way up the hill and Frank found himself on top of a small bluff that wasn't visible from below. There, in the middle of a large grassy area, he spotted Linda and Javier, sitting with their backs to him!

"Linda! Javier! I can't believe it—how did you two get here?"

"Frank!" yelled Linda. "Thank God you found us! Are we really in the Bahamas?"

When Linda spoke, Frank noticed that she didn't get up or even turn to face him, and he feared that she and Javier were injured. He ran to their position and circled around to face them.

"What's wrong?" he shouted. "Are you hurt?"

Javier attempted a laugh and replied. "Apparently we were drugged for our own safety during the trip, but I'm not sure how I know that. The feeling is slowly returning to our limbs, but neither of us can walk yet and twisting from side to side seems to be temporarily impossible. However, we're a lot better off then we were an hour ago."

"Are you in pain?" asked Frank as he knelt down in front of the two.

"No, just scared," replied Linda weakly. "One minute we were in an underground facility on Cuba and the next minute we were here! What happened, Frank?"

"I think you were 'rescued' by someone, Linda. Have either of you heard a strange voice but not been able to pin-point the source?"

"Yes!" shouted Linda. "It started in the elevator back in the warehouse but I thought it was coming through some kind of intercom system. It eventually directed us—*ordered* us, actually—into the device that brought us here. But then we heard it again after we woke up at this location. It seemed to be comforting us, in a strange sort of way, by telling us we were safe and to be patient."

"I've heard a voice, too," nodded Frank. "It started yesterday on a deep dive and it happened again just a few minutes ago. I was walking the shore line down below trying to find you two and it directed me up here."

"Frank, this is creepy! What's going on?" asked Linda with fear in her voice.

Frank sat cross-legged in the grass and described the dive he and Tony and Jill had made with Ian just a few hundred yards from their current position. When he repeated the note Ian had written on his dive slate before disappearing forever, Linda gasped.

"What do you think he had to do?" she asked. "And what did he mean by '*I'll come back if I can*'?"

"I don't know, Linda. I just don't know. The assumption was that his rebreather got the better of him and he suffered some form of narcosis, but now I'm beginning to wonder. Maybe he heard the same voices we've heard and they told him to do something stupid."

"But Frank," objected Javier, "the voice we've heard led us out of trouble, not into it. It even led you up here to us, right?"

"That's true," agreed Frank as he gazed out into Nicholas Harbor, "and there's only one way to know for sure what Ian encountered out there. As soon as you two are able to walk, I'm going to take you back to the Learjet, which is waiting at the airport, a short distance from here. I'm sure Susan has some snacks hidden away and she and Fitz can keep an eye on you while I test a theory."

"Frank, what are you going to do?" questioned Linda.

Without taking his eyes off the water, he said, "I'm going to look for Ian."

Chapter 24

Frank stayed with Linda and Javier until they had fully recovered the use of their limbs and then he helped them down the path and back to the waiting car. What ever drug they had been given was extremely powerful but once it wore off there were no apparent side-effects such as nausea or headaches. By the time the driver brought the car to a stop at the small South Bimini air terminal, both Linda and Javier were feeling as good as new.

Fitz, Susan and a tail-wagging Sandstrom waved from the open cabin door as the three climbed out of the car and up the stairs into the Learjet.

"Welcome to the Bahamas," greeted Fitz. "I can't wait to hear how you two got here!"

"Well, as soon as you get them fed you'll have your chance," said Frank, as he made his way towards the back of the plane to retrieve his dive gear. "I'm going for a quick swim while you get these two re-energized."

"Frank, are you sure you should do that alone?" worried Linda. "And what is that contraption?"

Frank held up the bright yellow device and replied, "This is my new favorite toy. It called a rebreather and, as the name implies, it allows a diver to reuse his air supply by continuously replacing the oxygen. It's the coolest thing I've ever seen!"

"What's the advantage over a standard air tank?" asked a curious Fitz.

"Well, for one thing, there aren't any bubbles because no air is exhausted into the water," explained Frank. "More importantly, though, it allows short dives down to nearly five hundred feet or shallower dives lasting up to ten hours. But I won't be that long, I promise! You two get some nourishment and rest. I'll be back in just a few minutes."

Frank piled his gear into the back seat of the small sedan and then climbed into the passenger's seat beside the driver.

"Back to the beach, please," he instructed.

Carefully, Frank waded out to the top of the wall. After inflating his BC, adjusting his mask and checking his air flow, he stepped off into the water that he knew was more than three hundred fifty feet deep. With one final check of the rebreather's console, Frank purged the air from his BC and began his downward descent.

At seventy-five feet, he passed the rectangular tunnel that was dumping cold water into the warm tropical sea and he shivered as he passed through the thermal anomaly. At one hundred feet he slowed his descent briefly to review the console. Frank was determined to make it to the bottom and he knew he wouldn't survive an equipment failure at that depth. Descending once again, he kept his eyes on the dark, smooth surface of the wall. He had his underwater light ready because he kept expecting to be immersed in darkness at any second. He was surprised when his feet hit the sandy bottom because he still had at least one hundred feet of visibility.

He gave his rebreather a minute to adjust, checked the console again and then turned away from the wall. Although it still startled him, Frank was not surprised to see the shiny sphere that was hovering about fifty feet away. He was tempted to approach it, but he didn't think it would let him get too close and the sphere wasn't really his objective on this dive, anyway. He was looking for the triangular, wall-like structure that he'd seen on Ian's camcorder.

Frank swam east, along the wall, with his body a few feet above the sand. He focused his attention to his right, away from the wall, and within a minute he spotted what he was looking for. It was no more than twenty feet from the base of the wall and it only protruded about three feet out of the sand. He slowly cruised back and forth over the structure, trying to capture a permanent mental image of its shape and size. The area inside the low, triangular wall was dark, and this puzzled Frank because the surrounding sand was such a brilliant white. His curiosity finally got the best of him and he dipped down to get a better look. By the time he felt the downward suction, it was too late and he was being pulled towards the triangular opening he had mistaken for dark sand.

Frank kicked as hard as he could and when he couldn't immediately overcome the downward pull, his thumb instinctively went to the inflator button on his BC. He heard air rush into the empty pouches and, just for an instant, his direction reversed but then the mysterious force intensified and he was once again headed down. He had managed to get his feet below him and as his fins dropped past the top of the triangular structure's outer perimeter, several alarms on the rebreather console went off all at once.

Frank looked up at the surface and spotted the sphere right above him.

"Help!" he yelled to no one in particular.

He felt a jerk, as if someone had grabbed the back of his BC, and he began to rise slowly out of the dark cavity. Before he could figure out what was happening, he found himself standing on the white sand a few feet from the wall.

Above the sound of the alarms, he thought he heard a voice say, *"You must control your breathing or your body will suffer permanent damage. Please calm down."*

As if in a dream, Frank realized that he was hyper-ventilating and that the rebreather was not able to provide the oxygen his body was demanding. Simultaneously, he concentrated on slowing his breathing while he manually increased the flow of oxygen into his re-circulated air supply. In a matter of seconds the alarms had silenced and Frank took mental stock of his situation. Apparently the air had been let out of his BC, because he was no longer buoyant.

"Are you still there?" he gasped.

"Yes," was the reply.

"Who are you? Where are you?" demanded Frank.

"Those are difficult questions to answer," came the reply. *"At least in terms you can understand."*

"Well try!" yelled Frank. "Did you just save my life?"

"Another difficult question," was the reply. *"It depends on how you define life."*

Frank looked at the rebreather console and then returned the oxygen flow to the automatic mode.

"Well, thank you, anyway," he said. "I don't have more than a couple of minutes before I have to return to the surface. What's that hole I was being pulled into?"

"You would call it an entrance," was the reply. *"You did not wish to enter, so we removed you from the area."*

"So am I talking to the sphere I saw?"

"Indirectly, yes. The spheres are what you would call our ears and eyes."

"Did you bring my friends here from Cuba?"

"Yes."

"Why?" asked Frank.

"They were in danger."

"And why did you bring them here, to Bimini?"

"Because the female wanted to rejoin you and this location was convenient for us."

"Just who is 'us'?"

"Enough questions. You must surface now, for your own safety."

Frank checked the console and realized that he'd overstayed the time he had allotted for the dive.

"Yeah, you're right but I have a million questions to ask you. Can we continue this later?"

"If you wish."

"I do, I do," replied Frank emphatically. "Shall I come back here?"

"No, we will contact you. Now please go."

Frank tapped the inflator button gently and began a slow, controlled ascent to the surface. He had intended to limit his bottom time to five minutes and it had already been nearly ten so he stopped every fifty feet on his way up to let his rebreather stabilize and adjust. He hung at thirty feet for ten minutes and at fifteen feet for another five minutes. When his head finally broke the surface, he saw his driver pacing the shore line and talking on his cell phone.

Frank floated over the top of the wall and stood up so the driver could see him. The man raced out knee-deep into the water shouting and waving his arms.

"My God, man, I thought you had drowned," yelled the driver angrily. "You said you'd be back fifteen minutes ago!"

"Sorry about that," apologized Frank. "I must have lost track of time. Give me a hand with this gear, will you? By the way, you do realize that your pants are all wet, right?"

When they arrived at the airstrip, Frank had the driver wait while he went aboard the Learjet and stowed his dive gear. Returning to the ground, he handed the driver a hundred dollar bill.

"I hope we can keep my poorly planned dive just between us," smiled Frank.

The driver looked at the bill and smiled broadly.

"What dive was that, sir?"

As the Learjet leveled off on its way back to Andros, Linda questioned Frank about his dive.

"When you left, you said you were going to look for Ian. Did you find him?"

"No, not exactly," replied Frank quietly, "but I'm not done looking." Changing the subject, he asked, "So, what did you find out about the inhabitants of the peninsula?"

"Not too much, I'm afraid," frowned Linda. "Our plan to get there worked out perfectly except that the truck we chose to hitch a ride in went directly into an underground warehouse and while we were trying to find our way to the surface, we got kidnapped by whoever brought us here."

"We did get a little second-hand information about the peninsula, though," interjected Javier. "It's apparently a rather lawless region where even the Castro regime doesn't have much control. We were told it was taken over by a group of Russian criminals-turned-construction workers who settled there after the missiles were pulled out because they weren't allowed to return to Russia."

"Are you sure?" asked Frank. Now that he knew more about how and why the pair had been transported to Bimini, the Russian connection didn't make much sense.

"What about the facilities?" he pressed. "Did they appear to look old or new?"

"A little of both," answered Linda. "The warehouse looked like it could be fifty years old. It was mostly wooden, with large beams supporting the ceiling, and the connecting offices looked like something out of the fifties. Even the waiting room where we discovered the first transporter reminded me of an old train station back in the States. But the vehicle—I guess that's what you would call it—looked much more contemporary. And I remember that it had strange symbols on the buttons. I just punched the top one because we were trying to get to the surface."

"Strange symbols?" repeated Frank, his interest suddenly peaked. "Did they by any chance look like Greek letters?"

Linda thought for a minute and then said, "Yes, I suppose that would be a good way to describe them. How did you know?"

"Just a guess. Miles Adderly, our hotel host, showed Jim and me some books he found in his library and Jim thinks they're written in a very early form of Phoenician, the language that eventually evolved into Greek."

"Wow, that's weird!" said Linda. "That would imply a connection between the Bahamas and the Cuban peninsula, wouldn't it?"

"Yes it would," nodded Frank. "But there's more to the story. One of the books has a drawing of a triangle on the last page and it's an exact copy of the real thing."

"You mean those triangles you found with the ROV," exclaimed Javier, "the ones that made me so sick?"

"Yes, and they've already resulted in one death on Andros," replied Frank. "It's odd, because some people have no reaction at all to them while others get very, very sick. We almost lost Jill three days ago and yet Jim plays with them all day long."

"Wow," said Linda. "Is Jill okay now?"

"Yes, she seems to be, but Jim has moved the triangles to the AUTEC facility so we don't endanger any more unsuspecting folks. He actually has a lab there and we only see him in the evenings. He thinks he's on the verge of a breakthrough with those strange changing symbols and he's even hooked up with a Navy researcher who speaks his tech language."

"Good for him!" replied Linda. "If you can't beat 'em, join 'em!"

"Listen, there's something else you two should know before we get back to the hotel," frowned Frank. "You remember Miles, right? He picked us up at the ship and we later found out that he owns the Bay Club Resort, where we're staying."

Both Linda and Javier nodded.

"Well, our friend Miles is apparently involved in a lot more than just operating a hotel. He always seems to know more than he lets on and I suspect he's connected to the U.S. government at a pretty high level. He's a former Navy SEAL and he's in cahoots with Buzz Edwards somehow. I'd bet a hundred dollars that Edwards already knows about your mysterious arrival on Bimini. Having said all that, Miles seems to be a pretty straight-up guy and yesterday morning he shared something with me that I wasn't supposed to know about. Apparently Edwards—or whoever he works for—has been compiling very detailed dossiers on each of us. Mine goes back to at least when I won the lottery, and probably further back than that."

"Couldn't it just be routine background information collected to support the security clearances we were granted last year in Las Vegas?" asked Linda.

"Oh, there's some of that, to be sure, but my file included some details about Alex and me that go way beyond a routine background check. In fact, the information could have only been obtained by planting an eavesdropping device in my hotel room in Merida!"

"Didn't Edwards show up in Mexico while you and Jim were down there?" asked Linda.

"Yup! That's already occurred to me, too. I understand the concept of national security, but when my alleged allies start recording personal and private conversations, it makes me mad."

"You know..." began Javier.

Linda snapped her fingers and shouted, "The hotel room in Pinar del Rio!"

"As I was saying," smiled Javier, "we're pretty sure our room was bugged and we know for sure it was searched while we were out for dinner one evening. We, of course, assumed the Cuban government was up to no good but maybe we suspected the wrong bad guys."

"And Olvera! He slipped up and called me by my real last name when he handed us off to his driver."

"Olvera?" asked Frank.

"The government official who hosted the environmental conference Javier and I used as a cover to get into Cuba," explained Linda. "And he also coerced us into doing some spying for him in Pinar del Rio. I'll bet our cover was blown before we ever left Cancun."

"Who arranged the trip and the cover stories?" asked Frank

"Edwards, of course! We've been unwittingly working for him since we arrived in Cancun," said an angry Linda.

"And maybe longer than that," said Frank. "A year ago, when I decided to dig into some unsolved archaeological mysteries, I never expected to become a pawn of my own government."

"I know what you mean," agreed Linda. "And, Frank, after seeing the way the regular people of Cuba are forced to live because of our embargo, it just makes me sick. Javier and I visited a beach restoration project in western Cuba that's as good as anything on this planet but nobody will ever know about it unless someone gets the word out."

"Well, NWIDI has the resources, if you have the ambition," smiled Frank. "You'd probably have to publish outside the U.S. though."

"Well, actually, Frank, there's something you should know before we land, too. While we were semi-paralyzed back there on Bimini, Javier proposed to me, and I accepted before he had the mobility to run away!" Linda squeezed Javier's hand and he hugged her back. "I'm going to move to the Yucatan and write about some of the really great work quietly being done for the sake of the environment. And Javier's going to continue his work with Centro Ecológico Cancun until my writing makes us rich and famous."

Linda's announcement caught Frank completely off guard and he was silent for several seconds.

Finally, realizing that the newly engaged couple was waiting for a response, Frank raised his plastic water bottle and toasted them. "To a long and happy life together! I'm very happy for you both and I wish you nothing but the best."

Linda and Javier breathed a collective sigh of relief and laughed out loud.

Seeing Frank's questioning look, Linda said, "We weren't sure how you'd take the news. You do realize this means that I'll be leaving NWIDI, right?"

"I do," frowned Frank, "but world-class champions of the environment are one in a million, and you're definitely one in a million, Linda. This calls for a big celebration when we get to the hotel. We'll have the whole team together—maybe for the last time—and I'll get Miles to cater the event. This is public information, isn't it?"

Linda and Javier looked at each other, shrugged and then laughed.

"Yes, I guess so," beamed Linda, "but I want to tell Jim privately before you make any big announcements. He and I have always considered ourselves the weaker but saner half of the NWIDI team and we became close friends when we stayed behind in Japan earlier this year."

"Understood," agreed Frank. "In fact, it's your news, so it should be up to the two of you to make any announcements. Just don't take too long, because I'm terrible at keeping secrets!"

When the Learjet taxied up to the Andros Town terminal, Frank spotted the familiar Bay Club van waiting just outside the fence.

"Don't mention the surveillance files in front of Miles, okay? I'd like to find out who's behind them without Miles knowing how concerned we are."

Frank, Linda and Javier waited in the van with Miles while Fitz and Susan secured the aircraft and gathered their bags.

"So, how was the dive?" asked Miles making casual conversation.

"How do you know I dove at all?" challenged Frank from the back of the van.

"Frank, you had a look of determination in your eyes that even a clump of sea grass could have read. And, besides, you took the rebreather. I didn't figure you needed it for ballast on the flight over. So, how was the dive? Did you find the young dive master?"

"Unfortunately, no," replied Frank honestly. "But I did look for him. The rebreather will need charging before it's used again because I went clear to the bottom—more than three hundred fifty feet down."

"Frank!" scolded Linda. "You didn't say you were going to do that!"

"For obvious reasons," replied Frank. "It's actually quite comfortable, once you get the hang of it."

"Frank, I think you should stop by the office this afternoon and let me run you through some routine rebreather maintenance because I'd like you to keep the unit you've been diving with," called Miles from the front of the van.

"I couldn't do that, Miles. Those things must cost a fortune!"

"That one is actually priceless, because I made some special Navy modifications to it, but I insist, Frank. If an Airman is going to pretend to be a SEAL, the least I can do is make sure he has top-notch gear."

"I really appreciate that, Miles. I'll take good care of it, I promise."

"You bet you will, Airman," laughed Miles, "starting at 1500 hours today!"

Frank called Tony and Jill from the airport and they greeted Linda and Javier as they climbed out of the van in the hotel parking lot.

"No luggage?" laughed Tony. "You must be traveling light!"

"I can't believe we're here at all," replied Linda. "But yes, most of our things are back in Cuba."

"It sounds to me like a shopping trip is in order," smiled Jill. "We haven't met, but I've heard so much about you from the guys that I feel like I've known you for years. How about if you and I drag the boys into town and get you two supplied?"

Frank pulled his wallet out and handed Linda his NWIDI credit card. "By 'boys' I assume she means 'boy friends' so I'll hang out here with the Fitzgeralds until you four get back. Maybe I'll work on the plans for that dinner we talked about earlier."

"Okay, but remember that I want to talk to Jim myself," said Linda. "Will you make sure he joins us tonight?"

"If I have to carry him there on my back," laughed Frank. "You guys have fun and try to stay out of trouble."

Frank had a light lunch with Fitz, Susan and Sandstrom at the pool bar and then he let them have some time to themselves to explore the hotel property and the marina. At 3:00 p.m. he knocked on Miles private office door and sat through an hour of training on how to change the lithium hydroxide scrubbers, the oxygen cylinder and the diluent canisters. During the training session, Frank's unit was completely refurbished and ready to go diving again. As Miles was reviewing the unit's console to confirm its status, he spotted something out of the ordinary.

"Okay, spill it, Frank. The console doesn't lie and it looks like you had every alarm on the system going off at once here. I'm curious about what happened, but I'm even more curious about how you survived!"

"Oh yeah, that. I meant to tell you about that. I found an underwater vent—only in reverse—and I got a little excited when it started pulling me in. I managed to get away, but my excitement upset the computer. I got myself under control pretty quickly and I added oxygen manually, but by then the alarms were going off."

"*An underwater vent in reverse?* Are you telling me it was sucking water in, rather than shooting it out?"

"Yes, I guess that describes it pretty well. It was a bit odd."

"No, Frank, that would make it a geological impossibility, not 'a bit odd' and it probably explains what happened to your dive master."

"Could be," said Frank, trying to get off the subject. "If we're done here, I need your help arranging a special dinner for my growing group. Linda and Javier are newly engaged and they're going to make the announcement tonight."

About 6:00 p.m. Frank called Jim's cell phone to see what time they could expect him.

"Frank, there's been an 'incident' here in the lab and I may not be able to leave for a while. Can I call you back later?"

Chapter 25

"What kind of incident?" Frank asked. "Are you alright, Jim?"

"Yes, yes, I'm fine, but I can't talk right now. I need to call you back, okay?"

"I take it you're not at liberty to speak freely," guessed Frank.

"Yes, that's correct," replied Jim evasively.

"Well, listen, Linda and Javier are back from Cuba, so try to make it by at least 8:00 p.m. We have a lot to talk about."

"They are! When... how did...? the last I heard, you and Tony were planning a rescue mission to go in after them," stammered Jim. "Did they get out on their own?"

"Well, sort of, but I'll explain it all later. Just be sure you're at the hotel by 8:00 p.m. See you in a couple of hours."

Frank wandered out to the pool bar, where he found Fitz and Susan enjoying a drink and the last few minutes of daylight.

"Beautiful weather, isn't it?" he greeted.

"It sure is," replied Fitz, "but I hear that's going to change soon. The storm that's bearing down on western Cuba is predicted to turn east over land and head this way. We should probably think about getting the plane out of here tomorrow."

"I'll leave that up to you," smiled Frank. "Pick out a couple of alternate airports in case we have to evacuate, but let's wait until the last minute to move, because I'd really like to hang around here for a few more days unless the weather chases us out. Besides, the storm could have a change of heart and head north, instead of east and then we'd be right in its path again."

"I'll look for some alternatives south of here," agreed Fitz. "The Virgin Islands or Puerto Rico might be good choices."

Miles had apparently spotted Frank at the bar and he jogged over from the main building to join them.

"Everything's all set up for tonight," he puffed as he caught his breath. "Did you talk to Jim?"

"Yes, but there's been some sort of 'incident' at the lab that he couldn't talk to me about. The best I could get out of him was a definite maybe."

"An incident?" questioned Miles. "That doesn't sound good. I'll make a few calls and see what I can find out. Anyway, I couldn't get anybody to cater here at the hotel on such short notice, but my friend Calvin has offered to host your group again, if you can put up with his bad jokes."

Frank groaned. "That will definitely make Tony happy, but I don't know if my stomach can handle all that spicy food twice in one lifetime."

"I guessed as much," smiled Miles, "so I talked him into adding steak and baked potatoes to the menu, just for you. I've got some errands to run, but I'll meet you all in the lobby at 7:45 p.m. and I'll run you over to Calvin's in the van."

Tony, Jill, Linda and Javier joined the group about thirty minutes later and Frank took Linda aside to tell her about the dinner party and to fill her in on Jim's situation.

"That sucks!" responded Linda. "We haven't said anything to Tony and Jill because we want it to be a surprise. Did you tell Fitz and Susan?"

"Not a peep," he replied. "Unless they overheard you talking on the flight down from Bimini, they're still clueless. Miles knows, of course, because I needed his help putting tonight's event together, but I swore him to secrecy. If Jim can't make it tonight, maybe you can call him before he finds out from the others."

"I suppose," frowned Linda, "but I'd rather talk to him in person. Maybe…"

Linda was cut off by the ring of Frank's cell phone.

"Hello," he answered. "Hey, that's good news! We'll see you there. Do you remember where it is? Oh, yeah, I suppose that's true. Okay, see you at 8:00 p.m. Bye."

"That was Jim," Frank announced to the group. "He's going to be able to make it after all, but he's going to meet us there. I suppose we should start getting ready, huh?"

Frank insisted that Miles join them for dinner, and as soon as they arrived at the restaurant, Frank disappeared into the kitchen to find Calvin. He handed the big man a folded stack of one hundred dollar bills and when Calvin tried to refuse the money Frank stood his ground.

"This is the second time in three days you've treated us to your hospitality and great food and I insist that you keep it. Share it with your staff, if you like, but I know it costs money to run an operation like this and my whole crew thanks you for accommodating us on such short notice."

Seeing that he wasn't going to talk Frank out of it, Calvin slipped the bills into his pocket and nodded humbly.

"My staff and I appreciate it very much, Mr. Morton." And then a huge smile spread across the black man's face and he shouted, "Now let's have some fun!"

The first round of drinks had just been served when Jim entered the room to cheers and applause and Linda tipped her chair over jumping up to greet him.

"You'd think she was engaged to Jim," whispered Miles.

"For a while I thought that might happen," grinned Frank, "but instead they just became very close friends. I want to talk to him about what's going on at AUTEC before the evening is over, but it looks like Linda is going to kidnap him for a while."

"I have some details about the so-called incident that I'll tell you about later but I'm interested in hearing his version first."

Before Jim even had a chance to sit down, Linda dragged him back out into the foyer and broke the news of her engagement to Javier. When they re-entered the dining room, both were smiling from ear to ear. Jim took a place at the table next to Frank and Linda stood behind Javier. Anticipating what was to come, Frank tapped his fork on the edge of his water glass to get everyone's attention. Even Calvin and the restaurant staff appeared in the kitchen doorway.

"Can I have your attention for a minute?" asked Linda after clearing her throat several times. "I would like to announce that Javier and I are officially engaged to be married."

Before she could continue, the group broke out in another round of cheers and applause. Even those who already knew clapped loudly and Linda held up her hand to quiet the noise.

"You're all invited—and expected—at the wedding, of course. We haven't set a date, but we're thinking about sometime between Thanksgiving and Christmas. That would give us—and all of you—a couple of months to prepare. The ceremony is going to be in Cancun, where we also plan to live, and hurricane season should be over by then so there will be no excuses!"

Although Frank knew about the engagement, the timing surprised him a bit.

"So when are you two heading back to Mexico?" he asked, trying to sound casual and hide his own emotions.

"Actually, Frank, we'd like to go as soon as possible. We don't want to leave you in the lurch here, but we have a lot of things to arrange before the wedding and I need to get back to Seattle and close up things there. Say, you wouldn't be interested in buying a condo, would you?"

"I was going to ask you the same thing," laughed Frank. Standing up, he raised his glass and said, "I'd like to propose a toast to the future Mr. and Mrs. Reyes. As my favorite alien often said, *'live long and prosper!'*"

Calvin and his staff served plate after plate of food and when the main course arrived, Frank took the opportunity to quietly query Jim.

"So tell me about this incident," he said in a voice only Jim could hear.

"Well, for one thing, I got caught hiding the other two triangles. I maintained that I had them stashed away as a control, in case our testing damaged the other three, but I don't think they completely bought my story. But more than that, chemical analysis has determined beyond any doubt that the objects didn't originate here on Earth, so now the government has once again stepped in and classified the entire investigation Top Secret."

"Damn them!" cursed Frank. "So you're out in the cold again, right? They'll confiscate the triangles, bury them somewhere and pretend this never happened!"

"Actually," whispered Jim, "I'm not being chased away, Frank. In fact, quite the opposite has happened—this afternoon I had to agree to become a 'civilian consultant' under contract to the Navy and to remain here at AUTEC for an 'unspecified period of time' while we get to the bottom of the triangle mystery. I'm sorry, but the fact that I had hidden away two of the triangles put me in a pretty weak bargaining position."

Frank chewed his steak and processed what Jim had just told him.

"You did what you had to do, of course, but what's the mystery if they already know the triangles are alien artifacts? It seems like the case is closed."

"Oh, no," replied Jim. "The real mystery is the messages that appear on the surface of the triangles—those changing messages we discovered back on the Atlantic Protector. It turns out that the messages on the triangles form a long repeating series and each of the triangles is repeating the same pattern. It took us a while to figure this out because the series is thirty-seven messages long and each triangle was at a different point in the series. However, my associate and I have been able to decipher some of the symbols and we're on the verge of a major breakthrough!"

"No kidding! You sound pretty excited about this work. What do you think the message is?"

"Do you remember the messages I decoded on the Loltun spheres?" asked Jim.

"Of course I do. They turned out to be the locations of total solar eclipses visible to the Maya. They were specified in polar coordinates, if I remember right."

"That's right! The numbers on the spheres provided a straight-line distance from a fixed point and an angle from a known reference line. In the case of the spheres, the fixed point was Loltun Cavern and the line was one that ran exactly east and west through the same point. Well, we think we've found the same type of pattern with the triangles! While most of the alphabet is still a mystery to us, we've got the numbers figured out and we think they represent coordinates—specific places on Earth."

"Really!" exclaimed Frank as he abandoned his meal and twisted in his chair towards Jim.

"Yes, but this was a much more difficult challenge because we didn't have any clue where the reference point was. Instead, I guessed at some destination locations and we reverse-engineered the problem."

"You mean you know where some of these locations are? Spill it Jim! Where are they?"

Almost whispering, Jim said, "On a hunch, I started with Loltun, Yonaguni and the underwater site near Cuba. With the help of the AUTEC computer center, we think we're on the right track. It's just a matter of time before we nail down the remaining locations."

"That's incredible!" replied Frank, trying to keep his voice down. "If my theory about alien intervention at Loltun, Yonaguni and Cuba is correct, that would mean there are thirty-four more sites to investigate! But the big news is the reference point. Where's that, Jim?"

"Frank, I know this is going to sound funny, coming from me, but I'm afraid I can't tell you that."

"Come on, old buddy! I promise I won't say a word to anyone, but you have to tell me where it is. This is huge!"

Jim carefully unbuttoned one of the middle buttons on his shirt.

"I'm sorry, Frank, but you know how this security stuff works. I was given very specific instructions about what I could and couldn't say tonight, especially to you."

Jim pulled his shirt apart just enough for Frank to see the elastic band around the younger man's chest.

"You're wearing a wire?" shouted Frank in surprise.

The words had barely left Frank's mouth when a pager on Jim's belt started beeping loudly. A second later, a Navy Shore Patrolman appeared in the doorway of the restaurant.

Sheepishly, Jim looked around the table.

"Oops!" he said. "I believe my ride is here. Good night everyone, and congratulations, you two. I hope to see you in Cancun."

And with that, Jim walked quickly to the door, followed closely by the SP.

The stunned group sat in silence for a long minute before Tony finally asked, "Did you say he was wearing a wire?"

Still staring at the door, Frank nodded.

"Yup!" replied Frank. Turning his attention to Miles, he continued. "Did you know about this? If anything happens to him, I swear, I'll..."

"I had no idea, Frank!" interrupted Miles. "I'll look into it. Excuse me."

Miles left through the same doorway Jim had just disappeared through and the room was silent again.

In an attempt to lighten the mood, Linda said, "That little twerp certainly knows how to steal the show, doesn't he?"

Forced chuckles from around the table did little to improve the mood and when Calvin came in from the kitchen carrying a tray of deserts, he noticed the two empty chairs.

"Where is everybody?" he asked. "Don't they like sweets?"

"Jim had to return suddenly to AUTEC and Miles went to find out why," explained Frank without looking up.

"No worries, then!" smiled the large man indicating the doorway. "He's back already!"

When Miles appeared, he was just closing his cell phone.

"Everything is fine," he announced with a weak smile. "The Navy has a particular interest in the work Jim is doing right now and they know he's relatively new to handling classified information. He really wanted to be here tonight and the monitoring device was the Navy's condition for allowing him to join you. But, I assure you, he's not in any danger or serious trouble."

The explanation seemed to satisfy the group and the three couples—Tony and Jill, Fitz and Susan, and the bride-and-groom-to-be—quickly resumed their chatter about the upcoming wedding.

Miles indicated that Frank should follow him and then disappeared into the foyer.

Outside, Frank shook his head.

"It was my fault," he frowned. "I was pressing him for some information that he'd already told me he couldn't disclose. He showed me the wire to explain why he couldn't tell me and I blew his cover."

"Don't sweat it," consoled Miles. "They know Jim has a loyalty to you and he'll get past this. I wouldn't expect to see him off the base anytime soon, though. He's on the verge of something big and they know how valuable he is to the project, so they're going to keep pretty close tabs on him. The good news is that he's really into his work and probably wouldn't leave if they told him to. He'll be fine, Frank, and I have someone keeping an eye on him, just in case."

"Thanks, Miles. I haven't figured out whose side you're on yet, but I appreciate your help."

"It's a complicated game, my friend, and there are more than just two teams playing it," smiled Miles, "but how about this as a peace offering? The location you wanted Jim to tell you about is just off the southern coast of South Bimini—very close to the place where you found Linda and Javier."

"The triangular opening that tried to suck me in!" shouted Frank. "That's the center of these thirty-seven points?"

"Quite possibly," nodded Miles. "And I think you and I should make a trip up there at our earliest convenience. However, we need to keep this just between you and me, okay? If word gets out that you've already been to the location Jim just discovered, you and I will find ourselves confined to AUTEC as well, and I don't think either of us would enjoy it as much as Jim does."

"Understood," replied Frank. "It sounds like Linda and Javier are almost ready to leave, so we may not have to wait too long. Let's get back inside—I don't want to miss Calvin's dessert tray."

The celebration lasted another two hours and Frank was dead tired by the time he got back to his room at 11:30 p.m. It had been a long day that had included a round trip flight to Bimini, the rescue of Linda and Javier, a dive to three hundred fifty feet, an alien encounter and a feast fit for a king. His eyes slammed shut the instant his head hit the pillow.

"*I believe you had some questions,*" said the voice. "*Is this a good time?*"

From a dream within a dream, Frank thought to himself, "Sure! Why not?"

"*You may begin whenever you like.*"

"Ah, okay. Let's start with the basics. How long have you been here?"

"*A long time. Hundreds of thousands of your years.*"

"Why are you here? I have a theory and I'd like to know if I'm correct."

"*You are.*"

"So you're here to keep an eye on things and make sure human civilization doesn't self-destruct?"

"*No, that has already happened many times. We simply monitor a civilization's progress and help a new one emerge after its predecessor fails.*"

"Many times? How many times, exactly?"

"*Thirty-seven times, exactly.*"

"Thirty-seven! That's the same as the number of messages on Jim's triangles—what a coincidence!"

"*It is not a coincidence. There is one message for each Initiative and, among other things, the message specifies each Initiative's point of origin. You are a member of Initiative Thirty-seven.*"

"So what happens when my civilization does what all the others before it did? Where's the location for number thirty-eight?"

"*There is no thirty-eight. Yours is the last.*"

"But my civilization is the most screwed up of them all!"

"*Agreed, but there will be no thirty-eight. When your civilization ceases to exist, our project will be over and we will move on.*"

"Project? Is this all just a game to you?"

"*Of course not. Even though time has no real meaning to us, we have invested a great deal of energy attempting to establish a permanent, self-sustaining civilization on this planet. Sometimes the process works and sometimes it doesn't. It appears your planet will fall into the latter category.*"

"Hold on! How can you be so cold about the fate of billions of people?"

"*We neither create nor destroy life. When a civilization crumbles, most of its members survive—at least for a while—but they tend to function at a very basic level. Our role here has been to provide the survivors with the knowledge and skills necessary to function as a group again. It's only with our help that humans have repeatedly been able to move beyond the wolf pack stage. Unfortunately, cataclysmic events of nature or internal strife have doomed each of our previous attempts."*

"And what about my civilization? Will it be nature or humans that do us in?"

"You have a saying, 'It's a crap shoot!' which seems to be very appropriate."

"So that's it? You're just going to abandon us? Don't you think some of the responsibility for the failed projects belongs to you? Maybe you should try harder!"

"We are trying harder. Initiative Thirty-seven is the only one in which we are preparing..."

"Frank! Are you in there? Wake up, Frank!" Tony was banging on the hotel room door and yelling at the top of his lungs.

Frank tried to block out the racket and slip back into his dream, but Tony was just too much to ignore.

"Hold on!" he called, shuffling to the door. "What's so important that you have to wake me up in the middle of the...oh, I guess it's morning, huh?"

"Morning?" laughed Tony. "It's 3:00 p.m., Frank! What did you have to drink last night, anyway? You need to get dressed and join us over in the lobby as soon as you can. That hurricane is definitely headed this way and we're trying to put together a plan."

"Okay, give me a few minutes to shower and I'll be right there. Are you sure it's afternoon?"

Thirty minutes later Frank joined Tony, Linda, Jill, Javier, Fitz, Susan and Sandstrom in the hotel's main building, which housed the lobby, the restaurant and the offices, including Miles' private library. The NWIDI team was gathered around the television watching a weather forecast.

"How does it look?" he asked.

"It looks pretty bad, Frank," offered Fitz. "The storm won't be here for another couple of days but by tomorrow every plane in the Bahamas will be looking for a safe haven. However, we have a plan to run by you."

Frank rubbed his eyes and checked his watch for the tenth time since being awakened by Tony.

"Go ahead," he said. "What's your plan?"

"Well, Linda and Javier would like to get back to Cancun as soon as possible, but a direct flight would mean going through some part of the storm." Fitz pointed to the television set. "However, if we dropped Jill off in the Virgin Islands first, we could then swing back west and north to Cancun and stay well behind the storm. From Cancun, we could bring you back here or head back to Seattle, whichever you prefer."

"So you're bailing on me, too?" Frank asked Jill.

"I'm sorry, Frank, but a situation has come up with some property I look after and it seems to make sense to hitch a ride back now, since your plane is headed my way. After my episode the other night, I'm not feeling nearly as adventurous as I was when I arrived. I'll leave that stuff to you and Tony, although I hate to leave him behind."

"Well, I'm sorry to see you go," frowned Frank, "but I don't think I'll let you leave Tony here. Somebody needs to keep an eye on you three and I have to take care of something here tomorrow, so I'm afraid you're stuck with him for a while longer."

"No way!" protested Tony. "If you're planning a trip back to that place Linda told us about on Bimini, I'm certainly not letting you make that dive alone again!"

"I won't be alone because I'm going to talk Miles into going with me—he just doesn't know it yet. Besides, there's still a possibility that the Columbians—or worse—are monitoring the Learjet's movements and I'd feel a lot better about this flight if I knew you were keeping an eye on things."

"Well, since you put it that way, I guess I can go along for the ride and see everybody safely home," Tony conceded. "But I'll be back here as soon as possible, so don't do anything stupid while I'm gone. I don't trust that Miles guy, you know."

"I agree, but, frankly, I don't trust anybody outside our own group anymore. When we get back to Seattle, maybe we should talk about cutting our ties with our current employer. As for coming back here, I'm not sure that will be necessary.

"Fitz, give me a call me when you get to Cancun and we'll figure the rest out then. Rather than having you fly all the way back over here to pick me up, maybe I'll meet you in Dallas or Houston."

"Okay, Frank, but we certainly don't mind coming back here, either," replied Fitz. "Wheels up in two hours, gang, so let's get packed. I'd like to be out of here before dark."

When the others had left for their rooms, Frank called Jim's cell phone and explained the evacuation plan.

"I'm sorry I won't be able to say good bye in person, Frank, but I'm sort of restricted to the base for a few days. Will you give them all my best and tell them I'll see them at the wedding?"

"Of course," said Frank. "I'm sticking around here, too, so maybe we can get together later in the week. I'm sure Miles can pull some strings to get me onto the base. I'm sorry I got you in trouble, but the wire you were wearing really caught me off guard."

"No, it was my fault," replied Jim. "I should have declined Linda's invitation but she was pretty persuasive on the phone. Anyway, it's already blowing over and things will be back to normal in a day or two. Call me Thursday or Friday and we'll see what we can work out. And please give my best to the others."

Frank had just sat back down to watch the news when Miles appeared.

"Why so glum?" he asked. "You look like you just lost your best friend."

"Best *friends*," corrected Frank. "They're all heading out in a couple of hours—all except Jim, of course, and he's been kidnapped by the Navy!"

"Jim's in a much better position than you think," smiled Miles. "His stroke of genius yesterday has allowed them to decipher fourteen more locations and you won't believe where some of them are!"

"Where?" asked Frank, his spirits suddenly lifted.

"Let's get together for a drink after we get back from taking your crew to the airport. I might have all thirty-four by then."

"How is it that you have such immediate access to Top Secret research taking place on a military installation?" asked Frank seriously.

"Join me for a glass of brandy and a Cuban cigar later and I'll explain that, too."

Chapter 26

Fitz' interest in getting into the air quickly eliminated any long, sad good-byes at the airport. Hurricane Dessie was growing by the hour and the weather in front of it was deteriorating rapidly so Fitz herded his passengers aboard as soon as they reached the small terminal.

Frank and Miles walked out to the plane with the flight crew, the four passengers and Sandstrom, the flight dog. After hugs and hand shakes, the others began filing into the plane. Frank pulled Tony aside and handed him a piece of paper.

"What's this?" asked Tony.

"It's the combination to the safe in my office back in Seattle," replied Frank. "Just in case."

"Just in case of *what*, Frank?" Tony asked, suddenly very serious.

"Well, I'm staying here, in the path of a hurricane and you never know what might happen. It's time you had it anyway. Just put it away in a safe place, okay? If anything ever happens to me, there are documents in the safe that will transfer NWIDI and its assets to you without a big legal hassle."

"Frank, it's just a storm! We've been through lots worse in the jungles of 'Nam. Besides, what makes you think I'd even want NWIDI?"

"Well, somebody would have to dispose of the assets and it would make me smile up there," Frank said, pointing to the sky, "just knowing that you were mired in the legal battles," laughed Frank. "I should have given you that a long time ago as a precaution. Now, you'd better get aboard or you're going to be walking to the Virgin Islands."

The two men shook hands again and the second Tony entered the plane, Fitz raised the stairs, waved and slammed the cabin door.

As Frank and Miles walked back to a safe distance, a light rain began to fall and by the time the Learjet pulled away from its parking place, it was raining hard.

They piled into the van laughing and Miles said, "I think they're getting out of here just in time. I'd better button down the hatches at the hotel before this gets any worse, but we're still on for this evening, right?"

"Sure, if we don't end up hiding in a storm shelter somewhere," replied Frank, wiping the rain off his face.

"I don't think you'd mind hanging out in the shelter at the hotel because it doubles as our wine cellar."

By the time Miles pulled into the hotel parking lot the rain was really coming down. He parked as close as he could to the lobby door and they made a run for it.

"How about if I stay here and help you?" asked Frank. "I'm not crazy about running back to my room in this."

"Sure, I can use a hand—follow me," replied Miles.

They went through a door marked "Employees Only" and down a long hallway to a utility room. Miles opened a locker and pulled out heavy yellow rain gear and boots.

Handing it to Frank, he said, "Did I mention that I need help outside?"

Together, the two managed to secure the storm shutters on all the windows in the main building just before the rain let up and by the time they got back to the utility room the sun was peaking out of the clouds on the western horizon.

"It never fails," laughed Miles.

Back in the lobby, several guests were gathered around the big screen television set and they didn't look happy.

"What's the latest?" asked Frank as he approached.

"It's turning north again," answered an elderly man. "It looks like it's going right up the western coast of Florida and there's no way for me to get back to Tampa before it hits!"

"It may change its mind again and turn back our way," suggested Miles. "I'm leaving the storm shutters closed until morning, just in case. These early season storms are really unpredictable."

Frank followed Miles back to his office and Miles ordered a round of drinks from the bar. While they were waiting for them to be delivered, Miles unlocked a drawer in his desk and took out a worn photo album.

"Here's something you should get a kick out of."

Frank paged slowly through the book, stopping to smile occasionally.

"Is this you when you were a new recruit?" he asked.

"As green as they came," replied Miles. "Great Lakes Naval Training Center, 1980."

Frank came to a picture of Miles and his class of fellow SEALs.

"Man, that's a tough looking bunch!"

"The only easy day was yesterday. That was our motto, and it was true for the entire twenty-five weeks of training," nodded Miles. "Graduation day was one of the proudest days of my life because there were so many times along the way when I didn't think I'd make it."

Frank flipped a few more pages and then stopped abruptly.

"Isn't that…" he stammered.

"President Reagan, yes. I received the Silver Cross in 1984 for a mission I was on in Grenada the year before. Do you recognize the guy behind the President, just to his left?"

Frank squinted and studied the photo. "It looks like a young version of Buzz Edwards!"

"It *is* Buzz Edwards. That was the first time I met him. At that time he was a member of the President's personal security detail."

"So he's in the Secret Service?" asked Frank.

"Not now, but he was then," replied Miles. "Later, when back injuries forced me out of the SEALs, he recruited me into my current position."

"And what is that?"

"It's a little difficult to explain," smiled Miles, "but I promised to try, and I will. Here come our drinks, so let me put that album away."

After the waitress had left the room, Miles continued.

"The Navy has always had a public relations problem with the locals here on Andros and every time a dead fish washes up on one of our beaches, the do-gooders get all revved up again. Even though I grew up in Florida, my parents were both Bahamian and I was born right here on Andros, so that makes me a Bahamian citizen. In mid-1990, I was recruited by the U.S. Government to act as a liaison with the locals. This hotel was for sale and I purchased it in my name thanks to a grant from the government. I moved to Andros and got involved in the community as quickly as possible and I was treated like the local boy who made it big on the mainland and then came home to settle down. The catch is that the locals think they recruited me to act as *their* liaison with the Navy!"

"So you're like a double agent," said Frank. "But in the PR business."

"Actually, it's a little more involved than that, Frank. Technically, I'm the Base Commander, although only one other person on Andros knows that. Captain Jefferies is the ranking military officer at AUTEC, but he reports directly to me."

Frank's jaw dropped. "And who do you report to?"

"The U.S. Government," replied Miles.

"Yes, I figured out that much, but who? Who's your superior officer?"

"Buzz Edwards."

"Ah-Hah! Now things are starting to make some sense. And who does he work for?"

"I don't know, Frank. My chain of command ends with Edwards. I have no idea who he works for."

"Well, what organization does he work for?" persisted Frank.

"I don't know. I don't even know which branch of government he works for. When I signed on, I was told not to ask those types of questions, so I don't. My disposable income comes from profits here at the hotel but the U.S. Treasury also deposits a substantial sum into my offshore account every month."

"Well, that certainly explains why you know so much about what's going on at AUTEC, but why a civilian boss and why do it undercover?" asked Frank. "What's our government hiding that requires such an unusual management style?"

"Nothing—and yet everything, Frank. Almost every test conducted at AUTEC is classified due to the national defense aspect of the mission." Miles held up his hand to stop Frank's objection. "I know, our government has lots of installations involved in classified work, but AUTEC is on foreign soil and it exists at the whim of the Bahamian government. In addition to the huge financial investment that AUTEC represents, it's also located on the Tongue of the Ocean—a place unique in the world. If local political issues forced the closure of AUTEC, our Navy would lose the huge advantage it's enjoyed since AUTEC was opened in 1965 and we just can't afford to take that chance."

"I see," considered Frank. "I guess there's more to world domination than I imagined. But what makes this place so different? There must be deep underwater basins similar to the Tongue elsewhere in the world."

"No, believe it or not, there aren't. And it's not just that. Scientists seem to work better here, Frank. I know it sounds silly, but there have been break-throughs here at AUTEC that would astound you. Just a few weeks ago, a team from Lockheed successfully tested a torpedo guidance system that had stumped them for months. They flew in one afternoon and when they met at their lab the next morning, the lead researcher had the answer!"

"Not unlike Jim's experience," nodded Frank.

"That's true! It's like people are just smarter when they're here."

"Or maybe they're getting some help," smiled Frank.

"What do you mean 'getting some help'? Who would be helping them?"

"I understand you've seen the shiny spheres on some of your dives, right?" asked Frank.

Softly, Miles said, "Yes."

"Have they ever talked to you?"

"What? No, of course not!" laughed Miles.

Frank leaned back in the over-stuffed chair in front of Miles' desk and smiled.

"Well, then I suggest you order more drinks and break out those Cuban cigars you promised, because I've got a story you're not going to believe!"

For the next hour, Frank told Miles everything he knew about the spheres, including the first sighting near Cuba, the mysterious 'cable' that seemed to connect the sunken city to Bimini, his own first encounter with the spheres, his rescue at the triangular structure off South Bimini and, finally, his mental 'dream state' conversation earlier in the day.

When he finished, he let Miles ponder his story for several minutes. Finally, Miles put his head back, closed his eyes, and said, simply, "Wow!"

"Would that be 'wow' to the fact that many ancient unknown civilizations have existed on Earth; 'wow' to the fact that we may be members of the last one; or 'wow' to the fact that there's an alien base camp right here in AUTEC's back yard?"

"Wow!" repeated Miles. "Just wow!"

The look of utter shock on Miles' face made Frank feel better than anything had in a long time. And yet, he felt sorry for the man who was so tied to the government that his only comment was "Wow!"

"I'm going to have to pass this information on, you know," Miles finally said. "And they're going to want to talk to you in person, Frank. A lot of people are going to want to talk to you."

"I'll bet none of those people represent the American public or the press corps, though. Or the Bahamians, who have been unknowingly hosting an alien culture for thousands of years. Or..."

"Frank," interrupted Miles, "you know this can never become public. Just the alien presence alone would cause widespread panic, but if people found out about the inevitable end of civilization, the world would self-destruct in days."

"But if people knew this was our last shot at success, maybe they'd take better care of the planet and of each other," objected Frank. "I've given this some serious thought and I think we owe it to the people of the world to get this story out as soon as possible."

"That's never going to happen, and you know it," replied Miles sternly.

Frank slumped in his chair sadly. "Yeah, I know. But make me just one promise. Promise me you won't pass the word up the line until after we dive the Bimini site tomorrow, or whenever the weather allows. I want you to see the structure that almost got me, and maybe you'll have a chance to make contact with them, like I did."

"This is too important, Frank. If my superiors found out that I..."

"Miles, right now it's just the story of one man who could have been suffering from any number of deep-water psychoses due to my inexperience. If you visit the site and if we can get them to communicate with you directly, the story will be much more credible. And you can tell them *your* story, instead of mine."

Miles' eyes brightened.

"You might be right, Frank. But understand that no matter what I see or hear during the dive, when we reach the surface I have to report this. I just *have* to!"

"I understand," nodded Frank.

The wind woke Frank twice during the night, but it was the sun that woke him up just before 6:00 a.m. Tuesday morning. Apparently he'd left the blinds open the last time he checked for wind damage and now the sun was blasting through the window that faced east. He climbed out of bed and went to the window to close the blinds but before he did he scanned the brilliant blue eastern sky. There was only one small cloud visible and the winds seemed to be calm. A good day for a dive, he thought to himself.

He turned on the television and then padded into the bathroom to shower. While he was drying off, he caught part of a weather report and learned that Hurricane Dessie had, indeed, turned north and made its way up Florida's western coast. The Fort Meyers area had sustained moderate damage but the storm had weakened as quickly as it had strengthened and by the time it reached Tampa it had been downgraded to a tropical storm. It was now so far north that it wasn't having any impact on the weather in Andros.

After a light breakfast, Frank went looking for Miles, hoping that the hotelier hadn't broken his word about releasing information to the government before their dive at the Bimini site. Frank had hoped he would be 'contacted' during his sleep again, but he'd heard no strange voices—only the wind.

Frank finally located Miles out on the dock next to the boat that had taken him diving several days earlier.

"There you are!" shouted Frank. "Are we diving today?"

"You bet we are," replied Miles. "I'm just getting some of my gear off the boat. Everything else, including your rebreather and mask, is already in the van."

"So what's the plan?"

"Well, air traffic still hasn't returned to normal after yesterday's storm scare, so I arranged for us to hitch a ride to Bimini on a Coast Guard helicopter that makes regular anti-drug patrols through the out-islands. They're going to pick us up at the AUTEC helipad at 10:00 a.m. sharp, so we need to leave here in about an hour."

"You can't beat that for service," smiled Frank. "What about getting back?"

Miles laughed. "I haven't figured that one out yet. The patrol route is a big circle that goes from here to Bimini, where it turns east and comes back by way of the Abacos and Berry islands. Most of the smaller planes joined yours and bugged out of here yesterday, but I'll figure something out. You should probably pack an overnight bag in case we can't get back until tomorrow."

"Okay, I'll go do that now. I also want to call the crew and see how they're doing. Shall I meet you in the lobby?"

"That works. See you there at 9:30 a.m.," called Miles as he disappeared below deck.

When Frank dialed Tony's cell phone number, he was actually surprised to get an answer.

"I thought you'd be in the air by now," greeted Frank. "How was the trip to St. Thomas?"

"Oh, it was fine," replied Tony. "It was a little bumpy climbing out of Andros, but by the time we reached cruising altitude we had left the storm behind. Jill is on the ferry crossing over to St. John right now and the weather is beautiful here. How is it there?"

"The storm turned north and missed Andros completely. This morning the sun is out and Miles and I are hitching a ride up to Bimini with the Coast Guard to dive the wall again."

"You be careful up there," cautioned Tony. "I'm too far away to save your butt if you get in trouble," he added with a laugh.

"I'm just going up to show Miles that triangular structure we saw on Ian's video camera. Besides, you have the combination to my safe so what are you worried about?" joked Frank.

"Hey, that's not even funny, old man! I'm beginning to think you sent me on this joy ride just to get rid of me."

"Not true," replied Frank. "Check in with Jill before you take off and keep a close eye on Linda and Javier. I'm concerned about them being on their own in Mexico but they're both adults and I can't tell them what to do."

"If your concerns are about the former owners of the plane, Jill, Linda and Javier should be fine. It's really Fitz, Susan and me that you should be worrying about, but so far I haven't seen any suspicious activity. When we get back to Seattle we should probably get to the bottom of this, huh?"

"Roger that," acknowledged Frank. "See you soon."

With Jim staying behind on Andros and Linda in Cancun, Frank wasn't sure why he and Tony were even going back to Seattle, except that it seemed like the normal thing to do. Besides, somebody has to take out the trash and pay the bills!

Frank packed a change of clothes, tidied up his room and hung out the 'Do not disturb' sign. As he walked across the grassy lawn to the lobby, he wondered how Miles balanced his life between a super-macho government agent and the owner of a hotel in paradise. He promised himself to never become like Miles—so controlled by the government that he didn't have the time to enjoy the morning breeze.

The helicopter ride to Bimini was long but very interesting to Frank, who constantly gazed out the window at the azure-blue water below. They passed over dozens of small, seemingly uninhabited cays and Frank couldn't help wondering if they had once been home to an ancient civilization nurtured along by whomever—or whatever—controlled the shiny spheres.

Miles spent most of the trip up front in a jump seat talking to the crew. Occasionally one of them would point towards the water and the helicopter would swoop down near the surface, but Frank never saw whatever it was that caught their attention.

As they approached the southern coast of Bimini, Frank guided them to the grassy area where he had found Linda and Javier. Once their gear was unloaded and moved a safe distance, they waved a "Thank you!" and the orange and white craft lifted off and disappeared over the small hill.

"This way," said Frank as he collected his gear and started down the now-familiar path to the shore. When they finally reached the water's edge, Miles was sweating profusely from carrying a heavy camera case along with his dive gear and a small travel bag.

"I need to cool down before I put on my wet suit," puffed Miles, "so why don't you tell me about this place while we wait? What exactly are we expecting to see?"

Frank pointed towards the water. "Well, I know it doesn't look like it, but just a few yards out from where we're standing there's a smooth vertical wall that descends more than three hundred fifty feet. The top of it is just below the surface and runs parallel to this side of the island. The Navy charted this area just a few years ago and those charts incorrectly show a gradual slope from here out several hundred yards. Any idea why they would do that?"

"None," replied Miles. "I've never heard of this wall or any other anomaly, for that matter. Maybe somebody decided this area wasn't important enough to actually measure and just made the data up in a bar somewhere."

"Possibly, or maybe they were covering up the existence of the wall to keep inquisitive divers like me away. At any rate, about seventy-five feet down there's a large rectangular hole in the wall that's spewing out very cold—and I believe fresh—water. We'll need to drift down at a slight westerly angle to see that and then we want to change our descent to take us east to reach the triangular feature I mentioned. Once we're on the bottom and can see the feature, I'm hoping we can make contact. After that, it's your call how long we stay."

"How will we hear this 'contact' if it decides to bless us with its presence?" asked Miles sarcastically.

"You'll hear a voice in your head. I can't describe it, but you'll know if it happens. I communicated by speaking out loud to help form my thoughts, but I'm sure that's not necessary. The second time, it was like I was dreaming, except I knew I wasn't."

Miles shook his head and said, "You know, if anybody other than you had told me that story last night, I would have ordered them to the psyche ward. Let's get going before I change my mind about you."

The minute Miles saw the wall, his attitude changed dramatically. He chattered constantly and Frank had a hard time getting him to shut up so he could point out the mouth of the fresh water exhaust.

"We checked a map after our first dive," explained Frank. "This point is on a perfectly straight line that runs through the only three sources of fresh water on the Bimini Islands. I believe they're just sink holes that open into an underground aqueduct which ends here. The other end is somewhere north of the Biminis."

"Amazing!" was all Miles could manage as they drifted through the cold water directly opposite the opening.

As they settled onto the bottom, Frank turned his back on the wall to look for the triangular structure.

"We may have to move along the base of the wall a little in either direction to find it, but I know it's nearby," he told Miles.

When there was no answer, Frank turned to find Miles standing at the base of the wall rubbing it gently with his gloved hand.

"Amazing, isn't it?" he asked as he joined Miles.

"Amazing doesn't even begin to describe it!" replied Miles. "You've probably noticed, but this isn't constructed from blocks— it's one continuous piece of rock or whatever it's made from."

"Yes, I've noticed, and it's like that all the way to the top. I paid particular attention to that characteristic the last time I was here. There's not a single seam or joint anywhere that I've seen."

Miles had his camera out and shot several angles and exposures before allowing Frank to lead him away from the wall. With a little swimming, Frank finally spotted the low triangular foundation that had almost sucked him in on his last visit. When Miles started for the area, Frank grabbed his arm and held him back.

"Hold on there, Miles. I haven't mentioned this yet, but you'll want to stay away from the top of that thing. It has an inward suction to it that almost cost me my life. If you want pictures, walk over and take them from the side."

Miles dropped his fins to the sand and approached the low wall. "Is this where you heard the voices?"

"Yes, about here. Someone—or something—had just pulled me out of harm's way."

"Is this where you set off all the alarms, Frank? Your oxygen levels were all over the place, according to the rebreather logs—you were probably just hallucinating!"

"*No he wasn't.*" said a voice in Miles head.

Miles spun and looked around him. "Who's there? Who said that?"

Inside his mask, Frank smiled broadly.

"I was afraid you wouldn't be here and he wouldn't believe me," said Frank out loud.

"So you heard it, too?" asked Miles. "Can you hear us?"

"*Yes,*" came the reply. And then to Frank only, "*Why have you returned here?*"

"I needed to make sure I wasn't imagining all this," replied Frank. "I needed another human to validate my experience."

"*Understood.*"

"Frank, I'm not hearing it anymore!" said Miles with panic in his voice. "I only heard your reply. What's going on?"

"I think it can selectively communicate with either or both of us as it wishes," guessed Frank, "and it may not know we can hear each other through the communications system in the full-face masks."

"*You are correct. Future responses will be directed to both of you.*"

"May I ask some more questions?" inquired Frank.

"*Yes.*"

"I'm curious about the feature that seems to connect a spot near here to a sunken city off the tip of Cuba. It appears to be a buried cable or pipe of some sort. Can you explain its purpose?"

"*Of course. Originally it provided power to our facility at the other end, but it has been disconnected now that we've abandoned that site.*"

"How long ago did you do that?" asked Frank quickly.

"*Thirteen of your days ago.*"

"The signals that mysteriously stopped and got me involved in this trip in the first place!" exclaimed Frank.

"*Correct.*"

"The what? You didn't tell me about signals, Frank," protested Miles.

"Ask your buddy Edwards about them," snapped Frank, annoyed by Miles' interruption of his conversation with the alien—or aliens.

"What about the city itself? Did you build it?" Frank continued.

"No, it was built by Initiative Thirty-five. It sank when a small object impacted the planet about fifty thousand of your years ago."

"But what about your facility? Wasn't it damaged?" asked Frank.

"Our facility wasn't there at that time. Our facility was installed more recently to monitor the activities of some humans nearby. We closed it because we were concerned about being discovered."

"The Russians!" shouted Frank. "The ones that live on the western tip of Cuba!"

"Correct. In an effort to improve the survival probability of Initiative 37, we chose to share some technology with them."

"You gave alien technology to the Russians?" cried Miles. "What kind of technology?"

"Water purification technology."

"Oh," mumbled Miles. "I was afraid it might have been weapons."

"After watching humans for hundreds of thousands of years, we know better than that! A small group in that area was in danger of extinction due to a lack of fresh water, so we intervened. We are doing whatever we can, wherever we can, to help keep humans alive, but you seem intent on self-destruction."

"Amen to that," agreed Frank. "I have another question. When I visited the underwater city, I saw a submarine lying on the bottom. Was that your doing?"

"That was an unfortunate accident. As I have already said, we can neither create nor destroy human life. However, sometimes it is necessary to defend ourselves against threats. The vessel discovered our monitoring facility in the sunken city and it insisted on interfering with our work. Eventually, it was necessary to neutralize it."

"So you sank it?" asked Miles. "What about the sailors inside? Not that I care about a bunch of Russians, but I'm just curious."

"They are with us. When their training is complete, they will be returned to serve as advisors."

"They're with you?" shouted Frank. "You mean they're physically with you?"

"In a manner of speaking, yes. They are physically well and they are with us the way you are with us now. The wall you were admiring earlier protects a large facility deep beneath the island you call Bimini."

"And what about Ian, the young diver who visited here a few days ago?" pressed Frank.

"He chose to join us voluntarily."

"Will he also return and serve as an advisor?"

"If he so chooses."

"I can't believe this," exclaimed Miles as he peered into the triangular structure. "I hate to cut this short, but I need to get topside and report this to the Navy ASAP."

Frank had moved to a position on Miles' right side and was also looking into the dark center of the structure.

Reaching over and pressing the inflator button on Miles' BC, Frank said softly, "I'm afraid I can't let you do that, Miles."

As the surprised Miles started to float off the bottom, Frank grabbed the other man's rebreather unit and pushed him out over the edge of the low wall into the center of the triangle. In less than a second, Miles was gone.

"I'm sorry," apologized Frank, "but I couldn't let him expose all this to the U.S. Government. That would have most certainly brought a quick end to Initiative 37."

"Understood. We will try to persuade him to join our cause."

In an instant, Frank knew what he had to do.

"He's a stubborn guy. I think you're going to need my help."

And with that, Frank dove over the wall and disappeared, too.

THE END

Final Words

It's New Years Eve, 2007 and Initiative 37 is still functioning, more than five years after Frank's last dive. Around the world, violence and destruction have become the norm and the future is uncertain, at best. Even nature seems determined to wipe us out, taking more than a quarter of a million souls in a Tsunami on Christmas Day two years ago. Will the new year that begins in a few hours be the last one for humankind?

More than seven years after its discovery, the world is still largely ignorant about the "lost city of Cuba" although bits of information can be found on the Internet.

The true nature of Bimini also remains a secret, but the ongoing work of researchers such as Greg and Lora Little, Bill Donato and others continues to inch closer to the truth. Already there are rumors of an "ancient civilization" that once inhabited the Bahamas and it won't be long before one of those resourceful individuals stumbles onto the wall off the south Bimini coast. At that point, the caretakers of humanity will be forced to either reveal themselves to us or terminate their final project early and leave Earth forever. Let's hope for the former!

Best Regards,
R.J. Archer
Initiative 37

Read the entire Seeds Of Civilization series:

Tractrix (ISBN 978-0977910908) Mysterious black spheres may provide a link between ancient Maya astronomers and visitors from another world!

Tsubute (ISBN 978-0977910915) Ancient ninja weapons may provide a clue to the origin of a 9,000-year-old sunken pyramid in southern Japan!

Triangle (ISBN 978-0977910939) Mysterious alien artifacts reveal the startling truth about the "lost city" recently discovered of the coast of Cuba!

For more information about this series, please join us at
http://www.SeedsOfCivilization.com